ROYAL DUTY

OTHER BOOKS AND AUDIOBOOKS BY TRACI HUNTER ABRAMSON

UNDERCURRENTS SERIES

Undercurrents

Ripple Effect

The Deep End

SAINT SQUAD SERIES

Freefall

Lockdown

Crossfire

Backlash

Smoke Screen

Code Word

Lock and Key

Drop Zone

Spotlight

Tripwire

Redemption

Covert Ops

Disconnect

ROYAL SERIES

Royal Target

Royal Secrets

Royal Brides

Royal Heir

Royal Duty

GUARDIAN SERIES

Failsafe

Safe House

Sanctuary

On the Run

In Harm's Way

Not Dead Yet

Unseen

DREAM'S EDGE SERIES

*Dancing to Freedom**

An Unlikely Pair

*Broken Dreams**

Dreams of Gold

*The Best Mistake**

Worlds Collide

FALCON POINT SERIES

Heirs of Falcon Point

The Danger with Diamonds

From an Unknown Sender

STAND-ALONES

Obsession

Proximity

*Twisted Fate**

*Entangled**

*Sinister Secrets**

Deep Cover

Mistaken Reality

Kept Secrets

Chances Are

Chance for Home

A Change of Fortune

The Fiction Kitchen Trio Cookbook

Jim and Katherine

* Novella

a novel

TRACI HUNTER
ABRAMSON

Covenant Communications, Inc.

Cover image: *Jewelry Crown Earrings* © Artem Sakharov / istockphoto.com. *Galaxy in the Night Sky Beach Scene* © Ahmed Rizkha / unsplash.com. *Palm Trees at Sunset* © Suhyeon Choi / unsplash.com

Author Photo by Jennifer Wolfe

Cover design by Tara Leong

Published by Covenant Communications, Inc.
American Fork, Utah

Library of Congress Cataloging-in-Publication Data

Name: Traci Hunter Abramson
Title: Royal Duty / Traci Hunter Abramson
Description: American Fork, UT : Covenant Communications, Inc. [2024]
Identifiers: Library of Congress Control Number 2023947893 | ISBN 9781524425388
LC record available at https://lccn.loc.gov/2023947893

Printed in the United States of America
First Printing: September 2024

32 31 30 29 28 27 26 25 24   10 9 8 7 6 5 4 3 2 1

for the Queens of the Court

You will always be royalty in my eyes.

Acknowledgments

Thank you to the many people who helped make this book possible, especially my fabulous editor, Samantha Millburn, as well as the rest of the Covenant family. Thank you to the incredible marketing teams and their fearless leaders, Shara Meredith and Amy Parker, and the many others who worked behind the scenes to bring this book into the world.

Thanks to my many critique group partners who have helped me polish this manuscript throughout those early days of drafting: Daniel Quilter, Eliza Sanders, Connor Olsen, Emma Jackson, H.Y. Gregor, Ashley Gebert, Steve Stratton, Jack Stewart, Millie Hast, Brian Godden, and Ann Feinstein. And thank you to Mandy Biesinger for your willingness to beta read for me and to Lara Abramson for all of your editing help.

I also want to thank the CIA Publication Classification Review Board for your continued support. And thank you to my family for sharing me with my computer and putting up with my crazy schedule. I couldn't do this without you.

Finally, thank you to the readers who have been so supportive of my fictional worlds. You make all the effort worth it. Happy reading!

CHAPTER 1

FLIGHT CANCELED. ALAN TIGHTENED HIS grip on Max's leash and checked the time on his watch. Typical. The one time he and Max didn't have to rush to make their connection and the airplane wasn't waiting to take them on the next leg.

Alan wished his current frustration could erase the ache deep inside him as he considered that this would be his last time traveling with his K-9 companion. He and Max had been together since Alan had first started with the CIA as a bomb disposal specialist. They had been rookies together, Max at three and Alan at twenty-one. That had been seven years ago, and their time was quickly coming to a close. After Alan had spent more than half his career in Europe, someone at headquarters had deemed it time for him to take another hardship tour, this time in the Middle East—with a new dog.

For six weeks, he would train with his new canine partner before spending the next two years in the Middle East. As for Max, he would go into retirement and be put up for adoption.

He would find a new home with someone else.

His heart heavy, Alan adjusted his leather duffel and his messenger bag so they were on opposite shoulders. Moving steadily forward, he made his way through the masses in London Heathrow International Airport. He knew better than to fly through this airport, but had his travel rep at the CIA listened when he'd asked for an alternate flight? Of course not.

They reached an escalator and a set of stairs. Even though Max was well trained and could easily navigate the moving escalator, Alan wasn't sure he trusted his fellow travelers to respect the German shepherd's space.

"Come on, Max." Alan headed for the stairs. With Max's leash still firmly in his grasp, he escorted his dog up to the next level. He spotted the crowd in front of the customer service desk several steps before the sign came into view. This didn't look good. With the time difference between London and DC, the CIA's travel office wasn't going to do him any good for another four hours. He and Max were on their own to get back to headquarters.

Alan took his place at the back of the line and glanced down at his companion. A lump formed in his throat, and he swallowed it. This wasn't the time to think about the next chapter in his career, especially since he couldn't imagine moving forward without Max by his side.

The line moved up slightly, and Alan moved with it. A little girl seated in a nearby stroller reached for Max.

Alan tugged on Max's leash so the dog would move to the spot directly in front of him. "Sit, Max."

Max complied, and Alan placed one foot on either side of the dog to protect him from the little girl and the other passengers pressing in on them. Max might not be working at the moment, but Alan preferred that his canine companion remain alert when in such public places.

Another fifteen minutes passed, with only three passengers moving through the line ahead of him. Alan's cell phone rang. He checked the caller ID before he answered it. Levi Marin, his former coworker, the new king of Sereno.

Alan smiled at the welcome distraction and nearly managed to keep the humor out of his voice when he said, "Hello, Your Majesty."

"Ha ha," Levi said dryly. "Cassie and I haven't been crowned yet."

"People are still calling you king."

"Technically, I'm king consort. I'm just married to the queen."

"Doesn't matter."

"Whatever people are calling me, for you, I'm still Levi."

Alan's grin widened. "I feel so special."

Levi's laughter carried over the phone. "While you're feeling special, any chance you can break away from your current assignment and come to Sereno until after the coronation?"

An opportunity to keep Max by his side a little while longer, not to mention postpone his permanent change of station to the Middle East? "If you can clear it with personnel, I'm all yours."

"Why personnel?" Levi asked. "I should only have to check with your station chief."

"You would, if I had one. I'm between assignments right now." Alan sighed. "They're retiring Max."

"Oh man. I'm sorry," Levi said. "I thought they would let him go for another year or two."

"So did I." The idiocy of the decision still rankled. "He should have been able to keep working since he's not having health issues, but someone decided ten was the cutoff age."

"How frustrating."

"Yeah." Alan swallowed, fighting against his rising emotions. Not able to give any more details with so many people nearby, he said, "I'm at Heathrow right now, but my flight was canceled. If you want, I can hold off booking my next flight until you can get in touch with someone who can give you an answer."

"Tell you what, go ahead and grab a taxi over to the Hampton Inn by London Stansted Airport. I'll have a room waiting for you."

"Why there?"

"Because tomorrow morning, the family jet will be picking up my sister-in-law to bring her home."

"Victoria?"

"Yes."

Alan's mind raced as he thought of Levi's oldest sister-in-law. Levi's generous, loyal, gorgeous sister-in-law. Alan likely would have asked her out when they'd first met, but her father had been so ill at the time, Victoria's sole focus had been on spending time with her family and filling in wherever she could. Plus, she had recently broken things off with an old boyfriend. Alan and Victoria's backgrounds were different enough that he hadn't wanted to deal with setting himself up as someone's rebound.

Levi spoke again, interrupting Alan's thoughts. "Victoria graduated with her MBA from Cambridge a few days ago."

Alan wasn't surprised. The woman was brilliant. "Why didn't she go home with you and Cassie?" Alan asked. "I assume you came out for her graduation ceremony."

"We did, but Cassie needed to be back the next day, and Victoria wanted a little time to celebrate with her friends," Levi said. "The plane tomorrow will also be transporting artwork that Sereno has had on loan to the British Museum."

"You want me to play security for the artwork?" He should have known Levi would put him to work right away.

"That's an added bonus. I'm more interested in having you here while we prepare for the coronation."

"You aren't worried someone will go after Cassie again, are you?" Alan asked. A string of assassination attempts two years ago had been the catalyst to Alan's six-month assignment in Sereno shortly before King Alejandro passed away.

"We haven't picked up any known threats, but I'd prefer to be overprepared than find out the hard way that security wasn't adequate."

"I can't blame you there."

"Victoria will have a basic security detail with her, but I want you to run the final security sweep of the plane and cargo."

"The royal guard doesn't always take well to outsiders being in charge."

"Don't worry. They'll work with you," Levi said. "Victoria's lead guard is a good man. He'll give you whatever support you need."

"Okay, I'll head over to the hotel." Alan moved out of the customer service line. "Call me after you talk to personnel."

"I'm not calling personnel," Levi said. "I'm calling the director."

"I guess it pays to be married to a royal."

Levi laughed again. "Sometimes, it really does."

CHAPTER 2

Princess Victoria of Sereno stepped out of the limousine onto the tarmac, where the family jet waited to take her home. The light breeze ruffled the red silk blouse she had chosen to travel in, and she couldn't resist stopping to appreciate her last few moments here in the United Kingdom, her last few moments of relative normalcy. Not that her classmates would have considered her graduate experience normal.

Holly, Lucy, and Sheldon, in particular, had done their best to get Victoria to socialize outside of their frequent study groups, but she'd rarely had time. School and career had come first. Personal life had been a distant second. Or maybe a distant third.

Despite the rigor of her master's program, Victoria had juggled the demands of her next career, as CEO of a new family enterprise. She and her older sister had long dreamed about turning the inaccessible stretch of beach near the palace into something usable. Now, after two years of planning and hard work, that dream was becoming a reality.

The Royal Sands Resort would open in a month, just in time for the first guests to arrive for her older sister's coronation.

Cassie would soon be crowned queen, and Victoria would serve her country in her own way, using her knowledge of finance and economics. Cassie had made her mark by overseeing the drilling efforts in the recently discovered oil fields off the coast of Sereno, but the resort was Victoria's pet project, and she was determined to make it a success. Besides being her chance to support her family's quest to be self-sufficient, without relying on tax support, the resort gave her a sense of independence, something she had always craved.

The work had been all-encompassing, but the finished product would soon be worth her efforts. She also couldn't deny that the ever-present plans for the resort and the demands of her studies had provided her with a welcome distraction over the past year since her father had passed away.

The familiar grief rose within her even as she tried to fight it back. Her father had ruled Sereno well, and it was up to her and her sisters to continue the legacy he had passed down to them.

The guard standing beside the plane stepped forward. "Your Highness, we'll be ready to depart in twenty minutes. We still need to load your luggage and some artwork we are transporting back to Sereno."

"Thank you, Giuseppe." Victoria shifted the messenger bag hanging from her shoulder and climbed the airstair to the plane.

The steward bowed his head in greeting. "Princess Victoria, may I take your bag for you?"

"No, thank you, Nicolo. I have a bit of work to do on the flight."

"Something to drink, then?"

"A sparkling water with lime would be wonderful. Thank you."

"Of course, Your Highness." Nicolo disappeared into the small galley.

Victoria set her bag on one of the two seats beside a worktable. By the time the steward returned with her drink, she already had her laptop open to the latest construction timeline for The Royal Sands Resort.

"Here you are, Your Highness." Nicolo set a coaster on the table and placed the drink on it.

"Thank you." She took a sip and glanced out the window. Several workers wearing reflective safety vests stood near the front of the plane. Giuseppe spoke to a man who appeared to be wearing some sort of military vest. He was taller than Giuseppe, maybe an inch or so over six feet, and his dense black hair was cut short. A German shepherd sniffed the ground as the man walked along her stack of luggage. Then the man looked up.

Victoria's eyes widened as recognition dawned. Alan Neisler and his dog, Max. Not military. CIA.

Victoria had gotten to know Alan peripherally when the CIA had allowed him to work at the palace for several months after a security breach a couple of years ago. At the time, so much of her focus had been on spending time with her father that little else had mattered to her. Still, it was hard to miss the man with the penetrating brown eyes and watchful stare. Not to mention the innate kindness he exhibited when working with his dog. Max wasn't simply a tool to Alan. The dog was his partner, one he clearly loved deeply.

Her own dog, Lazio, had passed away only a few weeks before Victoria's mother had been diagnosed with cancer. Even after more than three years, she still missed the Tibetan spaniel's sweet disposition and the way he had accompanied her wherever she'd gone.

Victoria turned her attention back to Nicolo. "What is Mr. Neisler doing here?"

"He will be accompanying us to Sereno." A flash of confusion illuminated Nicolo's face. "I'm sorry. I thought you were aware of the change."

"No." But if Alan was going to accompany her home, she had little doubt as to who had made the arrangements. "I must have missed a message from King Levi." It was most likely one of the seven she had ignored.

She had come to love her older sister's husband, but the man took overprotective to the extreme, especially since her sister had delegated the family and palace security responsibilities to him. She couldn't count the number of text messages and emails he had sent to her over the past few days, all counseling her on security protocols and safety measures she was already well aware of. She looked forward to getting on site at the resort so the security would be more focused on making sure tourists didn't infringe on the palace grounds.

After a quick check of her messages, where she found Levi had indeed informed her of Alan's impending presence, she picked up her bag and slid it into the spot behind her seat. Might as well make Alan feel welcome.

* * *

Alan gave the ground crew the go-ahead to load the princess's luggage onto the plane. All six suitcases. He supposed he would have more than a suitcase and a duffel, too, if he ever stayed in one place long enough.

Now Alan was dressed in a suit in the middle of summer because his ride to his temporary assignment would put him in the same cabin as royalty. Then again, his flak jacket wasn't exactly compatible with high temperatures. He'd have to adapt if he was going to survive two years in the Middle East.

Alan tugged at his collar.

Giuseppe, one of the royal guards Levi had worked with before, approached him. "The rest of our cargo is in the van over there."

Leaving the ground crew to deal with the baggage, Alan and the guard crossed the short distance to where the van was parked, the rear doors facing the plane's cargo hold.

"Luca, are we all set?" Giuseppe asked.

"Yes. I've already confirmed the inventory of the shipment." Luca opened the back of the van. "We simply need to load everything onto the plane."

Max sniffed the rear tires. Immediately, he sat and whined.

Alan's heart seized, and he held up a hand. "Wait!"

Luca's hand dropped from the crate he had been about to unload. "What's wrong?"

"That's what I need to find out." Alan waved at Max. "He's signaling a problem."

"A bomb?" Giuseppe asked.

"I don't know, but I don't want anyone moving anything until I check it out." Alan glanced in the open rear doors, the crates neatly arranged. Everything appeared to be in order. He turned to Luca. "Did you watch these being loaded?"

"Yes. I don't know how anyone could have planted a bomb in any of the casings. Each one was crated in my presence, and I haven't let them out of my sight since then."

"Were there any extra packages?" Alan asked.

"No."

His heart and mind racing, Alan knelt beside Max. If Luca was correct, the bomb wasn't planted in the packaging. It was somewhere on the vehicle. A quick search of the wheel wells didn't reveal anything, but the moment Alan expanded his search to the undercarriage, he spotted what he had hoped not to find: a small explosive device bolted to the exhaust manifold. Though the bomb itself was only about the size of a standard shoe box, the blast area would undoubtedly take out the van, the artwork, and possibly the plane.

"Found it." Alan struggled for calm. He was trained for this, but no matter how many times he faced a live explosive, he couldn't keep his heart from racing or the what-ifs from rushing through his mind. And he had faced the ticking clock of a bomb before. Oddly enough, since joining the agency, every time he had used his electrical-engineering knowledge to disable a bomb, the explosive had been intended to assassinate a royal.

He hadn't lost anyone yet, and he didn't intend for today to be his first failure. In truth, if Alan failed, he wouldn't live to remember it anyway.

He reached into his backpack and retrieved his tool kit. "You two clear out of here."

"I can't leave the paintings," Luca said.

When faced with a bomb, people's reactions never ceased to amaze Alan. The man was more worried about a bunch of canvases than he was his own life. If it weren't Alan's job to defuse explosives, he would hightail it out of here without a second thought.

"I'll have the pilot move the plane to another hanger," Giuseppe said. "I need to get the princess to safety."

"Negative. The vibration from the engines could set this off."

"Do I have time to walk her away from here?" Giuseppe persisted.

"I don't know. Stand by." Alan lay on the ground and slid under the van. He pulled a small flashlight from his kit and shone it on the crude YouTube 101 explosive. It might be simple, but it would still be deadly if he didn't succeed.

Alan analyzed the current threat. A simple timer angled downward to prevent the red numbers from drawing attention to the bomb. Three minutes and six seconds left. Three oh five. Three oh four.

If Giuseppe brought Princess Victoria into the open, she could be more vulnerable than if she remained on the plane.

"Keep the princess where she is," Alan instructed, opting to rely on both his instincts and his training. "I want you two to back away from the van. Slowly. And call the local bomb squad."

Not that the bomb squad would get here in time to help. Alan was on his own.

Trusting the other men to follow his directions, Alan placed the small flashlight in his mouth and used his lips to hold it in place. He then drew out his wire cutters with one hand while he used his other to follow along the tangle of wires.

His body tensed, and he had to remind himself to relax. He had time. Still more than two minutes.

He separated the wires with his free hand, tilting his head to aim the light more fully on the timing device. The black wire or the red? If he could just see which one connected to the detonator.

Alan shifted to his left, the pavement digging into his shoulder. Using the new angle, he tracked the wires again. The red wire. He was 90-percent certain. He wasn't going to think about the 10-percent chance that he was wrong, or the possibility that it was a dummy wire that would cause the bomb to explode the moment the circuit disconnected.

A few more seconds ticked by. Alan checked the device again to confirm his analysis. Only one more minute remaining until detonation.

Sirens sounded in the distance, growing louder with each second.

The bomb squad was quicker than expected, but it would still arrive too late. Alan sucked in a breath and pulled the red wire out enough for him to slip the cutters into place. Then he started his countdown. Three, two, one.

His breath shuddered out, and then he squeezed the wire cutters.

CHAPTER 3

VICTORIA BARELY DARED BREATHE. SHE didn't know much about what Alan did for a living, but it didn't take a genius to figure out that a bomb-sniffing dog sitting alert and still wasn't a good sign. Alan lying beneath a vehicle only added an exclamation point to her suspicion that Max had discovered a problem.

Giuseppe had taken position at the bottom of the stairs leading to the plane, but he hadn't come aboard to inform her what was going on. Alan must have made some sort of mistake.

That thought flitted away when Alan scooted out from beneath the cargo van and stood, a device with dangling wires gripped in his hand.

Sirens wailed nearby, and the lights of emergency vehicles flashed as a police van arrived.

Despite the possible threat, she remained by the window. Had Alan succeeded in neutralizing the bomb? His relaxed stance answered that question in the affirmative, and a new question filtered into her mind. With the constant security of the royal jet and the artwork being shipped today, how had someone managed to plant an explosive device? And why had they wanted to?

The possibility of her being a target bordered on ludicrous. After all, her death wouldn't serve any purpose other than to make headlines. But there were people in the world who committed hostile acts to draw that kind of attention. That sobering thought quickened her already rapid pulse.

Two police officers rushed out of their van and crossed to Alan. The three men spoke for several minutes. Then they secured the device Alan was holding in the back of the police van. A moment after the back doors of the van closed, Alan approached Giuseppe. After a brief conversation, Alan and Max circled the cargo van from the art museum.

The back of the van was then opened, and Max disappeared inside. In a painstakingly slow process, they removed each piece of artwork from the cargo van, Max and Alan examined them, and then they loaded the pieces onto the royal jet.

Nearly forty-five minutes later, Giuseppe boarded the plane.

Even though she suspected she already knew the answer, Victoria asked, "What happened?"

"We had a little delay," Giuseppe said. "Everything is fine now."

Typical. No one ever wanted to upset her, so they simply didn't give her details. That had happened when her father had learned of his illness and when an assassination attempt had been made on Cassie.

Victoria wasn't going to let this particular mode of operation continue. "Did that little delay have anything to do with the bomb Alan found?"

"Your Highness, I . . ." Giuseppe began, clearly not sure what he should say.

Alan boarded the plane with his dog. His gaze instantly met hers. He gave her a subtle bow of his head before he spoke. "Sorry to keep you waiting, Your Highness."

Victoria studied the man before her. He no longer wore his protective vest; in its place was a suit coat that didn't quite accommodate his broad shoulders. A smudge marred the cuff of his sleeve, and his tie was askew. He had grown a mustache and beard since Victoria had seen him last, both trimmed close to his face so they enhanced his naturally good looks rather than hiding his features.

Alan cocked an eyebrow, and her cheeks heated slightly when she realized she'd been staring.

"I'll forgive you if you tell me what happened." Victoria waved at the seat across from her. "Please, sit down."

Alan glanced at Giuseppe as though waiting for permission.

Giuseppe gave a subtle nod. "I'll inform the pilot that we're ready to depart."

Alan took his seat as Giuseppe moved to the front of the cabin. Alan signaled to Max, and the dog obediently sat and then stretched out on the floor. "I understand congratulations are in order. Levi told me you recently received your master's degree."

"I did." Victoria leaned forward in her seat. "And you're stalling. What happened out there?"

He tilted his head toward the window. "There was a small explosive device attached to the underside of the cargo van."

The confirmation of what she had witnessed sent a new ripple of fear through her. "How was that even possible? Surely we had additional security for the transportation of the artwork."

"I assume so." Alan leaned back in his seat as though it weren't a big deal that he had just single-handedly saved her life and the lives of those who would have been in the blast radius. "I was only requested to join the security detail yesterday."

"Yesterday?" she repeated. When he simply nodded, she focused back on the near-tragedy of moments ago. "Tell me about the bomb. How much damage would it have done?"

"You want to know if you were the target?"

"Yes."

"It's possible." The engines roared to life, and Alan waited until the plane started moving before he spoke again. "The blast would certainly have damaged the plane, but it's hard to know if the bomber assumed the van would have been parked closer to the cargo area."

"And if it had been?"

"Max still would have found the bomb."

"But if you hadn't been here . . . ?"

"Then you would have been in the kill zone."

* * *

Alan shouldn't have told Victoria the truth. He'd nearly kept it from her, but she had asked for details, and he'd figured she had a right to know.

He let the silence hang between them as the plane taxied down the runway and took flight.

He settled back into his seat, his legs and arms still restless from the remaining adrenaline running through him. He willed it to subside. A combination of Max's training and sheer luck had saved him today. Alan reached down and ran a hand over Max's head. He didn't want to think about the what-ifs from today's near-death experience, but he couldn't get his mind to shut off.

The plane leveled off, and Alan finally managed to settle his emotions enough to explore the possible motives of the would-be bomber. "I hate to ask this question, but can you think of anyone who would want you dead?"

Victoria's face paled. She shook her head. "I don't know of anyone who would benefit from my death. Even though Cassie hasn't been crowned yet, in all the ways that matter, she is already queen. I'm the heir presumptive for now, but once Cassie and Levi start having children, I'll continue to move down the line of succession."

Before Alan could continue questioning her, Victoria lifted a hand and signaled to the steward.

Instantly, the man moved to her side.

"May I have another water with lime, please?"

Alan couldn't help but wonder if anyone ever told the princess no.

The steward bowed slightly to Victoria. "Of course, Your Highness." He turned to Alan. "Anything for you, sir?"

"An apple juice, please." Alan pulled a collapsible plastic bowl from his backpack. "And some water for my partner here."

The steward nodded and moved to the forward galley.

Alan stared out the window, his mind whirling. Victoria was correct. The possibility that she would ever rule Sereno had decreased significantly when Princess Cassandra had married Levi, and from what Alan had seen of the three Rossi sisters, none of them had any inclination to try to climb into a position of power. Cassie would be queen, and both Victoria and Annabelle appeared content with the current status quo.

The steward returned with their drinks on a tray along with a basket of cookies. Methodically, he placed each drink on a coaster, even the bottle of water for Max, and set the basket of cookies on the table. "Will there be anything else?"

"We're fine for now," Victoria said, answering for both of them.

"Thank you." Alan ignored his drink and focused on Victoria once more. "Besides assassinating the heir presumptive, why would someone want you dead?"

"I have no idea." Victoria's lips pressed together as though she were trying to control her emotions. "Can we talk about something else?"

Alan didn't miss the way she blinked quickly to fight against the tears shimmering in her eyes. Searching for something else to talk about, he waved a hand to encompass the aircraft. "Do you always fly on a private plane?"

"Not always." Victoria took a sip of her water. "My sisters and I often fly commercial if we don't have anything we need to transport."

"That can't be easy for security."

"No, but with the increased focus on reducing flights around Europe, it helps show our commitment to respecting environmental concerns and reducing fuel costs."

"Seems to me that keeping you and your family alive should take priority," Alan said.

"This kind of thing has never happened before." Victoria paused. "Not to me anyway."

But it had happened to Cassie. Alan set Max's bowl on the floor and poured some water into it. Max stood up and lapped at the water until the bowl was empty.

"He was certainly thirsty," Victoria commented, the moisture in her eyes still evident. "I hope he isn't going to need to go out. The flight is over two hours."

"He'll be fine," Alan promised. "And I don't want him getting dehydrated. He did a lot of work outside before we boarded."

"You're right," Victoria said solemnly. "He did. And I'm grateful he was there."

"Me too." Alan's thoughts continued to churn as he sought for a motive behind today's bombing attempt. "You're assuming someone wants you dead because you're a member of Sereno's royal family," Alan finally said. "What about other reasons?"

"What other reasons could there be?" Victoria lifted both hands. "Except for my family connections, I've been a typical college and then graduate student for the past six years."

Alan ran through the events of the past hour again. Going after a member of Sereno's royal family right before the coronation could still be a possibility. The small island nation was on the brink of becoming one of the leading oil producers in the region. And once Cassandra was crowned, her role as queen would help provide a much-needed sense of stability as she fully took control of the government. Yet the bomb had been planted on the van, not inside a container being loaded onto the plane.

Another possible motive surfaced. "We should have the artwork authenticated once we reach Sereno."

A small line formed between Victoria's dark eyebrows. "You think someone could have been trying to destroy the artwork?"

"If someone wasn't trying to kill you, the artwork is the next most logical target," Alan said. "Had I not been here with Max, the likelihood is the bomb would have gone off while the artwork was still in the van."

Understanding sparked in Victoria's eyes. "You think someone might have substituted a forgery and then tried to destroy the evidence."

"It would make sense. If the paintings we're transporting aren't the real deal, what better way to get away with a theft than to make sure no one can verify that they're genuine?"

"I'll speak with Annabelle about having the paintings examined when we get back."

"Why Annabelle?" Alan asked.

"She's taken over our family's patronage to the local museums."

"Isn't she a bit young to have that responsibility?" Alan asked. "I mean, she can't be more than twenty."

"She'll be twenty-one next month, but she wanted to help ease some of Cassandra's duties." Victoria took a sip of her drink, and her expression turned wistful. "We both do."

Surprised by the glimpse into her personal life, Alan couldn't help but ask, "What duties are you taking off your sister's shoulders?"

The beginnings of a smile played on her lips. "I'll be managing some of the family's personal holdings, specifically The Royal Sands Resort."

"The new resort in Porto Blu?" Alan let out a low whistle. "I've heard a lot about the upcoming opening."

"I'm glad to hear our marketing team's efforts have paid off," Victoria said. "We'll have a limited opening the week before the coronation, with only VIP guests who are attending for the event."

"And after that, it will be open to the public?"

"It will."

"Sounds like your family is about to get even richer." Alan said the words and immediately regretted them. Her family's wealth and their ability to live off the earnings of others through taxes wasn't any of his business.

"The goal isn't to increase my family's wealth," Victoria said, her voice turning cool. "Quite the contrary."

Even though he had clearly hit a nerve, Alan couldn't help but try to clarify her meaning. "You're managing a business that isn't trying to make money?"

"We are trying to make money, but the profits will allow Cassie to keep the tax rates down so our family doesn't need to rely on our subjects for our support."

Contrite, Alan's gaze met hers. "That's very noble."

"Our family is in the business of serving the people of Sereno," Victoria said. "Unlike in many countries, the majority of our holdings serve the public. Half of all profits from our family-controlled businesses fund public works."

"So the more your family businesses make, the more money you have available to maintain your country's infrastructure?"

"Yes. My grandfather enacted a law to that effect shortly after your American president promised to build a naval base and pulled out after plowing over a good portion of our prime farmlands."

"That was quite a while ago," Alan said, aware of the naval base that had been promised by JFK, the same one that had been abandoned by the US government after JFK's assassination. "And it seems like the relations between our two countries have improved since your sister married Levi."

"Some." She tilted her head slightly. "But one marriage can't fix decades' worth of economic struggles that resulted from your country's broken promises."

"Hopefully time will heal those wounds," Alan said, "especially since your country is about to become one of the wealthiest in the region."

"The oil fields, wind fields, and resort will change a lot of things for our people," Victoria agreed. "Royal life is not all tea parties and lounging on the beach."

"I've been around royals enough to know that much," Alan said. "If you're taking over the resort, I guess that means you're moving home for good, then."

"Yes." Victoria glanced out the window briefly, a sudden cloud darkening her expression. "I am."

CHAPTER 4

Victoria gripped the arms of her chair in an effort to keep her arms from shaking. After his initial questions about who might want her dead, Alan had fallen silent, but the adrenaline running through her still hadn't completely abated despite the thirty minutes they had been in the air.

Someone had tried to kill her. She still couldn't wrap her head around it, nor could she fathom who might want to attempt such an attack. Who could want her dead? That question rattled around her brain until her head ached.

"Do you have any games on board?" Alan asked, breaking the silence. "Or maybe a book to read?"

Victoria lifted her eyebrows. "Why? Are you bored?"

"Not for me. For you." Alan gestured toward her hands. "You need a distraction."

Though instinct was to deny any weakness, she fought against it. Alan was right, and he was well aware of why she was uneasy. "I'm too on edge to read."

"What about a game?"

Victoria shook her head. The only two-person game on board was chess, and she certainly couldn't concentrate enough to play that. It wasn't a game she particularly enjoyed even when she wasn't obsessing over a possible assassination attempt.

Alan looked around the cabin. "Do you like dogs?"

"Yes, I like dogs." She furrowed her brow. "Why?"

"Good." Alan snapped his fingers. "Come here, Max."

Max stood and stretched before following Alan's direction and coming to the edge of the table.

"That's a good boy." Alan rubbed his head and motioned to the dog. "You can pet him. It'll help calm you down."

"I thought people weren't supposed to pet working dogs."

"They're not, but he isn't working right now." Alan swallowed and added, "Besides, Max here is going to have to learn how to be a regular pet soon. This is his last assignment before he retires."

"Max is being retired?" Victoria put her hand on the dog's back and ran her hand along his fur. "Why? He isn't that old, is he?"

"He's ten, and he's been working for seven years now." Alan shrugged in what should have been a casual gesture, but Victoria couldn't miss the tension in his posture.

"What will happen to him now?"

"He'll be adopted out. Although it's possible my agency will sell him to a breeder." Alan ran his hand over Max's head again. "He's the best detection canine I've ever seen."

"Can't you adopt him?" Victoria motioned to Max. "I mean, he's your dog."

"Technically, he's my partner," Alan corrected. "But to answer your question, I hoped to adopt him, but I wouldn't be able to take him on my next assignment. It wouldn't be fair since he'd spend most of the next couple years in a kennel."

"Where's your next assignment?" Victoria asked.

"I'm sorry, Your Highness. That's classified."

Victoria's gaze lifted to meet his. "But you'll still be looking for bombs?"

"Yes." Alan ruffled his dog's fur. "But with a new partner."

"Alan, I'm sorry. This must be terribly difficult for you." She petted Max again, and her fingers brushed against Alan's hand.

His hand stilled beside hers. For a moment, her mind went blank. Her gaze met Alan's again, and his eyes darkened. She could get lost in those eyes; it felt as though they held so many secrets. An unexpected spark rippled through her.

It was hard to believe she was sitting here with an American, an employee of the Central Intelligence Agency, no less, when only two years ago, her father had been so anti-American. How things had changed.

Alan's hand remained in place on Max's back, their hands still barely touching. His lips quirked slightly. "Did it help?" For a moment, she wasn't sure what he was talking about. Her confusion must have been evident because he added, "Petting the dog. Did it help calm your nerves?"

She held her hand up. The tremors had stopped. "It did. I didn't expect that."

"Max has a calming effect on people."

"I wasn't feeling so calm when I saw him sitting by that van earlier."

"That's understandable." Alan leaned back in his seat. "Max, go lie down."

Max happily circled the spot beside them twice and settled back onto the floor.

"How about you tell me more about the resort you're opening?" Alan suggested.

Not sure what to make of his question, she asked, "Are you trying to distract me?"

"I am," Alan admitted. "But I really am interested."

Anticipation rose within her. "Do you want to see the photos?"

"Yeah, I'd love to." Alan leaned forward.

Victoria turned her laptop toward him. "Just remember, you asked for it."

* * *

The woman was brilliant. Alan had seen glimpses of Victoria's intelligence during his last stint with the Rossi family, but listening to her detail her plans for the new resort was truly impressive. How she didn't have a dozen men lined up waiting to ask her out was beyond him. Or maybe she did.

Alan shook that uncomfortable thought out of his mind. Victoria's social life wasn't any of his business. She was a member of the royal family he had been asked to help protect. It wouldn't do for him to forget his place—or hers. After all, she was moving to Sereno permanently. He would only be there for a month.

Victoria motioned to the image of the new resort on her laptop screen. "If all goes well, I should have the rest of the staff in place within two weeks."

"I assume you're doing background checks on everyone," Alan said.

"Of course." Victoria tapped on her mouse pad to bring up a different screen. Employee names were listed in three columns, each color coded. She motioned to the blue column. "The employees here are fully vetted and cleared to work with royalty and high-ranking heads of state from other nations."

"And the green?" Alan asked.

"They've been cleared but don't have enough work history to determine whether they would be vulnerable to bribes or potential enticements by the paparazzi or others who might want to invade our guests' privacy." Victoria tapped on the last column, this one shaded in yellow. "These employees haven't been fully cleared yet. Until they are, they won't be able to do more than go through training."

"And if something pops up in their background checks that is concerning?"

"All their employment contracts are contingent upon passing their security screening. Depending on what the problem is, they'll either be paid for the hours spent training and be dismissed, or they will be eligible to work only jobs in low-security areas, like the grounds crew or cleaning staff on lower floors."

"But if you have anyone who isn't fully cleared, they could still access the resort when you have high-profile clientele."

"Actually, we're installing a badge system that can be switched to a high-security mode. When that's engaged, no one on the lower security tier will have access to any of our restricted areas, including the kitchen, the upper floors, and the guest registries."

"I'm impressed."

Victoria's cheeks flushed. "You're being polite. I'm sure you must be bored."

"Not at all." Alan plucked a shortbread cookie out of the basket between them and unwrapped it. "In fact, if there's anything I can do to help with security, let me know."

She pressed her lips together as though debating what to say.

"What? Is there something you already have in mind?" Alan took a bite of his cookie.

"I doubt you would have time to help at the resort."

"I can make time." Though the palace grounds and the spot on the beach where the resort was being built were separated by a natural rocky barrier, the drive between the two couldn't take more than ten minutes. Alan waved at Max sleeping comfortably on the cabin floor. "Max and I usually do a couple of sweeps every day, but it's not uncommon for me to have a few hours in the middle of the day open."

Victoria pulled up another photo of the resort, this time of a pretty garden area at the edge of the grounds. "I'm not really happy with this space here. Levi is insisting we have a double barrier plus an electric fence installed between the two walls to make sure no one can breach the royal grounds."

"That makes sense." Alan studied the topography. He could envision it easily. The double barrier, the electric fence, the rock barrier running along the back of both. "What's the problem?"

"I want these gardens to be inviting, someplace our guests can go to escape from the pressures of the day."

He focused on the rock barrier again; it was something an enterprising pedestrian could potentially cross. "But if you give them too much solitude, it could create a weak spot in the royal defenses."

"Exactly."

"I'm not a landscape designer, but I'm good at spotting potential security problems. I'd be happy to stop by and take a look."

The telltale sound of the landing gear lowering rumbled through the aircraft, and the pilot's voice came over the speaker. "We are beginning our final approach into Sereno National Airport. Please take your seats and fasten your seat belts."

Alan patted the seat behind him. "Max, up."

Victoria secured her belt and raised an eyebrow when she looked at Max now seated in the padded seat behind them.

"Sorry, but the landings are pretty uncomfortable for him if he's on the floor." Alan signaled for Max to lie on the seat and then clicked the seat belt into place around Max's girth before fastening his own.

The steward peeked at them to ensure they were property belted and then took his seat at the front of the cabin. Within minutes, the wheels touched the ground, and the plane cruised down the runway, ultimately slowing before turning toward the hangar.

Not quite ready for his time with Victoria to end, Alan asked, "Is there a good time for me to come by the resort tomorrow?"

"I have meetings until eleven," Victoria said. "If you're free, perhaps you can come by around noon. I'm sampling some of the food from the new chef for the restaurant at the resort. You can join me."

"Sounds like an offer I can't refuse."

CHAPTER 5

Victoria couldn't deny her disappointment when Alan didn't ride with her in the limo taking her from the airport to the palace, but she supposed her driver wouldn't have been pleased to have a dog in his back seat. She wasn't sure if she missed Alan's presence because of the way he had genuinely seemed interested in her work or if it was the way he had been able to distract her after the bombing attempt. Regardless, Alan wasn't here with her now because he had stayed with the artwork to help oversee its transport to the national gallery, where it would be inspected before being put back on display, assuming the paintings were authentic.

She clasped her hands together, her tension rising as the memory of those long moments on the plane in London crept in on her.

Oblivious to the inner turmoil churning through her, her driver kept his focus on the road. Not that he would have broken protocol and started a conversation with her.

The oddity that Alan had been comfortable speaking to her on the plane struck her. After all, technically, he, too, was in the service of the royal family. Yet over the past couple of hours, he hadn't seemed like an employee; he'd seemed like a friend.

Victoria straightened as her driver turned onto the portion of the road right before her home came into view. Within seconds, it appeared on the horizon.

Perched on a bluff overlooking the Mediterranean, the front of the palace resembled the castle that had inspired the Disney theme parks. Conical spires rose to the sky above the turrets that had once housed guards. Open turrets stood on either side, the walls a bright-white limestone against the greenery surrounding the palace.

Unlike the Disney version, beyond the core structure, battlements stretched along the side walls to create what now served as administrative offices.

To so many, the palace was a symbol of Sereno and the royal family. To Victoria, it was home, where her memories lived.

A sense of home flooded through her now. But with it came a fresh wave of grief. Before she left for college, the word *cancer* had simply meant a disease that affected other people. Now it was the curse that had robbed her of both parents.

The limo cleared the front gates and pulled up in front of the family entrance. A guard approached and opened the car door for her.

She gathered her messenger bag and stepped free of the car. By the time she passed into the private receiving hall, both of her sisters were there waiting. Victoria dropped into her customary curtsy to greet her older sister, the queen.

She'd barely straightened when Annabelle threw her arms around her. "You're home! I've missed you."

Victoria's dark mood instantly dissipated. "You saw me two weeks ago."

"For a few hours—most of which were spent doing your hair while you studied for finals."

"My hair did look great for the charity dinner." Victoria laughed. She released Annabelle and turned to hug her older sister. "How is our queen?"

"Happy now that you're safely home." Cassie drew her into a hug and held on. "And you saw me only three days ago."

"Yes, but we hardly had any time together."

"That's true," Cassie conceded. "But I will say it's been much too quiet without you here."

A needle pricked at Victoria's heart. "That's what Mom and Dad always used to say."

Cassie shifted so one arm was still around Victoria's shoulders. "We miss them too."

"I know." Victoria drew a deep breath and fought against the emotions clogging her throat. "It's just so hard to be here and know they're both gone."

"I know it will take some getting used to," Cassie said. "I still go into their apartment at least once a week thinking I can ask Papa a question."

"You never moved into the main residence?"

Cassie shook her head. "Maybe when Levi and I start having children we'll think about moving, but for now, my rooms are plenty big enough for the two of us."

Eager to speak of happier topics, Victoria asked, "Talking about having kids, are you?"

"Not quite yet," Cassie said. "For now, we need to settle into our new roles."

"It sounds like Levi's security consulting business is doing great."

Cassie's eyes lit up. "It is."

"Cassie even convinced him to set up his offices in the East Wing," Annabelle added.

"How did you manage that?" Victoria asked. "I thought he was set on keeping his business separate from our family holdings."

"He was, but I convinced him that the office space could be part of his negotiated fee for the work he does here at the palace," Cassie said. "Plus, it's way more convenient for him to have his offices near the security office than to have to run down from our rooms every time he needs to meet with someone."

"That's great." Victoria headed up the stairs toward the family quarters with her sisters flanking her on either side.

"How was your flight?" Annabelle asked. "I thought you were going to get here an hour ago."

Instantly, Victoria tensed. "The flight was fine once we got off the ground."

"What caused the delay?" Cassie asked.

"I figured Levi already told you about it."

"I've been in meetings all morning." Cassie stopped halfway up the wide stairway and rested her hand on the railing. "What happened?"

Victoria drew a breath before sharing the words that still seemed too surreal to be true. "Someone planted a bomb on the van that transported the paintings to the plane."

"What?" Cassie reached for Victoria's arm as though she were making sure she was really standing there. "Are you okay?"

"I was a bit rattled, but Alan did a good job of distracting me on the flight home." A wave of gratitude washed over her. "Thank goodness he and Max were there."

"They found the bomb?" Annabelle asked, also coming to a stop on the stairs.

"Max found it. Alan defused it."

"Thank goodness I approved Levi's request to have Alan join our security team." Cassie continued upward. "I want to hear all about this. We can talk in my apartment."

"Give me a few minutes to settle in first," Victoria said. "It's been a long morning."

"How about dinner in my apartment? That way Levi can give us any updates," Cassie said.

"I'd like that." Victoria's footsteps slowed when she reached her father's apartment. Doing her best to ignore the tightness in her chest, she turned to

Annabelle. "Alan already put the request in, but you should know that the artwork we transported back is being authenticated before being put on display so we can make sure no one was trying to destroy a forgery."

Annabelle's face lit with surprise. "What?"

The emotional turmoil of today's events caught up with Victoria. "I'll explain more tonight, but you may want to check with the museum."

"Okay," Annabelle said. "I'll make some calls."

"I'll be in my office if you need anything," Cassie said. "Otherwise, plan on meeting for dinner at seven."

Victoria nodded. "I'll see you both later."

She reached her living quarters and walked inside. The modest receiving room was about the same size as the living room in her flat at Cambridge. A sofa stretched along one wall, with a round occasional table between two cushioned chairs opposite it. A potted palm stood in one corner, and a large ceramic urn filled with silk flowers occupied another.

Victoria passed through the doorway that connected the formal space with the large living room beyond.

Light spilled through the floor-to-ceiling windows on the far side of the room, the curtains already open to invite in the view of the ocean. She passed by the massive marble fireplace to her left and lowered her messenger bag onto the rectangular table that ran along the back of the sofa. Without breaking stride, she continued to the french doors and pulled them open.

The scent of the sea carried on the breeze. She stepped onto the balcony and breathed deeply. Waves crashing against the nearby cliffs carried to her, the same sound that had once lulled her to sleep as a child.

A car motor interrupted the peaceful rhythm, and she realized it was the vehicle transporting her luggage when it came to a stop beside the residence entrance. The passenger door opened, and Alan stepped out. He pulled open the rear door, and Max joined him.

As though sensing her presence, Alan looked up. His eyes met hers, and he waved.

Victoria waved back, not sure what to think about the man who would once again be living in her home. He had saved her life today, and she enjoyed his company, but the fact remained: Alan was not only an American—he also worked for the CIA.

* * *

Alan's thoughts were still on Princess Victoria when he and Max passed through the main entrance of the palace, but he was instantly distracted by his ornate surroundings.

No matter how many times he walked these halls, he couldn't get over the intricate details and the historical beauty of the place. Marble floors, ridiculously high ceilings, suits of armor, decorative urns with potted plants.

A guard beside the door stepped forward. "Welcome back."

Alan took a moment to recall the man's name. "Thanks, Emil. It's good to be back." He looked around the enormous space again. "Can you tell me where I can find King Levi's office? I'm supposed to meet him there."

He pointed to the right. "Down that hall. Take a left at the first corridor. After you pass into the East Wing, go up the stairs on the right. His offices are the first ones on your right."

"Thanks."

Alan signaled Max forward, and his thoughts once again returned to Victoria. He couldn't say what it was, but something was different about her since the last time he'd seen her.

He had always admired the way she seemed able to juggle family and her royal duties with such ease. Today, he had sensed both a strength and a vulnerability in her that he hadn't previously witnessed. It wasn't like the grief of seeing her father wage a losing battle with cancer or even the shock of learning a bomb had been planted such a short distance from where she sat on the plane. No, this was different, almost as though she had something to prove, a single-mindedness to carve out her own identity.

He supposed it was natural to need a unique sense of purpose when your older sibling was about to be crowned the leader of your country. The thought of his own older sister brought a smile to his face. If Stephanie ever became president, he had no doubt she'd whip the United States into shape. But he wouldn't want to be seen as only an extension of her or her position.

Alan made his way through the maze of corridors and stairwells until he and Max reached Levi's office. A discreet name plate attached to the wall beside a doorway confirmed they were in the right place, and the oversized mahogany door was already open.

Alan led Max inside, surprised to find himself in a reception area.

A man in his midtwenties looked up from the two computer monitors on his desk and greeted Alan. "You must be Mr. Neisler."

Alan nodded, the salutation making him feel much older and wiser than his twenty-eight years.

"King Levi is expecting you." The man motioned to another ornately carved door. "Please go right in."

"Thank you." Alan managed to keep a straight face because not so long ago, he and Levi had been colleagues and considered equals. Then again, another former coworker, Janessa Rogers, was now a princess in Meridia. Had it not been for Janessa's previous assignment as Prince Garrett's fake fiancée, she never would have ended up a princess, and Levi and Alan never would have ended up working with the royals.

Ever the matchmaker, intentional or not, Janessa had ultimately introduced her brother-in-law to his wife, Alora, also a former CIA employee, and she had also put the wheels in motion for Levi to meet Cassie.

Alan knocked twice before he opened Levi's office door and walked in. As soon as he spotted Levi sitting at a round worktable in the corner, his suit jacket tossed haphazardly over the back of his chair, his sleeves rolled up, Alan closed the door and let his smile break free. "King Levi? What's the world coming to?"

Levi looked up and shot him a wicked grin. "Just think, in another month, Cassie and I will be crowned, and we'll take full control of the affairs of Sereno."

It hardly seemed possible that his friend, a former CIA undercover operative, was now a figurehead for this small island country that was quickly gaining popularity among American and European tourists alike. Alan lifted his eyes skyward and debated whether he should offer a sincere prayer about the state of this country's future now or if he should wait until he was alone.

Levi laughed at his obvious debate. "Trust me, God and I are on very intimate terms since I asked Cassie to marry me."

"I imagine so." Alan signaled for Max to sit before crossing the room.

Levi shook Alan's hand. "Thanks for coming."

"I'm thrilled to be here." Alan shrugged out of his suit coat and tossed it over the back of the chair beside Levi, just as he would have done back when they'd worked together at the agency. "What are you working on?"

"Trying to figure out where the security broke down today in London." Levi sat and gestured to the chair beside him. As soon as Alan settled into it, Levi said, "I thought bringing you here was simply an extra security measure. I had no idea you would save Victoria's life before you even reached Sereno." He paused. "How is she anyway?"

"A bit shaken up, but by the time we got here, she seemed to be doing pretty well, considering."

"And how are you doing?" Levi asked. "It isn't often you have to play bomb squad all by yourself."

"If it's all the same to you, I'd prefer not to go through that again."

"I don't blame you." Levi passed a photo to Alan, a close-up of the disarmed explosive. "Any idea who might have made this?"

"It was pretty basic. No secondary circuit, a simple detonator and timing device." Alan pushed aside the memory of the moment he'd clipped the wire, the moment he could have died had the device included a secondary circuit. He focused on the facts and delivered the bad news. "It could have been anyone who spent enough time watching YouTube videos."

"I was afraid you were going to say that."

"Did the police have any luck pulling any prints?"

"No. They assume our bomber was wearing gloves." Levi dropped the photo on the table and blew out a frustrated breath. "I can't believe someone penetrated our defenses."

"Where was the weak spot?" Alan asked, getting straight to the heart of the matter.

"Best guess is someone attached the bomb when the van was out for a delivery yesterday," Levi said.

"That would explain why the timer was the secondary detonator instead of the primary."

"You're lucky whoever planted it didn't trigger it the minute you found it."

"I know." That thought had raced through Alan's mind more than once since the incident. "But that does tell us that whoever it was, he or she wasn't there when Max found the bomb."

"Or they couldn't trigger it without drawing attention to themselves," Levi countered.

"I assume the police are checking the security feed?"

"Yes, and they're sending it to us as well," Levi said. "It can't hurt to have a few more sets of eyes on it."

"True." Alan settled into his seat while Levi brought him up to speed on the latest developments, ending with the examination of the artwork.

"The full authentication process will take several months," Levi told him. "But I've had staff reviewing the security feed of the storage area of the art gallery in London. So far, we haven't seen any evidence of tampering."

"I guess we work with what we've got for now," Alan said. "In the meantime, what did you have in mind for me?"

"For today, get settled in." Levi pushed back from the table and stood. "I put you in the ground-level tower apartment. It's easy access to get outside for Max, and it keeps you close to the family quarters."

"And tomorrow?" Alan asked as he rose to his feet.

"We'll start with sweeps of the palace morning and night. After a couple days, we'll reassess where you and Max will be most useful."

"Sounds good."

"My assistant will show you to your rooms."

"Your assistant." Alan shook his head with wonder. "Did you ever imagine you would end up with a life like this?"

Levi laughed. "Never."

CHAPTER 6

Victoria still couldn't believe she'd invited Alan to lunch. In the moment, it had seemed like the logical thing to do. After all, he was available in the middle of the day, and her morning had been booked with staff meetings. And he did offer to help her look over her security plans. Yet now, with the scents of grilled fish, freshly baked bread, and mouthwatering sauces lingering in the air, Victoria was experiencing the uncomfortable sensation of waiting for a date.

But it wasn't a date. Regardless of what the tabloids said, her social life had been nonexistent since she'd learned of her father's illness. Her boyfriend at the time had been less than understanding when she had decided to move home and take a gap year before starting graduate school, and she had been far too busy with her studies and the resort to entertain a new romance over the last year.

Victoria moved past the painters in the main reception area and made her way through the window-encased passageway that connected the main building to the restaurant. She peered inside.

Although the kitchen still had some inspections to pass, the dining area already stood ready to receive its first customers. Booths lined the far wall, and tables had been artistically arranged around the dimly lit room. Potted plants would be added within the next few weeks to add to the decor and to provide a more intimate setting for their diners.

Pleased with the progress, Victoria walked back through the passageway to the main building. She breathed in a little too deeply and fought back a cough. She looked forward to the day when the stench of drying paint wouldn't accompany the more savory aromas coming from the restaurant.

Lorenzo approached with a folder in his hand. "Your Highness, we just received the latest plans from the landscape architect."

Victoria held out her hand. "Thank you."

"Would you like to go over them while we review the menu?" he asked.

She fought to keep her surprise from showing on her face. She hadn't anticipated that her assistant manager would join her for the tasting, nor had she invited him to do so. Opting for a diplomatic answer, she said, "I'm sorry, but I had to schedule a security meeting during the tasting."

The front door of the resort opened, and Alan walked in with his German shepherd beside him.

Instantly affronted by a dog's presence, Lorenzo stepped toward them. "I'm sorry, sir, but we aren't open."

"I know." He looked past Lorenzo and bowed to Victoria. "How are you doing today?"

"I'm doing well, thank you." She glanced down at Max. "Perhaps we should meet on the terrace. Max will likely be happier outside."

"It is nice out."

Victoria turned to Lorenzo. "Can you please tell Félix that Mr. Neisler and I will take our samples outside?" Hoping to smooth any ruffled feathers, she added, "You and I can compare notes on the menu this afternoon."

"Of course, Your Highness." He bowed his head slightly.

Victoria led Alan to the wall of french doors that lined the dining area. The terrace beyond was much like the one outside the ballroom at the palace, the wide doors inviting the outside in.

Alan stepped onto the terrace beside her. "Do you want me to leave these doors open? It will help get rid of the paint smell."

Victoria nodded. She chose a seat at a table by the grassy area beside the swimming pool.

"This is really coming together." Alan waited for her to sit before he took his seat. "Other than the painters and the bare floors in the lobby, this place already looks like it could be open to the public."

"We still have so much to do." Victoria pointed at two gardeners planting a palm tree on the far side of the property. "Another dozen trees to plant, finalizing and printing the menus, figuring out the security and landscaping of the section by my family's land. And then there's the furnishings for the guest rooms and the artwork that needs to be hung."

Alan pointed at the grass beside him, and Max stretched out on the ground. "I'm not the greatest at hanging pictures, but I'm happy to look at the security plans."

Victoria opened the landscape architect's plan and spread it out between them. "This just arrived."

Alan leaned forward and stared at the blueprints for a moment. Then he looked around the exterior of the resort before studying them again.

"So these trees would be planted over there?" Alan pointed at the twelve-foot barrier wall that protected the palace grounds from anyone at the resort.

Victoria leaned close, her hair falling over her shoulder. She pushed it back again and nodded. "Yes. The idea was to create a natural barrier so the wall wouldn't be as noticeable to our guests."

Alan shook his head. "Sorry, but that won't do."

"Why not?"

"Those trees will eventually grow above the top of the wall. That gives a potential intruder a perch to climb. Whether someone is aiming a gun or a camera, I don't think your family wants anyone spying on them."

"No, they don't." Victoria suppressed a sigh. Levi had shut down the idea of shrubs in front of the wall. A place for someone to hide. A gazebo would create a potential listening post station. "Someone in security shoots down everything I try to use to hide that wall."

"Then don't hide the wall."

Victoria turned in her chair to face the plain cinder-block wall. The very ugly, plain cinder-block wall. "This is supposed to be a five-star hotel. I can't have that be part of the backdrop."

"Sure you can. Just throw some paint over it, and it'll be fine."

"Fine?" Victoria should have known better than to ask a middle-class American for advice. Alan was as bad as Levi about going to extremes on security measures. "Establishments of this caliber have to do a lot better than fine."

The chef and one of his servers approached, interrupting any response Alan might have made.

"Here are the appetizer selections for today, Your Highness." Félix motioned to the serving tray the waiter held, then described each of the dishes as he transferred them from the serving tray to the table: pan-seared scallops on a bed of greens, with cooked lentils; grilled portabella mushrooms stuffed with a crab-and-cheese mixture; beef carpaccio topped with mozzarella and a pesto sauce; cucumber-stuffed cherry tomatoes; and grilled Mediterranean octopus.

"Wow. These look amazing," Victoria said.

The chef placed two plates on the table with napkins and silverware. Then he clasped his hands together, clearly waiting for their reactions to each of his offerings.

Victoria picked up her fork and cut a large sea scallop into quarters. She took a bite and hummed her approval. "You have to try this."

Alan took a bite twice the size of hers. "Oh." He nodded. "That's a winner."

Victoria nodded her agreement. One by one, they sampled the appetizers, each one just as good as the last.

When Félix left them alone to retrieve the next samples, Alan said, "This restaurant alone is going to put this place on the map."

"We were very lucky Félix was willing to come here." Victoria didn't want to think about the risk she had taken by putting so much of her budget into his salary.

She glanced at the Mediterranean, the water rolling over the sandy beach a short distance away. They'd package the restaurant, the ambiance of the common areas, and the luxurious rooms with state-of-the-art security, high-quality service, and incredible views to launch The Royal Sands Resort to the top of the list for best resorts in the Mediterranean. At least, that was what Victoria hoped would happen.

Alan interrupted her thoughts. "I was serious about painting the wall."

"Painting isn't going to help." Victoria shook her head. "I need something that will hide it so no one knows it's there."

"I'm not talking about just giving it a new color," Alan said. "Make it a mural. Invite one of your local artists to create a seascape on the wall so you see the natural beauty of the actual ocean and beach and then see it mirrored in the mural."

Victoria narrowed her eyes and looked at the ugly wall. With a little effort, she could picture it. Waves rolling over sand, the mural ending where the landscape began. "I could leave a grassy area there, maybe put a bocce ball court in front of the wall."

Alan nodded. "It's simple, and it keeps the visibility of the wall intact. Security cameras at the resort and more on the royal-grounds side of the wall will ensure no one goes where they aren't welcome."

"And my family can maintain their privacy."

"Exactly."

"It's such a simple solution." Victoria tilted her head as she studied Alan. Her earlier irritation faded. "Thank you."

"You're welcome."

Félix reappeared holding another tray, this one filled with main-dish selections.

Alan breathed deeply and picked up his fork. "For the record, I'm available anytime you need a taste tester."

Victoria couldn't help but smile. "That's good to know."

* * *

Alan sampled a last bite of mango cheesecake and reminded himself that this wasn't a date. Just because he was sitting beside Victoria and eating with her didn't mean he could pretend she was now someone he could be interested in romantically.

But he was interested, and he didn't want to be. She was royal, and he was far from it.

He turned to the chef. "Félix, truly, this has all been amazing."

The man's stern features relaxed into a satisfied smirk. "Your choices for the main menu, Your Highness?"

Victoria studied the selection of eight desserts in front of her. "I hate to admit this, but I can't decide."

Alan took a last bite of mango cheesecake. He needed to make this his last bite, or his stomach might explode. "Maybe this decision is best left to the chef."

A light dawned in Victoria's eyes, as though she had never considered delegating the choice to another. After pondering a moment, she nodded. "I think Alan's right. Everything we've had today has been award-worthy. I'd like you to create a balanced selection that you feel is manageable for the main menu, and you can incorporate the other dishes as specials."

Félix took a step back, and his jaw dropped for a brief moment before he managed to press his lips together again.

Alan scooped more cheesecake onto his fork. Okay, this was really going to be his last bite. "I know some of my favorite restaurants create their specials based on which fruits and vegetables are in season."

Félix gave a definitive nod of agreement. "That would help us keep our supply costs more consistent."

"And it would allow us to procure more produce locally." Victoria nodded. "I like it."

"Giulia will appreciate that," Félix said.

"Who's Giulia?" Alan asked.

"She's our kitchen manager," Victoria said. "She takes care of procuring our supplies and hiring the kitchen and serving staff so Félix can concentrate on his strengths."

"Like making magic in the kitchen." Alan pushed his plate back. "You'd better take this away from me, or I may not be able to walk out of here on my own."

Félix's lips quirked into a half smile. He lifted his hand to signal a nearby server, who promptly stepped forward and stacked the dishes onto a tray.

"I'd like a draft of the menu by Monday," Victoria told Félix.

"Yes, Your Highness." Félix stepped away from the table. He and the server had barely disappeared from view when Lorenzo emerged onto the patio and made a beeline for the princess.

Alan fought back his unexpected annoyance. Had he really thought he and Victoria would have time alone together? Their two hours on the plane had been an anomaly and would likely not repeat itself. He shouldn't forget that.

Lorenzo reached their side. "I have my notes on the menu. When would you like to discuss them, Your Highness?"

"Let's meet on Monday afternoon, say, three o'clock," Victoria said. "By then, we should have Félix and Giulia's draft menu."

Lorenzo's mouth opened and closed twice before he managed to find his words. "But I thought we were going to determine the menu."

"As Alan wisely pointed out, who better than the chef to guide this decision?"

Lorenzo straightened his shoulders and tilted his chin up slightly. "If you have delegated that task elsewhere, perhaps now is a good time to look over the landscape plans."

"Meet me in my office in two hours," Victoria said. "I'd like to show Alan around before we finalize those details."

Lorenzo's jaw tightened briefly, but he nodded. "As you wish."

Victoria pushed back from the table and stood. "Shall I give you that tour?"

Time alone with a fascinating, gorgeous woman? Alan rose to his feet. "I'd love that."

CHAPTER 7

Victoria's impression of Alan was changing by the minute. During his previous time working at the palace, she had viewed him simply as a necessary member of the security force, one who stood out because of his canine partner.

Today, as they walked along the perimeter of the property, she came to understand that he was far more than a glorified guard. The man's ability to identify potential problems was truly mind-boggling.

They reached the spot on the beach where dry sand gave way to wet. Max trotted alongside them, his leash now tucked away in Alan's pocket.

Alan pointed at the rope attached to buoys that stretched out into the water to delineate the resort side of the beach from the royal side. "Are there any motion sensors or other security measures to pick up movement if someone tries to bypass the guards on the beach?"

"Levi had some kind of sonar detectors installed last year to protect us from anyone approaching our land from the water," Victoria said. "In truth, the family never uses the beach on the other side of the rocks. It's too visible to people in town."

"I figured you would prefer the beach on the far side of the cliffs," Alan said. "We just have to make sure this beach can't be used as an infiltration point."

Victoria stopped and turned toward the palace grounds. From here, the rock barrier and short stretch of beach beyond the wall weren't visible, nor were the cliffs that lay immediately beyond. "The reason we created the barrier where we did was so Levi could install the electric fence but leave the natural protection of the rocky area and the cliff walls."

"It was a smart choice," Alan said. "But if you rely solely on the natural barriers, you still run the risk of someone climbing the rocks at night and slipping past the guards."

Victoria looked over her shoulder to ensure that they were still alone. "Did you work in a security unit with the CIA before you started working with the canine unit?"

"Actually, I started out studying electrical engineering. I also used to work part-time with my dad's architectural firm. It's amazing how much staring at building blueprints teaches you how to identify the weak spots."

"I can imagine, but how did you end up going from engineering to doing—" She waved her hand toward Max, not quite sure how to phrase her question without offending him.

"To playing with bombs and dogs?" Alan's low laugh chased away any awkwardness that might have encroached upon their budding friendship. "I guess you could say I stumbled into it."

"How?"

Alan fell silent for a moment, as though debating how much to say.

"I'll understand if you can't tell me."

"It's not classified." Alan shook his head. "In fact, you could probably still find the story in the newspaper if you looked hard enough."

"What story?"

"Let's just say my first experience with explosives wasn't planned."

Victoria tilted her head to one side. "You aren't going to make me search the internet to find out, are you?"

He drew a deep breath. "I was interning for a civilian contractor on an army base when the fire alarm went off in the building we were renovating. Everyone headed for the exits, assuming it was just a fire drill."

"I'll venture a guess that it wasn't."

"No." Alan leaned down and ran his hand over the top of Max's head. "I was working in the basement and made it to the stairwell, where I noticed a dog sitting beside the water heater. I called to him, but he didn't move."

"Whose dog was it?"

Alan glanced down at his dog. "It was Max. He was operating as a bomb-detection canine for the army." Alan stroked his dog's fur again. "When I went to get him so I could take him out of the building, I found his handler on the ground, shot twice. And there was a bomb attached to the main gas line."

"Oh my gosh." Victoria put her hand on her chest, unable to fathom what she would do in such a situation. The mere prospect of facing a live explosive was outside the realm of her wildest nightmare. "You must have been terrified."

"That's an understatement," Alan said. "But that moment changed my life."

"What did you do?"

"There was less than two minutes on the timer. I knew I couldn't get out of there fast enough, especially if I tried to take the injured man with me." Alan shrugged and blew out a breath. "So I disarmed the bomb."

"You"—Victoria's eyes widened—"disarmed the bomb?"

"I didn't have much of a choice."

"How did you even know how to do that?"

"Like I said, I studied electrical engineering."

Victoria lifted her eyebrows. "I don't think they teach people how to disarm bombs in school."

"No, but I'm pretty good with circuitry." Alan rubbed his free hand over his thigh. "I borrowed some wire cutters from the toolkit Max's handler had dropped. Then it was just a matter of determining which circuit to disrupt to ensure the detonator could no longer signal the explosive," he said.

"Did Max's handler survive?"

"Yes, but it was a long road to recovery, and he ended up taking a medical retirement."

"And then you and Max joined the CIA?"

"Yeah. Turns out Max had only been on the job for a few months when I met him," Alan said. "The CIA recruited us both, and we've been at this ever since."

"Do you like it?"

He hesitated ever so slightly. "Most of the time."

"Well, I'm grateful you're so good at your job. Your background has certainly served you well."

"Yeah, I guess so." Alan stopped walking and turned back toward the resort. "This really is a gorgeous place."

Victoria followed his gaze to the white, castle-like structure. The conical spires on the corners of the resort building had been designed to resemble the palace, the rounded turrets creating unique guest rooms with incredible views of the water and surrounding countryside. "Come on. Let me show you the inside."

"I'd like that."

* * *

Alan stepped into one of the tower guest rooms and let out a low whistle. "Wow. This is incredible."

The arched windows on one side framed the view of the Mediterranean. On the other side, the lush green of the mountains was interrupted only by the tower on the opposite corner of the building.

"The architect did a wonderful job protecting the views for as many of the rooms as possible."

Max sat on the thick carpet and stretched out his legs in front of him.

"And clearly Max approves." Alan grinned. "Did you steal one of the tower rooms for your office?"

"I thought about it, but I couldn't justify taking a premium room for myself." She waved toward the hall. "My office is on the first floor and doesn't even have a window."

"So you're pretending to be ordinary while your guests pretend to be royalty."

Victoria laughed. "I guess so." She crossed to the closest window. A slight edge came into her voice. "This is what people will pay for, to come here and feel like they're living in a dream."

The way she said it caught Alan's attention. "The typical person doesn't have a clue what your reality is like, do they?"

Surprise illuminated her features. "No." She turned to face him. "They don't."

Without thinking, Alan put his hand on her shoulder. For a brief moment, he forgot about his upcoming transfer and the title that came before her name. Her brown eyes met his and held. "We'll find out who was behind the bomb attempt yesterday."

"I hope so." Victoria remained where she was for several seconds longer before she stepped back, forcing him to break contact. As though lifting a shield between them, her voice took on a professional tone once more. "Now that you've seen the most expensive room, let me show you what our typical guest rooms look like."

Alan fell in behind her, Max following obediently.

Victoria showed him the various room types, ranging from multiple-room suites to classic European hotel rooms that didn't contain much more than a bed and a bathroom.

"This really is impressive," Alan said.

"Thanks." Victoria headed toward the sweeping staircase that led from the first floor to the ground level. "Lorenzo has done a great job keeping everything running in between my visits home. Most of the rooms haven't been furnished yet, but we'll work on that in the next few weeks."

"How often were you flying back here while you were in school?"

"Every other weekend."

Alan stopped at the top step and stared. "Seriously? How did you manage to keep up with your studies?"

"I did a lot of homework on the plane." Victoria moved past him. "And thankfully, I didn't have any bomb threats last year."

"That would help too." Alan walked beside her, and they reached the entrance to the courtyard that made up the center of the building. The grass had already been groomed, and tables, chairs, and benches had been placed strategically throughout to create conversation areas and spots where someone could simply escape for a moment of solitude.

"This turned out great," he said.

"I think our guests will enjoy it." Victoria led the way into the reception area.

Alan took in the packages that filled the space by the glass front doors, packages that looked very much like the ones in the back of the cargo van yesterday.

A worker picked up a box that looked to be the size of a small painting and carried it toward the elevator. Alan caught sight of the stamp on the box: Sereno National Gallery.

He'd seen that stamp before, only moments before he and Max had disarmed a bomb. The possibility of artwork being used to plant another bomb flooded his mind.

Alan rushed forward. "Whoa! Has anyone run a security check on that yet?"

The worker looked from Alan to Lorenzo. "He told me to take this upstairs."

"Have these packages been examined yet?"

Clearly confused as to Alan's concern, Lorenzo said, "The workers know to document any breakage when they unwrap them."

"That's not what I'm worried about." Alan turned to Victoria. "This isn't safe."

"I'm doing my job as efficiently as possible." Irritation and indignation merged in Lorenzo's expression.

"And you can get back to doing your job in a few minutes." Alan pushed past Lorenzo and spoke to his dog. "Max. Search."

Max instantly sniffed at the nearest package.

"What are they doing?" Lorenzo asked Victoria, his irritation carrying into his voice.

"They're helping me," Victoria said calmly. She turned to the man who had been carrying the package. "Riccardo, how many packages have already been taken upstairs?"

"None. We just finished our inventory."

"Without opening the boxes?" Victoria asked.

Alan wasn't sure if she understood his concern about potential explosive devices being hidden inside or if she was focused on ensuring everything had arrived intact. Regardless, she was keeping Lorenzo out of his way, and for that he was grateful.

Lorenzo huffed out a breath. "The contents are clearly marked on the outside."

"And sometimes they are marked incorrectly."

"Which is why I instructed everyone to do a count and check for damage every time they open a new one."

Max completed his inspection of the boxes closest to him, and Alan guided him to the next stack of packages.

"From now on, I want everything inspected before going beyond the lobby," Victoria said.

Max sniffed at the largest of three, sniffed the other two, and came back to the biggest one again. Alan's heartbeat quickened. He'd seen this behavior before. Sometimes it turned out to be nothing, but often, it happened right before Max identified a problem.

"We'll have far less breakage if we take the artwork upstairs in their shipping containers," Lorenzo protested.

"Yes, but—" Victoria cast a glance at Max as though she, too, sensed a problem. Max sat down and whimpered. The princess gasped. "Oh no."

CHAPTER 8

Victoria's heart seized. Her breath caught. Not again. There couldn't be another bomb.

"What's wrong?" Lorenzo asked, clearly missing the significance of Max's motionless state.

Alan didn't give Victoria the chance to respond. He waved her toward the back terrace. "You need to get out of here. And call the police."

Victoria pulled her cell phone from her pocket and dialed 112 for emergency services.

Alan turned to Riccardo, the staff member who had been carrying a package to the elevator. Reaching into his pocket, Alan retrieved a set of car keys. "I need you to go out to the black sedan parked out front. Get me the silver plastic box from the trunk. It's about the size of a toolkit." Alan tossed his keys to Riccardo. "Make it quick."

He nodded and rushed out the front door.

A woman answered Victoria's call with, "Emergency services. What is your emergency?"

"I need the police and a bomb squad at The Royal Sands Resort."

"The bomb squad?" Lorenzo backed away from the crates and boxes. "There's a bomb?"

"As soon as I have my tools, that's what I'm going to find out," Alan said.

"I'm dispatching the police right now," the emergency operator said. "Have you discovered a bomb, or was a bomb threat called in?"

Before Victoria could answer, Lorenzo backed up farther. "I'll pull the fire alarm."

"No." Alan looked up from his examination of the box. "If there really is something here, we don't want to alert anyone that we're aware of it. If there's a secondary detonator, they could set it off."

"Signorina," the operator said, pulling Victoria's attention back to the phone call.

"We have a trained bomb-detection canine that has signaled a problem," Victoria said as Riccardo returned with Alan's tools. "His handler believes there may be a bomb."

"A bomb?" Riccardo's eyes widened. He dropped the toolbox, turned, and ran back out the front door.

Ignoring him, Victoria asked, "How long until the police get here?"

"Three minutes," she said. "Have you already evacuated the building?"

"No."

"Do that now," the emergency operator said.

Victoria turned to Alan. "She wants us to evacuate."

"No. Get everyone to the restaurant." Alan flipped open the lid of his toolkit.

"They may already know we found the bomb if they saw Riccardo run out of here," Victoria said.

"One person running outside isn't the same as a whole building emptying out," Alan said. "The restaurant is a separate building, and it's far enough away that everyone should be protected."

"Everyone except you," Victoria said.

"I'll be fine."

Victoria hoped so. She turned to Lorenzo. "You heard him. Get everyone to the restaurant."

Lorenzo quickly disappeared from the room.

Alan pointed at her phone. "Make sure you tell the operator that the bomb squad needs to come in an unmarked vehicle."

Victoria repeated the instructions to the woman on the phone.

As soon she finished relaying the instructions, Alan said, "You need to go too."

"Be careful."

"I will." Alan flipped open the lid of the toolkit and retrieved a flashlight and a box cutter. "Go on." He tilted his head toward the doorway. "I need to know you're safe before I see what I've got here."

Though she hated to leave him, Victoria backed into the hotel lobby and forced herself to leave Alan and Max alone.

* * *

Alan waited until Victoria's footsteps faded before he made his first cut in the tape securing the flaps on the box. His examination of the exterior hadn't revealed any tripwires or booby traps, but he wasn't about to take chances that a mistake on his part might get Victoria killed, especially when he didn't have access to any portable scanners or X-ray technology.

The words *Fragile — Artwork — The View of Sereno* were stamped on the side, but if Max was right, that wasn't all that was inside this box.

A flash of doubt surfaced. It was possible something inside was a substance Max was trained to detect instead of an actual explosive device. It would be embarrassing, for sure, to have caused others stress for no reason, but in this case, Alan preferred that over the alternative.

"No offense, buddy," Alan said to Max. "But I'm really hoping you're wrong on this one."

Slowly and steadily, Alan peeled away the tape on the narrow end of the oversized cardboard box. Then he gently pulled the top section as far as it would go without cutting more of the tape. He shined his light inside, and he caught his first glimpse of a potential problem: a red wire running across the center of the box, right where he would have cut had he opted to start on the center piece of tape.

Holding his thin flashlight in his mouth, he carefully used his box cutter to cut away the portion of the top flap closest to him, taking off a small piece at a time to make sure he didn't inadvertently cut through any other wires that might be hidden within the packaging.

When the hole reached six inches in diameter, he pulled the flashlight from his mouth and examined the visible contents. The wire he had first spotted ran from where it was attached to the tape at the top of the box, along either side, and disappeared into some corrugated cardboard packaging. A few inches farther down the center strip of tape, a blue wire ran parallel to the red one, and a green wire ran beyond that.

He adjusted the light so he had a clearer view of the wires running down the side of the box, and his heartbeat quickened. A spiderweb of wires lined the inside of the box where his light shone. And here he was without any protective gear and with only a handful of basic tools to navigate his way through a device unlike anything he had ever seen before.

Uneasy that he had no idea what kind of detonator he might be dealing with or how much time he might have, Alan diverted his attention to the narrow side of the box. With no wires in sight there, he cut away a large section, essentially creating a door into the box by removing the majority of the side panel.

The door to the building opened, and two men entered, both wearing protective gear, complete with the full-body suits and helmets that left them resembling astronauts dressed in green. Alan's throat closed up. So much for keeping everyone from knowing they'd identified the problem.

"What do you have?" the first man asked.

"Still trying to figure that out," Alan said. "It looks like a bomb encased in the cardboard."

"Detonator?"

"I can't see it, but there are wires lining the center. Looks like it would have gone off if someone had cut through the tape to open the box."

"Clever." The shorter of the two men squatted beside Alan and looked over his shoulder. "I'm Officer Ortega. This is Officer Morales."

"Alan Neisler, royal guard," Alan said, opting to use his current role rather than make something up to hide his true employer. "Any chance you have another bomb suit in your van?"

"Yeah," Ortega said. "Morales, go get it."

Keys jangled as Morales disappeared out the front door.

"Once I suit up, we need to cut away the other side and support the interior while I work my way through the packaging to find out what's really inside."

"This is going to take a while," Ortega said.

Alan's stomach twisted uncomfortably. "I hope we've got a while."

* * *

An hour and seventeen minutes. Why was it taking so long? The last time Alan had disarmed a bomb, it had taken less than five minutes.

Victoria paced the length of the kitchen again, her personal guard standing between her and the door leading to the resort. She had already sent home six workmen who were getting ready to break for lunch. They had no idea why she had given them the rest of the day off, but they hadn't been too upset about the prospect of waiting until tomorrow to finish caulking the rest of the bathtubs on the third floor.

The police had escorted Lorenzo and the rest of the staff to the beach. Victoria assumed they had taken refuge in a gazebo on the deck or in the boathouse.

As for her, she had made the conscious choice to remain inside. Or more specifically, Giuseppe, her personal guard, had offered the wisdom that if the bomb by the front door was meant for her, it was possible someone could be using an explosion to drive her outside, where she would be most vulnerable.

Victoria doubted that was the case. After all, she and Alan had been outside for much of the afternoon, and no one had been visible besides the gardeners planting trees, Félix, and some of the kitchen staff.

Giuseppe's phone rang, and he answered it. "Giuseppe." He paused, clearly listening to whoever was on the other end. "Nothing yet, sire."

Sire? It must be Levi.

The conversation continued, with Giuseppe explaining that they didn't have anything new to report since first informing Cassie of the possible threat.

Giuseppe was still on the phone when footsteps against tile carried to them. The kitchen door opened, and Alan walked in with Max. At least, Victoria was pretty sure it was Alan beneath the astronaut-looking suit. And if he was here, did that mean they were safe now?

Alan removed his helmet and spoke to Giuseppe. "Are you still talking to the police?"

"No. It's King Levi," Giuseppe said. "Is everything okay?"

Alan used the back of his hand to wipe at the sweat on his brow. "It is for now."

Relief washed over Victoria.

Alan reached out his hand. "Let me talk to him." He took the phone from the guard and lifted it to his ear. "Hey, it's Alan. We need to meet."

Victoria's stomach lurched when Alan focused on her.

"Send a car for us. I want the bomb squad to check out all of our vehicles before anyone drives them." Alan said his goodbyes and hung up.

"Tell me what you found," Victoria said, needing to know the extent of the threat.

"I'll tell you all about it when we get back to the palace." Alan handed Giuseppe's phone back to him before speaking to Victoria again. "Is there anything you need from your office? We may need to keep you away from here for a few days."

Even though her body still trembled, Victoria took a step toward the door. "I'll get my laptop and my files."

"Wait here until Max and I clear your office," Alan said. "I'll call you as soon as we're done, and Giuseppe can escort you there." Without waiting for a response, he tugged on Max's leash, and the two of them disappeared back through the door.

CHAPTER 9

ALAN WAITED FOR VICTORIA TO slide into the back of the limousine before he ordered Max into the vehicle. Alan sat across from Victoria and stroked Max's head. The dog had saved one life today. Maybe more.

The bomb squad would take over the analysis of the explosive, but Alan had left orders that he and Levi both receive reports on their findings.

Giuseppe took the spot in the front passenger seat, and the moment that last door closed, the driver pulled away from the resort.

"Tell me everything," Victoria said.

The scene was a little too much like when Alan had first boarded her private plane.

He glanced at the two men in the front seat. Even though they both had high security clearances to gain their current positions, Alan wasn't prepared to give details in front of anyone who didn't have an absolute need to know.

As though sensing the reason for his hesitation, Victoria pressed the button on the control panel beside her to raise the privacy window between them and the driver.

When it slipped into place, Victoria said, "Tell me." She swallowed hard before she asked, "It was another bomb, wasn't it?"

"Yes." Alan ran both hands along his thighs, grateful to be free of the protective gear he had borrowed.

Victoria pressed her lips together before she spoke again. When she did, her voice quivered. "Was I the target?"

"It's possible."

She nodded, not in agreement but as though she were fighting against her rising emotions. When tears shimmered in her eyes, Alan reacted on instinct. He slid into the seat next to her and put his arm around her. She leaned into him.

Her hair brushed against his cheek, the silkiness sending a shiver through him. The fragrance of her perfume tickled his senses, something floral with an underlying hint of spice.

"You're okay," he murmured, trying his best to ignore the way she fit so neatly against him.

"That's twice you've saved my life." She leaned her head on his shoulder, burrowing into him. She sniffled. "If you and Max hadn't been there today . . ."

Alan didn't want to think about what might have happened today or yesterday had Levi not put him in Victoria's path. Needing confirmation of his suspicions, Alan asked, "The package containing the bomb said it had artwork in it, *The View of Sereno*. Where was that supposed to go?"

"My office." Victoria swallowed hard. "It was a painting for my wall."

"So if Lorenzo had gone through with his original plans, Riccardo would have delivered it there," Alan said. "Would he have opened it and hung up the artwork?"

She shook her head. "No. I specifically asked that it not be opened until I was present because of the value of the painting," Victoria said. "Was the painting even in the package?"

"No. Besides the bomb, there was a lot of packaging and a bunch of wires that would have triggered the explosive."

She shifted away from him and tilted her head up so she could see his face. "How would the wires have triggered it?"

"They were taped to the center seam. Whoever opened the box would have needed to use scissors to cut the tape. When they did, they would have cut one of the wires and detonated the bomb."

"I could have peeled the tape off."

"The tape had a wire connected to it that would have also detonated it," Alan said. "Would you have opened the package yourself?"

She shook her head. "Probably not. I would have been there when it was opened, but Riccardo or Lorenzo probably would have taken care of it for me."

"So, if someone knew that you asked to be present when the package was opened, you were the target," Alan said. "How many people knew that?"

"I don't know." She sniffled again. "The director at the museum, Lorenzo, a few staff members. It's possible the delivery crew might have known as well."

"I want you to make a list of everyone you can think of who may have had that information."

"If one of them is behind this, it's someone who's working closely with me."

"Yes, which is why I don't want you anywhere near the resort until we get this sorted out."

Victoria straightened, suddenly indignant. "How am I supposed to coordinate the opening if I'm not ever on site?"

Alan pulled the arm that had been around her back to his side. "I don't know, but it will be a heck of a lot easier than if you're dead."

She sucked in a quick breath.

"I'm sorry." Alan put his hand on hers. "I didn't mean to sound harsh, but you need to know what we're dealing with here. If you are a target, whoever is after you is determined," Alan said. "Bombs aren't items you can just pick up at the market. They take planning, and they take access. For this to happen twice in two days is very unsettling."

"On that, we can agree." Victoria blinked against the tears in her eyes.

Sympathy welled inside him. "We'll figure this out."

"And while you do, I'll be kept prisoner."

The palace came into view. "I can think of worse places to be locked up."

"That's beside the point." She lifted her gaze to meet his, the depth of her fear swimming in her eyes. "Who would want me dead?"

"That's an excellent question, and it's one Levi and I will explore fully."

The limo passed through the gates and pulled up to the family entrance.

He waited for the driver to open the door before he stepped out and patted his leg to signal for Max to follow. Even though he was certain the guards had already secured the area, he looked around the grounds before he offered Victoria his hand.

She put her hand in his, and attraction rose within him at the simple contact. He did his best to ignore it.

"Giuseppe will escort you up to your room," Alan said. "I'll let you know how my meeting with Levi turns out."

"No." Victoria shook her head. "I need to be there too."

"Why?"

"If someone was trying to kill you, wouldn't you want to know everything you could?" Victoria asked.

Alan didn't have to ponder that question. "Yeah, I would." He looked down at her hand that was still in his and gave it a gentle squeeze. "Let's go."

* * *

Victoria fought against the tears still threatening as she walked with Alan down the hall to Levi's offices. The moment they entered, Levi stood and crossed to her. He pulled her into a brotherly hug and held on for a long moment. "Are you okay?"

She started to nod but immediately abandoned the premise to shake her head. Tears carried through her voice when she asked, "Why is someone doing this?"

"I don't know." Levi walked her to one of the chairs across from his desk.

She sat, immediately missing the comfort of having Levi's arm around her. She'd always wanted an older brother, and Levi lived up to everything she had ever hoped for. Besides making Cassie happy, he made them all feel safe.

Victoria turned her gaze to Alan. He had that same effect on her, yet the comfort he'd given her in the limo hadn't felt brotherly.

Levi leaned against the front of his desk and gestured for Alan to take the remaining empty chair. "I already spoke with Cassie, and she's asked me to head this investigation personally. I also received a call from the police chief. From what he described, this bomb wasn't anything like the first bomb you disarmed."

"It wasn't." Alan glanced at Victoria as though he were debating how much he should say in front of her. A moment passed before he continued. "The first device was simple. Anyone with enough time and the right tools could have made it," he said.

"And the second?"

"Well-thought-out, creative." Alan shook his head slightly. "If I didn't know better, I'd say the second device was the initial explosive, and the one in London was a panic job."

"They're out of order."

"Yes," Alan said. "And I don't know why."

Victoria fought back her emotions and struggled to follow Alan and Levi's conversation. "What do you mean by 'they're out of order'?"

Levi answered instead of Alan. "When someone uses an explosive as a weapon, there's a significant amount of planning that goes into it."

"The bomb I disarmed today was meticulously planned to detonate only when that package was opened," Alan said. "It wasn't something someone could have created after the first one missed." He glanced at Levi. "Assuming the first one missed."

"You still think it might have been to destroy the paintings?" Levi asked.

"Maybe." Alan pushed out of his seat and paced to the window and back. "Either way, we have two bomb makers. The first one was likely in the UK. The one who built the one that showed up today could be from any country familiar with your shipping methods."

Victoria had no idea how Alan could be so specific about where the bomb makers were from, but Levi seemed to agree with his assessment.

"But you do think the two incidents are related?" Levi asked.

"Absolutely. They both used the transportation of artwork as their delivery method," Alan said.

"Now we just have to figure out who would benefit from these bombings." Levi flicked a glance at Victoria.

And who would want me dead. The unspoken words hung heavily in the air. She swallowed and asked, "What would this bomber's motivation be?"

"Artwork is still a possibility," Alan said. "The painting that was supposed to be in the package today wasn't there."

"Which begs the question, Where is it?" Levi picked up his phone and hit a button. "Lorenzo, I need you to find out if the artwork for Princess Victoria's office at the resort is still at the museum." He paused. "Yes. Use discretion."

Levi hung up the phone.

"Any chance of getting an early finding from whoever is authenticating the paintings?" Alan sat back down beside Victoria.

"I already asked about that." Levi circled his desk and settled into his office chair. He flipped through several papers. "They plan to give me a preliminary report on Wednesday, but unless it shows clear evidence of a forgery, it won't do us much good."

"One week." Alan turned toward Victoria. "Can you work from here for that long?"

"I can maybe manage a few days, but even that will be hard," Victoria said. "You saw what happened when Lorenzo was in charge of receiving the shipments. He hasn't been trained to take potential security issues into consideration before making a decision."

"Seems odd that you have someone working for you who isn't more security conscious," Alan said.

Her cheeks flushed. Hiring Lorenzo had been her decision. "He's good at his job in every other aspect."

"Victoria was lucky to steal him from The Imperial Blu before she left for school last fall," Levi said. "But I do think I should have one of my contractors provide a security lesson to the hotel staff."

"That's a good idea," Alan said before Victoria could speak. He looked at her. "Would you be okay with that?"

"After today, I think it's prudent to train the staff in every aspect of preventing future issues."

"I'll set it up." Levi jotted down a note on the pad of paper at his elbow.

"I also think you should consider buying a portable scanner for the royal guard. It would be good to have in case we run into any more problems," Alan said.

"I'll get Darius on that," Levi said, referring to the captain of the guard. He looked up and focused on Victoria. "For now, let's plan on having you work here at the palace for the rest of the week. We'll reevaluate on Monday."

"Are you going to let the work continue at the hotel while I'm here?" Victoria asked.

"I'd like to minimize the staff there for a few days," Levi said.

"I'll see what I can do to juggle schedules, but I really need the contractors to continue if we're going to open on schedule."

"What if I go over and run a sweep of everything the workers bring in every morning?" Alan asked.

"That may be our best option," Levi said.

Relief filled her. "Thank you. I'll work on those schedules this evening."

"Alan, I know you and Max have already had a full day, but would you mind helping her?" Levi held up his hand as though expecting Victoria to protest. "I know you're capable, but I'd like for you to have Alan's insights to make sure he can cover the areas where you'll have workers."

Victoria turned to Alan. "If you're willing, I'd appreciate the help."

"Yeah, I'm willing."

CHAPTER 10

Alan dropped onto the sofa in the living room of the apartment he had been assigned. Unlike the last time he'd lived at the palace, his quarters were far more expansive than a bedroom and a bathroom. The living room alone was double the size of the room he'd had in the servants' wing, and the kitchen was large enough to seat two people at the counter and another four at the kitchen table.

Had Alan been heading back stateside instead of to the Middle East, this was exactly the type of place he would rent for himself and Max. Max sniffed along the base of the coffee table before he sat and rested his chin on the cushion beside Alan.

"You did good today." Alan ruffled the fur between Max's ears. The moment he withdrew his hand, Max plopped his chin on Alan's leg.

"You want some more attention, huh?" Alan stroked Max's back several times before settling more comfortably onto the sofa.

He closed his eyes and contemplated the bomb he had disarmed today. The bomb maker really had been clever. If anyone besides a trained bomb tech had opened the box, the lobby would have ceased to exist, and the blast area would have been extensive.

Sitting here alone with Max, he could admit that he wasn't looking forward to going back to the resort, not because he was afraid of what might happen to him but because he feared someone might succeed on the next attempt if he didn't do his job well enough.

And there would be another attempt. He had no doubt about that.

Artwork or Princess Victoria. Which was the target?

Max whined, a reminder that it was approaching dinnertime.

"It's that time, huh?" Despite his weariness, he pushed to a stand.

Max wagged his tail and followed Alan into the kitchen.

Alan opened up the pantry, where he had stored Max's dry dog food. The large bag filled the bottom shelf. The other shelves remained bare. "Tomorrow, no matter what, we're going grocery shopping."

Max looked up at him as though he understood. Alan suspected that he did.

He scooped food into Max's dish and set it on the floor. After he refilled Max's water, he opened the refrigerator. Why he'd expected food to magically appear, he couldn't say. It remained empty, except for two bottles of sparkling water. Even after all these years living in Europe, he had never developed a taste for it. He much preferred still water.

He pulled a glass out of the cabinet and filled it with tap water. After he drained the glass, he set it in the sink. His stomach growled. He had two choices: go to the other side of the palace and eat with the servants or borrow another car and go to the store.

Max lifted his head, his ears raised.

Someone knocked on the door.

Alan crossed the room, and Max abandoned his food to investigate who was on the other side. Alan pulled the door open, surprised to find Victoria standing across the threshold. A woman stood behind her holding a large tray.

"I hope you haven't eaten dinner yet."

"I was just debating my options," Alan admitted.

"Now you don't have to." Victoria nodded at the servant. "May we come in?"

"Sure." Alan stepped aside and grabbed Max's collar to keep him clear of the doorway while the two women walked inside.

"Triana, you can put that on the table."

"Yes, Your Highness." The woman, who appeared to be in her midthirties, crossed into the kitchen and set the tray down. When she returned to the living room, she asked, "Will there be anything else?"

"Not for now. Thank you."

Triana curtsied and left the apartment, closing the door behind her.

"I hope you like shrimp scampi." Victoria headed toward the kitchen.

"Right now, anything that I don't have to cook myself or go out and get sounds fantastic." Alan let go of Max's collar and joined Victoria at the table. "I thought you would be eating dinner with your family tonight."

"Annabelle had a video call with some friends from school, and I wanted to give Cassie and Levi some time alone." She lifted the cover off both of their plates. Shrimp scampi, broccoli and carrots, and a thin stack of potato pancakes. "I hope you don't mind eating with me."

"I'm glad you came." And he was. While the food smelled amazing, he rather looked forward to having someone to talk to who could actually talk back. The fact that the someone was a fascinating, attractive woman was a bonus, one he shouldn't get too accustomed to.

Alan pulled out a chair for Victoria and waited for her to sit before he took the seat beside her. "What do you say, Your Highness? Do you want to look over the work schedules while we eat?"

"You've saved my life twice. I think you should call me Victoria." She gestured toward her messenger bag. "And the schedules can wait. Let's enjoy our meal first."

A little surprised by her response, Alan picked up the water decanter in the center of the table and filled both of their glasses. "How are you doing after all the excitement today?"

"My body finally stopped shaking about twenty minutes ago." She took a sip of her water. "I don't know how you do this every day."

"If you're talking about disarming bombs, I don't do it every day."

"You have lately," Victoria said.

"I say tomorrow we break our streak."

"What if we don't?" The vulnerability was back, both in Victoria's voice and her expression.

"Levi has worked hard to secure the palace grounds. You're safe here."

"This is supposed to be my home, not some sort of gilded cage." Victoria gestured toward the door. "I can't spend my life knowing that every time I leave, someone will try to kill me." Tears welled up in her eyes, and one spilled over. She didn't bother to wipe it away, nor the next one that trickled down her cheek.

Alan pushed back from the table. "Hey. Come here." He took her hand and drew her to a stand. Then he pulled her into his arms.

Victoria's arms wrapped around his waist, and she clung to him as though he were her only lifeline as she fought against a current pulling her out to sea.

The protectiveness he had experienced earlier magnified. This woman in his arms was brilliant, hard-working, dedicated. Why would anyone want her gone? Who could possibly benefit if she were no longer here?

Her reaction today revealed a new aspect he hadn't fully seen before. She cared as much for the people around her as she did for herself. She hadn't run from the bomb as so many would typically do. She had taken the time to make sure everyone was safe. She'd even worried about him.

Alan stroked his hand down her back in an effort to soothe. "We're going to put a stop to this. It's going to be okay."

She burrowed her head into his shoulder, and tears dampened his shirt. Her body trembled against him.

Alan simply tightened his hold, an increased tenderness welling within him.

A minute stretched into two and then three before she finally lifted her head. He expected to see smudges of mascara beneath her eyes and on his shirt, but only tears glistened on her dark lashes. Maybe she used the waterproof kind, unlike his sister.

"I'm so sorry," she said.

"Don't apologize."

"Our food is getting cold." She eased back.

"And I have a microwave." Alan loosened his hold, but he didn't release her. "We are going to catch whoever is behind this. Trust me."

She blinked several times, the last of her tears subsiding. "I do trust you."

* * *

She trusted him. Victoria didn't stop to analyze how the bond had been created between her and Alan. It was simply there, and it was something she so desperately needed right now.

The dishes from their earlier dinner remained on the kitchen table, pushed aside so she and Alan could work together on her laptop.

Over the last two hours, she had somehow managed to push past her earlier emotional storm to finish adjusting the work schedules.

"The timeline is going to be tight getting those final inspections," she said. "The last of the carpeting won't even go in until two weeks before we open."

"You can get your occupancy permits before then," Alan said. "You don't need carpet to make a place safe to live."

"That's true." Victoria studied her current timeline. "If I have them come in after the plumbers finish, they could do the inspections at the same time they do our final approval for the kitchen."

"There is one more precaution I would like to put in place."

Victoria looked up from her laptop screen. "What's that?"

"I want to put up a temporary storage unit at the far edge of the parking lot to receive deliveries."

Victoria grimaced. She needed the resort to look like it was already finished, not like they were starting a new phase. "That's not going to create a very positive curb appeal."

He lifted his eyebrows. "I'm not worried about aesthetics right now."

"Obviously, and I understand what you're saying." Victoria leaned back in her seat. "It's just that at this point, we need the resort to look like a place people want to stay, not a construction zone."

"I get that, but if we put in a storage unit, we could have all the deliveries made there so I can go over and clear the packages before anything is taken inside the resort."

Though she still wasn't thrilled with the prospect, Victoria let out a resigned sigh. "Okay, that makes sense."

Alan pointed at her screen. "Most of your deliveries arrive by two o'clock."

Victoria adjusted the work schedules in her head. "If I have a moving crew arrive at that time, they can take everything into the hotel after you and Max check it out."

Max lifted his head from where he lay on the floor. When Alan didn't give him any command, he lowered his head back down to rest on his front paws.

"If your moving crew can work later hours, you'll stay on schedule."

"It's a good idea." Her mobile phone rang, and she lifted it from where she had set it on the table. "It's Annabelle. I'd better take it."

"Do you need some privacy?" Alan asked.

"No, it's fine." Victoria pressed the Talk button and greeted her sister.

"Where have you been?" Annabelle demanded. "I've been looking everywhere for you."

Victoria ignored her first question and focused on her second. "Why are you looking for me?"

"Prince Garrett and Princess Janessa from Meridia just arrived. They came to visit for a few days since they won't be able to attend the coronation," Annabelle said. "Cassie wants us in the reception hall to greet them."

"I'll be right there." Victoria hung up and stood.

Alan stood as well. "Is everything okay?"

"Some guests just arrived. I need to go to the reception hall." She closed her laptop and slid it into her bag. Then she grabbed her small makeup case from inside. "May I use your bathroom to freshen up? I must look awful after that crying jag."

"You look beautiful, but if you need to see that for yourself, go ahead." Alan waved toward the short hallway to his left.

The compliment surprised her, especially delivered in such an offhanded way. "Thank you." She headed to the bathroom and checked her makeup. Her mascara had held up remarkably well, considering. She added a little blush to her cheeks and a fresh coat of lipstick. When she finished, she returned to the living room, where Alan waited near the door.

"I'll walk you down there."

"Thank you." She slipped her makeup bag back into her messenger bag. "Would you mind if I leave this here until after the reception? I'd prefer not to bother any of the servants with having to run it back up to my room."

"That's fine." Alan nodded at his dog. "Max can guard it for you."

She smiled at the idea that she was entrusting her resort plans to a dog. "I appreciate it. I'll pick it up on my way back to my room."

Alan opened the door for her, and they walked out into the corridor that connected the tower rooms to the gallery hall. "How long is this little gathering supposed to take?"

"I don't know. Sometimes they only last a few minutes. Sometimes they stretch out for hours."

"If you need an escape, just have Levi text me," Alan said. "I can come rescue you."

"Are you planning on making this a habit?" Victoria asked.

"What?"

"Rescuing me."

He seemed to contemplate her question. "I wouldn't mind, as long as we make it rescuing you from social situations rather than life-threatening ones."

She smiled. "That would be preferable."

They reached the wide hallway where family portraits and various artwork hung on display. Benches and side tables had been strategically placed for anyone to sit and enjoy the beauty of what the artists had created. The last rays of daylight spilled in through the windows on the far end of the hall.

A guard stood at the reception hall entrance, and voices carried from inside.

Alan looked at her quizzically as they approached the doorway. He lowered his voice and asked, "Who are you meeting with tonight?"

Victoria didn't get a chance to answer.

A woman's voice carried to them. "Alan?"

Alan moved through the wide doorway, and his face lit up. "Janessa!" He gave a slight bow of his head before he abandoned protocol and pulled her into a hug. "I didn't know you were here."

"I didn't know you were here either." Despite her pregnant belly, Janessa drew him close before pulling back to look at him. "When did you arrive?"

"Just yesterday." Alan released Janessa and turned to Prince Garrett, the second in line for the throne in Meridia. "Have you been taking good care of her?"

"Whenever she lets me." Garrett stepped forward and shook Alan's hand. "It's good to see you again."

"You too." Alan motioned to Janessa's protruding stomach. "How's the little one?"

"Kicking up a storm." Janessa rested her hand at the top of where her belly swelled. "You are coming to visit after the baby is born, right?"

"You know it," Alan said. "I've already put in for my leave."

Janessa turned to Victoria. "Princess Victoria, it's good to see you again."

"You as well." Victoria nodded to Janessa and Garrett in turn. "I didn't realize you were acquainted with Alan."

"I worked for a while in Meridia before I came to Sereno," Alan said.

"He and Max saved my life," Janessa added.

"I'm afraid that's something we have in common." The sincerity in Victoria's voice cut through her typically reserved demeanor.

"What?" Janessa looked from Victoria to Alan as though needing confirmation. When Alan gave a subtle nod, she reached for Victoria's hand. "I am so sorry. If you ever need to talk, please reach out."

Touched by the offer and the genuine emotions behind it, Victoria nodded. "Thank you."

CHAPTER 11

Less than five minutes into the casual social event, Alan ended up at the side of the room with Janessa and Levi. The three of them had been the closest of friends since their early days together working for the CIA.

"Want to fill me in?" Janessa asked. "Clearly, something has been going on here that I haven't heard about yet."

"Two bombing attempts in two days," Alan said, his voice low.

Janessa put her hand on Levi's arm, concern reflected in her eyes. "Someone is going after Cassie again?"

"Not Cassie." Levi shook his head. "Victoria."

Janessa's eyebrows drew together. "Why would someone go after Victoria?"

"That's the royal question," Alan said. "Both attempts were facilitated through art deliveries."

"Garrett and I plan to stay through the weekend, but I can extend for a few more days if you need another set of eyes on the intel."

"We may take you up on that," Levi said. He went on to fill Janessa in on the second possible motive, the artwork.

When he finished, Janessa said, "Logically, the timing makes sense that this would have something to do with Cassie's coronation."

Levi looked across the room to where Garrett was chatting with Cassie, Victoria, and Annabelle. "I had a similar thought."

"Any chance one of the Escobar heirs might be going after the royal family again?" Alan asked, referring to the family who would take over Sereno if Victoria and her family were no longer able.

"I've been exploring that possibility," Levi said. "The next in line to the throne would be Theo, but he denounced the throne when he came to Cassie's father for protection from his brother. Since we're the only ones who know that, the motivation doesn't seem likely."

So the Escobar family would assume Theo was the heir behind Victoria and her sisters, but in fact, he had been working as a servant to the family for years and was not in the royal line anymore. "Someone has to have a reason for planting these bombs," Alan said.

"Someone does," Janessa agreed. "And with the three of us working together, we'll find out what their motivation is."

Alan's gaze drifted over to Victoria. "I hope so."

Janessa put her hand on Alan's shoulder. "Come on. Let's join the others. We can talk shop tomorrow."

"You two can talk shop," Alan corrected. "Max and I will be doing security sweeps of the grounds and the new resort."

"Let's meet after the reception tomorrow night," Levi said. "We can compare notes."

"What reception?" Alan asked.

"It's one of these fancy get-togethers where I get to wear a pretty dress," Janessa said.

"And I have to wear a tux," Levi added with a grimace.

Not exactly the kind of dress code Alan had to worry about. "You two have fun with that."

"Oh, we will." Levi shot Janessa a conspiratorial look. "Seems to me that it would be wise to have an extra member of the security team as Victoria's escort tomorrow night."

Janessa grinned and turned her attention to Alan. "I agree."

"Wait. What?" Alan shook his head. "I can't go to some fancy party, not if Max and I need to clear the area."

"You'll be done with that long before our guests arrive," Levi said. "And the kitchen staff is preparing the food in-house, so we won't have any caterers or outside help coming in."

"But I don't have a tux."

Janessa slipped her hand through Alan's arm. "You know what one of the best parts of being royal is?"

Sensing a trap, he slowly shook his head. "What?"

"It only takes a phone call to get whatever you need."

"I'll call the tailor tomorrow to arrange for a tux for you," Levi said. "You can swing by to pick it up on your way to do your sweep at the resort."

"I bet you'll look quite dashing." Janessa smiled sweetly at him.

"You're enjoying this, aren't you?"

"Oh yes." She tugged on his arm. "Come on. Let's go chat with the others. I'd love the chance to get to know Victoria and Annabelle better."

"Is Annabelle going to have a date?" Alan asked.

"Not exactly, but Prince Khalid will be attending without a plus-one," Levi said. "Cassie likes to have an even number at the table, so you attending will take care of that little issue."

"I have to wear a tux so Cassie's seating chart will work?"

"That's just a side benefit," Levi said. "I want you there to help Victoria feel safe."

Alan's resistance melted. "That I can do."

* * *

The last thing Victoria had expected tonight was to enjoy herself, but she had immensely. Janessa had thrown all sense of formality out the window when she'd greeted Alan with a hug. The fact that Levi and Cassie had spoken to Janessa and Garrett as genuine friends had served to further put Victoria at ease.

Now here she was, nearly three hours later, finally making her way back down the hall with Alan at her side.

His strong profile shone beneath the wall sconces that spilled light into the wide corridor. What would it be like to have such deep friendships like the ones Alan clearly shared with Janessa and Levi? Victoria wasn't jealous, she assured herself. She simply found herself yearning for trusted relationships that went beyond her immediate family.

The grandfather clock down the hall struck ten.

"I'm sorry we stayed so late," Victoria said. "I know you plan to be up early tomorrow."

"It was worth it." Alan glanced at her, the expression on his face confirming that his words were genuine. "I haven't seen Janessa since her gender-reveal party in Bellamo. That must have been two months ago."

The oddity that Alan had been invited to such an intimate family event confirmed her suspicion that Alan and Janessa's relationship went far beyond former employer/employee. "It sounds like you and Janessa are quite close."

Alan nodded. "She's one of my closest friends."

"Do you always bond with the people you save?"

"I rarely meet the people I save." Alan shrugged. "If you want to call disarming a bomb saving people. Usually, it's the people clearing the potential victims out of the danger zone who are the real heroes."

"I beg to differ. Those people have an important task, but you're the one who stays on the front line to the very end."

"My job is pretty simple. I do it right, or I won't be around to defend myself if I make a mistake."

Victoria stopped walking, and those tense moments she had experienced earlier resurfaced with a vengeance.

Alan stopped and looked back at her. "What?"

"How can you be so cavalier about that? You could have died today. You could have died yesterday."

"And I could die tomorrow." Alan stepped toward her so he was standing directly in her path. "Any of us could. I've simply come to learn that I can't let the reality keep me from moving forward, especially when I'm doing my job."

His job disarming bombs that could explode at any moment. "Forgive me, but your attitude is terrifying."

Alan reached for her arm and tugged it gently to put her back in motion. Victoria fell into step beside him.

"Mine may be a simplistic view of life, but it's the one I need when I'm looking for something I hope I'll never find."

"Something you've found twice in the past two days."

"We're breaking our streak tomorrow, remember?" Alan said, his hand once again by his side.

"Right." His gesture of a moment ago caught up with her. Even though he had demonstrated an understanding of royal protocols in each of their meetings, he had broken those rules when he'd taken her arm. Then again, hugging Janessa had hardly been a proper response either.

"I should have a break for about an hour tomorrow around eleven if you want to chat some more about the security measures for the next few days," Alan said.

"I thought you weren't going over to the resort until around two."

Alan grimaced. "I have to stop by and pick up a tux on my way over."

She arched her eyebrows. "Really?"

"Levi asked if I would be your escort to the reception tomorrow night," he said. "Apparently, there's a dress code."

"My brother-in-law set us up on a date?"

"I guess he thought it would be easier for you to go with someone you already know."

"I don't really know you." But she wanted to, and that was a sensation she hadn't experienced in a very long time.

They reached his apartment, but instead of opening the door, he turned to face her once more. "Do you mind if I'm your date tomorrow night?"

"No." She offered a slight smile. "Not at all."

"Good." He reached into his pocket for his key and unlocked the door. "It's a date."

She had a date with Alan. That thought flitted through her head with new significance. With it came an idea to spend a little more time with this intriguing man. "Stop by my apartment at eleven. I'd love to get your opinion on a few things."

"I can do that." Alan opened the door for her, and Victoria entered his living room.

Max stood at attention and sniffed the air before he crossed to Alan and greeted him by rubbing his head beneath Alan's hand.

"Hey, boy. Did you miss me?"

Max barked once.

Alan squatted and rubbed Max's neck with both hands. "Come on. We'll go outside after we walk the princess back to her room."

Alan straightened and grabbed Max's leash. He clipped it to the dog's collar and straightened.

"Are you ready?" Alan asked.

"Yes." Victoria retrieved her bag and slipped the strap over her shoulder.

Together they left Alan's rooms and moved down the hall. He and his dog were walking her home. Was it too much to ask that he think of her as more than a royal obligation? She truly hoped not, because whether he realized it or not, she had already come to consider him a friend. Or perhaps even more than a friend.

CHAPTER 12

Alan sat across the table from his two best friends, a pitcher of orange juice, a plate of pastries, and the latest intel reports on the bombings spread out between them.

"I was really hoping the cops would be able to pull fingerprints off the latest bomb," Alan said, not thrilled at the early-morning news that neither bomb had revealed any useful information that would lead them to the person behind the two attempts.

"I had hoped so too." Levi shifted a file over to Janessa. "Have you ever seen anything like this one?"

Janessa held up a picture of the second bomb. "Whoever built this was clever, in the scariest possible way." She shook her head. "I've never seen one like this before."

"What about security footage at the local art gallery?" Alan asked. "There are cameras everywhere. One of them had to pick up something."

"Two of them actually." Levi reached behind him to pick up a remote off his desk. He aimed it at the television on the wall and pulled up the video feed.

The image of a storage room came into view. A shadow crossed the floor near the edge of the screen, and a figure appeared for a brief moment, only the back of the person's head visible.

"That doesn't give us anything," Janessa said.

"Other than the guy having a black baseball cap on," Alan added. "What about the other one?"

Levi hit a button on the remote, and a new image popped up, this one of the loading dock. The same person appeared briefly at the edge of the screen, their clothing simple dark slacks and a dark shirt, the black ball cap in place, and their face away from the camera. He, or a tall she, carried a box, but the camera didn't pick up anything beyond that.

Frustration welled up in Alan. "This is all you've got?"

"I'm afraid so," Levi said. "Best we can tell, someone came in around two in the morning on the day of the resort bombing attempt. It looks like they swapped the bomb for the original painting intended for Victoria's office."

A painting that was supposed to have been opened in her presence. Alan suppressed a shudder. "Was the painting valuable?"

"It's worth about thirty thousand euros. It's expensive but not worth the thief's effort to secure it."

"What about the security system?" Janessa asked. "There has to be some clue as to who accessed the museum during the time of the theft."

"According to the security company, no one's access card was used during the time in question, but there was a power surge around 1:45 a.m."

Alan shook his head. "The thief figured out a way to override the system."

"That's my guess."

"So, no fingerprints on either bomb. No clear images of our suspect." Alan rubbed at the knot forming at the back of his neck. "We're back to square one."

"The police are looking into the museum employees, but so far, they haven't found anything," Levi said.

"I assume they're also watching for the possible sale of the painting," Janessa said.

"They are." Levi clicked off the television screen. "But if the thief is smart, he won't try to unload it for a year or two."

"I hate to say it, but this guy is smart." Alan sighed.

"Yeah, he is," Levi agreed. "But we're smarter."

* * *

Victoria stared at the piece of paper with six names on it. After a conversation with the museum director, she had managed to determine that only he and one of his employees had been aware of Victoria's instructions that her painting not be opened until she was present.

Besides the two museum employees, only Lorenzo, Riccardo, and Giulia had been aware of her instruction. So had Giuseppe. At least, those were the only people she was aware of. Supposedly, the delivery crew had not been given any special instructions beyond the standard protocols of securing valuable cargo.

With her list in hand, she left her room and stepped into the hall, where Giuseppe stood guard. "Do you know if Cassie or Levi is in their rooms?"

"I don't believe so, Your Highness. Queen Cassandra was meeting with Theo this morning, and King Levi is in his offices."

"Thank you." Victoria folded her list in half. No need to show Giuseppe that he was one of only six who could very well end up on Levi's suspect list. She started toward her brother-in-law's offices, and Giuseppe followed her.

Her chest tightened, and her body began to tremble. She struggled to fight for control. She was being paranoid. Giuseppe had spent the past several years assigned to her. He had kept her safe during her last two years at university. He had stood by when she had needed to escape the confines of the palace during her father's final year of his life. He had watched over her during her time at Cambridge.

Her hand tightened on the paper in her hand. Six names might be listed on it, but only five would truly be suspects. Giuseppe wasn't involved. Of that she was certain.

By the time Victoria reached Levi's office, the worst of her panic attack had subsided.

Levi's assistant stood when she entered.

"Good morning, Your Highness."

"Good morning, Renato. Is the king available?"

Renato picked up the phone on his desk. "I will let him know you're here."

A moment later, Levi's office door opened. Concern lit his eyes. "Come in." He looked past Victoria. "Giuseppe, you need to report to the security office. I'll make sure Princess Victoria is watched after until you return."

"Yes, Your Majesty." Giuseppe bowed his head in acknowledgment and disappeared into the hallway.

Victoria passed into Levi's office and handed him her list. "These are all the people who knew I wanted to be present when *The View of Sereno* was unboxed. I thought you would want it."

"I do." Levi unfolded the paper and skimmed over the names. "I know the museum director, Lorenzo, and Giuseppe, but who are these others?"

"Riccardo and Giulia are both on staff at the resort. Riccardo was there when the bomb was discovered, and he was quick to get out of there when he learned about it. I'm not sure he could fake that kind of terror."

"What about Giulia?"

"She was off the day the bomb arrived at the resort."

"What's her role?"

"She's my kitchen manager." Victoria shook her head. "I have a hard time believing she could be involved. It was coincidental that she was even in the room when I told Lorenzo that I wanted to be there when the painting was opened."

"What about Matei Barone?"

"He's an employee at the museum. Apparently, the director informed him that the package was to be delivered directly to me."

"So he's the only person on here who hasn't been cleared by us somehow," Levi said.

Victoria nodded. "The only other name on there is Giuseppe, but I have a hard time believing he would try to hurt me."

"I agree, but he's going through a polygraph this morning just to make sure he didn't inadvertently share information he shouldn't have."

She wasn't the only person acting paranoid. "I feel terrible that he has to do that."

"Don't feel bad," Levi said. "Giuseppe will understand. The royal guard goes through them regularly. It's not going to come as a surprise."

Victoria sighed and motioned to the paper in Levi's hand. "What happens now?"

"For now, we try to enjoy our weekend and pretend that life is normal."

"I don't know if I can do that."

"You can." Levi motioned toward the main part of the palace. "Your sister has a wonderful reception planned, and we're all under orders to have a good time."

"Well, if Cassie has given us royal orders, I guess I'll have to try."

Levi gave a definite nod. "Yes, you will."

* * *

Alan admitted it. He had been looking forward to seeing Victoria this morning. Of course, that had been before he'd learned she planned to turn him into a human pincushion.

He stood in the center of her spacious living room, a wooden stool beneath his feet and a tailor at his side.

"Hold your arms out," the tailor instructed, his pincushion once again in his hand.

Alan complied.

Victoria sat on the couch in front of him, Max stretched out on the rug at her feet.

"Is all of this necessary?" Alan asked for the fourth time since arriving at Victoria's suite and learning that the tailor had come to him.

"I'm almost done." The tailor tucked a pin in the sleeve. He then wrote something in his notepad before moving back. "You can step down now."

Alan slowly lowered his hands to his sides to make sure the pins didn't prick him. Then he looked down at the pant legs, which were also pinned. This operation was more intricate than defusing a bomb. "I'm afraid to move."

"You'll be fine." The tailor pointed at the doorway to the bedroom Alan had used to change his clothes. "Go take this off. I'll get the adjustments made this afternoon and have your tux delivered by five."

"Thank you, Darío." Victoria stood and crossed to shake his hand. "I appreciate your willingness to come out on such short notice."

Gingerly, Alan stepped down from the stool and headed for the bedroom. He changed out of the pants and jacket, exchanging them for the polo shirt and slacks he had been wearing before being ordered into the formalwear.

Careful to keep the pins where the tailor had left them, Alan carried the clothes into the living room and handed them over to the tailor.

As soon as the older man left, Victoria asked, "Now that we have that out of the way, do you have time to look at the delivery and work schedules? I wanted your opinion on the furniture deliveries."

"Sure." Alan waved toward the door the tailor had just disappeared through. "You really didn't have to call the tailor. I was going to stop by his shop later."

"Now you don't have to."

"I guess I should thank you for taking that task off my to-do list."

"Or I can thank you for agreeing to be my escort tonight."

"I think I got the better end of this deal."

Victoria's face lit with a smile. "I'm glad you think so." She led the way through the wide archway that led to the dining room and settled at the mahogany table, where several file folders lay beside her laptop.

Alan sat in the upholstered chair beside her.

She slid a file folder to him. "I made a list of the deliveries that are still scheduled. Right now, I have the majority of the bedroom furniture arriving two weeks from Thursday, right after the last of the carpeting goes in."

Which would leave them two weeks after the carpeting was done to prepare for the grand opening. "How many rooms still need carpet and furniture?" Alan asked. The rooms she had shown him had all been furnished.

"I believe we still have a hundred and eight guest rooms left and three of the meeting rooms on the second floor."

Alan didn't want to think about the amount of time it would take him and Max to clear over a hundred mattresses and box springs. Add in chairs, desks, couches, and who knew what other decorative furniture Victoria had planned, and he wasn't going to have time for anything else. "Is that enough time to get everything in place before the grand opening?" he asked. "That's a lot of furniture to move in a short amount of time."

"I had planned to bring in some movers to help get everything in place, but with what happened yesterday, I think we need to make some adjustments."

"I agree." Alan flipped open the file she had given him. The schedule was outlined precisely, as were the completion dates for the bathrooms, the carpeting, the kitchen, and the laundry room. He focused on the carpeting.

"You said the plumbers will finish in the guest rooms on Monday, right?"

"Yes."

"According to your schedule here, the carpeting will be installed in sections."

"That's right." Victoria edged closer so she could also see the schedule. "They're starting on the upper floors and working their way down."

He pondered the timing and the logistics of the work that still needed to be accomplished. "What are the chances you can get some of those furniture deliveries early?"

"How early?"

"If you can get the beds for the top floor next Wednesday, Max and I could clear those, and your staff could get them set up that afternoon and the next morning." Alan nodded as the schedule solidified in his mind. "The next day, we have the deliveries of couches, chairs, and desks for that floor. By the end of the week, you would have one entire floor ready to go. Then, as soon as the next floor is carpeted, we start on furnishing that one."

"That would be more efficient, but I'm not sure if I can get those deliveries moved up that soon."

Alan cocked an eyebrow. "I found out last night that I needed a tux, and you had a tailor here barely twelve hours later."

"Yes, but that was easy. Some of this furniture is being shipped in from overseas."

"Then you bring in what you can now and add the other furniture when it gets here," Alan said.

Victoria tilted her head to the side, her expression thoughtful. "The beds are already in a local warehouse. So are most of the sofas."

"Every piece of furniture we can move in early will ease the burden on you and your staff," Alan said. "And it will make it way easier for me and Max to clear them."

"I'll make some calls this afternoon to see what I can do," Victoria said.

Max lifted his head, his ears pricked.

"Are you expecting someone?" Alan asked.

"Lunch should be delivered any minute."

A knock sounded on the door.

The protectiveness Alan had experienced over the past few days crested. "Do you mind if I get that?"

"Not at all."

Alan crossed through the living room and opened the door. A member of the kitchen staff stood on the other side of the threshold with a tray in her hand.

"I can take that." Alan reached out and took the tray. "Thank you."

"Yes, sir." She gave a slight nod. "Please have Princess Victoria ring the kitchen if she needs anything else."

"I will. Thanks." Alan closed the door and carried the tray into the dining room. After he set it in the middle of the table, he gathered the papers and slid them into the folder. "I should get going."

"Aren't you going to stay for lunch?" Victoria asked. "I ordered enough for both of us."

"You didn't have to do that."

"I was hoping for some company."

"This is getting to be a habit."

"I guess it is." Victoria slid her laptop aside. "Do you mind?"

Alan sat beside her. "I can't say that I do."

CHAPTER 13

Victoria blinked her eyes against the dryness that came from staring at a computer screen too long. For the last two hours, she had sorted through work orders and emails in an attempt to keep the resort on track, despite her absence.

Her phone rang, and she immediately thought of Alan. She shook her head. As far as she knew, he didn't even have her phone number.

She glanced at the screen on her mobile and smiled. Sheldon Burton, one of her classmates from Cambridge. "Hello, Sheldon. How are you?"

"I'm living the dream." The smile in his voice was easy to visualize on his face. "I just arrived in Sereno yesterday. How about we get together, and you can show me the sights?"

"I'm sorry, but I don't know that I can tear myself away from work right now." Or could she? At the moment, she couldn't go anywhere near work, and most of her duties had been delegated to others.

"I'm sure it can wait," Sheldon said. "You're royalty. You can take some time off. Besides, I'm only asking for one day."

Typical Sheldon. Play first, work later.

In truth, she probably could take some time off, but after the recent bombing attempts, Victoria couldn't imagine leaving the grounds, not without Alan. "I'm sorry, Sheldon. I just don't think—"

"Come on, Victoria," Sheldon interrupted, his tone persuasive. "What's the point of being a princess if you can't take advantage of delegating your work every now and then?"

"I'm afraid one of the disadvantages of being a princess is that security is never happy when I spring an unexpected outing on them," Victoria said. "And I really do have a lot of work to do. My family's resort opens a month from tomorrow."

"If you need any help with that, let me know," Sheldon said. "I did score the highest in our hospitality class."

Second highest, Victoria thought. Behind her. Sheldon's overinflated ego sometimes exaggerated *almosts* into facts.

The oddity that he would offer his help caught up with her. "You aren't asking for a job, are you?" she asked. "I thought you were going to work for that hotel chain in London."

"I am, but I don't start until next month," he said. "I thought, what better place to spend the last of my freedom than here with you?"

She nearly rolled her eyes. She would have had she not been trained to avoid expressions that might be caught on camera and cast her or her family in a negative light. "That's a very sweet thought, but I'm afraid my time isn't my own right now."

"If you can't come out today, what about tomorrow?" Sheldon persisted. "You don't have to work on a Saturday. Your hotel isn't open yet."

How little her university friends understood about royal life. The reception tonight would be only the first in a series of events that would celebrate Garrett and Janessa's presence in Sereno.

Not interested in extending the conversation, Victoria said, "I'll have to check my schedule."

"Great. I'll call you later." He hung up, giving her no chance to respond.

Would it be terribly rude to block Sheldon's number until after the weekend was over? The man was charming when he wanted to be and was always attentive on the occasions Victoria had joined her classmates for study sessions. Of course, he had always seemed more interested in socializing than studying.

Someone knocked on her door, and Victoria crossed the room to answer it. Ludovica, the family's press secretary, curtsied and greeted her.

"Your Highness, I'm sorry to bother you, but we do have some scheduling items to discuss."

"Come in." Victoria stepped back and waited for Ludovica to enter before she closed the door. Victoria took a seat on the sofa and gestured for the other woman to join her. "I know about the reception tonight, but I haven't looked at my schedule beyond that."

"I'm afraid that with Prince Garrett and Princess Janessa here, we have a very full weekend." She offered Victoria a printout of the events that would take place over the next several days—the dinner tonight with the ruling council, a brunch tomorrow with several key business leaders in the region, and a ball tomorrow evening, which would benefit the new hospital in Porto Blu.

"The visit to the art museum tomorrow was canceled," Ludovica continued, "but your sister hasn't decided yet whether to put something else in its place."

"Thank you." Victoria scanned the calendar again before she set it aside. "Is there anything else?"

"Yes. Princess Janessa has requested an audience with you. I took the liberty of setting up a meeting at four o'clock in the salon."

Curious as to why Janessa would want to meet with her, she said, "I'll look forward to seeing her then."

"Very good." Ludovica jotted a note in her phone. "I will confirm your appointment."

Victoria stood. "Thank you."

She escorted the press secretary to the door, relieved when she was once again alone. She checked the time. Only an hour until she would meet Janessa. Only three hours until Alan would arrive to escort her to the reception tonight.

That thought brought a smile to her face. She couldn't wait to see him in his new tux.

* * *

They broke their streak. For the first time since agreeing to work in Sereno again, Alan had made it a full twenty-four hours without needing to disarm a bomb.

He drove along the winding road that led from Porto Blu to the palace. A breeze rustled through the palm trees on either side of him, shadows stretching out across the pavement. The road curved to the right, and the beach came into view. The Mediterranean sparkled beneath the afternoon sun and brought with it a sense of peace.

He reached the crest of the hill at the base of the mountains and slowed when he reached the palace grounds. After passing through the security check, he parked his borrowed sedan in the twelve-car garage beside a host of other vehicles the royal family used. He was well acquainted with the variety of limos, SUVs, and luxury cars Victoria and her family used on a regular basis.

Out of habit, Alan exited the vehicle, clipped Max's leash into place, and began a search of the car parked beside his. For the next fifteen minutes, he and Max examined the contents of the enormous garage. Once satisfied that all was as it should be, Alan used his personal code to open the panel on the wall that hid the rack where the keys to the various vehicles were kept.

He stepped free of the garage as Levi approached with two guards trailing behind him.

"I was wondering if you were back." Levi stopped by the garage entrance.

"Got back a few minutes ago."

"Everything okay at the resort?"

"Yeah. The plumbers have a couple more days before they'll be finished, and I cleared the carpeting that will be installed tomorrow."

"They're laying carpet on a Saturday?"

"It was supposed to be today," Alan said, "but I asked Victoria to push the installation off so we would have time for Max to inspect it."

"Sounds like the two of you have been doing quite a bit of juggling."

"I expect we'll be doing a lot more by the time the resort opens." Alan glanced at the two guards now standing a short distance away. "You going somewhere?"

"Janessa is craving baklava." Levi grinned. "I told Garrett I'd save him the trip to the bakery."

"You know that you have an entire kitchen staff in the palace, right?"

"Yeah, but it will take them hours to prepare it. It will only take me thirty minutes to make a quick trip into town."

"And is there a reason you aren't sending someone else to pick it up?" Alan asked.

Levi gave a slight shrug. "Sometimes it's good to do things for yourself."

Now certain that there was more to Levi's outing than he was saying, Alan asked, "Want some company?"

"Sure." Levi walked into the garage and pulled a set of keys from his pocket. He clicked the fob, and the lights flashed on the nearby SUV. He glanced down at Max. "Want to have him do his thing before we go?"

"No need to." Alan opened the back door and signaled Max to get in. "We checked out the garage when we got back."

Alan took his spot in the passenger seat, and Levi climbed in beside him. As soon as the guards were inside their car, Levi started the engine and pulled into the drive.

"Are you going to tell me where you're really going?"

"I need to play big brother for a few minutes."

"You lost me."

"Victoria received a call from one of her former classmates a few hours ago. Then he called her two more times, but she didn't pick up." Levi waved at the guards manning the gate as he passed through. "I've been tracking his phone, and he's on the move. I want to see what he's really doing here."

"Did he say something to make Victoria suspicious?"

"She doesn't know I heard the call."

Alan's jaw dropped. "You cloned her phone?"

"I had to. She's been in England for the last year. I had to make sure no one tried to take advantage of her."

"You know she'll kill you if she finds out you're spying on her."

"Oh, I know," Levi said. "Come to think of it, so would Cassie."

"I never thought I would say this, but I think you may be taking this security thing a little too far."

"I might agree with you if it weren't for Sheldon Burton."

"Who is this guy?" Alan asked, irritated by the jealousy that surfaced.

"He was in the same master's program as Victoria. He also attended Oxford two years ago with Marguerite Dubois."

"Sorry. I'm not up-to-date on the society pages. Who is Marguerite Dubois?"

"Her father owns a dozen car dealerships in Canada."

"And?"

"And shortly after the two graduated together, Sheldon paid the young heiress a visit. Two weeks later, her father sold one of those dealerships, the proceeds of which apparently made it into Sheldon's pockets."

"Blackmail?"

"That's our guess." Levi turned down the road that afforded the tranquil view of the Mediterranean. "The CIA caught the funds transfer because of the sheer amount of it, but no one knows what kind of dirt would warrant that kind of payoff."

"I can't think of anything," Alan said. "In today's world, no one is shocked by anything that hits the media."

"The Dubois family is known for its strong moral values." Levi shrugged. "There are also rumors that Marguerite's father is considering a move into politics. With the depth of his pockets and his party's backing, he could be the next prime minister."

The implications of Sheldon's presence in Sereno sank in. "You don't really think this guy has dirt on Victoria, do you?"

"No, but I guarantee he's not here to work on his tan."

"You sure he isn't just reaching out to Victoria to gain social status?" Alan asked. "If he already had a huge payout, he may be out of the blackmailing business."

"I doubt it. He may be a successful blackmailer, but he is a complete flop when it comes to managing money," Levi said. "Bad investments, gambling debts, expensive homes, and exorbitant vacations. Word is, he's sinking fast and won't likely be able to keep up with his property taxes, much less keep the utilities in all those properties turned on."

"How many properties did he buy?"

"Four. A flat in London, a penthouse in New York, a villa in the south of France, and a beach house in the Azores."

"That's a lot of real estate."

"Yes, it is." Levi's mouth pressed into a hard line. "But if Sheldon Burton thinks he's going to support his lifestyle by tapping into Sereno's royal funds, he has another thing coming."

CHAPTER 14

Victoria approached the parlor, Giuseppe at her side. As expected, her guard had passed his polygraph with flying colors, reaffirming her conviction that he wasn't a threat to her or anyone else. He took his typical post in the hallway as she passed through the door.

The room was empty when she walked inside. Unlike the reception hall, where the chairs were all pushed back against the walls to allow for space to mingle, this particular room boasted several clusters of chairs to create intimate conversation areas.

The paintings on the wall displayed the works of both classic artists and local favorites. Victoria stopped beside a portrait of her parents when they were newly married. Her mother seated in a chair, her father standing behind her, his hand resting lovingly on her shoulder. The expressions on both of their faces revealed what she had always observed firsthand. Her parents truly had been so happy, so in love.

A heaviness pressed in on her, and she struggled to focus on the good moments rather than the losses.

Fabric rustled behind her, and she turned. Janessa stood a few meters away with an understanding look on her face.

"That's such a lovely painting." Janessa stepped to Victoria's side. "I wish I could have met your mother. I've heard such wonderful things about her."

Victoria let her gaze return to the portrait. "She was an incredible woman."

"Your father once said she was the best part about him."

"That was his favorite saying." The sweet memory brought a smile to Victoria's face. She gestured to a nearby cluster of chairs and took a seat. "Are your parents still with you?"

Janessa sat beside her. "They're both alive and kicking." Humor flashed in Janessa's expression. "Although, most of their kicking these days is trying to get my younger brothers and sisters to find a significant other. I'm starting to think my mom should start a dating service."

Victoria couldn't help but laugh at the mental image. "I remember meeting your brother Jeremy and his wife at my sister's wedding, so they must be doing something right."

"Actually, I'm the one who was responsible for that meeting." Janessa pursed her lips. "Maybe I need to have the rest of my siblings come visit more often."

"How many brothers and sisters do you have?"

"Five. Jeremy, my sister Mary, and I are the only ones who are married." She waved her hand to encompass the room. "I'm not sure the others would feel very comfortable in a royal setting. My wedding was quite an interesting challenge for them."

Genuinely interested in how others lived outside the palace walls and the confines of advanced educational institutions, Victoria asked, "How so?"

"Royal protocols can be a bit overwhelming if you haven't grown up around them," Janessa said. "When you're raised on a farm, you're more concerned about getting the work done than who is supposed to extend his hand first in a handshake or which fork to use at the dinner table."

Victoria tried to imagine growing up in simple circumstances but couldn't. "You have certainly adjusted to royal life well."

"Thank you, but I was fortunate to have traveled a good deal before I met Garrett." She waved her hand again, this time in a dismissive gesture. "That's enough about me and my family. I wanted to talk about you. How are you?"

"I'm doing well, thank you."

Janessa lifted both eyebrows. "You were the potential target of two bombing attempts in the space of two days. I doubt 'doing well' is an accurate description of your current emotional state."

Janessa was right, but Victoria had yet to identify her own emotions, much less find a way to describe them to others. "You mentioned that Alan saved your life before. What happened?"

"Alan was working at the royal château in Bellamo when Garrett and I were engaged." Janessa shifted in her chair as though trying to get more comfortable. "I walked downstairs one day and saw Max sitting at attention a second too late."

"Too late for what?"

"I stepped on a pressure-triggered bomb." Janessa shook her head. "It's pretty terrifying knowing that if you move, you'll not only die, but you'll also take one of your best friends with you."

Alan and Janessa were best friends. Victoria wanted to figure out how Garrett's then-fiancée had become so close to a man who spent the majority of his time working with his dog. "What happened?" she finally managed to ask.

"Alan disarmed the bomb with Levi's help."

"Did they figure out who was behind the bombing attempt?"

Janessa nodded. "We followed the clues."

"We? You helped?"

Janessa tilted her head slightly. "I can be stubborn when I need to be. I wasn't about to just sit by and watch someone try to kill Garrett."

"Garrett? I thought you were the one who was almost killed by the bomb."

"I was, but that particular explosive wasn't meant for me."

Janessa's candor brought with it an inherent trust.

"Alan isn't convinced I was the target of the bombing attempts," Victoria said.

"But he's worried you could be." In a gesture as natural as it was soothing, Janessa took Victoria's hand and squeezed it. "Trust that Alan will keep you safe. He and Levi have a lot of experience with this sort of thing." Janessa withdrew her hand and settled back in her chair.

"I appreciate their experience, but they can't spend all of their time babysitting me," Victoria said. "My sister's coronation is in four weeks. They're supposed to be focused on keeping her safe."

"Trust me, they'll make sure Cassie is protected, but really, if something happened to you or Annabelle, the coronation wouldn't go on as scheduled."

"You're right." What would Cassie do if her sisters met an untimely death? She would go through a mourning period like she did when their father died. "Who would benefit if my sister weren't crowned for another year?"

"I don't know," Janessa said. "But I'd love to find out."

* * *

"There he is." Alan resisted the urge to point at the well-dressed man sitting at the outdoor café. The seat across from him remained vacant, but judging from the empty glasses on the table, Sheldon had been there for some time.

Several of the nearby tables were occupied, but the one directly behind Sheldon remained empty.

"Looks like he's waiting for someone." Levi passed by the café and parked in front of the bakery two doors down.

"I have a sudden urge to take an early dinner at that café down the road." Alan glanced at Max in the back seat. "What do you say, boy? I'll bet they'll let you come with me if we sit outside."

Levi reached over and opened the glove compartment. He pulled out a ballpoint pen and a communication device disguised as a set of earbuds.

Alan had only to glance at the pen to see that it, too, was not what it appeared. A small microphone made up the top portion of it.

"I see you're still carrying your toys around with you." Alan slipped the first earpiece into place. He held up the pen. "What's the range on the audio?"

"It would be best if you can get within ten meters," Levi said. "Of course, it won't matter if whoever he's meeting doesn't show up."

"Just in case there's anything to hear, I'll go snag that open table while I can." Alan put in the other earpiece and climbed out of the car. He opened the back door and clipped Max's leash into place. "Come on, boy."

"I'll go grab Janessa's baklava while you get settled," Levi said.

"Was Janessa serious about that?"

"Knowing Janessa, probably," Levi said. "But either way, it will be best to keep up appearances for the staff."

"If you're going in anyway, you can grab me a piece too."

Levi laughed. "Already planned on it."

Alan left Levi behind without a backward glance. He spotted a young couple approaching from the other direction, the man focused on the café.

Alan quickened his step to reach his desired table first, then pulled out the chair facing Sheldon and used a hand signal so Max would sit beside him.

A waiter approached with a menu in hand. He greeted Alan in Italian, and Alan fought the instinct to try to blend in. After all, American tourists frequented this area often, and Alan's Italian wasn't good enough for him to pass as a native. "Do you have an English menu?"

"Of course, sir," the man said in heavily accented English. He moved to a small cart nearby and exchanged the Italian menu for an English one.

"Thank you." Alan gave the waiter his drink order and opened the menu. He then pulled a small notepad out of his pocket and grabbed the microphone pen. He set both on the table while he slowly read through the various dishes.

The waiter returned a little too quickly, and Alan asked for another minute to peruse the menu. When the waiter returned a second time, Alan started at the appetizer menu and ordered a dish. Uncertain how long he would need to stretch out his time here, he then ordered a pasta that included a side salad. That should take him a while to eat.

The waiter left him alone, and Alan took a sip of his water. He feigned writing notes, he texted an update to Levi, he nibbled on the slightly overcooked calamari his waiter had brought him ten minutes after he'd put in his order.

He was nearly halfway through his appetizer when a woman approached. Sheldon stood and pulled out the seat opposite him.

"I'm so sorry I'm late." The woman spoke in English with a subtle British accent. "I had a dreadful time finding a taxi."

She settled into her chair and waited for Sheldon to reclaim his seat. "Have you made any plans yet for your time in Sereno?"

"Not yet, but I spoke with our friend last night and suggested we get together."

"And?"

"And nothing." Sheldon leaned back in his chair as though he didn't have anything better to do than sit and watch the traffic go by. Then again, maybe he didn't have anything better to do.

"This isn't going to work unless you spend time with her."

Her. As in Victoria.

"Don't worry. It always takes a few invitations before she gives in." He shook his head. "Poor girl. She really does need to learn how to relax a bit."

"You can hardly expect her to relax with everything that's been happening."

"Clearly she just needs a trusted friend to confide in," Sheldon said smugly. "It's only a matter of time before that friend is me."

Not if Alan could help it.

The waiter approached with a tray in hand. He stopped between Alan's table and Sheldon's.

"Here you are, sir." The waiter set his dinner in front of him. "Will there be anything else?"

Even though Alan's water glass was nearly empty, he shook his head. "No, thank you."

"Enjoy." He nodded and turned to Sheldon's companion. "May I get you something?"

"Yes. I'll have a tequila sunrise."

As soon as the waiter moved away, Alan picked up his phone. Using the guise of taking a photo of his food, he snapped a photo of Sheldon's dining companion.

Sheldon and the woman continued their conversation, the topics turning to the weather and possible diversions for while they were in town.

Despite his desire to return to the palace to prepare for his date, Alan ate slowly. He ordered another drink. He sampled his dessert. All the while, Max lay at his feet, and not once more did the couple at the next table discuss anything of interest.

When they finally paid their check, Alan pulled out his wallet and set several bills on the table.

With Max walking at his side, he returned to where Levi sat in his car.

Alan put Max in the back seat and climbed into the car. "I really don't like that guy."

"We're on the same wavelength there," Levi said. "Only the first few minutes sounded like anything that might have been of interest."

"I agree. It sounds like Sheldon is up to something, but he was smart enough not to give any specific details in public."

"Any idea who the girl is?" Levi asked.

"They didn't act like a couple, but they clearly know each other well." Alan held up his phone. "I took the woman's photo. I'll text it to you."

"Thanks." Levi started the car and pulled onto the road. "I'll try to figure out who she is."

"It sounded like they were classmates." Alan pulled up the image and sent it to Levi.

Levi's phone chimed with the incoming message. "If that's the case, maybe I can pull the graduate photos."

"Trying to keep Victoria in the dark?"

"Only about me having a clone of her phone."

"I can't blame you for that. I know I wouldn't be happy if I found out my brother-in-law was spying on me."

"Your brother-in-law is an accountant."

"Doesn't matter. The outrage would be the same." Alan glanced behind them. "Where's your security detail?"

"They're following Sheldon and the girl. I want to know where they're staying."

"And what they're up to."

"Yes, but uncovering that truth may take a bit more effort than taking a trip to the bakery for baklava." Levi motioned to the white bakery box on the floor by Alan's feet. "Speaking of, yours is in the box."

"Thanks," Alan said and rubbed his stomach. "But I'm stuffed."

"That's going to make for an interesting evening," Levi said. "Dinner is being served in less than an hour."

Alan leaned his head back. "I should have just ordered the salad."

CHAPTER 15

Victoria sat on the padded chair in her bathroom while Annabelle pinned her hair up in a complicated updo.

Annabelle slid another bobby pin into place. "I hope Alan didn't plan to stay out of the limelight tonight, because when he walks in with you, he's going to get noticed."

"I don't think he's the type who wants to be gracing a magazine cover with me."

"Then it's a good thing the press won't be there tonight." Annabelle teased the wisps of hair framing her face. "There. All done." She stepped aside so Victoria could see her reflection in the mirror.

"Thanks, Annabelle. I don't know what I'd do without you."

"If I weren't around, we'd need a hairdresser on staff instead of only bringing someone in when we need a haircut."

"You're right." Victoria stood so she could check the line of her dress. The deep purple complemented her dusky complexion. With her enhanced makeup and her hair pinned back, she looked every bit the princess. She hoped Alan would approve of the royal version of her.

Her stomach fluttered. She had a date with a handsome, fascinating man. She had a date with an American spy. But it didn't squelch the anticipation humming through her.

She enjoyed his company. Certainly there wasn't anything wrong with exploring their blooming friendship. It wasn't as if anything could come of it on the romantic front, since he would be leaving soon.

She walked with her sister through her bedroom and into the living room.

A knock sounded on the door.

"Your date is here."

The butterflies inside her multiplied and took flight. "It's not a real date. Levi asked him to escort me."

"He didn't say no. And neither did you." Annabelle gave her a cheeky grin before continuing into the entryway. "I'll see you down there."

Victoria nodded.

Annabelle opened the door. "Hello, Alan. Don't you look dashing tonight."

"Thanks. You look quite stunning yourself."

"Why, thank you." Annabelle glanced over her shoulder at Victoria before she said, "Have fun tonight."

Annabelle moved past Alan, and Victoria got her first good look at her date. Her jaw didn't drop open, but it was a close call. The man looked incredible.

Witnessing Alan's session with the tailor hadn't prepared her for how he would look in the finished product. The fitted jacket enhanced his broad shoulders and athletic build. His beard and mustache had been trimmed, and his brown eyes were staring intensely at her.

"Wow." He took a step back as though trying to get a better look at her. "You are beautiful."

The simple compliment shouldn't have sent her pulse racing, but it did. She offered him a genuine smile. "Thank you."

Alan extended his arm. "Shall we?"

Victoria nodded and slipped her hand through the crook of his elbow. "Thank you again for escorting me tonight."

"Coming with you certainly isn't a hardship." Alan lifted his free hand and tugged at his collar. "Well, except for the whole bow-tie thing."

She glanced at him again, his tie perfectly in place. "You've obviously tied one of those before."

"Yeah, but not very well. Cassie tied this one for me."

Her grip tightened on his arm, and her steps slowed. "She used to do that for my father after my mother passed away."

"It must be hard being back here again with your father gone."

She nodded. Emotions pressed to the surface. This would be her first formal event since her father's funeral. She would sit in the formal dining room, but her father wouldn't be the one at the head of the table. It would be her sister.

As though sensing her churning thoughts, Alan stopped. "I'm sorry. I didn't mean to upset you."

"It's not your fault." Victoria sniffled and lifted her chin in an effort to push away the nostalgia. "Tonight was bound to be difficult no matter which words were spoken."

Alan angled his body so he was facing her. "Why is tonight harder than any other?"

She dropped her hand from his arm. "It's the first formal dinner without Papa here."

"I can't imagine how hard this is for you."

She blinked rapidly against the excess moisture in her eyes. "I'll be okay."

Alan took her hand and settled it on his arm once more as they started forward again. "If you need to make an early exit, just let me know. I'm good at slipping away unnoticed."

"I don't think you'll go unnoticed tonight," Victoria said. "As my sister said, you are quite dashing tonight."

"It must be the new tux."

"I don't think that's it."

They walked downstairs and approached the entrance to the main salon, where everyone would gather before dinner. Voices and a muted selection from Chopin spilled into the hall.

"Are you ready?" Victoria asked.

"I was about to ask you the same thing."

Victoria straightened her shoulders. "Let's do this."

* * *

Alan had never experienced anything like it. The moment he and Victoria had walked into the salon, all fifty people in the room had turned to stare. Each of them had sported similar reactions—an admiring glance at Victoria and a speculative one at him.

He was an unknown to the rest of the guests. After spending so much time around the royals in this part of Europe, he understood how that alone could fuel conversations in the upper echelons of society.

Victoria tugged gently on his arm. "Come on. There are some people I would like for you to meet."

Alan crossed the floor with her as she approached a couple in their forties. "Lord Romero, Lady Romero, it's so good to see you."

"Princess Victoria. I'd heard you were back in Sereno," Lord Romero said.

"Yes, I just arrived this week." Victoria nodded at Alan. "May I present my friend, Alan Neisler."

"Mr. Neisler," Lord Romero said, his tone reserved.

"Please, call me Alan."

"Alan, then." Lord Romero shook Alan's hand.

Lady Romero shook his hand in turn. "Tell me, Alan, how do you know Princess Victoria?"

"We met through some mutual acquaintances."

"Oh?" Lady Romero's eyebrows rose, clearly hoping for more details.

Victoria tilted her head toward the older man. "Lord Romero has been overseeing the economic development committee for Sereno for the past several years."

"That must be quite a challenging job with so many businesses coming into Porto Blu," Alan said.

Lord Romero's cool demeanor remained intact. "It's nothing I can't handle."

Movement near the entrance caught Alan's attention. He glanced over his shoulder as Garrett and Janessa walked in.

They greeted someone near the doorway without stopping as they approached Alan and Victoria. At the royal couple's arrival, Lady Romero dropped into a neat curtsy, and her husband and Alan both bowed to acknowledge Garrett and Janessa's status as working royals.

Garrett shook Alan's hand. "Alan, I was hoping you would be here tonight."

Janessa brushed his cheek with a kiss, using the greeting common in Meridia among friends. "I'm so glad you're here."

"Me too," Alan said.

Garrett greeted Victoria and the Romeros.

Lord Romero cast a speculative glance at Alan. "I wasn't aware you were acquainted with Prince Garrett."

"Alan has been a trusted family friend for many years," Garrett said.

"Yes." Janessa smiled. "He even attended our wedding."

"I had no idea." The lord's disposition changed instantly.

"In fact, I'm glad I ran into you tonight," Garrett said, still focused on Alan. "My brother would appreciate it if you could give him a call at your earliest convenience."

"I'd be happy to," Alan said, not sure if Garrett was serious or if he was just making a show for the pompous lord. "I'll give him a call tomorrow."

Lord Romero took a half step forward. "Alan, I'm surprised we haven't met before tonight."

Alan wasn't sure how to respond. Thankfully, he didn't have to.

Victoria inclined her head toward a foursome a short distance away. "It was lovely seeing you again," Victoria said. "If you'll excuse us, I have a few more people I'd like Alan to meet."

"Of course," Lord Romero said.

Alan, Victoria, Garrett, and Janessa all excused themselves from their current conversation and moved toward the next group.

Alan lowered his voice and spoke to Garrett. "Did Stefano really want to talk to me?"

"Actually, yes. He'll be our family representative at Cassie's coronation. He wants your thoughts on whether it's safe to bring his boys."

"I heard the two of you weren't coming?" Alan asked. "Is it because of Janessa's pregnancy?"

Garrett shook his head. "My father is being increasingly protective of us lately. He doesn't want both of his sons in the same place for security reasons."

"I can't blame him there," Alan said. "I'll call your brother in the morning."

"Thanks." Garrett looked down at Janessa with adoration. "Shall we go mingle?"

"Right after we find the waiter with the appetizers." Janessa placed a hand on her stomach. "Our child is hungry."

"I think we can take care of that problem." Garrett lifted a hand to flag down a nearby waiter.

The man quickly made it to their side and lowered his tray.

Janessa selected one of the finger sandwiches. Victoria took something that looked like a minipastry. Garrett opted for steak on a skewer. Alan kept his hands at his side.

"Don't you want anything?" Janessa asked. She finished her sandwich in two bites.

"No thanks."

Before the waiter could get away, Janessa took a steak skewer for herself. "We'll see you later."

Victoria and Alan resumed their course toward the two couples chatting near the terrace doors.

Alan lowered his voice and leaned down. "Is everyone going to act like the lord and lady over there?"

"No. Most are much nicer." Victoria paused. "And some are much worse."

"Do I get to meet some nice ones now?"

Victoria smiled. "Yes, you do."

She was right. The two couples they met next were friendly. The mayor of Porto Blu and his wife shared their excitement about the new resort. Lord Cattaneo and his wife echoed the sentiment.

After making the introductions, Victoria said, "Lord Cattaneo is probably the hardest-working member of parliament at the moment. He heads the energy commission."

"That must be an enormous job, especially with the new oil venture."

"We have also begun construction of a new wind field off our north shore," Lord Cattaneo said. "It's an exciting time for us all."

"It looks like they're about to serve dinner." Victoria looked up at Alan. "Shall we?"

Alan fought the urge to lift his hand to his still-full stomach. "Sure."

They walked into the dining hall, where little seashells were inscribed with each guest's name. Victoria must have known where they were sitting because she led him halfway down the length of the long table.

Cassie moved past them to the head of the table. She waited until all the guests arrived before she lowered into her seat. The rest of the guests followed suit.

Within moments, members of the serving staff stepped forward and placed a bowl in front of each guest.

Alan eyed the creamy soup in front of him and whispered to Victoria, "How many courses is this dinner?"

"Only nine."

"Nine?" Alan repeated. This was going to be an interesting night.

CHAPTER 16

Victoria stepped into the dining hall, the scent of fresh pastries carrying on the air. She breathed in deeply, and her stomach rumbled. Even though it was only ten thirty, breakfast had been over four hours ago and had consisted of only an apple.

She swept her gaze over the room. Approximately two dozen guests mingled about, businessmen and royalty occupying the generous space. Several round tables had been set up in the dining hall, each topped with white tablecloths and floral arrangements.

Victoria scanned the room again. It wasn't until she'd confirmed that Alan wasn't present that she realized she had been searching for him.

Disappointment swept through her, and she accepted the emotion for what it was: a confirmation that she was developing feelings for him.

She couldn't let this happen, yet the thought of not seeing him on a regular basis left a hollow sensation inside her.

She lifted her chin. She could think about this later. This morning, she had to be a princess.

One of the local restaurant owners approached and bowed to her. "Good morning, Princess Victoria."

"Good morning, Elias. It's so good to see you again." Victoria slid into the expected idle chitchat for a minute before she moved to greet the next guest, a local bank president.

She chatted with four guests before she reached the spot where Cassie was deep in conversation with Keith Maloney, the CEO of Axion. The man's company had won the drilling rights two years ago, and he had become a frequent visitor ever since.

At Victoria's arrival, Cassie excused herself from her current conversation. "We can meet later this afternoon."

Keith nodded and moved away to chat with another guest.

Victoria spotted Garrett and Janessa across the room, chatting with one of the local business owners. "It looks like everyone is enjoying themselves."

"Yes, it does." Cassie gestured to a nearby staff member. "They will enjoy it even more once brunch is served. The kitchen staff outdid themselves."

"Dimitri must be exhausted with all these events back-to-back," Victoria said, referring to the palace chef.

"He wisely delegated the management of the brunch to his pastry chef."

Victoria inhaled the mouthwatering scents of eggs, sausage, and fresh bread. "If the food tastes anywhere near as amazing as it smells, that decision was a good one."

"I agree." She leaned close and whispered, "I hope you're okay with sitting next to Nico Amando this morning."

Victoria lifted her eyebrows. "You want me to have brunch with the resort's biggest competition?"

"I know he wasn't thrilled when we announced our plans to build The Royal Sands Resort, but as I explained to him when we started, we have the potential to attract enough tourists to allow both of our hotels to thrive."

"And you want me to remind him of that fact," Victoria said.

"I do." Cassie smiled. "You can be charming when you want to be."

Victoria didn't bother to answer. It was best to save sarcasm for the confines of their private quarters.

Within moments, the meal was announced, and everyone made their way to the tables. Victoria found her spot, her name inscribed on a small place card. Nico Amando's name was right beside hers.

Seriously? It was one thing to sit at the same table, but did Cassie really have to put them right next to each other? She briefly debated swapping Nico's place card with the one beside his to give them a buffer, but Nico arrived a moment too soon.

Dressed in a three-thousand-euro suit, he bowed his head slightly. "Good morning, Your Highness."

"Good morning. It's good to see you again." Victoria extended her hand to him as though they were friends.

"I understand your resort is coming along nicely."

"It is." Victoria offered her practiced smile. "I hope you will be able to attend our grand opening."

His lips curved into an equally insincere smile. "I wouldn't miss it."

Victoria's stomach clutched at the prospect of conversing with this man for the next hour. She glanced over her shoulder to make sure Cassie had already taken her seat before she lowered into her own. She then turned to the seat on the other side of her. Empty.

Victoria read the place card at the vacant spot. Hubert Derosche, the banker who had fallen ill this morning and had sent his regrets. Fabulous.

"Have you already finished with your inspections?" Nico asked as he settled into the chair beside her.

"Nearly. Just a few more small items to tend to first."

"I hope you're able to open on time. The inspectors can be brutal on that final walk-through." Nico tilted his head. "Then again, I'm not royal, so maybe those issues will be easier on you."

"I assure you, the inspectors do not take my title into account when they are doing their job," Victoria said. "After all, their role is to ensure the safety of the building and everyone who enters it. I wouldn't dream of interfering with such an important responsibility."

"That's a refreshing attitude."

A waiter set a plate of food before her, and she broke off a piece of her croissant.

"How is Lorenzo working out for you?" Nico asked.

"He's doing good work." Victoria glanced across the room at where Janessa and Garrett sat with several other prominent businessmen. Why couldn't Cassie have let her have them at her table? Hoping to ease the subtle hostility exuding from Nico, she said, "Did you hear that a new marketing campaign for Sereno will be launching this fall? We hope to increase tourism during the winter months."

"I had heard rumblings about that." He picked up his fork and cut into a piece of sausage. "Maybe that will help me replace the bookings I'm losing to your new place."

Victoria chose her words carefully. "If the queen's initiatives are successful, we will both be turning people away."

"If." He shook his head. "That's a dangerous word."

"Yes," Victoria said soberly. "It certainly can be."

* * *

Alan passed through the third-floor hallway of the resort, pausing when he and Max reached a toolbox someone had left outside one of the corner rooms.

Max sniffed at it and then lifted his head. No issue.

Alan continued forward, his thoughts wandering to the night before. The idea that he had accompanied a princess to a royal event hadn't really sunk in until after he had walked her back to her room last night, after he had resisted the urge to kiss her.

She was royalty, he reminded himself. He was only in Sereno for a short time. The two of them could never work.

But that didn't keep the memories of his time at Victoria's side from replaying through his mind and warming his heart. She had been so attentive all evening, making a point of introducing him to their guests, always treating him as though she were the one who was lucky to be there with him instead of the other way around.

Was this how the relationship between Levi and Cassie had started? He had been there on the front lines when Janessa and Garrett's romance had gone from a fictional engagement to a real one. Yet the magic of watching two people falling in love always seemed like a fairy tale that never touched his life.

His sister insisted his lack of a dating life resulted from his constant travel. He suspected it had more to do with simply never finding someone who shared his love of travel as well as his love of animals. He also hadn't found someone he wanted to spend time with.

A sense of dread washed over him at the thought of spending two full years in the Middle East. He would start in Turkey, near the Syrian border. Not exactly a hopping social scene for an American who was constantly escorted by a K-9 partner. Where he would go after that, he wasn't sure, but it was common for such assignments to include multiple moves. He just hoped he was able to live somewhere with indoor plumbing. During his previous hardship tour in Africa, he had ended up living in a tent for a good portion of his time.

Alan continued down the hall with Max and headed down to the next level. A quick sweep revealed no one was present beyond the plumbers finishing the guest bathrooms. They would complete their task today.

The resort was so close to being done. Victoria would be thrilled to check another item off her list.

He reached the atrium, where Félix and Giulia sat at a small table, a platter of pastries between them.

The two spoke in Italian, but with Félix's French accent, Alan picked up only a few words here and there. If he was correct, they were discussing which breads to serve with dinner, and the two didn't appear to be in agreement.

Félix spotted him and waved him over. "Alan, come here." The forcefulness of his tone reminded Alan of a general on a battlefield.

With his latest security sweep complete, Alan complied. "What can I do for you?"

"Taste these. Which one is better?"

Alan studied the options before him. Two kinds of rolls and slices of rye bread. He picked up one of the golden-brown rolls, broke off a piece, and took a bite. The bread practically melted in his mouth. "That is amazing."

"And the others?" Félix asked.

Alan took a bite of the rye bread. "That's good, but I'm not a huge fan of rye."

"And the last?"

Alan broke off a bite of the final offering. It had a unique nutty flavor, one that was more common in many of the European countries he had visited.

"Well?" Félix prompted.

"If you could only have one, which would you choose?" Giulia added.

"That's a hard choice. I'm not a fan of rye, so personally, that one is my least favorite." Alan studied the remnants of the two rolls he had broken pieces off of. He picked up the white roll. "This one is my favorite, but the other roll is really good too. A lot of your European visitors might like that one better."

"See?" Félix held both hands up as though punctuating his point.

"Fine." Giulia rolled her eyes. "You win."

Alan looked from Giulia to Félix and back again. "What just happened?"

"I wanted Félix to limit himself to only one type of roll on the weeknights, but he insisted he needed both to accommodate the varying tastes of our international clientele."

Alan broke off another bite of the roll in his hand. "Sorry, Giulia, but I think Félix is right."

"I am always right," Félix said, his eyes flashing with triumph.

Alan chuckled. "Enjoy celebrating your victory. I'm going to head back to the palace."

"You will be back tomorrow?" Félix asked.

"I hadn't planned on it." Alan's eyebrows drew together. "There shouldn't be anyone working on Sunday."

"I have a few more dishes to work on," Félix said. "But if no one else is coming, perhaps I'll be able to create undisturbed."

Alan nodded. "Feel free to save me some leftovers."

"I will."

Alan headed for the exit. He was nearly to his car when his cell phone rang. He pulled it from his pocket and checked the caller ID. Prince Stefano from Meridia, Garrett's older brother.

Alan hit the Talk button. "Good morning, Your Highness."

"Alan, how are you?" Stefano asked. "Am I catching you at a good time?"

"You are. I just finished my early-morning sweep of the new resort."

"I hear it's going to be quite the destination."

"Yes, it will," Alan said. "I assume this is where you're staying when you come for the coronation."

"Yes. That's actually why I was calling," he said. "I had hoped to bring my wife and sons with me, but Garrett mentioned some security concerns."

"I'm afraid we have an unidentified threat," Alan admitted.

"How significant?" Stefano asked.

"It appears to be focused on one target," Alan said, even though he still wasn't sure. "Unfortunately, the risks haven't yet been reduced."

"I'd love to ask you how soon the situation might change, but I suspect you wouldn't be able to give me an answer."

"No, I wouldn't," Alan said. "I can let you know when the status does change."

"I would appreciate that," Stefano said. "And if I may ask one more favor."

"What's that?"

"Keep my brother and sister-in-law safe while they are in Sereno."

"I'll do my best."

"Thank you."

Alan ended the call and slipped his phone back into his pocket. He would do his best to protect all the royals present, but he couldn't deny that the one who worried him most was the woman who was quickly becoming the center of his thoughts.

CHAPTER 17

Victoria had spent the last two hours reviewing progress reports from her various department heads and watching her phone. She had given Alan her mobile number last night when he'd dropped her off at her room so he could update her on his visits to the resort. She had hoped he would take advantage of using her number for personal reasons as well.

She let out a sigh and pushed back from her dining room table. She had thoroughly enjoyed her time with Alan last night. He had been cordial to everyone, even Lord Romero when he'd made a point of visiting with them after dinner. He had also kept the conversation from growing stale during dinner, despite their close proximity to the minister of fish and wildlife. The man rarely managed to talk about anything beyond trade routes and fishing regulations.

Someone knocked at her door, and Victoria experienced a quick surge of anticipation. She immediately chastised herself. She couldn't assume it would be Alan. More likely, her social secretary was stopping by to remind her of the upcoming ball tonight, which she would attend alone.

She opened the door.

Alan stood in the hall, a large serving tray in his hand and his dog standing by his side. "Did you know your chef graduated from Le Cordon Bleu?"

"I did know that." She stepped aside to let him enter. Max trotted in behind him, his leash noticeably absent. "What's all this?"

"I ran into Triana when Max and I were checking out the kitchen. She mentioned you hadn't eaten yet, so I thought I would bring something up to you."

"That's an awful lot of food."

"I may have been hoping you'd let me join you."

Her insides fluttered. "I'd like that."

They walked into the dining room, where she had left her laptop and several of her notes scattered on the table.

Alan set the tray on the opposite end of the table. "How come you're working in here? Don't you have an office somewhere in the palace?"

Victoria couldn't count the number of times her parents had asked her a similar question. "I have a desk in one of my spare bedrooms, but I like to be able to spread out a bit more and see everything at once."

"It's your way of staying organized."

"My family never sees it that way, but yes, I suppose it is." She sat next to the tray. "What did you bring me?"

"We have an assortment of leftovers from last night and some croissants and meat and cheese in case you'd prefer a sandwich."

"I thought you didn't like the food last night," Victoria said. "You hardly touched your dinner."

"It was nine courses, and I had a very late lunch." Alan began setting the food out. "I had to sample everything so I would know which leftovers to go after today."

Judging from the spread before her, Alan had chosen seven of the nine courses. "So you liked everything besides the salad and the fish."

"I liked everything," Alan corrected. "There weren't any leftovers of the salad or the fish."

Victoria plucked a croissant out of the basket and put it on her plate. She then proceeded to add a small serving of steak. "What have you and Max been up to this morning?"

"We did an initial sweep over at the resort to make sure the carpet installers could get to work. Then we spent some time down at the main gate."

"Why the main gate?" Victoria tore off a piece of her croissant and took a bite.

"I needed to review the security procedures for tonight's event."

The hope that Alan would ask her to the ball withered. "So, you have to work tonight?"

"I'll work the gate until all the guests arrive," Alan said. "The entrance will be sealed an hour after the ball begins so the guards don't have to divide their attention between people coming and going."

Her hope rekindled. "What happens after the first hour? Are you coming to the ball?"

"I would, but I have one significant problem."

"What's that?"

"I need a dance partner." He set his fork down. "I don't suppose you would be willing to go with a date who will have to arrive late, would you?"

Delighted, she bit back a smile. "I supposed I could meet you there."

"This means I'm going to have to wear my tux again, doesn't it?"

"Yes." She tilted her head toward the door. "If you need it cleaned before tonight, let the staff know. They can take care of it for you."

"Theo already took care of it this morning." Alan took a sip of his water. "I'm starting to understand why Levi has more than one tux now."

"The formal events do tend to cluster together. Once Garrett and Janessa leave on Sunday night, the focus will shift to the coronation, but if we're lucky, life will settle down for at least a little while." Victoria paused. Life had been far from settled since she had arrived home. "I hope life will settle down anyway."

"We've made it almost forty-eight hours without sighting another bomb. That's a good sign."

"Yes, it is." Two days since the last moment of terror, but was the threat behind them, or was it just beginning? "I really wish we knew who was doing this."

"Me too, but we'll figure it out."

"That's what Levi always says." Victoria's phone rang, and she checked it to see that it was Sheldon again. She ignored it.

"Who is it?"

"A guy I went to school with."

Alan cocked an eyebrow. "A boyfriend?"

"No. Nothing like that." The phone rang again, and Victoria silenced it a second time. "He asked me out a few times during graduate school, but I never accepted. Now he's here in Sereno and keeps insisting we get together."

"What did you tell him?"

"I told him it wasn't a good time." The phone rang again. "Obviously, he isn't taking no for an answer. He's been calling constantly since yesterday."

"Maybe it's time to block his number."

Victoria sighed. "I hate to do that, but you could be right."

* * *

Alan stood in the center of Levi and Cassie's living room while Cassie did her magic with his bow tie.

Levi, already dressed and ready to go, sat on the chair across from him. "You know, eventually, you're going to have to learn to tie one of these on your own."

"It's not that I can't tie it," Alan countered. "It's just that Cassie does a much better job."

Cassie finished her work. "There you go." She tugged at both ends to straighten it. "All done."

"Thanks."

"You're welcome." She made another last adjustment to his tie and stepped back. "Try to keep from pulling at it while you're working. You don't want to look mussed up when you arrive at the ball."

"Is this your way of saying you'll be too busy to come fix it for me?" Alan asked.

"I'm afraid so." She gave him a little smile. "Of course, you could always ask another princess to help you if you need it."

"Janessa *is* pretty good with bow ties," Alan said. "I've had her help me before."

"I wasn't talking about Janessa." Cassie sat beside Levi and motioned for Alan to join them in the sitting area. "You and Victoria looked like you had a nice time last night."

"We did." Alan settled into the armchair across from her. "It was nice spending some time together when neither of us had to worry about security threats."

Cassie slipped her hand into Levi's. "It's been quite a while since Victoria has dated anyone, since before my father died. With the way she looked at you last night, I can't help wondering if that's about to change. And I hope you know you have my blessing if you choose to date my sister."

"Me and Victoria?" Alan couldn't deny that the image had popped into his head more than once since his arrival, but he wasn't comfortable discussing his private life, especially the speculation of it. "Are you sure she hasn't dated anyone lately? Some guy named Sheldon has been calling her a lot over the last couple days."

"I'm quite certain," Cassie said. "Victoria may be private when it comes to her dating life, but she usually tells me and Annabelle when she's interested in someone. Not to mention, she had a security detail with her at Cambridge. They would have known if she was dating."

Alan glanced at Levi. The blank stare told him his friend hadn't confided in Cassie where they had been before dinner last night. Curious to know if Cassie had any knowledge of the subject of their stakeout, Alan said, "Whether they dated or not, this Sheldon guy is persistent. After he called the third time during lunch, I suggested she block his number."

"And did she?" Levi asked.

"Yeah." Alan couldn't tell if Levi approved of the suggestion, but neither of them would want Victoria anywhere near Sheldon if he was hoping to find something to blackmail her with.

"Better let the guards at the gate know to keep an eye out for him," Levi said. "We don't want him trying to slip in as a friend of hers."

"I will." Alan stood. "Speaking of which, I'd better go get Max. The guards are opening the gates in fifteen minutes."

"Oh, one more thing," Cassie said. "You should join us for our family brunch after church tomorrow."

"But I'm not family."

"Janessa and Garrett will be there too," Levi said.

"It's just a simple meal," Cassie said. "It's our time to step away from our duties for a while and enjoy each other's company."

A small, intimate affair where no one would be trying to put on airs. It sounded perfect. "In that case, I'd love to join you."

"Great. We'll eat out on the terrace by the family chapel," Cassie said.

The family chapel that was as large as the ballroom and would be the location of Cassie's coronation.

"And feel free to bring Max," Levi added. "No reason to leave him cooped up when he can be outside with the rest of us."

"I'm sure he'll appreciate that." Alan moved toward the door. "I'll see you later." He patted his bow tie. "And, Cassie, thanks again."

"You're welcome."

Alan left Levi and Cassie's quarters and turned toward his own. He slowed when he reached Victoria's door.

Unable to resist, he stopped and knocked.

"Coming!" Victoria called from inside. The door swung open, but her focus was on the table beside the door. "I just need to grab—" She looked up, and surprise illuminated her expression. "Sorry. I thought you were Annabelle."

Alan grasped for words, but the sight of her disconnected his mouth from his brain. Her hair had a windswept look tonight, with most of it pulled up and wisps falling down to frame her face. Her dress, a deep blue, hugged her body before flaring out at her hips and flowing to the floor.

"I thought you had to work tonight," she said.

Alan nodded and struggled to untangle his tongue. "I'm heading down to get Max now."

"So you stopped by to tell me you're going to work?"

The truth spilled out. "I just wanted to see you." He focused on her face, the high cheekbones, the expertly enhanced eyes, the full, painted lips. "You look incredible."

Those lips lifted into a smile. "Thank you."

Alan took her hand and brought it to his lips. His lips lingered for a brief moment on the smooth skin before he straightened. "I'll do my best not to keep you waiting."

Her smile widened. "And I'll do my best not to watch the clock."

Reluctantly, Alan released her hand and stepped back. "I'll see you later." He forced himself to leave her. As soon as he arrived at his apartment, he traded his tuxedo jacket for his protection gear.

"Come on, Max." Alan clipped the leash onto Max's collar. "Let's get this job done so I can go to a ball."

CHAPTER 18

Victoria watched the time. She could hardly do otherwise with the grandfather clock in the hall chiming every quarter hour.

Annabelle left the dance floor, where she had been dancing with a prince from Denmark, and came to her side. "You haven't been dancing."

"I'm afraid my dance partner is running late."

Annabelle's smile was instant. "I told Cassie you liked him."

"It's not like that," Victoria said even as the memory of Alan kissing her hand brought a flush of color to her cheeks. "He's become a friend."

Annabelle's focus shifted to someone behind Victoria. "Judging by the way he's looking at you, I think he wants to be more than just friends."

Victoria turned toward the terrace doors and spotted Alan moving toward her.

Alan reached her side. "Sorry I'm late."

"That's okay."

He put his hand on her back before he greeted her sister. "Princess Annabelle. Are you having a good time?"

"I am."

A new song started, and Alan held out his hand. "May I have this dance?"

"You may." Victoria put her hand in his.

Annabelle leaned close and whispered, "Have fun."

Victoria smiled and nodded. She joined Alan on the dance floor and turned to face him. He pulled her into his arms, his hand firm on her waist.

Her breath caught in her throat when her gaze lifted to his. He stared at her for a brief moment, and then they were dancing.

He twirled her around as though he spent his days practicing ballroom dancing instead of sniffing out bombs.

"Where did you learn to dance?" Victoria asked.

"My parents were on the ballroom dance team in college. My sisters and I didn't have a choice but to learn." He released her to twirl her away from him before drawing her close once more.

"You learned well."

"Thank you."

Victoria tilted her head back and trusted her partner as she arched away from him.

As though they had danced together dozens of times, she continued to follow his lead. The joy of being in Alan's arms, of moving to the music, flowed through her and brought a smile to her face.

When the last notes faded, Alan's hand remained on her waist. He leaned in. "You are an incredible dancer."

"Thank you." Her gaze lifted to his once more. "Dance lessons were always one of my favorite diversions."

"It's obvious you enjoy them." The notes of the next song rang out. "Care for another?"

"Yes." She smiled. "I would."

Victoria couldn't remember the last time she had spent more time on the dance floor than socializing with their guests, but she loved every moment she spent with Alan.

The music came to an end again, and the conductor of the orchestra announced that they were taking a break.

Victoria motioned toward a server who was circling with a tray of fluted glasses and water goblets. The server stopped beside them and lowered his tray.

"Water?" Alan asked.

"Please," Victoria said.

Alan took two goblets from the tray and thanked the waiter, then passed a glass to Victoria.

"Thank you." She took a sip of the cool liquid.

"It's a little stuffy in here. Do you want to go outside for a few minutes?"

She caught sight of Lord and Lady Romero working their way toward them. "That's a wonderful idea."

Together they weaved through the ballroom to the french doors leading outside. Several guests already occupied the wide terrace that stretched between the ballroom and the family chapel. Victoria greeted several as they passed by.

Alan led her to the far edge, where the light faded and the shadows began. Guards stood at attention on the paths leading away from the terrace. Her eyes narrowed when she spotted a dog beside one of the guards.

"Is that Max over there?"

"Yes. Federico offered to keep Max with him," Alan said.

"I didn't think you would let anyone else work with Max."

"Federico trained with me the last time I worked here," Alan said. "And trust me, Max would much prefer to be out here than locked up in my room."

"I don't blame him." Victoria took another sip of her water. "It's such a beautiful night; everyone should get the chance to enjoy it."

Alan glanced over her shoulder. "Don't look now, but Lord and Lady Romero are heading our way."

"Would it be terribly rude of us to go for a walk to avoid them?"

"No, but I think we already missed our chance."

Lord Romero's voice sounded behind her. "Princess Victoria. I was hoping to see you tonight."

Victoria turned to face the older couple, a practiced smile on her face. "Hello. Have you been enjoying the party?"

"Oh, very much so," Lady Romero said.

"I neglected to ask you the other night if you have set the date for the grand opening for The Royal Sands Resort," Lord Romero said. "I like to keep the economic council informed on significant events such as this."

"I'm sure you do," Victoria said. "As of now, our plans are to hold the grand opening the week after the coronation."

Lord Romero furrowed his brow. "I don't understand why you are waiting until you've already hosted guests to hold the grand opening. I would think you would receive far more interest in the media if the main event included the distinguished guests who will be in attendance for the coronation."

"I'm sure the media would enjoy that," Victoria said politely. "Our security team, however, would not."

Lord Romero looked over his shoulder to where Cassie and Levi currently stood chatting with Janessa and another couple. "I believe your brother-in-law's obsession with security is creating quite a few difficulties when it comes to economic development."

"In what way?" Alan asked.

"Take tonight, for example," Lord Romero said. "Everyone had to arrive within an hour window, or they would be denied entrance; only the official palace photographer is present to document the event; and I'm sure the press release will be little more than a generic statement about the royalty in attendance."

"That is true," Victoria said, "but how does that impact our economic development?"

"The more Sereno is in the news, especially in other countries, the more tourists we'll have coming into our cities," Lord Romero said.

"It is a delicate balance," Victoria said.

Lord Romero opened his mouth to speak at the same time music carried through the open terrace doors.

"I believe they are playing our song." Alan took Victoria's hand. "Shall we?"

"Yes." Victoria nodded to Lord and Lady Romero. "If you'll excuse us."

Victoria and Alan moved back inside, both of them depositing their empty glasses on a passing waiter's tray. Then Alan swept her into another dance.

"Thank you."

"Oh, believe me," Alan said. "It was my pleasure."

CHAPTER 19

Alan supposed he should give Victoria the chance to socialize more, but every time they started to leave the dance floor, Lord Romero seemed to be hovering nearby.

Another waltz started, and Victoria whispered in his ear, "Is it just me, or do you feel like we're being watched?"

They were being watched, not only by the Romeros but by many guests who seemed to be speculating as to who he was and why he was here with Victoria.

He twirled her around and edged closer to the center of the dance floor. "Everyone is appreciating how beautiful you look tonight."

She lifted an eyebrow. "That's not the reason."

"I wouldn't be so sure about that." Out of the corner of his eye, he caught sight of Levi and Janessa. Levi lifted his chin ever so slightly, a subtle signal that he wanted to speak to Alan.

Alan replied by tilting his head toward Victoria, his silent question whether Levi wanted to speak to both of them or Alan alone.

Levi shook his head in response.

The dance continued, and Alan debated how to best separate himself from Victoria so he could speak with Levi without leaving her alone.

When the dance ended, he took Victoria's hand. A ripple of attraction flowed through him. Not bothering to fight it, he asked, "Would you like something to drink?"

"I would, thank you."

They cleared the dance floor, and almost instantly, a waiter appeared at their side with a tray of drinks.

Alan released her hand and waited for Victoria to indicate which one she wanted before he passed a glass to her. He selected another for himself as Janessa appeared at Victoria's side.

"Victoria, I hate to ask, but would you mind introducing me to Lord Cattaneo? I haven't had the chance to meet him yet, but Cassie and Levi are tied up at the moment."

"I'd be happy to."

Alan put his hand lightly on Victoria's waist and said quietly, "I'll be back in a minute. It looks like Levi wants to talk to me."

Before Victoria could respond, Janessa said, "We'll see you in a bit."

Alan nodded and crossed to the corner of the room. A couple had approached Levi, but it took only a minute for the new king to excuse himself and move to Alan's side.

"What's up?" Alan asked.

"Janessa got the reports back on the woman with Sheldon."

"And?"

"No hits on facial recognition for Interpol or law enforcement agencies in the US."

"Did we ask MI6 to run her image through their database? She sounded British."

"We're still waiting on them. It's unlikely we'll hear anything back until Monday, at the earliest."

"I'd really like to know who this woman is."

"That makes two of us."

"Do we know where she's staying? Or where Sheldon is staying, for that matter?" Alan asked.

"Sheldon is at the Imperial Blu," Levi said. "The woman went there, too, but no one has spotted her since last night."

"How many people did you have on surveillance?"

"Two," Levi said. "We're trying to access the guest registry, but Nico hasn't been very helpful."

"I don't think she's staying there. If she's at the same hotel as Sheldon, it doesn't make sense that they would meet somewhere else."

"I had the same thought," Levi said. "That's why I haven't pushed hard about the records. For all we know, the woman could be staying anywhere on the island."

"Sounds to me like you may want to put your effort into checking security cameras at the airport."

"We already have," Levi said. "I was hoping to narrow down her arrival time so we could identify her through passport control."

"And?"

"And she didn't come through the airport."

"If she didn't fly here, she must have come by boat."

"Yes, like thousands of other tourists every day."

Alan let out a sigh. "Cruise ships."

"I'm afraid so. She could have come here on one of those, but we have no way to be certain that she is still here or if she arrived for one day and left."

"If she was only here for one day, we know when it was."

Levi nodded. "I already requested the passenger manifests for the ships that were docked at the time she met with Sheldon."

Alan replayed the overheard conversation in his mind. "I hate to say it, but I don't think she was here for just a day. I got the impression that she was part of whatever Sheldon had planned."

"I don't disagree with you, but we have to explore every option to identify her."

"Maybe you should start with passengers who arrived through the port but who haven't left yet."

"I had the same thought." Levi's gaze swept over the room until it landed on his wife. "If they don't turn up something soon, we may need to shake a few things loose."

"Just let me know if you need my help."

"With the way things are going, I don't think it's a matter of if. It's a matter of when."

* * *

Victoria couldn't remember an evening she had enjoyed more. Even though Alan had been late to the ball, he had spent practically every moment since his arrival by her side.

The last of the guests lingered near the exit, and the orchestra worked to pack up their instruments across the room.

Alan put his hand on her waist, and the warmth radiated through the thin layer of silk. "Do you want me to walk you up to your room?"

Victoria spotted Giuseppe near the doorway leading to the hall. Her guard could keep her safe, but she couldn't resist drawing out her time with Alan a little longer. "I'd like that."

"Do you need to say goodbye to anyone before we leave?"

Victoria glanced at Annabelle chatting with several of the remaining guests. "No. It looks like my sister is taking care of wishing everyone a good night."

"Do you take turns being the one who stays late?" Alan asked.

"We do," Victoria said, struck by the fact that Cassie and Annabelle hadn't discussed that task with her beforehand. Usually, it came down to a game of rock paper scissors. She was terrible at that game.

Alan guided her to the exit, and Giuseppe fell in behind them, following at a discreet distance, close enough to keep them in sight but far enough to allow them a private conversation.

"What were you talking to Levi about tonight?" Victoria asked.

"He was just giving me an update."

Even though Victoria didn't want to ruin this perfect evening with thoughts of the bombing attempts, she couldn't keep herself from asking, "Did he discover anything new?"

"No. It was more a conversation on how to eliminate possibilities."

Victoria sighed. "I don't think I would be very good at law enforcement."

"Why's that?"

"I'm not patient enough." She glanced over her shoulder at where Giuseppe had stopped beside one of the chairs lining the wide hallway. She stopped as well. "I want answers now."

"We all do."

Victoria started forward again. "I know Levi doesn't want to worry me, but I wish he would tell me more about what he knows."

"If he had anything significant to share, he would tell you about it," Alan assured her.

They passed by the main entrance, with its ornate chandelier hanging from the ceiling and suits of armor posed as though standing guard. "Sometimes I wonder what it must have been like when guards had to wear armor to protect themselves from potential invaders and travel from one country to another could take weeks or even months."

"I didn't think Sereno had ever been involved in a major conflict."

"We haven't. Sereno is far enough out of the shipping lanes that we were able to avoid getting dragged into the world wars, and we didn't have sufficient financial resources to enter into the other major international conflicts."

"So you've been like Switzerland—stay out of everyone else's business, and hope they'll leave you alone."

"Something like that." She shrugged. "Obviously, our visibility in world politics has changed since the discovery of the oil field."

"Your family has also created a thriving tourism industry here," Alan said. "I visited Sereno on a vacation once a few years ago."

"Before you came to work with the royal guard?"

"Yes. It was during a holiday when I was living in Meridia." Alan looked down at her and grinned. "I had to see who had the best beaches."

"Who did?"

"At the time, I favored Meridia, but that was because I had access to the private royal beach," Alan said. "I'd forgotten what it was like to have to share with a bunch of tourists."

Victoria laughed. "I imagine that would factor in on your opinion." She motioned in the general direction of the Mediterranean. "What do you think now that you've had a chance to enjoy our royal beaches?"

"I think I may need to make another visit." Humor danced in Alan's eyes. "You know, just to make sure I've spent enough time to really make a fair comparison."

"I'm sure that can be arranged." Victoria envisioned a quiet picnic on the beach, just the two of them. "Do you want to take a ride out to the beach tomorrow afternoon?"

Alan stopped beside her apartment door and turned to face her. Regret flickered over his face. "I'd love that, but it wouldn't be wise to have you out in the open until we know more about who is behind the bombs."

Her heart sank at her current lack of freedom. "I'm sorry. I wasn't thinking."

Alan took her hand in his. "I hope you know that I'd love nothing more than to spend the afternoon with you on the beach."

A wistfulness came over her. "Maybe someday."

"Someday will happen." Alan stepped closer, cutting the distance between them in half. "And when it does, I hope I'm here to enjoy spending more time with you."

Victoria lifted her eyes to meet his. A flash of uncertainty reflected there, but she wasn't sure if it was because of the growing bond between them or because he knew he would be leaving soon.

He stared for several long seconds before glancing at where Giuseppe now stood guard down the hall.

Alan lifted her hand and pressed his lips against her skin, his gaze never leaving hers. The familiar tingle that came from his touch started at where he'd kissed her and crept up her arm and into her very core.

Alan stepped back, still not releasing her hand. "I'll see you tomorrow."

She nearly asked when before remembering tomorrow was Sunday. "You should come to brunch with my family tomorrow," she said. "Unless Levi changes it, we'll eat on the terrace after church."

Alan's lips twitched into a half smile. "Cassie already invited me."

"Then I'll see you there?" Victoria asked.

Alan nodded and squeezed her hand once more before releasing it. "I'll see you there."

CHAPTER 20

Alan must be crazy. Or he had spent too much time around Victoria. Either way, the woman was on his mind far too much, and he wasn't sure how much longer he'd be able to resist the temptation to move beyond friendship.

He opened his refrigerator and poured a glass of juice. He was letting Cassie's comment from last night get to him. Sure, Victoria had been sweet and attentive when they'd been together at the past few events, but he suspected Cassie was confusing Victoria's gratitude for affection. Too bad. Or was it?

Alan's assignment here would last only a few more weeks, and once he started his work in the Middle East, his vacation time would be limited, at best. Not to mention, the high security threats at his new post would make it impossible for Victoria to visit him.

Alan's mood clouded at the idea that this connection between him and Victoria would have a finite end after Cassie's coronation. Max scratched at the door, signaling that he needed to go out. Alan checked his watch.

"Just a minute. It's time to go to brunch anyway." He debated briefly whether he should discard the tie he had worn to church. Cassie had said it would be only her family there, along with Janessa and Garrett.

Alan loosened his tie and slipped it over his head, then tossed it onto the sofa. He grabbed Max's leash and tucked it into his pocket. "Come on, boy."

He opened the door, and Max wandered down a short hall and to the side exit. The moment the dog was outside, he made a beeline for the nearby trees; then, after a moment, he trotted back to Alan's side.

"Ready to go?" Alan asked.

Max gave him his goofy dog grin, apparently aware that today was his day off too.

"Come on." Alan signaled for Max to fall in beside him. Together they walked along the thick side wall to the palace, around the rounded wall of the corner tower, and down a path past a large stone gazebo.

They were nearly to the terrace when voices carried to them.

"I'll take care of it, Your Highness," a woman said.

"Thank you," Victoria said.

Alan reached the terrace, empty except for Victoria and the guard standing near the steps. "Are we the first ones here?" he asked.

Victoria turned to face him. "We are." She smiled fully. "Janessa and Garrett are running late. I guess they went to church in town and haven't made it back yet."

Alan took in the large round table covered with a bright-yellow tablecloth and set for seven. "What about Levi and your sisters?"

"They know Janessa and Garrett are late, so they're taking their time." Victoria took a seat at the table. "I'm sure they'll be here in a few minutes."

Alan took the spot beside her. Even though he had seen her at church, he asked, "How has your morning been?"

"Blessedly uneventful." She looked down at Max lying in the shade of the table beside Alan. "He looks like he's happy to have the day off."

"Yes. He hasn't had a lot of those lately."

"It's hard to imagine you and Max not being together after this month."

"I know." Alan didn't want to think about it. "He's loving life here though."

"We love having him around." Victoria reached down and stroked the fur between his ears. "I tried to convince Papa to let us get another dog a few years ago, but he didn't want to deal with it since all of us were either in college or about to be." She paused. "When Mama got sick, we stopped asking."

Alan looked down at his canine friend, and an improbable solution needled through his thoughts. "Maybe you should be the one to adopt Max."

Victoria's eyes widened, first with surprise and then with hope. "Could I?"

Even though the last thing he wanted was for someone else to take Max, the solution took root. He gazed around the vast grassy area behind them, at the nearby trees, at the stables just barely visible from where he sat. A lump formed in his throat, but he forced it down. "If you're willing, I'm sure we could make it happen." He reached down and ran his hand down Max's back. "Maybe you'd even let me visit him."

Victoria reached out and put her hand on his. "There's nothing I would like more."

Max perked his ears up and rose to his feet at the sound of a high-pitched yip.

"That sounds like a puppy." Alan turned to face the french doors leading from the house at the same time Levi and Cassie walked outside. Annabelle trailed behind them with a black furball in her arms.

Instantly, Victoria rose to her feet. “Oh, how adorable.” She hurried to Cassie and stroked the pup’s fur. “Where did he come from?”

“She,” Annabelle corrected, a grin lighting her face. “And she’s yours. Welcome home.”

“Mine?” Victoria held her hands out as Annabelle passed the puppy.

Unable to resist a closer look, Alan stepped beside her. “How old is she? About eight weeks?”

“Nine weeks tomorrow,” Levi said. “Cassie insisted she be fully potty trained before she came home.”

“I can’t blame her there,” Alan said. Max pressed closer, and Alan stroked his head. Alan suspected the puppy’s arrival would quickly change Victoria’s mind about taking Max in.

The puppy squirmed in Victoria’s arms and licked at her cheek.

Victoria giggled and cuddled her tighter. “I can’t believe this. In only a few minutes, I went from not having any pets to having two.”

“Two?” Cassie asked. “What do you mean?”

“Alan is going to help me adopt Max.”

Levi shot Alan a surprised look, but Alan focused on Victoria. “You still want to adopt Max even though you have a puppy?” Alan asked.

Victoria rested her chin on top of the puppy’s head. “Yes.” She looked down at Max. “That is, if you think they’ll get along okay.”

“Let’s find out.” Alan pulled the leash from his pocket and clipped it on Max’s collar. “Bring the puppy out onto the grass.”

Victoria walked down the short steps leading to the lawn. Alan followed. As soon as they were a few steps from the terrace, he said, “Put her down, and let’s see how she reacts to Max.”

“And how Max reacts to her,” Victoria said.

“That too.” Alan signaled for Max to sit.

Victoria set the puppy on the grass. Instantly, the puppy started sniffing the grass and moving toward Max. Max stretched out his neck and did his own bit of sniffing. Then the puppy lifted her front legs as though trying to play with Max.

“Easy, girl.” Alan scooped the puppy up with one hand and held her in front of Max.

Max sniffed her again. Then he licked the puppy’s head.

Victoria laughed. “It looks like they’re going to get along just fine.”

Alan tried not to think of what he was losing and instead focused on the gift Victoria was giving Max. “Yes, it does.”

* * *

They were the first to arrive and the last to leave. Victoria sat beside Alan at the table on the terrace, the two dogs resting in the shade beneath the table.

Her sisters and Levi had left to go horseback riding with Janessa and Garrett, but Victoria hadn't wanted to leave her new friend quite yet.

"Have you decided what you're going to name her?" Alan asked.

Victoria shook her head. "I think I may need to get to know her a little better before deciding on that."

"Don't wait too long, or her name will end up being Puppy."

Victoria gazed down. "She is so adorable."

"I hope you still think so at three in the morning when she needs to go out."

"I hadn't even thought about that."

"I don't think Levi did either. It'll likely be a few more weeks before she can make it through the night." Alan furrowed his brow. "Maybe you should let me take the puppy at night. It's not a good idea for you to be walking the grounds at that hour, and it would be best not to disrupt the guards' routines."

"You're offering to get up in the middle of the night with my puppy?"

"I'm the logical choice. I do know dogs."

He did know dogs, and Victoria couldn't deny that she appreciated a good night's sleep. Still . . .

"I know it sounds crazy, but I'd really like to be the one to take care of her," she said.

"I get that, but your safety has to come first. Levi will agree with me on that."

"There's a guard stationed right next to the door by your apartment. It shouldn't cause an issue for me to take her out on the lawn right there."

The puppy stirred. She stretched her little paws in front of her and let out a huge yawn.

"Let's take these two for a walk. We can see how much training she's had," Alan suggested.

"I don't have a leash."

"You can use Max's. He won't run off, and I have a spare in my apartment." Alan unclipped Max's leash and reattached it to the puppy's collar, then handed the end to Victoria. "Shall we?"

Victoria gripped the leash and stood. "Is this a test for whether I can take care of her by myself?"

"No." Alan walked until they reached the path that led to the gazebo in one direction and the stables in the other. "This is to satisfy my curiosity."

Max walked at Alan's side. The puppy trotted after him, tugging on the leash when she got too far away from Victoria.

"Force her to walk at your side." Alan signaled Max, and the older dog took his place on the grass beside him. Alan reached into his pocket and gave a treat to Max as well as the requisite praise.

Victoria tugged on the leash to keep the puppy beside her as they headed toward the gazebo. The puppy trotted along for a few feet before lowering her nose to the ground and trying to veer off into the grass.

"Looks like she needs some more training," Victoria said.

"She'll learn." Alan reached into his pocket again and offered Victoria a handful of dog treats. "Labs are food driven. Give her a treat and some praise every time she does something right, and she'll learn in no time."

"I hope so." They walked slowly down the path, stopping several times so Victoria could either refocus or reward the puppy.

When they reached the gazebo, Alan said, "I think we all deserve a break."

"I agree." Victoria moved into the gazebo and settled onto a bench. She motioned to the puppy the way she had seen Alan do when he wanted Max to sit. "Sit."

The puppy wagged her tail for a few seconds and then finally sat.

"Good girl." Victoria fed her a treat and looked up, a smile tugging at her lips.

"She's a smart little thing." Alan sat beside Victoria. "Are you sure you want to be the one to take her out at night?"

Victoria nodded.

"Since you'll be passing my apartment to go outside anyway, maybe I can come out with you," Alan suggested. "That way there's someone with you, and the guard can stay focused on his duties."

"Are you sure about this? It will only take me a few minutes to take her out. Plus, I'm working from home right now. I can take a nap if I need one. You don't always have that luxury."

"I'll be fine," Alan said. "And it will make me feel a lot better knowing you aren't outside alone."

"Okay, if you're sure," Victoria said. "I can call you when I leave my room so you're awake when I get there."

"Sounds good."

They fell into a comfortable silence, and Victoria pondered the recent changes in her life. Graduating, taking over the resort, the bombing attempts, Alan's return, her new canine companion, and the prospect of a second one soon.

"Are you really okay with me adopting Max?" she asked. "I can't imagine it feels right letting anyone take him besides you."

"I wish there were a way I could keep him." Alan gazed down at her. "But since that's not possible, I can't think of anyone I would want him to be with more than you."

CHAPTER 21

They'd spent the entire day together. Alan walked alongside Victoria that evening, the dogs on either side of them. Victoria had issued an unexpected invitation to join the royal family for dinner shortly after they'd returned from their earlier walk with the dogs.

Alan and Victoria reached the gardens, several of the rose bushes in full bloom.

"Do you think it's safe yet for me to go back to the resort?" Victoria asked.

"I don't know," Alan admitted. "I'd like to have you stay away for a few more days so I can spend some more time observing the day-to-day activities."

"You don't think someone at the resort had anything to do with the bombs, do you?"

"I don't know," Alan said. "I keep going over possible motives, and wanting you dead doesn't seem like a logical one. Not unless someone is trying to get to your sisters through you."

"How would someone get to my sisters through me?" Victoria asked.

"If that last bomb had killed you, your sisters would have been at your funeral."

"That's terribly morbid."

"And accurate." Alan stopped beside a stone bench in front of a climbing rosebush. "But let's assume for a minute that your death isn't the goal. Then what's the objective?"

Victoria sat on the bench and commanded the puppy to sit. The delighted surprise on her face when the puppy obeyed the command distracted Alan from his question, and he lowered onto the bench beside her.

"What other motives have you come up with?" Victoria asked. "I know art theft was one possibility."

"Yes. As far as I know, that missing painting hasn't been found," Alan said.

"What else?"

"What would happen with the resort opening if something happened to you?" Alan asked.

"It might be delayed, but I have to think it would still go forward." Victoria straightened and shifted on the bench so she was facing him more fully. "You don't think Nico Amando could be behind this, do you?"

"Who is Nico Amando?"

"He's the owner of the Imperial Blu, the Royal Sands' biggest competition," Victoria said. "He wasn't thrilled when Cassie announced we were building a resort. Judging from his behavior at brunch yesterday, his attitude hasn't changed."

"We can look into it, but I'm not sure the timing makes a lot of sense," Alan said. "If he were going to try to sabotage the resort, he would have had better opportunities when the structure was first being built."

"I guess that's true." Victoria pushed to a stand and paced across the gazebo. "If not Nico, then I doubt the resort has anything to do with the motive behind the bombing attempts."

"I'm not so sure about that. If something happened to you or if there were significant damage to the structure, the opening would be delayed until after the coronation." Alan let that thought roll over in his mind. "The security at your hotel is better than any hotel I've ever been to."

"Levi insisted that it be safe enough for high-profile clientele to stay there," Victoria said. "He designed the security system himself."

"But if someone were able to keep the resort from opening, where would your out-of-town guests stay for your sister's coronation?"

"I imagine they would go to the Imperial Blu or the Grand Hotel," Victoria said. "Both are five-star resorts, and both have good security."

"Good security but not great security."

"You think someone could be trying to keep the resort from opening so they'll have easier access to one of our guests?"

"Royals and heads of state are more vulnerable when they're traveling."

"That's true, but if I'd been killed by one of the bombs, the coronation would have been postponed," Victoria said. "A coronation is supposed to be a celebration. It wouldn't be held while the family is in mourning."

"So we should look into what would happen in the next year if your sister remained uncrowned."

"While you're speculating, I have a question." Victoria paced back to the bench and sat beside Alan once more. "Why does the bomber keep coming after me? Why not go after Cassie or Annabelle?"

"Simple. It's a matter of access," Alan said. "Your return to Sereno was anticipated. It wouldn't have been hard for someone to figure out when you would be traveling."

"But it wasn't public knowledge that I would be working at the resort."

"Then maybe that's where we should start."

"Start what?"

"Narrowing down our suspect list." Alan stretched his arm across the back of the bench, his fingers brushing against Victoria's back. "Do you think you could spare a couple hours tomorrow to help me compile a list of people who knew you would be at the resort?"

"Tell me when you're available, and I'll adjust my schedule accordingly."

"I need to escort Janessa and Garrett to the airport in the morning, and I'll swing by the resort to check on things on my way back."

"Want to meet me for lunch?"

"Sounds good."

The puppy stretched up on her hind legs and tried to reach the bench. Victoria leaned down and picked her up.

Alan reached over and petted the puppy. "We should plan on taking a walk afterward too."

"I have a feeling we'll be taking a lot of walks over the next few weeks."

Alan didn't fight the pleasure that thought brought with it. "I'm sure you're right."

* * *

Taking on the responsibility of a puppy had sounded like a good idea—until two in the morning. The puppy whimpered and scratched at her bedroom door.

Victoria groaned and rolled out of bed. "I'm coming."

She donned her silk robe and belted it at her waist. A quick glance in the mirror ensured she was decent, although makeup-free. She ran her fingers through her hair. She clearly hadn't been thinking when she'd accepted Alan's offer to share puppy duty with her tonight. No one besides her sisters ever saw her without her makeup on.

She eyed the cosmetics on her dressing table. The puppy whimpered again.

Victoria was fast at putting on her makeup, but she doubted the puppy would wait that long.

She grabbed her phone and the puppy's leash—she really needed to give her a name—and headed into the hall with her new charge.

The puppy pulled at the leash, leading Victoria toward the back stairs. Alan was right. She was a smart dog. After only traversing the path between Victoria's room and the outer door twice, the puppy already knew which way to go.

Victoria pulled up Alan's phone number and hit the Call button.

He answered, sounding far more alert than she'd expected. "Time to take the dog out?"

"Yes. I'm coming downstairs now."

"I'll meet you by the door."

She hung up and slid her phone into the pocket of her robe. She reached the top of the stairs and leaned down to scoop the puppy into her arms. No need to have her stumble and possibly hurt herself.

By the time Victoria stepped into the downstairs hall, Alan was already waiting for her. His attire—a pair of shorts and a faded T-shirt—could have easily been workout clothes rather than sleepwear, and they showcased his muscular physique a little too well for comfort.

His gaze landed on her, and he stared.

Her cheeks flushed. Maybe she should have slept with her makeup on.

She lowered the puppy to the floor and tugged the belt of her robe a little tighter.

The puppy strained against her leash and pulled Victoria toward the exit.

"I already checked outside and let the guard know we were coming." Alan opened the door and waited for her to pass through before following.

The moment the puppy reached the grass, she squatted to relieve herself. "Looks like she wasn't going to be able to wait much longer."

Victoria combed her fingers through her hair again. "Sorry I'm such a mess."

"Are you kidding?" Alan glanced at the guard standing a short distance away before he whispered, "You're gorgeous."

Her breath caught at his nearness and the huskiness of his voice. Even though his words sounded sincere, she shook her head. "I looked in the mirror before I came down here. I know better than that."

Alan reached out and ran a finger along her jaw. "Gorgeous," he repeated.

The puppy pulled at her leash again, forcing Victoria to follow. The dog sniffed the grass as though debating whether she was finished with her business or not.

For the first time, Victoria noticed Alan was without his dog. "Where's Max?"

"He's still inside. I don't want him to get in the habit of going out in the middle of the night."

"I hope Puppy loses this habit soon."

"Please tell me you're going to give her a real name."

"I am, but not in the middle of the night."

"Middle of the night," Alan repeated. "You could call her Midnight. It fits with her current habits and her color."

"Maybe, but I'm hoping this habit will be short-lived."

Alan glanced at the dog before bringing his gaze back to her face. "I don't know. I kind of like seeing you like this."

"You can't be serious." She shook her head. "If the paparazzi took a photo of me right now, they might not even know it was me."

"Maybe that's not such a bad thing."

An idea sparked. "I could disguise myself."

"What?" Alan eased back so he could see her more clearly. "Disguise yourself for what?"

"So I could go back to the resort." Victoria lifted her shoulders. "If no one knows I'm there, I could oversee the progress without anyone trying to kill me."

"I don't know. That may still be too risky." Alan shook his head. "Give me a few more days of keeping an eye on things."

"I'm going to go crazy sitting around the palace indefinitely," Victoria said. "There's so much work to do."

The puppy tugged on her leash, now heading back toward the door.

"For now, I think you need to let your puppy be your distraction."

"But—"

"And I'll talk to Levi about your idea. Maybe we can plan a time for me to take you in after hours."

"Thank you." Victoria yawned.

Alan escorted her back inside. "Want me to walk you back to your room?"

"No. That's okay."

Alan grinned at her. "I'll see you in a few hours."

A few hours. Victoria looked down at the puppy. It was a good thing she was cute.

CHAPTER 22

ALAN CIRCLED THE BLACK SUV with Max for a second time before sending a text to Janessa that the vehicle was clean. He rubbed Max's head, his thoughts instantly going to Victoria.

Max would have a new home now, a good home, as long as the agency gave the approval. Surely, they'd say yes.

Alan smiled at the image of Victoria taking the puppy out last night. She had looked so flustered in her robe, her face free of makeup, a scatter of freckles visible on her nose and cheeks for the first time since he'd met her.

Even though his body would have preferred a solid seven hours of sleep without interruption, he had been disappointed that the puppy had only gotten up once during the night.

The side door to the garage opened, and Janessa walked in with Garrett.

She took one look at him and lifted an eyebrow. "What has you in such a good mood this morning? Glad we're finally leaving?"

Alan laughed. "Not at all. Having you here has been enlightening."

"Enlightening?" Garrett asked. "How so?"

Alan opened the back door and pulled back on Max's leash so he would know he needed to stay still. "This weekend was the first time I've been to any of your fancy royal events. It gave me a very different perspective."

"You were at our wedding."

"Yes, but I spent most of the time before it started searching cars with Max and the rest of the security team. During the reception, we mostly circled the perimeter to make sure we didn't have any security concerns."

"We should have had someone else on duty that night," Janessa said.

"You did offer," Alan reminded her. He'd even been tempted to take her up on the offer, but after so many security concerns leading up to Janessa's wedding, he never would have been able to live with himself if someone had managed to slip a bomb past security because he and Max hadn't been on duty. "And I'm not complaining. I kind of liked being in the background." Alan waited for them to get in before he circled to the passenger side to put Max in the front seat.

He checked his phone and sent a text to the security team that would escort them to the airport. Once he received the confirmation that the team was ready and waiting, he climbed behind the wheel and clicked his seat belt in place.

As soon as Alan opened the garage door and turned on the engine, Garrett asked, "How did you like mingling with the ruling class?"

Alan pulled forward behind the sedan that carried half of the security team. A second security vehicle pulled up behind them. "I will admit, I did enjoy seeing the expression on Lord Romero's face when you two came over and greeted me. Until then, he seemed to think I was some sort of social pariah."

Janessa laughed. "It's amazing how quickly people change their mind about your value when they know you're connected to someone they think can improve their own social standing."

"Janessa certainly went through that when she first moved to Meridia," Garrett said.

"Yes, but most of the people who treated me poorly were jealous that I was there with you."

"I don't know about that," Garrett said.

Janessa leaned forward and put her hand on the back of Max's seat. "Alan was there. He saw it."

"I have to side with Janessa on this one." Alan passed through the gate and pulled onto the road. "There were quite a few women who seemed very intrigued by the idea of becoming your princess."

"Thank goodness those days are over for me," Garrett said.

Janessa leaned back in her seat. "They aren't over for Victoria yet though."

"Any suitors on her horizon?" Garrett asked.

"Or should we say competition?" Janessa put in.

"It's not like that." Not yet. Alan shook that thought from his head. More likely, it never would be. "According to Levi and Cassie, Victoria hasn't dated anyone since before her father passed away."

"Ooh." Janessa's tone turned playful. "You're talking to her family about her dating history. Sounds to me like you're interested."

"Levi and I were just trying to figure out what some guy is up to. He started calling her a few days ago and was very persistent."

"What did he say he wanted?" Garrett asked.

"He said he wanted to get together with her while he's in town." Alan relayed the conversation and what he saw and heard at the restaurant Friday night.

"Still no idea what he's really up to?" Janessa asked.

"No, and I have to admit, it's bugging me." Alan came to a stop at a red light, and he instinctively scanned the area for potential threats. When he glanced in the rearview mirror, he noticed Janessa doing the same thing.

"Do you think you'll ever stop thinking like a CIA officer?" Alan asked.

Janessa's gaze met his in the mirror, and she laughed. "I doubt it."

"We've been married three years, and I still have a hard time keeping her out of the security office," Garrett said.

"Rachelle had some big shoes to fill when she replaced Levi as chief of security at our château," Janessa said. "I just wanted to make sure she had all the support she needed."

"It's hard to believe I have two friends, both former CIA, who are now royalty."

"Technically, three," Janessa said. "Don't forget about Alora."

Princess Alora, Prince Stefano's wife. "Yeah, but I never worked with her while she was still CIA." Alan cast a glance at Janessa in the rearview mirror. "Have you ever thought about how crazy it is that you not only ended up as a princess but that because of you, Alora and Levi are royalty too?"

"Royalty or not, I don't think you'll see Levi sitting on a throne unless Cassie forces him to."

Alan chuckled. He cleared the security gate at the airport and pulled to a stop beside the private plane that would take Garrett and Janessa to Meridia. A luggage tug was parked a short distance away, each of the three luggage carts behind it filled with boxes.

"What's all that?" Alan asked.

"Some imports we're transporting back with us," Garrett said. "We try to double up the usage of our private plane whenever we can."

"Ah. Trying to be environmentally conscious," Alan said.

"While maintaining our security at the same time," Janessa added.

Alan parked beside the plane and turned off the engine. He swiveled in his seat so he was facing Janessa and Garrett. "I assume you want me to check those boxes out before they're loaded."

Janessa smiled sweetly. "It's like you're reading my mind."

Alan laughed. He clipped Max's leash into place. "I'll do another check of the plane first. Then I'll get on the cargo."

"Another check?" Garrett asked. "You already came over here today?"

"Yeah. Victoria and I got up with her puppy around five thirty. I decided to take care of the in-depth search then."

"You got up with Victoria to take care of her dog?" Janessa turned her smile on her husband, and her eyes filled with speculation. "Sounds to me like we might have another CIA/royal matchup."

"You're getting ahead of yourself," Alan said. "I'm only here for a month."

Janessa pressed her lips together.

Alan knew that look well. She was trying to keep from saying something.

"What?" he asked.

She remained silent for a moment. Then she said, "Send me the intel you have on this Sheldon guy. I should have some time to do a little digging for you and Levi."

Even though Alan was certain she had intended to say something else, he nodded. "I'd appreciate it." He climbed out of the car and signaled for Max to follow him. "Come on, Max. Time to go to work."

* * *

Victoria held her favorite black Prada heels in her hand. Or rather, what was left of them. Sitting in front of her, Puppy looked up with her adoring brown eyes and wagged her tail.

"Bad dog." She shook the shoe in front of the dog's nose. "Did you have to chew up my favorites?"

Granted, those were the only shoes she had left outside of her closet last night, but still.

Victoria pushed the shoe in front of Puppy's nose. "This is a no-no."

The dog's expression changed, as though she were confused.

The chime of Victoria's cell phone carried from the dining room.

"Come on." She dropped the shoes and picked up the dog. "I can't trust you in here alone."

She hurried into the dining room and slipped her AirPods into both ears.

As soon as she answered the incoming call, Lorenzo greeted her.

"How's everything going so far?" Victoria settled the dog on the floor and sat at the dining room table.

"The electrician finished installing the last of the washing machines in the laundry room a few minutes ago, and the carpet installers are working on the third floor. The foreman seems to think he can meet your revised schedule."

"Good." The puppy lifted both front paws and rested them on the side of Victoria's chair. Victoria nudged her back to the floor.

"Félix has updated the menu," Lorenzo continued. "You should have the email with that from him within the hour."

Victoria glanced through the wide archway to where the grandfather clock stood in the living room. Eleven forty. "Has Mr. Neisler come by yet?"

"Yes, Your Highness. He left some time ago."

She had hoped to hear he was already on his way back to the palace, but if he had left some time ago, why hadn't he come to see her yet? Pushing aside the sliver of disappointment, she said, "I gather there weren't any security issues."

"No, Your Highness," Lorenzo said. "He cleared the latest carpet and furniture deliveries."

"Have Riccardo and Enzo do what they can to start moving the beds into the upstairs rooms."

Lorenzo's voice was stiff when he said, "They already started."

"Thank you. I appreciate your overseeing that."

"Will there be anything else, Your Highness?"

"No. Thank you." Victoria ended the call, pulled her AirPods free, and set them on the table. Puppy stretched her paws out and yawned.

"You really are adorable," Victoria said. "But I'm still mad at you."

Puppy wagged her tail.

Unable to resist, Victoria leaned down and lifted the dog into her arms. Instantly, her face was bathed in puppy kisses. A giggle escaped her. "You certainly aren't worried about how to treat a princess or her shoes."

More puppy kisses.

"Okay. That's enough." Victoria tilted her chin upward so her face was out of reach. The puppy took the movement as a challenge and tried to climb up higher in Victoria's arms.

Victoria set her back on the floor. "I think we have quite a bit of training left to do."

Someone knocked at her door. Maybe Alan could help her teach Puppy some basics.

Victoria crossed to the door, the puppy following along behind her. Her heart lifted when she opened the door to discover Alan in the hall with Max by his side.

Alan lifted his hands to bring two enormous shopping bags into her line of sight.

"I hoped that was you. Come in." Victoria stepped aside to let Alan and Max enter. Instantly, the puppy darted into the hall and jumped up on her hind legs as she pressed her front paws against Alan.

"Get down," Alan said gently but firmly. He shifted the large bag from one hand to the other and nudged the puppy back on all fours. Alan walked in, and the two dogs trotted behind him.

Victoria closed the door. "What's all this?"

"Just a few necessities." Alan set the bags on the sofa, then pulled a round dog bed out of the largest of them and set it on the floor. "This will help keep dog fur out of your carpet."

The puppy raced to the bed and climbed inside it. She plopped down and rested her head on the edge.

Victoria laughed. "I think she likes it."

"It appears so." Alan reached into one of the smaller bags and retrieved several packages of dog treats. He handed them to Victoria. "For training."

She took the offering. "Do you really think I'll need this many?"

"Labs love to play, and they love food," Alan said. "If you use the two together when you train her, she'll learn quickly."

"I was actually hoping you might be willing to help me teach her a few things."

"I'd be happy to." He reached into the bag again, this time producing several chew toys. "These will hopefully save your furniture. And your shoes."

"My shoes?"

"Shoes are often a favorite chew toy," Alan said. "You should probably keep your closet door closed from now on."

And all her shoes inside it. She grimaced. "I'll remember that."

CHAPTER 23

Alan knelt on the rug in Victoria's living room in front of the puppy, a treat in his hand. "Sit." He spoke the verbal command as he held out the treat in front of the puppy's nose and lifted it upward.

The puppy sniffed and tilted her head to follow the treat before she plopped her hind quarters on the floor.

"She did it!" Victoria's excitement carried in her voice, even though the puppy had demonstrated yesterday that she had already learned the simple command.

Alan bit back a smile. He wasn't sure which gave him more satisfaction: Victoria's delight or the successful training tactic. He leaned down and gave the puppy the treat. "Good sit. I suspect the breeders worked with her on some basic commands."

Curious as to how much more she knew, Alan gave the signal to the dog to lie down. Sure enough, despite the absence of a treat in his hand, she stretched her little paws in front of her, her tail wagging.

"Good girl." Alan pulled another treat from his pocket and gave it to her.

"I think Max wants a treat too." Victoria pointed at Max, who had also stretched out into a horizontal position.

Amused, Alan reached for his backpack that he had left on the sofa. "He's going to have to work a bit harder than that for a treat."

"Sorry, Max." Victoria lifted both hands. "I tried."

"Do you mind if I use your kitchen for a minute?"

"Help yourself." Victoria waved toward the dining room and the kitchen that lay beyond. "If you're looking for a snack, though, I'm afraid I don't have much in the way of food in there."

"I'm not looking for food." Alan signaled for Max to stay. "Want to help me?"

Victoria stood. "What are we doing?"

"We're setting up a little training for Max." Alan carried his backpack into the kitchen. He glanced around the large kitchen. Cabinets lined the far wall, and a long island stood in the center of the room.

Victoria joined him, the puppy trailing behind.

"Looks like your shadow is joining us."

An odd expression emerged on Victoria's face. She glanced at the puppy and then looked back up at him. "Shadow." She repeated the word, a giddy excitement lighting her eyes. "That should be the puppy's name."

"Shadow." Alan nodded his approval. "I like it."

Victoria knelt in front of the puppy. "What do you think, Shadow? Is that a good name?"

The puppy reared up on her hind legs in an attempt to lick Victoria's face. Victoria laughed. "I think that's a yes."

"I would say so." Alan pulled a treat bag out of his pack.

"What are you doing in here anyway?" Victoria asked him.

"We're going to play a little game of hide-and-seek with Max." Alan held up the treats. "I'm going to hide a treat in one of your cabinets. If he signals he found it, he gets the treat."

Victoria lifted the puppy into her arms and straightened. "Can Shadow play too?"

"Sure. Take her into the other room. I'll tell you when I'm ready."

"Okay." Victoria carried the puppy into the dining room.

Alan hid two treats in the lower cabinet next to the refrigerator. He then returned to the living room. "Max, come."

Max stood and crossed the room to him.

Alan escorted him to the kitchen doorway.

"What should I do with Shadow?" Victoria asked, still holding the puppy.

"Set her down by Max." Alan stepped into the center of the doorway. He signaled for Shadow to sit and spoke the command. The puppy complied, and Alan handed her another treat.

Even though the puppy clearly wouldn't understand the command, Alan stepped aside and pointed into the kitchen. "Max, Shadow, search."

Max's nose instantly went to the floor. He sniffed along the bottom of the cabinets.

Shadow sniffed the air in general, her tail wagging.

Victoria followed the dogs into the kitchen, her expression a combination of curiosity and fascination.

Max reached the objective first and sat beside the cabinet containing the treats. A few seconds later, Shadow must have smelled them because she rushed to Max's side. Instead of sitting, though, she jumped up, placing her two front paws on the cabinet containing the treats.

"Sit," Alan commanded. He pulled her back and pushed her hind quarters down so she would sit beside Max. "Good dog." Alan stepped back. "Stay." He waited a few seconds before he pulled open the cabinet and handed a treat to each of the dogs. When he straightened, he caught sight of Victoria. She was smiling.

"How often do you get to play with Max and call it work?"

"Oh, about 90 percent of the time." Alan laughed. "Want to see what his normal play looks like?"

"I thought you wanted to talk about who might have planted the bombs."

"I do, but we can talk while we play." Alan grabbed his backpack and moved toward the door. "Come on."

"Where are we going?"

"Over by the stables," Alan said. He waited for Victoria to clip Shadow's leash into place before he opened the door. "We just need to stop by the security office on our way."

"What for?"

"That's where I secured my training supplies." Alan said. "I don't want to risk keeping bomb materials in my quarters. It might get too overwhelming for Max."

Her eyes widened. "We're going to get bomb materials?"

"Bomb materials and a tennis ball." Alan nodded. "It's amazing how hard Max will work if he knows he gets to play afterward."

"But bomb materials?"

"Don't worry," Alan assured her. "Materials only. No detonators."

"I'm trusting you."

The simple words evoked an unexpected warmth that spread through him. "Good."

* * *

Victoria had never considered how one would go about training a dog to detect explosives. The scene before her was fascinating.

Alan had set up a hundred bottles in two lines on the lawn beside the stables. While Victoria looked on with Shadow, he gave the command for Max to search.

With Alan holding his leash, Max sniffed along the base of the bottles. He made it nearly to the end of the row before he sat.

"Good boy." Alan gave the praise in a sing-song voice, as though speaking to a baby, then he rubbed Max's neck enthusiastically to demonstrate his pleasure. When he finished, he straightened and gave the command to search again.

This time, Max made it past only four bottles before he sat again. "That's a good boy." The praise repeated.

They completed the course again with success. Then Alan pulled a tennis ball from his pack and sent it flying.

Instantly, Max tore off with impressive speed in pursuit.

Victoria closed the distance between her and Alan. "Did he miss any?"

"Not one." Alan beamed with pride. "He rarely does."

Shadow sniffed at the nearest bottle.

"Could you teach Shadow to do that?"

"These dogs go through months of training, and that's usually after they've gone through a type of puppy boot camp." Alan looked down at Shadow. "Then again, it can't hurt to work with her too."

Max returned with the ball and dropped it on the ground at Alan's feet.

Alan picked it up and held it out to Victoria. "Want to play with Max while I set up a new course for Shadow?"

Victoria eyed the slobbery tennis ball. She caught the way Alan lifted an eyebrow in challenge.

Using only her thumb and forefinger, she took the ball from him. Then she adjusted her grip and threw it over the bottles and toward the riding ring. Again, Max chased after it.

Alan moved several bottles around, loading two thirds of them into the wagon he had used to transport them to the field. The rest, he spread into a half circle.

"Okay, let's see what we can do." Alan held out his hand. "May I?"

Victoria nodded and passed Shadow's leash to him.

Alan went through two basic skills: sit and lie down. He rewarded her with treats for both. Then he guided her to the first bottle on the challenge course. He waited patiently for the puppy to sniff at the bottle before he guided her to the next one.

Max returned with the ball, and Victoria threw it for him again. She repeated the cycle more times than she could count while Alan continued guiding Shadow along the line of bottles.

When they reached the third one from the end, Alan waited for the puppy to sniff at the bottle. Then he pushed her rump to the ground.

As though she had chosen to signal the new scent on her own, he praised Shadow with the same baby talk he had used with Max. He gave her a treat and petted her. Then he guided her to the next couple bottles.

Max arrived yet again with the ball. He dropped it and panted happily, as though he could play like this all day.

Alan approached and handed Victoria Shadow's leash. "Hold on to her. I want to switch the target around."

Alan leaned down and grabbed the ball. He rubbed Max's head. "Last time." He hurled it across the field. Despite the distance of Alan's throw, by the time Alan had switched two of the bottles, Max was back at Victoria's side only a moment after Alan.

Alan took the ball and tucked it away in his backpack.

Max wagged his tail and circled excitedly.

"Sorry, Max. That's enough for now." Alan pointed at the ground. "Lie down."

Max stretched his body out on the grass beside Victoria.

Relieved that she could give her throwing arm a rest, Victoria knelt beside Max and petted him while Alan started on the training course again.

She didn't realize how much she had been hoping Shadow would identify the bomb substance until Alan reached the objective and had to force the puppy to sit again.

In the next twenty minutes, Alan repeated the challenge twice more, but both times, he had to show Shadow where she was supposed to signal.

"I think they've had enough for now." Alan retrieved two tennis balls from his pack. "Here you go."

He held Shadow's leash while he threw the ball for Max. Then he leaned down and let Shadow sniff the second ball. He unclipped her leash and lobbed the ball a short distance away.

Shadow yipped excitedly and chased after it. She leaned down and tried to pick it up, not quite able to fit it into her mouth. She finally managed to grip one side of it, the rest hanging awkwardly out of her mouth.

Victoria laughed. "I think we need a puppy-sized one."

"Not for long. She'll be as big as Max before you know it." He pulled a treat from his pocket and leaned down as Shadow returned with the ball. He grabbed the ball while it was still in her mouth. She didn't release it, instead growling playfully.

"Drop it," Alan said in the same moment he held out the treat.

Shadow instantly dropped the ball so she could take the treat.

"Good girl." Alan praised her and ruffled her fur.

He threw the ball again for Shadow and then repeated the fun for Max.

"As much as I hate to say it, I should probably go in and make some calls," Victoria said.

"Do you want me to keep Shadow with me while I clean up?" Alan asked.

Victoria glanced down at the puppy. "Actually, that would be great, if you don't mind. I should be able to check in with Félix to finalize the menu by the time you're done," Victoria said. "I'll call and have some lunch sent up too." She paused. "That is, if you want to join me."

"I'd love to."

CHAPTER 24

ALAN FINISHED STORING THE TRAINING bottles and returned them to where he had left the two dogs in Federico's care.

"Thanks for keeping an eye on them," Alan said.

"I'm happy to watch them anytime." Federico hesitated briefly as though debating whether to say something else. Finally, he asked, "Do you think I could help with the training exercises sometime?"

Alan recognized the eagerness now, the same enthusiasm he had experienced when first working with Max. "Let me know when you're available, and I'm sure we can work something out."

"That would be great. Thank you."

"No problem." Alan took both dogs' leashes and signaled them to come. Max complied immediately. Shadow followed his lead an instant later. She really was a smart dog.

Alan made his way from the security building toward the palace. He was nearly to the terrace doors when his cell phone rang. He glanced at the screen before he answered it. "Hey, Levi. What's up?"

"Can you and Max go down to the front gate? We have a delivery truck that's an hour behind schedule."

"Yeah. We'll go check it out." Alan continued past the palace entrance toward the gate. "What's the truck delivering?"

"It's returning a painting that was being cleaned at the museum."

With the recent issues all being tied to artwork deliveries, Alan didn't have to ask why Levi wanted the extra security. "I'll let you know if I find anything."

Alan looked down at the puppy and debated what to do with her. Not wanting to risk a delay, he scooped her into his arms so he and Max could move faster than Shadow's little legs would allow.

He crossed to where a guard stood in the guardhouse beside the front-gate barrier. A second guard stood beside the driver's-side door of the delivery truck.

Alan set the puppy down beside the guard in the secure structure, complete with bulletproof glass. "Here. Keep an eye on her for a minute."

The guard took the leash and scowled, clearly not thrilled at being reduced to a dog sitter.

Alan moved forward with Max. "Search."

Max responded by sniffing at the front wheels and then the bottom of the cargo truck. After they circled the vehicle without incident, Alan stopped beside the driver's side. "Go ahead and open the back."

The driver climbed out and proceeded to slide a key into the lock that secured the back door. He turned and bumped his elbow against the back of the truck. "There you go," he said as he stepped back.

The guard started to move forward to open it, but the oddity that the driver hadn't done it himself sent an alarm ringing through Alan's head. Alan reached out and put a restraining hand on the guard's shoulder. "Have him do it."

The guard stepped back and took position at the rear of the truck on the passenger side. He motioned to the driver.

The man shrugged and stepped forward. His elbow bumped against the back of the truck again as he pulled the latch mechanism to open it.

Alan drew the pistol from the holster at his belt. The elbow against the back panel of the truck could have been incidental, or it could have been a signal.

The driver pushed the door upward to reveal the cargo compartment. A row of boxes lined the back. Thick, fat boxes, not the tall, thin, protective crates that typically contained artwork.

"Check the manifest," Alan told the guard.

"I already did. The delivery only includes a single painting."

The fur on the back of Max's neck rose, and he let out a low growl.

Max's danger warning sent adrenaline pulsing through Alan.

He wasn't the only one. The guard took a step back. "Is there a bomb?"

"No." That was as far as Alan got before the boxes tumbled forward. Four men burst forward, all dressed in royal guard uniforms, AK-74s in their hands.

"Gun!" Alan shouted the warning to Max and the two guards in the same instant he darted around the edge of the truck with Max at his side.

"Throw down your weapons!" the guard nearest him shouted.

Gunfire erupted. Footsteps clanged against the metal floor of the truck.

Alan lifted his pistol and peeked around the edge of the truck. One intruder was already on the ground, and the guard wasn't anywhere in sight.

The gunman nearest him turned his weapon toward Alan, and Alan squeezed the trigger. The man stumbled and fell to the ground.

Alan pulled back and leaned against the side of the truck. Bile rose in his throat at the thought that he may have just taken a life. He swallowed hard and drew a deep breath. These men had to be stopped. Victoria was inside the palace. So was the future queen of Sereno.

Bullets sparked in his direction, and he held his position for several seconds. Then he leaned down and took aim beneath the truck with the intention of shooting at the gunmen's legs. Three sets of pant legs were visible, but all of them were the same color as the royal guard uniform. With the man Alan had shot still sprawled on the ground, one of those sets of pant legs must be a guard. Which one, he couldn't tell.

More footsteps pounded against the pavement. Another shot fired, this one from a smaller-caliber weapon.

A man cried out. Shadow barked in earnest.

Alan moved along the driver's side of the truck and peeked over the hood. The guard in the guardhouse had wisely remained inside, his weapon pointed at the driver's side of the truck. Shadow stood beside him, her barking incessant.

Leaning down again, Alan looked under the truck. The second guard lay on the ground, and the legs of the driver and the remaining gunmen revealed their positions. One at the back corner of the driver's side of the truck. The other two men taking cover on the passenger side.

Alan straightened and sent a warning shot toward the back of the truck. Then he raced toward the guardhouse. Max sprinted alongside him. The guard laid down cover fire toward the back of the truck as Alan approached.

Alan leaned down and grabbed Shadow on his way through the doorway and pushed past the guard to make room for Max.

"What's the situation?" the guard asked.

"Four gunmen plus the driver," Alan said. "I dropped one of them, and the other guard is down."

"I already alerted the security office. Reinforcements are on the way."

Alan set Shadow down in the back of the guardhouse. "Stay." Then he moved to the guard's side. "I'm Alan. Contracted as part of the royal guard for the events. What's the plan?"

"Fausto here. For now, we keep them pinned down and hope the bulletproof glass holds and that our reinforcements get here quickly."

* * *

Victoria pushed away from her dining room table. What was going on outside? It had sounded a lot like gunfire.

Suspecting that Alan might have decided to subject Shadow to more training, she moved to the window and looked outside.

Two guards sprinted toward the front gate. Several more rushed toward the garage.

Her insides seized, and her throat tightened. Something was wrong, and she had no idea where Alan was right now. Was he safely inside the palace, or was he in the middle of whatever conflict was taking place outside?

A heavy-handed knock sounded at her door. An instant later, it flew open as Sabine, one of the female members of the royal guard, rushed inside.

"Get away from the window," Sabine commanded.

The lack of protocol reaffirmed what Victoria had already observed for herself. The gunfire she had heard moments ago wasn't from a training exercise. This was real.

Two more shots fired, and Victoria forced herself to step to the side of the window so she would no longer be visible from outside. Though she was afraid to know the answer, she asked, "What's happening?"

"We have gunmen trying to breach the front gate."

"Alan's out there." So was Shadow.

Sabine ignored her comment. Instead, she spoke into the communication device in her ear. "Princess Victoria secure." She fell silent for a moment before she gave a subtle nod. "We're on our way." Sabine turned to Victoria. "The king wants you and your sisters in the panic room."

Before Victoria could protest, Sabine ushered her out of her apartment. Annabelle and another guard were already in the hall.

The moment Annabelle saw Victoria, she rushed to her side. "Someone's out there shooting!"

The alarm in Annabelle's voice mirrored Victoria's own tumultuous emotions. "I know."

"Your Highnesses, this way." Sabine motioned down the hall. "Quickly."

Victoria and Annabelle rushed to the doorway just beyond the apartment that had once belonged to their parents.

Sabine pulled it open and led the way inside. Victoria and Annabelle entered, with the second guard falling in behind them. Sconces lit the narrow hallway, the thick stone walls reminiscent of centuries past.

The guard secured the door behind them, shutting out what little light had spilled in from the main corridor.

"This way." Sabine hurried through the passageway that guards had once used to alert the king from the watchtower. After Levi had married Cassie, he had converted the watchtower into a panic room.

They reached the spiral stairs, and Victoria put one hand on the interior wall to keep from getting too dizzy as they ascended. All the while, her thoughts raced. Twice last week, she had been within the blast range of a bomb. Now this. The likelihood that the three incidents were related fell into the highly-probable category.

Who was behind this, and what did they want? What purpose would her death serve?

She reached the top of the stairs, where a thick metal door contrasted against the surrounding structure of the palace wall. Sabine typed in a code on the cipher lock beside it, and the door clicked open.

Annabelle rushed inside first, with Victoria right behind her.

Cassie and Levi waited inside the tower room, with its thick, curved walls and a set of living room furniture.

Levi motioned to the two guards who had escorted them. "Guard the door."

Sabine nodded and pulled the door closed so only the royal family remained inside.

Annabelle stepped into Cassie's embrace, clearly needing comfort. Cassie guided Annabelle to the sofa on one side of the windowless room.

Victoria focused on Levi. "Did you know something was about to happen?"

"I didn't know we had gunmen trying to get through." Levi put his hand on Victoria's shoulder and guided her to one of the two chairs opposite the sofa. "Tell me everything you know about Sheldon Burton."

"Sheldon?" Victoria wrinkled her brow. "How do you know about him?"

"It's my job to know about people who are harassing you," Levi said.

Victoria wasn't sure if he was talking about his job as her brother-in-law or as the person who had been entrusted with the security of the palace and her family. Taking a different approach, she asked, "Why do you want to know about him?"

"Because he's the only person I've identified who was everywhere you were when your life was endangered."

"I can't imagine Sheldon being involved in anything like this," Victoria said, hardly able to consider the absurdity of what Levi was suggesting.

"Tell me everything you know," Levi repeated.

"I don't know much beyond that he attended Cambridge with me," Victoria said. "He's several years older than me, probably twenty-eight or twenty-nine, but he mentioned that this wasn't his first advanced degree."

"What was he like during your time in school together?" Levi pressed.

"Fun-loving, always the life of the party," Victoria said. "That's the impression I got, but I rarely had time to socialize with him or anyone else."

"Did you ever date him?"

"No."

"But he did ask?"

"Yes." Victoria gripped the padded arm of her chair. "You don't think he wants me dead because I wouldn't go out with him, do you?"

"I'm exploring all possibilities, but I think it's more likely he may have been trying to exploit you somehow."

"I don't know why he would think that would be possible. I've barely done anything besides work and study the whole time I've known him."

"That may be so, but he somehow managed to end up with a very large payout from a previous female classmate," Levi said. "The right photo taken out of context, a staged indiscretion, and who knows what accusations someone would be able to create."

Levi's words were more accurate than she cared to admit. Royalty was held to a higher standard than many others in the world. Still trying to reconcile Levi's words with her impressions of Sheldon, Victoria asked, "Do you have any idea what Sheldon's previous classmate was being blackmailed for?"

"According to the information Janessa sent me earlier and if our suspicions are correct, it was murder."

CHAPTER 25

Alan pressed his body against the narrow space between the doorframe and the corner of the guard booth. The three gunmen had settled into their positions around the truck, two at the back corner and one at the front.

Shots fired, one bullet impacting the bulletproof glass of the guardhouse window. Alan sucked in a quick breath. Given the choice between facing a ticking bomb or people shooting at him, he'd take the bomb any day.

Max barked. Shadow yipped, but both dogs remained safely at the back of the tiny shelter.

Alan expelled the magazine from his SIG and reloaded as more gunfire sounded outside. Bullets impacted the concrete wall currently protecting him. Alan jerked back. He definitely preferred bombs.

From his spot on the opposite side of the door from Alan, Fausto spoke into his comm set. "We'll lay down cover fire." He then turned his attention to Alan. "We have four guards behind the guardhouse, ready to assist. The two of us will lay down cover fire while one of the guards pulls Bernardo to safety. The other three will try to flush out the driver."

Alan ran through the terrain in his mind. The open space between the gate and the truck was dangerous at best, deadly at worst. "Do they have any vehicles they can use for protection?"

"A couple of armored SUVs should be here shortly."

"Might be best to wait." Alan glimpsed the fallen guard. He tilted his head toward the delivery truck. "They're too protected for any of us to get a clean shot, and your men will be far too vulnerable."

Fausto pondered for a moment before he relayed Alan's suggestion. Silence followed, except for the sound of the truck door opening and closing and a vehicle approaching from the garage.

Alan extended his arm outside the doorway long enough to fire at the back of the truck twice and once at the truck window.

The glass cracked but didn't shatter.

The driver ducked, leaving his door hanging open. The truck engine roared to life.

"They're in the truck!" Fausto shouted into his microphone. "Block the entrance!"

The SUV barreling from the garage sped toward the gate and skidded to a stop in the path leading onto the palace grounds.

The truck driver must have reached out for his door because it slammed shut. More shots sounded, this time in the direction of the SUV that had created another barrier between the shooters and the royal family.

One of the assailants at the back of the truck fired several shots as a frenzy of movement blurred beside the gunman. It took Alan a moment to determine the source. The other gunman had grabbed their fallen comrade nearest them and pulled him out of sight.

One of the guards in the SUV returned fire without success.

Anticipating that the driver would be visible behind the windshield at any moment, Alan took aim at the driver's side. Sure enough, the driver's head and shoulders appeared as the truck went into motion. But instead of moving forward, it jolted into reverse.

Alan squeezed the trigger. The driver's body jerked, and he hit the brakes.

Tires skidded, the truck rocked to a stop, and then the engine roared again.

Alan and the guards fired, but their efforts didn't prevent the driver from throwing the vehicle into drive and stomping on the gas. Tires squealed as the truck surged forward with surprising speed.

Fausto hit the button to raise the gate. The moment it lifted, the SUV sped off in pursuit.

A guard rushed forward to check on his injured colleague, while the others took defensive positions and the second guard vehicle drove after the first.

Alan checked on the two dogs, grabbing their leashes before he exited the guardhouse as Fausto lowered the security gate back into place.

By the time Alan reached the fallen security guard, a member of the royal medical staff already knelt by his side.

"How is he?" Alan asked.

"Alive." The medic pulled an IV and a medicine vial out of his bag. "I'll do my best to keep him that way."

Sirens wailed in the distance, rapidly drawing closer.

Fausto approached. "The ambulance is less than a minute out."

"I'll stay and clear it before I take the dogs inside and check on the royal family."

"I appreciate it," Fausto said. "And thanks for your help today."

Alan glanced at the spot by the gate where the truck had been parked. "They took their dead with them."

"Maybe they weren't really dead," Fausto said.

Alan fought back his frustration and a wave of helplessness. "Or they wanted to make sure we couldn't identify them."

* * *

Sheldon involved in blackmail? Her classmate potentially responsible for a suspicious death? Victoria struggled to reconcile the facts Levi had laid before her with the man she knew from grad school. All the while, her mind raced with concern for Alan, Shadow, Max, and the men and women sworn to protect her family.

A silent prayer looped through her mind that they would remain unharmed, that the people behind this current threat would be stopped permanently.

"Sheldon must have had a plan involving you for him to be here now."

"I don't know what it would be," Victoria told Levi for the third time. "Alan suggested I block his number when he wouldn't stop calling, so I did."

Annabelle lifted her head from where it had been resting on Cassie's shoulder. "It stopped."

Levi lifted his chin and listened to the silence.

"Levi." Cassie only had to say his name for Levi to rush into action.

He grabbed the phone on the counter beside the big-screen television on the wall. Why anyone would take the time to provide a source of entertainment in a panic room was beyond Victoria's comprehension. Obviously, no one could think about anything beyond what was going on outside the palace walls.

Levi spoke into the phone. "Status?"

Victoria strained to hear the other side of the conversation, but she couldn't distinguish the words carrying through the phone.

"Why didn't he use his mobile?" Annabelle asked, posing a question that hadn't even occurred to Victoria.

"It won't work in here. There's a dampening field to make sure no one can track our movements through electronic devices." Cassie gave Annabelle's hand a squeeze before she stood and moved to Levi's side.

"Clear the ambulance," Levi said, "but don't let it through the gate."

An ambulance. Someone was injured or worse. The possibility that the someone was Alan raced through Victoria's mind. She gripped her hands together in her lap.

Levi went silent for a moment longer before speaking again. "As soon as you're able." He hung up the phone.

"Who's hurt?" Victoria asked, her words rushing out of her.

"Bernardo." One of the guards.

"How badly?" Cassie asked.

"It's not good, but the medical staff is already down there treating him." Levi's voice was grave. "We'll know more after they get him to the hospital."

Annabelle straightened in her seat. "Can we leave here now?"

"Not yet," Levi said. "The guards need to do a thorough sweep of the grounds and check the perimeter before we risk going back into the main part of the palace."

"How much longer?" Annabelle asked.

"A couple hours."

"Hours?" Victoria repeated the word incredulously.

"We have to make sure the incident at the front gate wasn't a diversion for someone trying to infiltrate the grounds somewhere else," Levi said.

"You make it sound like we're in a war zone," Annabelle said.

Levi turned his attention to Victoria, his concern evident.

A chill ran through Victoria. "You think whoever tried to get in here might be the same person who planted the bombs."

"I don't know, but this is the first aggression against the royal family since we identified the threat against Cassie two years ago," Levi said. "It makes sense that this is all somehow related."

"But how?"

"I have absolutely no idea."

CHAPTER 26

Alan had tried multiple times to go back to the palace, but between inspecting the ambulance when it had arrived, helping with the inspection of the wall on the east side of the grounds, and writing up his report for the head of the royal guard, nearly three hours passed before he'd finally made it to the front door.

He'd left Shadow in Federico's care two hours ago, but the puppy now trotted along at Alan's side again. Max sniffed at the ground as though he, too, were afraid that today's aggressions weren't yet over.

"Come on, boy." Alan gave Max's leash a little tug as they reached the front door. They made it only a few steps inside before Alan spotted Theo, King Alejandro's former steward. "Where's—" He broke off before he said Victoria's name. "Where's the family?"

"Still in the panic room," Theo said. "The guards aren't finished checking the area yet."

"Show me where they are."

"I'm sorry, sir. I can't do that." Before Alan could press for an answer, Theo added, "I don't know where it is."

"How do you not know?" Alan asked. "You must have been briefed on emergency protocols when you worked for King Alejandro."

"I was, but changes have been made since the attack on the palace, including the addition of a new panic room."

Levi. He must have created a new one to protect Cassie. "Who does know where it is?"

"Only a few members of the royal guard," Theo said.

Alan pulled out his cell phone and called Victoria. It immediately went to voice mail. He dialed Levi next. Same result. "Do you have a phone number for the panic room?"

"I'm sorry, sir, but I don't."

Alan tapped another number on his phone, this time for Darius, the captain of the guard.

"Status?" Darius asked, clearly concerned that Alan had uncovered another threat.

"Everything's fine," Alan assured him. Except that he needed to see for himself that Victoria was okay. "What's the latest on the royal family?"

"King Levi is bringing them out now."

Relief swept through him. "Thanks." Alan ended the call, and within moments, the clicking of high heels against tile echoed down the nearby hall.

Alan turned as Levi and Cassie came into view.

"What happened out there?" Levi asked, even though Alan had no doubt he'd already been briefed by his security forces.

"I'll give you the blow-by-blow after I get Shadow back to Victoria."

"I can take her up." Cassie held out her hand to take Shadow's leash.

Disappointment rose within him, increasing the unexplained need to see for himself that Victoria was safe.

As though sensing Alan's inner turmoil, Levi put his hand on Cassie's arm. "Maybe we should let Alan take Shadow up to her."

Cassie glanced at Alan briefly before nodding to her husband. "Maybe that would be best."

Levi put his hand gently on Cassie's back before he spoke to Alan. "Meet me in my office when you're ready."

"Thanks, Levi." Indescribably relieved, Alan ushered the dogs down the hall to the back staircase. He reached the residential wing, where guards were stationed at both ends, with a third positioned a few yards from Victoria's door.

Alan nodded a greeting to the guards as he passed and knocked on Victoria's door. It opened slowly, as though she needed to assure herself that it was safe before pulling the door wide. Then suddenly, she was in front of him, rushing into his arms.

Alan pulled her close as much to comfort her as to assure himself that she was safe and whole. Her breathing hitched, and her body trembled.

Shadow yipped and tried to push between them. Alan ignored the puppy and held Victoria for a long moment before he pulled back to look at her face. Tears streaked her cheeks, and she quickly lifted both hands to wipe the moisture away.

All too aware of the presence of the guards, Alan released Victoria and escorted her into her living room.

As soon as the door closed behind them, Victoria sniffled and reached for a tissue on a nearby table. "I was so worried about you."

"I'm fine." Alan unclipped the leashes from both dogs. "We're all fine."

"Levi said that someone was trying to get through the front gate."

"Four men were hiding in the back of a delivery truck," Levi said. "We identified the problem and stopped them."

Victoria stared at him for a moment. When Alan didn't expound on his account of the events, she asked, "How bad was the guard's injury?"

"He's still alive," Alan said. "I don't know how long it will be before we know more than that."

Victoria sniffled again. "They were coming after me, weren't they?"

"I don't know."

"Levi seems to think I was the target." Victoria leaned against the back of the sofa. "He was asking about Sheldon, the old classmate I told you about, who kept calling me."

"Sheldon is the only person we know of who has been nearby for every incident."

"That's what Levi said." Victoria paused. "Wait. How did you even know he was involved before now?"

"Levi mentioned him as someone he was concerned about," Alan said. "Have you heard any more from him?"

"No. I blocked his number, like you suggested."

"Maybe it's time we unblock it."

Victoria looked at him, horrified. "Why?"

"Because it might help us figure out what he's up to." Alan glanced down at the dogs, Max lying quietly on the floor, the puppy snoring softly beside him. "I need to meet with Levi in his office. I'll talk to him about options."

Victoria straightened. "I should come with you."

Alan wavered. Levi would speak more freely if Victoria weren't in the room, but Alan also wasn't thrilled with the idea of leaving her alone. He was still wavering when Victoria spoke again.

"I want this to stop, and I have a right to be part of whatever decisions are made to make that happen."

"Levi might be more open with me about his plans if you aren't in the room."

Victoria leaned down and picked up the snoozing puppy. "I'll put Shadow in her crate."

Alan watched her disappear into the bedroom. He leaned down to Max and clipped his leash into place. "I guess she's coming with us."

* * *

Victoria didn't miss the surprised look on Levi's face when she walked into his office. Even she still wasn't quite sure what had pushed her to accompany Alan.

Levi looked past Victoria to where Alan now stood with Max.

Alan shrugged. "She insisted on coming."

Before Levi could protest her presence, Victoria faced Levi. "I need to know why these men came today and if they were coming after me."

"We don't know if you were the target." Levi circled his desk before he faced her again. "It could have been any member of the royal family." He paused. "Or all of you."

All of us, Victoria thought, but the words caught in her throat, and she had to concentrate on breathing for several long seconds. She fought against the fear and forced herself to ask, "What do you know?"

Levi gestured for Victoria and Alan to sit. As soon as they lowered into the seats across from him, Levi took his spot behind his desk. "The delivery van was carjacked a few blocks from the museum. The driver was drugged and left in the woods along the road."

"That explains why the shipment was running late." Alan leaned forward. "What about the painting that was supposed to be delivered?"

"It's missing." Levi balled his hands into fists and stuffed them into the pockets of his slacks. "It was a new Taylor Palmetta. Just arrived from the US a couple days ago."

Another thirty thousand euros' worth of artwork missing. "What about the painting that was supposed to go in my office at the resort?" Victoria asked.

"Still no sign of it," Levi said.

"Do the cops or Interpol have anything on our attackers?" Alan asked.

"We're running the images of the driver and the other man who came into view through facial recognition. Hopefully, we'll have something back on that by the end of the day."

"How does Sheldon fit into all this?" Victoria asked.

"Like I said before, he's the only person we know of who was present when all the threats occurred," Levi said.

Even though the thought of her recent classmate being involved fell into the ridiculous category, she pressed on. "If you're right, that he was trying to blackmail me somehow, why would he plant a bomb in London? Or at the resort, for that matter?"

"She's right," Alan said. "Blackmail and murder don't go hand-in-hand, especially not when the murder attempt comes first."

Levi focused on Alan. "Maybe we should have a chat with him."

"Maybe *I* should have a chat with him," Alan corrected. "If you're right about this guy, he doesn't deserve an audience with the king, especially if he could be wired or have cameras nearby."

A hint of frustration flashed in Levi's expression. "Fine. You handle it, but be careful. This isn't the type of work you usually do."

Victoria had seen Alan disarm bombs—twice—while hardly breaking a sweat, but how much experience did he have investigating crimes? She tried to tamp down her rising ripple of concern as she shifted to face Alan. "Maybe you should let the royal guard handle this."

"I'll have Federico come with me for backup."

"Why Federico?" Levi asked.

"Because he can handle Max while I chat with Sheldon, and I'd prefer not to be without Max after finding two bombs in the past week."

"I can understand that," Levi said.

The analytical side of Victoria went into overdrive. She tried to put the puzzle pieces of the past week together in her mind, but nothing seemed to connect. "Whether it's Sheldon behind today's attack or someone else, what are they after?"

Levi leaned back in his chair. "I still don't know."

Was Levi saying that because he was truly at a loss as to the criminals' motives, or was he determined to keep her in the dark? "You must have some idea."

"I have a lot of ideas, but none of them make any sense."

"Tell me about them," Victoria insisted.

"The first two bombings could have been to cover up art thefts," Levi said. "The painting that was supposed to be delivered to the resort still hasn't been recovered."

"And the paintings we brought back from London haven't been verified yet."

"Nor will they for several months," Levi said. "The initial findings were inconclusive."

"The truck that carried the gunmen today was supposed to be delivering artwork," Alan added.

"Art has been a common thread in all these crimes, but three different attempts, three different MOs." Levi shook his head. "We're missing something."

"And you're hoping Sheldon can help you provide the missing link?" Victoria asked.

"I am." Levi pushed out of his chair and paced to the window before turning back to face them. "We need to figure out why all this is happening now."

Why now? Victoria repeated Levi's words in her mind. Levi and Alan circled through the same questions they had already posed several times before, with no one coming to any helpful conclusions. When they finally exhausted their usual suspicions, Victoria said, "The timing of all this has to be important. It must have something to do with the coronation."

"Delaying Cassie's coronation doesn't serve any useful purpose," Levi said, "With or without the crown, Cassie is already queen."

"That's right," Victoria said. "The only thing that changes after her coronation is that a few responsibilities will shift for some of the higher positions in the ruling class, but those are all minor."

"How many people are we talking about?" Alan asked.

"Three or four," Victoria said. "They're simply situations in which Cassie wants to reorganize responsibilities."

"Why can't she do that now?" Alan asked.

"Technically, until she is crowned, Cassie can't make changes without the ruling council's permission. There are a few on the council who are resistant to change, so she decided to wait until after her coronation."

"Who is slated to change?" Alan asked.

Levi spoke now. "Lord Romero will move from the economic council to agriculture, Lord Cattaneo will take over the economic council. He's doing most of the work anyway since the energy commission reports to the economic council. The other main change will be putting Jeanette Bonheur in as Cassie's new chief of staff."

"I know it's a long shot, but it's worth looking at those people whose positions will change," Alan said.

"I'll do some digging." Levi turned his attention to Victoria. "In the meantime, I'm afraid you'll need to stay on the palace grounds."

Victoria had expected this, but the finality of Levi's statement still brought on a wave of frustration. "How am I ever going to get this resort ready to open if I can't visit it?"

"Your safety is more important than the resort opening on time," Levi said.

Victoria sighed.

Alan turned to face her more fully and put his hand on hers. "I know it's not what you want to hear, but you may have to let Lorenzo take on more responsibility."

"You're right." Victoria sighed again. "It's not what I want to hear."

CHAPTER 27

Alan and Levi approached the office where Theo sat behind a desk, the man's focus on the computer screen in front of him. Alan had planned to walk Victoria back to her room before starting the investigation, but Levi had handed his intended escort duty off to one of the royal guards.

The thought of what could have happened today had that delivery truck come through curled his stomach, and even now, he just wanted to get this current assignment over with so he could ensure that Victoria remained safe.

Levi entered the office first. "Theo, do you have a minute?"

Theo stood and bowed his head before answering. "Of course, Your Majesty."

Levi angled his head toward the door, and Alan complied with the silent request to close it.

Theo glanced at Alan before focusing on Levi once more. "Is everything okay? I heard there was an incident today at the front gate."

"Yes, there was."

"Any idea who was behind it?"

"That's what we're hoping you can tell us." Levi motioned for Theo to sit before lowering into one of the chairs opposite him. Alan remained on his feet by the door.

"You can't possibly think my family had anything to do with this."

"We are simply exploring all possibilities." Levi leaned forward in his chair, as though preparing to share a confidence. "Obviously, the royal family is aware that you have renounced your claim to the throne. Does anyone else know about this?"

"I haven't told anyone, but it was my understanding that King Alejandro shared a copy of my declaration with the British intelligence service."

This was news to Alan, but Levi didn't look surprised.

Apparently sensing Alan's confusion, Theo looked up at him. "The king wanted to ensure that my denouncement remained confidential so my family wouldn't know I was no longer in the line of succession. Sharing the documentation with a neutral party also ensured that I wouldn't be able to pretend I never made the agreement."

"Sounds like the king covered all his bases," Alan said.

"He was a very wise man." The sorrow in Theo's voice hummed through his words.

Levi nodded. "Yes, he was."

"Who would be in line for the throne behind you?"

"I honestly don't know. As far as I'm aware, I'm the last of the Escobar heirs."

"So, what would happen if the royal family were wiped out?" Alan asked. "If you are no longer eligible to take the throne, who would?"

"If there is no eligible heir, the constitution would allow for one of two things to happen," Theo said. "The ruling council could either appoint a new king . . ."

"Or?" Alan prompted.

"Or they could eliminate the monarchy and opt to elect a president to govern."

"And everything would change."

"Yes." Theo nodded solemnly. "The centuries of tradition that have been in place since Sereno gained its independence would all come to an end."

Alan focused on Levi. "Who would benefit from the end of the monarchy?"

"I have no idea." Levi tapped his fingers on the arm of his chair. "What about you, Theo? Any ideas who would like to see the monarchy come to an end?"

Theo shook his head. "I don't, but if there is anyone who would know, it's Queen Cassandra."

"You're right." Levi stood, and Theo followed suit. "Thank you for your time."

"Of course, Your Majesty."

Alan opened the office door and waited for Levi to walk out before joining him in the hall. "Do you believe him?"

"It won't be hard to check with MI6 to make sure they really have a copy of the documentation."

"Where to now?" Alan asked.

"Time to talk to my wife." Levi started down the hall.

"While you do that, do you want me to track down Sheldon?"

"Let's talk to Cassie first."

"Do you really think someone could be trying to wipe out the royal family?"

"I think we still have far too many motives and not enough suspects." Levi traversed the halls until they reached his wife's private offices. As soon as they stepped into the outer office, the two secretaries inside stood.

"Please sit." Levi waved for the two women to reclaim their seats. "Is my wife available?"

"She's on a call with the Prime Minister of the United Kingdom," one of the women said. She glanced at the phone on her desk. One of the lights switched off. "It looks like she just hung up."

"Thank you." Levi didn't wait to be announced; he headed for the door to Cassie's inner office and rapped twice before he pushed it open. "Got a minute?"

"For you, always," Cassie said.

Levi pushed the door wide and motioned for Alan to join him inside.

As soon as the door was closed behind them, Cassie asked, "What have you learned so far?"

"We just came from Theo's office," Levi said. "According to him, British intelligence is aware that he is no longer in line for the throne."

"They are." Cassie leaned against the front of her desk. "I just got off the phone with the prime minister. They have a duplicate copy of his declaration in their possession."

"So, Theo isn't a threat," Alan said.

"No." Cassie shook her head. "And I still have no idea who is. We don't have any evidence of another member of his family being a potential threat, and as far as we know, they are unaware of his current status anyway."

"I'll have Renato do a deep dive into Theo's family to make sure we aren't missing anyone," Levi said. "In the meantime, who would be the most likely to benefit if the royal family were no longer able to rule Sereno?"

Cassie took a moment to ponder her response. "It depends on if the motive is profit or power."

"Let's assume profit."

"The most lucrative holdings we have at this point are the gas and oil rights. Half of those funds goes directly into the national treasury, and the other half remains under the family's control."

Levi spoke to Alan. "Cassie has set up a significant portion of the profits to funnel into education and social programs as well as reducing taxes on Sereno citizens."

"If a new king or queen were appointed, would they be able to access those funds?" Alan asked.

"Technically, a fund trustee manages the family's portion. Depending on how the ruling council is organized, it's possible."

"Who would be the most likely to gain power?" Alan asked.

"I have to think that if my family were killed, Lord Cattaneo would be the most likely appointee. He's been heading the natural resources committee for years."

"I thought he was taking over the economic council for Lord Romero."

"He is, but that won't happen until after my coronation."

"Because you knew you would have resistance if you tried to make a change," Alan said.

Lord Romero was moving solidly up the suspect list.

"Yes. Lord Romero wants to be in the middle of the action, and he isn't very happy about my decision to move him."

"Why are you making the change?"

Levi and Cassie exchanged a look.

"What aren't you telling me?"

"Lord Romero has suffered some financial struggles over the past few years," Cassie said.

"And?"

Levi leaned against the desk beside his wife. "Let's just say we don't feel comfortable having him managing the billions of dollars the gas field will produce when he was being unwise in his personal financial decisions."

"Gotcha." Alan rocked back on his heels before he asked Levi, "Am I checking him out, or are you?"

"I'll look into Lord Romero's recent movement and contacts," Levi said. "For now, I want you to have a chat with Sheldon."

"That I can do."

CHAPTER 28

Victoria paced the length of her dining room, her assistant manager's voice carrying through the wireless earbuds in her ears. Her body had yet to stop shaking since the scare earlier, and so far, work was the only distraction that had helped her fight against the memories looping through her brain.

She made a note on her schedule to adjust her log of which employees had received an updated security clearance. She hated that she had to throw so much responsibility on Lorenzo's shoulders, especially right now, as they were preparing to bring on new staff and begin training.

"I show nine more deliveries scheduled this week, but only one is for artwork," Lorenzo said.

"When is that due to show up?" Victoria asked.

"Day after tomorrow."

"I'll speak with Alan to make sure he is available to come check the delivery before it's brought into the hotel."

"Do the authorities have any idea who is behind the bombing attempt?" Lorenzo asked.

Bombing *attempts*. Plural. Victoria refrained from correcting him. Her assistant didn't need to be told about the first bomb.

"Nothing yet," Victoria said. "Unfortunately, there was another incident at the palace today."

"I heard sirens. Is everyone okay?"

Victoria's thoughts went to the injured guard. "We aren't sure yet." Eager to change the subject, she said, "I want you to email me this week's delivery schedule. And can you also take photos and video of the common areas and the kitchen and send those to me?"

"Of course. I'll take care of that this morning."

"Feel free to delegate the photos and videos to one of the new employees," Victoria said. "I know you have a lot to do to prepare for the upcoming training."

"I'll have Sandra take care of it."

The marketing director. Smart. "Sounds good."

"I do have one request for you, though, if you have the time," Lorenzo said.

"What's that?"

"Since you won't be present for our employee orientation tomorrow, I thought perhaps you could record a welcome video for us to share with them."

A little seed of disappointment planted inside her. Still, she couldn't deny that Lorenzo's suggestion had merit. "That's a good idea. I'll take care of that today and get it right over to you."

"Wonderful," he said. "I'm sure we'll talk soon."

"Lorenzo, thank you for everything. I hope you know how much I appreciate all you're doing to keep everything on track."

"You're welcome, Your Highness," he said, sincerity in his voice. "It's truly my pleasure."

Victoria ended the call and headed into the living room. Shadow lay curled up in her dog bed in the corner of the room, and Victoria couldn't resist leaning down to pet her. She stroked the puppy's fur, taking comfort in the simple connection.

Male voices outside carried to her, the words muffled. She crossed to the balcony and pulled open the french doors. When she stepped out, she spotted Alan at the family entrance below, along with Max and the guard who had helped them earlier with the training materials.

Max's ears went up, and instantly, Alan looked around until he spotted her. His gaze met hers, and her stomach leaped with pure, sweet attraction.

Though she could hardly deny the underlying connection between her and Alan, she fought for logic. He would be leaving soon.

Alan smiled and waved. Flutters erupted inside her.

Even as her heart betrayed her, she returned his smile. Surely it wouldn't hurt to enjoy the bond between them. After all, once the resort opened, her social life would be little more than making appearances whenever her royal duties overshadowed her private life.

Alan opened the back door of a sedan parked near them and waited for Max to climb in before opening the front passenger door. He gave her a last wave before he climbed into the car.

The guard climbed behind the wheel, and a moment later, they pulled away. She watched them approach the front gate before turning onto the main road and disappearing from view.

He must be going to see Sheldon. Once again, Alan was potentially facing danger to keep her safe.

A knock sounded at Victoria's door, and she forced herself to walk back inside. When she answered the door, her sister Annabelle stood in the hall.

"Sorry to bother you, but I don't want to be alone." Annabelle shot her a hopeful look. "Do you mind if I hang out with you for a while?"

"No, come on in." Victoria pulled the door wide and waited for her sister to pass through before she closed it again. "I thought you were with Cassie."

"I was, but she wanted to go to her office. I tried watching a movie to distract myself, but it didn't work."

"We've had a rough day," Victoria said, wincing at the understatement. "I was just about to record a welcome video for our new employees at the resort. Want to help me?"

"Sure." Annabelle motioned to the open balcony doors. "Were you going to record it on the balcony?"

"No. I went outside when I heard voices. Alan was just leaving."

Annabelle smiled. "You like him."

She started to deny it but couldn't. No matter how much she wanted to protect her heart, when Alan left, she would miss his presence. Victoria changed the subject. "I'll get my cell phone. You can help me decide what we should use for the background."

"Avoidance." Annabelle grinned. "You *really* like him."

Victoria couldn't deny it. "Yeah, I really do."

* * *

Alan only had to go as far as the swimming pool at the Imperial Blu Hotel to find Sheldon Burton. As though he didn't have a care in the world, Sheldon sat in a lounge chair, an umbrella protecting his fair skin from the sun's rays and a fruity drink in a fancy glass perching on the round table beside him.

"Is that him over there?" Federico asked.

"Yeah." Alan kept Max's leash in his hand as he took in the rest of the scene.

A few other guests waded in the water. More lounged in chairs, and a group of tourists chatted around a large table. Unfortunately, none of them resembled the woman Sheldon had met with three days ago.

Sheldon reached for his drink and took a sip through a straw.

"What now?" Federico asked.

"Wait here for a minute." Even though Sheldon didn't appear to have anything with him besides the towel that hung from the back of his chair and a backpack on the deck by his side, Alan leaned down and spoke to Max in a low voice. "Max, search."

Alan guided Max behind the chairs and tables that lay between him and Sheldon, giving Max a little more slack in his leash when they reached the spot behind the man Alan planned to interrogate.

Max sniffed at the base of the chair, sniffed the backpack, and pulled against his leash to keep going. Alan continued for another few meters before he turned back and returned to where Federico waited.

Alan spotted two uniformed police officers approaching across the wide lawn that separated the pool area from the beach. "Looks like our backup is here." Alan debated how to proceed, then he handed over Max's leash. "Keep an eye on him. I'm going to see if our friend is willing to talk. And tell the police to stay back until I signal for them."

Federico nodded. "Good luck."

"Thanks." Alan needed luck if he was going to uncover exactly what Sheldon was doing here. He strolled back to where the Brit sat and took a seat beside him.

Sheldon glanced over, a smile on his face. The smile disappeared when he focused on Alan. "I'm sorry. That seat is taken."

"I won't be here long," Alan said casually. "I'm just waiting for a friend." He jutted his chin toward the pool. "Who are you here with?"

"She hasn't arrived yet." Sheldon lifted an eyebrow, and his tone turned haughty. "There are plenty of other chairs. Why don't you use one of those?"

"I'm exactly where I need to be, Sheldon."

His eyebrows drew together. "How do you know my name?"

"We have a mutual friend." Alan paused. "Princess Victoria."

Sheldon straightened and looked around. "Is she here?"

"No, but she is very interested to know why you're in Sereno."

Sheldon leaned back in his seat and studied Alan openly. "I told her. I'm here on vacation."

"And you just thought you could drop in on her while you're in town?"

Irritation filled Sheldon's expression. "Who are you?"

"I'm with the royal guard."

Like a chameleon, Sheldon's demeanor changed in an instant. "Then maybe you can help me get in to see Victoria. I think there must be something wrong with her phone."

"Why are you so anxious to see her?"

"Like you said, I'm in town. So is she. We're old friends."

"I believe she told you she wasn't available anytime soon."

"If she can't go out with me, it's not a problem. All she had to do was say so."

"She did, yet after she said no, you called her fifty-six times. Why?"

"You must be mistaken. I only tried her a few times," Sheldon said. "I was worried when she didn't answer my calls."

Taking a different tactic, Alan asked, "Who was the woman you had dinner with on Friday night?"

"How did you know—" He broke off, and his eyes narrowed. "Have you been following me?"

"You have shown an unusual interest in the princess. I simply want to know why."

"This is ridiculous." Sheldon swung his legs over the side of his lounge chair and pushed to a stand. "I'm not going to sit here while you insinuate I've done something wrong."

Alan stood as well. He retrieved his phone from his pocket and the recording Levi had provided for him from Friday night. He hit Play.

"This isn't going to work unless you spend time with her," the woman said.

Sheldon's voice came next. *"Don't worry. It always takes a few invitations before she gives in. Poor girl. She really does need to learn how to relax a bit."*

"You can hardly expect her to relax with everything that's been happening."

"Clearly, she just needs a trusted friend to confide in. It's only a matter of time before that friend is me."

Indignation turned Sheldon's face red. "You were spying on me!"

"What was your friend talking about?" Alan asked. "What did she mean that *it* wasn't going to work?"

"That was a private conversation. It had nothing to do with Victoria."

"Oh really?" Alan didn't believe that for a minute.

Sheldon's attention drifted to the entrance leading from the pool into the hotel. Alan turned. The woman who had dined with Sheldon stood just outside the door, her eyes scanning the area.

"Looks like your friend has arrived." Alan motioned to Federico, who moved forward with one of the police officers. "I think we need to take a little ride so we can continue this conversation."

Sheldon protested as Federico took him by the arm, but Alan tuned him out. He was already focused on the woman.

She spotted Sheldon when Alan was halfway to the door, a mere twenty meters between them. She took a step back and turned. Before she could disappear the way she had come, Alan sprinted toward her. "Excuse me, miss. I need to talk to you for a minute."

"I'm sorry. I'm late for an appointment."

Alan took the woman's arm as a police officer approached. "Yes, you are."

CHAPTER 29

"MARGUERITE DUBOIS." VICTORIA REPEATED THE name as she sat at Cassie's dining room table across from both of her sisters. Cassie's suggestion to have the entire family eat together hadn't come as a surprise. Levi's question about a woman she had never heard of, however—that fell into the category of the unexpected. "Who is this woman?"

"We spotted her talking to Sheldon on Friday." Levi settled in the seat at the table between her and Cassie.

"We?" Victoria looked from Levi to Cassie. She couldn't imagine her sister had been involved in spying on her former classmate.

"I had a colleague listen in." Levi didn't offer who the colleague was, but Victoria had her suspicions. She hadn't seen Alan on Friday after he'd been fitted for his tux until he'd picked her up for dinner. Not that she had been paying attention, of course.

Levi set his cell phone on the table and pressed the screen. Instantly, Sheldon's voice came on as he spoke to a woman who sounded to be around Victoria's age.

The conversation was short and somewhat cryptic, but it didn't take a genius to read between the lines. Alan and Levi were right. Sheldon had planned something nefarious concerning her, and had she given in to his insistence that they spend time together, she could have fallen victim to any number of vulnerable situations.

"This guy was supposed to be your friend?" Annabelle asked.

"I thought so." Victoria turned back to Levi. "Did Alan find out anything when he talked to him?"

"He's at the police station, questioning him now." Levi glanced at the grandfather clock across the room. "I assume he's still there."

A knock sounded on the door, and Levi went to answer it. The fact that he did so himself suggested that he had dismissed their personal servants for the night. Levi returned a moment later with Alan trailing behind him.

Myriad emotions pulsed through Victoria at the mere sight of him: joy and security as well as the bond of friendship. Overriding them all was a sense of home. She nearly pushed out of her chair to greet him with a hug, but she caught herself. She and Alan might have technically been on two dates, but thus far, nothing between them had indicated their relationship would ever go beyond a simple friendship.

Alan's gaze locked on hers, and he circled the table to where she sat. He lowered his hand to her shoulder and gave it a comforting squeeze. "How are you doing?"

"Work was a good distraction this afternoon."

Before he could respond, Cassie said, "Alan, please sit down. You must join us for dinner."

"I'll grab an extra plate." Levi headed for the kitchen while Alan lowered into the seat beside Victoria.

As soon as Levi returned, he asked, "What did Sheldon have to say?"

"Only that he wanted to call his lawyer." Alan shook his head.

"And the girl?"

"Marguerite asked for a lawyer before we even reached the police station." Alan stretched his hand out and rested it on Victoria's back as though he needed to make sure she was still okay. "I think she's the key to all of this though."

"How so?" Annabelle asked.

"We've been operating under the premise that Sheldon somehow manipulated Marguerite or at least manipulated a difficult situation for financial gain."

Blackmail. That was what Levi had told Victoria in the panic room. Awareness dawned.

"In the recording Levi played for me, it sounded like Marguerite was working with Sheldon," Victoria said.

"I watched them together," Alan said. "They seemed friendly, but I would put their relationship into the business-partner category."

From where he once again sat at the head of the table, Levi said, "We need to find out why the Dubois family paid Sheldon."

"You're assuming they'll be willing to talk about it," Cassie said. "If they have something to hide, they aren't going to tell you about it simply because you ask."

"Maybe not." A gleam glinted in Levi's eyes. "But Marguerite may not know that."

Alan's hand rubbed along Victoria's back before he dropped it to his side. "You want to try interrogating her as though we know everything?"

"It's worked before," Levi said.

"Yes, it has." Alan leaned forward in his seat. "Her attorney won't arrive until tomorrow."

"It sounds like the two of us may need to make a stop at the police station after dinner," Levi said.

Cassie reached out and put her hand on Levi's arm. "Is it really wise for the king to spend time at the police station?"

"Probably not." Levi leaned over and kissed Cassie's cheek. "But if you're worried about appearances, I'll make sure I'm not noticed."

"I don't suppose staying home is an option, is it?"

Victoria wasn't surprised when Levi shook his head and said, "Not a chance."

* * *

Alan had wanted to stay at Victoria's side at the palace, but an hour after dinner, he and Levi entered the police station through a side door, Max trotting along between them.

With the ease at which Levi navigated the halls between the door and the interrogation room, Alan suspected this wasn't the new king's first time using this route.

"How do you want to play this?" Alan asked.

"I think I'll have a nice chat with her, and we'll see what shakes out."

"I know you have more experience with interrogations than I do," Alan said, "but it might work better to let me play bad cop for a few minutes before you come in to rescue her."

Levi looked through the two-way mirror. Marguerite sat motionless in the single seat facing the camera, the table empty before her. "She is looking a little too calm in there."

"That was my thought."

"Okay. Do what you can to get her to talk, but don't give away anything about us talking to her father."

"I'll leave that to you." Alan headed for the door and signaled for Max to follow.

"You're taking a dog into the interrogation room with you?"

"He's going to help me." Alan smirked. "Watch this."

Alan led Max into the interrogation room. "Miss Dubois, thank you for being here." Alan signaled for Max to sit at attention beside him.

"This situation is unacceptable. I demand to be released."

"We'll be happy to let you go after you tell us a bit more about your relationship with Sheldon Burton."

"There is no relationship," Marguerite said. "We went to Oxford together. That's it."

Alan used his hand to signal for Max to bark.

Marguerite startled.

Alan continued as though no noise had occurred. "Why are the two of you here in Sereno?"

"I'm not answering any of your questions without a lawyer."

Alan signaled again. Another bark from Max.

"Why is your dog here?"

"He's my partner." Alan leaned back in his chair. "In the recording we have of you chatting with Sheldon, you said it wasn't surprising that Princess Victoria was cautious because of everything going on. Exactly what were you referring to regarding what was going on with the princess?"

Silence. Until Alan clenched his hand into a fist and Max barked again.

"Were you involved in the bombing attempt against the princess?"

Her eyes widened. "What?"

Alan took a moment to evaluate the woman's expression. Her surprise appeared to be genuine.

"You understand the severity of what will happen to you if you are tied to a terrorist attempt against a member of Sereno's royal family."

"I—" She swallowed. "I did nothing wrong."

"The recording, your presence at the site of the incident, your past dealings with Sheldon Burton . . ." Alan shook his head. "Those don't bode well for you."

Marguerite swallowed hard, and tears glistened in her eyes. She was rattled, but she still wasn't talking.

Alan glanced over his shoulder at the mirror behind him. Only a few seconds passed before the door opened and Levi walked in.

Alan stood and made a show of bowing to the king. "King Levi. I didn't expect you here."

Marguerite stared at Levi for a moment. Then belatedly, she stood as well. She blinked rapidly, as though caught between confusion, surprise, and terror.

"Perhaps you should give me a minute with Miss Dubois." Levi gave a surprisingly regal gesture of his hand, effectively dismissing Alan from the room.

Alan swallowed the urge to wish his friend luck. Instead, he bowed again. "Yes, Your Majesty." He tugged on Max's leash and said, "Come, Max." Alan escorted his K-9 partner to the observation room as Levi and Marguerite settled into chairs at the table.

Levi's voice carried over the speaker into the room. "I had a nice chat with your father a few minutes ago."

Marguerite's surprise appeared to increase another notch. "My father?"

"That's right. I needed to know what would prompt him to give such a large sum of money to Sheldon Burton when there was no clear reason for such a payment." Levi leaned back. "I must say, I was quite surprised by his answer."

Marguerite's mouth opened and shut, but no sound came out.

Alan had to give it to Levi. He knew how to bluff. Alan made a mental note to never play poker with the man.

Levi continued, understanding and compassion carrying in his voice. "The thought of his daughter, his only child, being involved in a murder must have devastated him, especially with his political aspirations."

Marguerite swallowed hard. "I'm sure I don't know what you're talking about."

"I don't know what your involvement is with Sheldon now, but it's only a matter of time before the prosecutor offers a deal to whoever gives us the information first on the assassination attempt and the motivation behind it."

"I didn't have anything to do with an assassination attempt. I had never even heard anything about one until just now."

"I expected you would say as much." Levi shook his head, and his voice took on the tone of a parent scolding a small child. "I had hoped you would be the one to help us."

"I don't know anything."

"Oh, but you do," Levi said. "You know why Sheldon Burton was trying so hard to see Princess Victoria, and you know what your role is in his plot."

Alan leaned forward, praying the suspect would share the truth.

A tear spilled over and streaked down Marguerite's cheek. "Sheldon never said anything about a bomb or an assassination." She shook her head in denial. "I swear I didn't know."

"What did he tell you?" Levi asked gently.

A tear trickled down Marguerite's cheek.

Levi pressed harder. "I can only help you if you help me."

Silence filled the room. Max moved restlessly beside Alan, as though he, too, were anxiously awaiting Marguerite's answer.

"Tell me what you know."

Marguerite's resignation registered in the way her shoulders slumped before she spoke. "Sheldon said he'd be able to get close to Princess Victoria. With her sister's coronation coming up and with the new resort opening, he was sure she would pay to keep her family name intact."

"He was planning to blackmail her?"

She swiped at the fresh tears streaming down her face and nodded.

Fury bubbled inside Alan, and he fought the urge to storm back into the interrogation room.

"What did he intend to blackmail her with?"

"I don't know. I was supposed to follow them around and take photos. He seemed to think there would be something I would be able to catch on camera that would be valuable enough for her to pay."

"When were you supposed to start taking photos?"

"At the airport in London. Sheldon thought he could get a ride with Princess Victoria to Sereno," Marguerite said.

"Were you at the airport?"

Again, she nodded. "I took photos from the terminal, but I don't know what Sheldon was hoping for me to find. I saw a couple of police cars, but I never saw Sheldon. The next day, he called and told me to catch a flight to Sereno."

Levi glanced over his shoulder as though he could see Alan through the glass. Then he turned back to Marguerite. "I want you to tell me everything that has happened since Sheldon first spoke to you about Princess Victoria." He paused. "And then I want your side of what happened to cause your father to pay so much money to Sheldon."

CHAPTER 30

Victoria couldn't work. She couldn't sit still. Giuseppe wouldn't let her go outside, not even to take Shadow out to go to the bathroom. Not that she could blame him. She wasn't sure she was ready to step out into the open, even if she were surrounded by members of the royal guard.

As though sensing her unease, Shadow had snuggled up beside her on the chair closest to the living room window. Darkness had fallen, and Victoria hadn't heard any cars coming in or out of the palace grounds since Levi and Alan had left over three hours ago.

The grandfather clock behind her chimed the half hour. Ten thirty. She needed rest, but how could she sleep while Alan and Levi were still out, while she still had so many questions that remained unanswered?

Victoria shifted Shadow off her lap and lay her in the chair before she moved to the window. She stared at the grounds below, where the number of guards had increased significantly since last night.

The events of the past week tumbled through her mind. The bombing attempt at the airport meant someone had known her itinerary. The one at the resort indicated the culprit had had some insight into her return to Sereno and the job she intended to do there. Sheldon qualified on both accounts. But the shooting today? Would he even have the resources to orchestrate such an attack? And even if he did, why would he?

The headlights of an approaching car cut through the darkness. It turned into the drive and cleared past the guards.

For a brief moment, anticipation fluttered inside her. Then she looked at the clock. The likelihood of Alan coming to see her at this hour was miniscule, even if he and Levi had managed to learn more about Sheldon's motives.

Disappointment swept over her, along with an unexpected sense of despair. Her life had been on a roller coaster since the moment she'd left for Sereno.

Was it too much to ask for her to be able to create a normal life, for her to establish her career and perhaps even find someone to spend her time with?

Shadow lifted her head and yipped. A moment later, a knock sounded at her door.

She pulled it open to reveal Alan and Max in the hall. Her heartbeat instantly quickened.

"Sorry for coming by so late, but I thought you might want to know what we learned tonight."

"I was hoping you would stop by." The truth had spilled out of her before she could stop it. Her cheeks heated, and she lowered her head to hide her blush. She motioned him inside.

Shadow sniffed at Alan's shoe and wagged her tail.

"Hey there." Alan scooped the puppy into his arms and walked with Victoria into the main parlor.

"Did Marguerite tell you anything?"

"Not me, but Levi got quite a bit out of her."

Hope leaped inside Victoria. Was it possible that this ordeal was finally over? "What did she say?"

Alan motioned to the sofa and waited for her to sit before he spoke. "Apparently, Sheldon did have blackmail plans." He set the puppy down beside Max and lowered to the sofa beside Victoria. "According to her, she didn't know anything about a bombing attempt or even what Sheldon planned to use as the source of blackmail."

"Is it possible Sheldon didn't have anything to do with the bombs or the shooting?" Victoria asked.

"He must have known about the first one."

"Why do you say that?"

"Because he sent Marguerite to photograph you at the airport. She was inside the terminal, watching through the window, when Max and I found the bomb. She just didn't know what she was seeing."

"So Marguerite was working with Sheldon but didn't know what he was up to?" Victoria shook her head. "That doesn't make sense."

"It does when you consider that they had worked together before and he was using their previous crimes against her."

"When I listened to the recording of her talking to Sheldon, she didn't sound like she was distressed."

"No, she didn't, but she admitted that she had helped Sheldon coerce her father into making a hefty blackmail payment when she was at Oxford."

"Wait." Victoria reached out and grabbed Alan's arm. "She was involved in blackmailing her own father?"

Alan nodded. "From the sound of it, she wanted a certain lifestyle without all the restrictions her parents wanted to put on her." He stretched his arm out and rested it on the sofa behind Victoria, his body angled toward her. "When a classmate was murdered, she and Sheldon came up with the idea to use the murder as a way to gain financial freedom."

Victoria's eyes widened. "They pretended she was a murderer?"

"They pretended there was evidence that could point to her being involved," Alan corrected. "She always maintained her innocence."

"I can't imagine deceiving my family that way." The new information rolled through Victoria's mind, and she struggled to make sense of it all. "If Marguerite was there when the first bomb was supposed to go off, do you think Sheldon was the one who planted it?"

"I don't know. It's certainly possible, but so far, he isn't talking."

A glimmer of hope sparked. "If Sheldon was the one behind the bombings, does that mean I'm safe now?"

Apology lit Alan's eyes. "Marguerite was at the airport in London. She also admitted to being at the resort the day the second bomb was delivered."

"I'm sensing a *but*."

"But she wasn't anywhere near the palace today."

Emotions clogged Victoria's throat, and she swallowed hard as she fought against the tears trying to form.

"It's possible the attack today was intended to be either a theft or a kidnapping," Alan continued. "But at this point, we have no way to be sure if Sheldon was behind it or if it was someone else entirely."

Victoria lifted her hands and pressed her fingers to her eyes. She wasn't going to cry. She wasn't. After a moment, she lowered her hands and asked, "Is this ever going to end?"

"Levi and I are going to make sure it does." Alan put his hand on her shoulder. His eyes darkened as he stared down at her. "I'm not going to let anything happen to you."

Victoria met his gaze, and the air backed up in her lungs. She didn't know what had changed between them, but when Alan's eyes lowered to her lips briefly, all thoughts scattered.

Alan's fingers slid up to caress the back of her neck, and he leaned closer. Her pulse quickened in anticipation. Then his lips met hers.

Everything faded in that moment, and a shiver worked through her.

The kiss was brief, and confusion lit Alan's face when he pulled back. He stared for a long moment. Then he lifted his free hand to her cheek and leaned in again.

She let herself get lost in the sensation of Alan's lips on hers. The bond between them bloomed, expanding as Alan changed the angle of the kiss.

The pounding of the surf roared from the beach outside, but that was nothing compared to the tumbling sensation of her heart. Breathless, she drew back and looked up at Alan.

"Sorry." Alan's voice grew husky. "I tried to resist."

Despite the turmoil of the last week, Victoria's heart lightened. A smile stole across her face, and she leaned in for another brief kiss. "I'm glad you stopped trying."

CHAPTER 31

Alan couldn't keep the smile off his face as he navigated the palace halls and made his way to Levi's office. The impulse to see Victoria last night had been too strong to ignore. Now everything had changed between them, and he couldn't be happier.

The added news that the injured guard had survived his surgery was another bright spot in his day. Though the guard would likely be out of commission for several months while he recovered, according to Levi, his prognosis was good.

As an added precaution, Alan had insisted on keeping Shadow with him last night to make sure Victoria wouldn't be outside when the puppy needed to go out. He'd missed seeing Victoria in the middle of the night, with her face free of makeup and her long hair tumbling loosely over her shoulders, but he hadn't minded the good-morning kiss when he had dropped Shadow off a few minutes ago.

He smiled again. It had been far too long since he'd dated and longer still since he had come across someone who had consumed his thoughts like this.

Even though he knew he was supposed to transfer soon, he couldn't quite bring himself to look that far into the future. Was it so terrible to live in the moment, to enjoy their time together?

Another thought popped into his head, one he had never truly considered before. What if he asked the CIA for a reassignment? Was one even possible?

Even if he had to partner with a new dog, there had to be somewhere in Europe he could be stationed, somewhere he could use his current language skills, somewhere safe enough for Victoria to visit.

He took in the paintings on the walls and the ornate furnishings. A little seed of guilt planted inside him, accompanied by an overwhelming dose of reality. Who was he kidding? The only way the CIA was going to let him avoid going to the Middle East was if he left the agency or if one of his royal friends made a call on his behalf. Levi and Janessa both had the titles and the contacts to influence the director of the CIA, but Alan wasn't sure how he felt about taking another premier post while someone else had to step into the hardship duty he had been assigned.

He was also assuming Victoria would want to pursue a relationship beyond the next few weeks. He hoped she would.

The thought of her many responsibilities came to mind, and he readjusted his hopes for the future. If he did manage another European post, he would have to visit her rather than the other way around. Not to mention, she would be managing a resort, one that had pretty amazing views and was only a ten-minute drive from the palace.

Possibilities continued to whirl through Alan's mind as he continued up the stairs leading to Levi's office.

First things first. Victoria's safety still needed to be ensured before she could start the life she had planned. They were getting closer to finding answers. Even though they still didn't know why or how Sheldon had been involved in the bombing attempts, they finally had a lead. Yet another reason to hope that he and Victoria would be able to navigate their way through a relationship.

Alan reached Levi's office, and Levi's assistant waved him through. Alan knocked twice on the door before pushing it open.

Levi already sat at the round worktable by the window, several photographs spread out before him. "I've been looking through Marguerite's photos. These are the ones from before you arrived."

"I assume you haven't found anything."

"No. I think our assumption is correct that the bomb must have been planted while the van was out making a delivery the day before."

"That's the only place that makes sense," Alan said.

"I also talked to our friends at Interpol this morning."

"And?"

"They sent over the file on the murder from when Sheldon and Marguerite were at Oxford."

"Any chance either of them was involved?"

"It's hard to say. The girl was last seen at a party, but there were dozens of students there. Her body was found in the river two days later."

"What was the cause of death?"

"She had a head wound, but the coroner couldn't determine conclusively if it was inflicted by someone else or if it occurred due to a fall."

"So it could have been an accidental death."

"It's possible, although her roommate was convinced that the girl never would have gone out to the river alone."

"Whether it was murder or an accidental death, it's possible Marguerite is telling the truth, that she and Sheldon really did capitalize on the situation."

"It's looking that way," Levi said. "Marguerite may have swindled her father out of money to gain her independence, but I don't think she's a killer."

"Her story is a bit too farfetched to be fiction." Alan scanned the photos on the table. "These are from the airport. What about her other photos? Did you pick up anything at the resort?"

"She had a few of the outside of the resort, and some of deliveries being made, but there weren't any of Victoria."

"It's possible she tried to catch images of the bomb going off."

"Maybe, but we're still missing a motive." Levi grabbed a pen and pad of paper off his desk and tore off the top sheet. "Who do we still have on our suspect list?"

Alan sat across from him. "I originally thought someone might be trying to keep the resort from opening so that a specific world leader would be forced to stay somewhere else for the coronation, somewhere less secure, but that doesn't mesh with the attack on the palace yesterday."

"I agree, but keeping the resort from opening is the most logical reason to go after Victoria," Levi said. "Either that, or someone was trying to cover up art thefts."

"It's hard to imagine the attempted break-in yesterday was really a robbery gone wrong."

"It's possible. The men in the back were dressed in royal guard uniforms. If they hadn't been found, it's possible they could have slipped in without being noticed, or they might not have been noticed in time to prevent them from leaving."

"We really need Sheldon to talk."

"I agree, but for now, we need to determine who really would benefit from going after Victoria or keeping the resort from opening."

"You're the king of this country. You tell me."

"Janessa and I have already eliminated the possibility of someone in line for the throne. The documentation from Theo renouncing his claim to the throne is in the hands of enough people that he wouldn't be able to deny its existence. Theo also passed his polygraph with flying colors."

"And his relatives?" Alan asked.

"Our security has been monitoring everyone who could potentially succeed Cassie and her sisters. No red flags on any of them."

"Then we really are down to either the art or the resort." Alan leaned back in his seat. "The motive behind the art theft is obvious, but who would benefit the most from the resort not opening?"

"Nico Amando, the owner of Imperial Blu, wasn't thrilled when we announced the plans to build the Royal Sands, but I don't know that he would spend this much money to hire someone to disrupt the opening."

"Victoria and I talked about that too," Alan said. "It would have been more logical to try to disrupt the construction in the early stages."

"I hate to say it, but I think we still have to consider that we're missing someone who wants to hurt Victoria." Alan's voice turned grave. "She has been a possible target in every attack. Whoever is behind this has to know her schedule." His stomach curled. "It has to be someone in her inner circle."

"That narrows down our suspects considerably, but so far, I haven't found any member of the staff who could have been involved."

"Maybe not the palace staff, but what about the resort staff?" Alan asked.

"Lorenzo did work for the Imperial Blu before he came to the Royal Sands." Levi shook his head.

"But why go after Victoria? And how is he connected to Sheldon?"

"I don't know, but I think you just gave me my research project for the day."

"What do you want me to do?" Alan asked. "I need to go to the resort anyway this morning. Should I make an excuse to stay longer?"

"For this morning, do your regular scan. Tonight, you can go back over after Lorenzo leaves for the day."

"What are the chances that you'll be able to get Sheldon to talk?"

"After sitting in jail all night, I'm hoping he'll be a bit more agreeable," Levi said. "In the meantime, I want you to stick close to Victoria. If she's the target, I want someone close by who I can trust."

"She has her regular security team. I would imagine you trust them."

"I do, but she trusts you. You're the only person who can act as protector and also make sure she doesn't let that new puppy make her a target outside."

Alan lifted his eyebrows. "You want me to babysit her puppy to keep Victoria safe?"

"It's not just that, and you know it," Levi said. "I can double the number of guards at the gate. I can increase the number of people watching the surveillance feed. What I can't do is give Victoria a sense of comfort while the danger is still out there. You can."

CHAPTER 32

Victoria watched the clock, hoping Alan would stop by her apartment before heading over to the resort this morning. Or maybe he wouldn't need to continue with his daily security sweeps now that they had suspects in custody. She should have asked him about his plans when he dropped Shadow off a little while ago.

Her heart lifted at the sweet memory of the way he had leaned in and greeted her with a kiss when she had opened her door to him. Was this what the next few weeks could be like? Uncertainty rushed through her. Alan was here for only a few weeks. What would happen when he needed to leave?

A knock sounded on her door, but it opened before she could get up to answer. Annabelle poked her head inside. "It's just me."

"How are you doing this morning?" Victoria sat on her sofa and patted the spot beside her.

"I'm a little better now that I know the police arrested a suspect, but even that didn't help me sleep last night." Annabelle settled onto the sofa, facing Victoria. "Why didn't you tell me about this Sheldon guy?"

"I thought he was just looking for a way to use me to get his five minutes of fame. I had no idea he might be trying to kill me." The thought sent a shudder through her.

"Well, I'm glad he's behind bars."

"Me too." Footsteps sounded in the hall. Victoria listened for a moment, disappointed when they continued past her apartment. "What are you doing today?"

"I have a video conference with someone from the insurance company today about the missing paintings. Lady Romero seemed to think they might be more cooperative if a member of the royal family is in attendance."

"Are you sure you're up for that?"

"I think so." Annabelle clasped her hands in her lap. "Lady Romero promised the attorney would handle the details. She even offered to postpone the meeting after she found out what happened."

"I don't think Levi wants us talking to people about yesterday," Victoria said.

"It's not like I gave her details. I just said there was an incident and that someone was arrested," Annabelle said. "I wouldn't have even brought it up, but I was on a video call with her when Cassie called to tell me what happened."

Victoria's phone rang, and she checked the caller ID to see it was Lorenzo on the other end. "I'm sorry, but I need to take this."

"That's fine. I'll talk to you later."

Victoria nodded and answered the call as Annabelle left the room.

"Your Highness, I'm sorry to bother you, but I received a call this morning from the secretary for the economic development committee. She wanted to set up a time for the committee to tour the resort."

Victoria let out a sigh. Lord Romero had asked about a tour a few days ago, but she had yet to find a time that would work well in the construction scheduled. "I think we need to push that off until the day before our grand opening."

"I suggested that, but apparently, Lord Romero is insistent that they see the facility before the first guests arrive."

Which would happen only three days before her sister's coronation.

Though her instinct was to grant the request to avoid the potential backlash from the economic development committee, the potential security concerns weren't worth it. "Call the secretary back and tell her you spoke with me and that their private tour can be held the day before our public grand opening."

"Are you sure about that? Lord Romero isn't going to be happy."

Of that, Victoria had no doubt. The man tended to complain to all the right people in Parliament when he didn't get his way.

"I'm afraid we'll just have to deal with his disappointment," Victoria said. "Set up the tour, preferably before two. I don't want to have anyone besides staff present after three so we can do a final security sweep prior to our first guests' arrivals."

"I'll take care of it."

"Thank you, Lorenzo." Victoria chatted with him for a few minutes longer to go over the latest developments. It wasn't until she hung up that she lifted her hand and noticed that all the tremors she had suffered after yesterday's attack had subsided sometime during the night.

Shadow whimpered from somewhere in the formal living room. A scratch of her nails against the door followed.

Victoria walked to the door where the puppy stood. "Do you need to go out?"

Shadow's tail wagged.

"I'll take that as a yes." She grabbed Shadow's leash out of the drawer in the entry room table and clipped the leash into place.

She walked into the hall, and Giuseppe fell into step behind her as she headed down the stairs. Halfway down, her chest tightened painfully, and the events of yesterday flooded through her mind. Fear rose within her. Someone had tried to infiltrate the palace walls less than twenty-four hours ago, and she still didn't know why.

With some effort, she forced herself to keep moving forward. Sheldon was in custody. If he really was the person behind all these attacks, that meant she was safe, right?

She reached the bottom of the stairs and drew a deep breath. Shadow strained against her leash and pulled Victoria forward. They made it all the way to the spot where the main hall intercepted the corridor leading to the exit before her steps slowed again. She would pass Alan's apartment, but he had likely already left for the resort to do his usual security sweep. Could she go outside without him?

The puppy pulled her another step forward, but Victoria resisted Shadow's attempts to keep her in motion.

Giuseppe stopped beside her. "Your Highness, perhaps I can take her out for you."

Victoria pressed her lips together and nodded. "Thank you."

Giuseppe motioned to a nearby guard to join them so Victoria wouldn't be in the hall alone. Giuseppe headed for the exit with Shadow, the second guard standing a short distance from Victoria.

Despair washed over her. She was in the palace, surrounded by people committed to keeping her safe, and she couldn't even walk outside by herself.

She glanced at Alan's apartment door. She couldn't say what it was about him that made her feel safe, but already, she couldn't imagine what life would be like here at the palace without him.

* * *

Alan guided Max through the outdoor dining area. Only a few of the tables were already in place, but planter boxes containing trees had been interspersed strategically to provide shade and privacy for anyone who chose to eat outside.

Max sniffed at the base of a table and continued on until they reached the low wall that separated the dining area from the pool. Alan took a moment to appreciate the view before him. White sand, the sun peeking through the thin layer of white clouds overhead. The scent of something fruity carried on the air, evidence that Félix was once again experimenting in the kitchen.

Alan's phone rang, competing with the waves crashing against the shore.

For a brief moment, Alan hoped Victoria would be on the other end. Then he remembered that Levi would likely be listening in. Having his friend carrying a clone of Victoria's phone was not exactly conducive to keeping his budding romance private.

Alan checked the screen. Levi.

"Hey, what's up?" Alan asked.

"A couple things. The police just found the abandoned delivery truck used in yesterday's attack."

Hope rose within him. "Did forensics pull any fingerprints?"

"No, and they aren't going to be able to. It appears the truck's surfaces were bleached, and then the van was burned."

"Bleached and burned? These guys really don't want us to know who they are."

"It reeks of hired professionals."

"So they'll continue to be a threat as long as someone is paying them."

"That's my take on the situation."

"Great." Unable to stand still, Alan walked across the sand toward the water. "What else have you found out?"

"The judge just signed off on the search warrant of Sheldon's and Marguerite's hotel rooms. I want you and Max to do a sweep of both their rooms. I doubt Sheldon would have anything on him, but if anyone can find anything, it'll be you and Max."

"I'll head over to the Imperial Blu now." Alan ended the call and took one last look at the beach before he turned away from the tranquil setting and headed back into the hotel.

His drive from the Royal Sands to the Imperial Blu took only ten minutes, and he was greeted by the police chief in the main lobby.

Like the Royal Sands, the Imperial Blu exuded wealth, but the decorator's taste for the Imperial Blu ran more toward the ornate rather than the subtle. Alan preferred subtle.

After greeting Alan, the police chief motioned him toward the elevator. "This way."

"Were both Marguerite and Sheldon staying here?"

"Yes. Marguerite was on the sixth floor. Sheldon was on the eighth," he said. "I thought we could start at the top and work our way down."

"That's fine with me." Alan stepped into the elevator with the chief and pulled a pair of crime-scene gloves out of the little pocket beside his holster. He put them on as they rode up the elevator with glass on one side so he could see the lobby below.

When they reached their floor, a police officer stood guard beside an open door.

"Has anyone gone inside?" the chief asked.

"No, sir. Forensics is unloading their gear."

"Good." The chief waved Alan inside. "It's all yours."

"Max, search."

They cleared the deluxe bathroom first. Nothing. Max sniffed the chair and sofa positioned across from a flat-screen TV on the wall. He barely slowed as he passed them. The bed and nightstands also didn't seem to warrant more than a cursory search.

Alan circled the bed, and Max sniffed at the base of the closet door. He kept sniffing.

With his gloved hand, Alan slowly opened the door so Max could access the contents.

Clothes hanging inside, shoes on the floor beside a carry-on suitcase, a luggage rack, a thin box about the same size as the one that had contained the bomb delivered to the resort, and a small safe.

Max sniffed the shoes; he sniffed the air. Then he sat down and whined.

Alan was still processing the possible find when the chief rushed forward. "Did you find something?"

"Maybe." Alan did a quick analysis. It was possible Max had picked up the scent of bomb residue on Sheldon's clothes, but the suitcase and box were the more likely hiding places. Or the safe.

"Do we need to evacuate the building?" the police chief asked.

"I doubt Sheldon would plant a bomb in his own room." That logic didn't prevent Alan from pulling his small flashlight from his pack. He checked the safe, the box, and the suitcase for any booby traps. "Can you get the override code for the safe?"

"I already have it." The chief passed him a paper key-card holder with four digits scribbled on it.

Alan tucked it in his pocket. "Best get back."

The chief disappeared from the room. Alan knelt and examined the contents of the closet again.

"Which one is it, Max?"

Max's ears perked up, and he sniffed at the suitcase. Following his partner's lead, Alan carefully unzipped the suitcase a few inches.

He shined his light into the interior but could see only a box inside. Alan unzipped the suitcase a little more, again stopping to further examine the interior. He repeated the process twice more before he undid the zipper completely.

"Let's see what we've got here." Alan pulled the top open slightly to get a better look at the box inside. No wires were visible, and the flaps weren't secured.

He did another inspection for booby traps before he opened the box completely.

Wires, wire cutters, potassium chlorate, sugar, a prepaid cell phone. All the items needed to create another bomb.

"Looks like we found our guy." Alan moved on to examine the narrow box that leaned against the wall by the safe. Ever cautious after the last run-in with a package that was more than it appeared to be, Alan cut into the side of the box and removed a small piece of the cardboard so he could examine the contents. He breathed a sigh of relief when he shined the flashlight inside and saw nothing beyond packing materials around what appeared to be a piece of artwork.

He cut more of the box away to review the contents more clearly. After another examination, Alan pulled away the packing materials. Nestled inside the protective wrapping was a painting, the same painting that had been scheduled for delivery yesterday.

Alan stood and called out. "Hey, Chief? You're going to want to see this."

The chief appeared at his side a moment later. "Looks like Sheldon Burton was involved in a whole lot more than blackmail."

"Yes, it does."

CHAPTER 33

Victoria sat in the living room chair, Shadow curled up on her lap. The curtains billowed in the light breeze, and sunlight streamed into the room.

It was the perfect weather to go for a ride or perhaps stroll through the gardens, but the mere thought of walking outside sent another wave of panic crashing over her.

She leaned forward so she could see the front gate at the end of the circular drive. The guards were in place, and two armored SUVs were parked on either side of it, each with an armed guard beside it.

Four guards at the gate, several more visible on the grounds. She was safe. Her mind knew it, but her body wasn't listening. A tremor worked through her, and she fought against another panic attack. Victoria stroked Shadow's head.

The sound of a car engine carried to her, and she straightened in her seat. Shadow's ears perked up, and she sat up in Victoria's lap.

Victoria stood, the puppy in her arms. She identified the vehicle when it came into view. Alan was back.

She hugged Shadow as Alan drove into the garage. If he adhered to his typical routine, it would be twenty or thirty minutes before he came inside.

Even though a dozen tasks demanded her attention from work, she sat back down in her chair. She would work later.

Only five minutes passed before a knock sounded on her door. Was that Alan already?

Victoria set Shadow on the floor and hurried to answer the door. She opened it, and an instant later, she was in Alan's arms.

He held her in silence for a moment before speaking. "Federico said you had a rough morning."

Victoria's cheeks heated at the thought of the guards discussing her. "I'm okay."

Alan released her long enough to walk inside and close the door. Then he pulled her into his arms again. "What happened?"

Another wave of embarrassment washed over her. She fought the instinct to keep her emotions buried and private. "I don't know. One minute I was walking down the hall to take Shadow outside. The next, I couldn't even move."

Alan eased back so he could see her face. "You had a traumatic experience yesterday."

"Yes, but why am I freaking out now? I had two other scares last week, and I managed after those."

"You managed, but neither of those happened here at the palace." Alan released her and guided her to the nearest sofa. He waited for her to sit before he took the spot beside her. "Those men violated your safe space. It's understandable that you would struggle."

"I'm so embarrassed." Victoria motioned toward the door. "Giuseppe and Federico must think I'm crazy."

"Hey." He slid his arm around her shoulders and moved closer. "No one thinks you're crazy. Quite the opposite. You've been very stoic through all this. It's okay to also be human."

Victoria didn't want to think about how often one of her "human" moments had ended up in the tabloids. "I'm royalty. I'm not allowed to be human."

"Yes, you are." Alan lowered his lips to hers for a sweet kiss. "This is your home. And everyone here only wants you to be happy."

He was right. Giuseppe and Federico had been incredibly sympathetic when she'd had her first panic attack. Focusing on the bigger problem, she asked, "How do I get past this?"

"Would it help if I told you I found evidence in Sheldon's room that indicates he was behind all this?"

"What?" She pulled back so she could see him more clearly. "You did?"

Alan nodded. "He had bomb materials and the painting that was supposed to be delivered yesterday."

"Sheldon Burton?" Victoria said his name with disbelief. "You're sure?"

"The evidence is pretty compelling," Alan said. "My guess is he paid someone to create the second bomb and found out when you were flying out, so he tried to take advantage of an earlier opportunity."

"And you don't think this was about the artwork?"

"It's possible he was stealing some, but I suspect that it was more of a side benefit," Alan said. "I'm going to talk to Levi about having him investigate everyone at the local art museum for connections to Sheldon."

Victoria could put the clues together well enough to guess Sheldon had either a cohort or a resource who was sharing shipping information, but a more important detail still eluded her. "What was Sheldon's motive? I thought he was trying to blackmail me."

"I don't know, but now that we have this much evidence against him, I hope he'll talk."

"I hope so too." She leaned back against the soft cushions of the sofa and grasped for the sense of security that should have come with this newest information.

"What do you say we go for a walk? It's a gorgeous day."

Victoria shifted away from him. "I don't—"

"Where is your favorite place on the palace grounds?" Alan asked, cutting her off. "The beach? The gardens? The cliffs?"

"There is a little spot in the woods that I love to ride to." Victoria pondered the little spot where Levi had proposed to Cassie. "It's not visible to the public."

"We need horses to get to it?" Alan asked.

"It's the easiest way." Victoria paused. "Do you know how to ride?"

"Janessa taught me, but it's been a while."

Janessa taught him. "The two of you really are good friends."

"Yes." His lips quirked up into a half smile. "You may already know that she grew up on a farm in the US."

"I had heard that."

"She loves to ride and is pretty determined to make sure her friends don't miss out on the joy of being up on top of a thousand-pound animal."

"Does that mean you don't like to ride?"

"I like it okay, but it took a while before I felt like I knew what I was doing," Alan said. "I could use some more practice though. Want to come with me and show me how it's done?"

He was asking her to spend time with him where he knew she would have to face her fears.

When she didn't speak, Alan gestured in the general direction of the stables. "Tell you what. Let's have the stables saddle a couple horses. We'll cut through the servants' residence so we can stay inside until the last possible minute. Then we'll see if you're up to walking down the path to the stables."

His plan sounded easy enough, but her pulse was already racing.

"I don't know if I can do this."

"Are you willing to try?"

Victoria drew a deep breath and let it out. "Yes, I'll try."

* * *

Alan waited beside the servants' exit and studied Victoria. Her face was paler than usual, and with the way she clung to Shadow, he had no doubt she was still fighting her demons. If only he could slay them for her, but he had witnessed post-traumatic stress before and knew he could only hand her the sword. She would have to make the decision to use it.

"Ready?" he asked.

She swallowed hard and nodded.

He pulled on the door handle and tugged on Max's leash to guide him forward. "Just stay right with me and Max. We'll let you set the pace."

Victoria gave him a stiff nod.

Alan escorted her outside, and instantly, Victoria quickened her stride. He matched his steps to hers, and within a few short minutes, they reached the stables, where two horses were already saddled and waiting.

A stablehand approached, holding some sort of small harness. "Your Highness, I thought you might want this for the pup there."

Some of the tension eased out of her body. "I forgot we even had this."

"It's been a while since we've had need for it."

Alan studied the black straps that looked like some sort of complicated seat belt or baby carrier. "What is it?"

"It's a harness that I can use to strap Shadow to me so she can come with us."

"Let's get her hooked in, then," Alan said. Hopefully, the puppy would give Victoria both a needed sense of comfort and a distraction.

Victoria held Shadow out so the stablehand could help her attach the harness.

Even though Alan suspected that Victoria would do well to keep the pup with her, he asked, "Do you want me to ride with Shadow?"

As he hoped, she shook her head. With the stablehand's help, she strapped the harness to her body so Shadow was safely tucked next to her chest. She led her horse to a mounting block and used it to mount her horse.

"You all set?" Alan asked.

She looked out at the open space surrounding the stables and the trees that lay beyond. "I think so."

With Janessa's voice echoing through his head from his dozens of riding lessons, he placed his foot into the stirrup and swung himself onto his horse. The gelding sidestepped, and Alan tightened the reins to keep the horse in place. "Which way?"

"The trail is over there." Victoria moved toward an opening in some nearby trees.

Alan called out, "Come on, Max."

Max trotted beside him, exploring the nearby woods the moment they reached the trees. The path widened as they passed a fallen log, and Alan urged his horse forward until he reached Victoria's side.

"It's pretty out here."

"Cassie used to bring me and Annabelle out here when we wanted to escape the palace for a while." A faint smile alighted her features. "Papa was never thrilled when he found out we were playing hide-and-seek from the guards instead of each other."

Alan laughed. He could imagine it all too well. Three young girls conspiring together, the guards frantically trying to do their jobs without admitting to the king that they had lost his daughters.

"I'm glad I wasn't working security back then."

"Me too." Victoria motioned toward where Max was currently sniffing a nearby bush. "If you'd had Max with you, you would have found us."

"You've got that right."

Max flushed a squirrel out of its hiding place, and Shadow barked; Victoria startled and reined her horse to a stop.

The squirrel scampered up a tree, leaving Max behind.

"Sorry," Alan said, apologizing for the disturbance Max had created. He stopped beside her.

Victoria took a deep breath. "It's not your fault I'm so jumpy."

"I feel like it is. If we had connected Sheldon to the bombs sooner, you wouldn't have gone through the trauma of an attempted breach yesterday." Alan urged his mount forward again, pleased that Victoria did the same.

"You couldn't have known what he was up to."

"No, but he was on our radar as a potential threat. We just didn't think he was trying to physically harm you."

"I still don't understand how you all had him on your radar in the first place."

Preferring to avoid sharing details that might cause conflict between Victoria and Levi, Alan sidestepped the underlying question. "Levi will undoubtedly have his best interrogators questioning Sheldon."

"Do you think he'll talk?"

Alan pondered the question for a moment. If Sheldon really was guilty, the likelihood of him admitting it wasn't high. "I doubt it."

"So we may never know why he tried to kill me."

"I don't know," Alan said. "Marguerite has been somewhat cooperative. With any luck, she'll have more insight to share."

They reached a clearing that held a gazebo in the center. Alan had come through here often enough, especially during his first time working at the palace. "This is Cassie's favorite place."

"It is. How did you know that?"

"I used to check out the area before she and Levi would come up here when they needed some time alone."

Victoria came to a stop. "Can you take Shadow before I dismount?"

"Sure." Alan dismounted and tied his horse to one of the posts of the gazebo. By the time he reached Victoria's side, she already had the puppy out of her harness and was handing her down to him.

Alan set Shadow beside Max at the edge of the woods. Immediately, the puppy jumped up on the older dog in an attempt to play.

Victoria stepped beside Alan and slid her arm around his waist. "I'm glad they get along so well."

"Me too." The possibilities for the future flitted through his mind. Him and Victoria together, a couple of dogs. He stopped those thoughts before they could go any further. This wasn't a time for worrying about what-ifs. It was a moment to enjoy the present.

He turned Victoria into his arms and lowered his lips to hers. Leaves rustled from the dogs playing, but all that faded as Alan pulled Victoria closer.

She lifted her hands to encircle his neck as his lips explored hers. She leaned into him. The many moments they had spent together, the friendship they shared, expanded and created something new, something vivid, something essential.

Even as he struggled to define the changes happening between them, Alan couldn't resist trailing his hands up her back and tangling his fingers in her hair. This was what he wanted, this connection, this sensation that he was the center of Victoria's world, the same way she had become the center of his.

Slowly, he eased back and brushed her hair back from her face. "Thanks for coming out here with me."

Victoria reached up and kissed him again. "Thank you for bringing me."

CHAPTER 34

VICTORIA STOOD AT THE EDGE of the high cliffs that split the two royal beaches, Alan at her side and the two dogs playing on the grassy area behind them.

Waves crashed against the stone wall below, the water churning much like the turmoil swirling inside her. To one side, a white stretch of sand led to the dock where the royal yacht was currently docked. On the other side, the beach was broken up by the rock barrier and the security wall that separated the royal grounds from the resort. Would she ever feel safe enough to leave the palace grounds again?

The spires and turrets of the resort really did resemble her home, a replica of sorts that would soon host guests from all over the world for her sister's coronation.

"The coronation can happen on schedule now that Sheldon is behind bars, right?" Victoria asked.

"I assume that will be the case," Alan said. "I'm sure Levi will keep investigating Sheldon and any accomplices he might have had until we have more answers, but with the increased security and Sheldon in custody, I don't think Levi will want to push it off."

"Sheldon's accomplices? I don't like the sound of that."

"We already know the driver from yesterday was a hired gun, and we believe the crew was as well," Alan said. "That's good news."

"How is that good news?"

"Because it means they were here for a paycheck. No paycheck, no additional threat."

"Maybe there's a way to track payments from Sheldon to the people working for him."

"We already have both Interpol and the CIA looking into it."

"Why would the CIA help us?"

"The same reason they let me come here on temporary assignment," Alan said. "They want peace in this region, and having your family in power is in all our best interests."

Victoria couldn't deny her inherent desire for her family to continue to fulfill their legacy, but to have a superpower support that wish so openly didn't quite make sense. "Why does the US want to keep my family in power?"

"Are you kidding?" Alan's eyebrows lifted. "Your family has ruled peacefully for centuries, and we've seen firsthand that your loyalties lie with protecting your citizens. That's impressive."

"That's all they want?"

"That's all." Alan took her hand and led her back toward the woods. "I know your father didn't trust Americans, but I like to think some of those prejudices faded before he died."

"Levi had a lot to do with that."

"I agree, but your father deserved a lot of the credit too. He wanted Cassie's happiness more than he wanted to hold on to those old wounds."

"You're right. He did." A wave of nostalgia washed over her and uncovered the grief always brewing beneath the surface. Her father wouldn't be here to walk her down the aisle when it came time for her to marry. He wouldn't even meet her future husband, whoever that would be.

Alan released her hand to push aside a low-lying branch to protect her as she walked by. Once she passed, he slid his arm around her waist. A tingle worked through her, and she looked up at him. His dark shirt against smooth skin, his neatly trimmed beard, his handsome face. Far too easily, she could picture him in a tux, waiting for her as she walked down the aisle in a billowing white dress.

Her heart stumbled at the image, and her steps echoed it when her toe caught on a tree root.

Alan's firm grip kept her upright. "Are you okay?"

She nodded, not quite able to get any words out. Her and Alan? Married? She shook away the thought. Even though they had met almost two years ago, they had only known each other well since her return home.

"What's going to happen to us when you have to leave here?" Victoria asked.

"I don't know yet." Alan stopped when they reached the gazebo and turned to face her. "I've thought about asking for a reassignment, but I don't know if it will be granted."

"It can't hurt to ask though, right?" She sensed his hesitation. "Unless you don't want to."

"Of course I want to, especially if it means I can be close to you." Alan linked his hands behind her waist. "But it's my turn for a hardship post. I feel bad that someone else would have to take my place."

A hardship post. Victoria didn't like what that implied. "I know it's selfish of me, but I hope you can stay here."

"I hope so too." Alan leaned down and kissed her.

Victoria leaned into him, wishing this moment could go on forever.

Alan pulled back and looked around the clearing. "We should probably get back."

"I guess so." Victoria was struck by the fact that she wanted to stay out here when less than two hours ago she had barely managed to leave the palace walls.

Alan helped her put Shadow in the harness and stood by while she mounted her horse. A moment later, he swung into his saddle with ease.

"You don't look like someone who is uncomfortable around horses," she said.

"Janessa forced me into a lot of lessons."

"It's still hard to believe a royal was able to spend so much time teaching you."

"I bet you would have taught me if I didn't know how to ride."

"Yes, but that's different," Victoria said. "We're dating." She hoped that was what they were doing.

"That's true, but that doesn't change the fact that you would make the time to help me if it were something you wanted to do."

"You're right." Her admiration for Janessa increased. "That was kind of Janessa to make you a priority that way."

A flicker of humor and something else crossed his face. "Like I said, she's a good friend."

"And that all she's ever been?"

"Janessa is like a pesky older sister, one who tends to think she needs to look out for me." From atop his horse, he leaned closer and gave Victoria a quick kiss. "And no, I never dated her."

"Good to know."

"You ready?"

Victoria nodded. She led the way down the trail, relieved that their conversation about Janessa had been short-lived.

Shadow snoozed in her harness while Max explored the woods beside them. Rabbits and squirrels scampered from the underbrush; birds took flight. Victoria startled only twice during the ten-minute ride back to the stables.

Squirrels, rabbits, and birds. No people with guns.

"Hold up," Alan said when they approached the clearing surrounding their destination. He pulled to a stop beside her and retrieved his mobile. He tapped on the screen and spoke into the phone. "We're heading your way." He paused before thanking whoever was on the other end and hanging up. "Giuseppe said the guards are in place."

Her earlier fears resurfaced. "They're sure it's safe?"

"I'm not going to let anything happen to you." Alan reached out and put his hand on her arm. "I promise."

CHAPTER 35

Alan picked up Max's tennis ball and sent it flying over the grassy knoll at the edge of the palace gardens. Max raced after it, practically tripping over his own feet when he came to a rapid stop. This little bit of downtime was much deserved, a reward for the long hours Alan and Max had put in over the last few days.

They had split their workday, inspecting the deliveries at both the resort and the palace, and they'd spent their free time primarily in Victoria's company. Alan had hoped that after their ride on Tuesday, she would be able to push past her fears, but every time they went outside, she seemed to struggle all over again.

At least she kept trying. She had managed to go on a ride again with him yesterday and a walk in the woods the day before. She'd even consented to join him for his daily training sessions with Max, which he had adapted to include Shadow. Yet every time they traversed the open space that crossed within view of the palace gates, Victoria tensed.

Alan was ready to help her move beyond the palace walls, back to the life she had planned for herself before the threats against her had begun. Unfortunately, Victoria wasn't going anywhere until he and Levi were certain the threat against her was really behind bars.

Max dropped the ball in front of Alan, and Alan threw it toward the trees that separated the open space from the stables.

A pair of guards came into view, Levi walking between them.

Levi motioned for the guards to remain behind as he approached Alan.

"Any new developments?" Alan asked.

"Sheldon is finally talking, but he hasn't given us any information other than to say he's being framed."

"I'd say I was being framed, too, if I were arrested for terrorism."

"So would I, but I'm still not thrilled that we haven't identified a clear-cut motive," Levi said. "He went to a lot of effort and expense to get to Victoria if his only motive is some twisted payback for Victoria not going out with him."

Alan had entertained similar thoughts more times than he cared to admit. "You're afraid someone hired him."

"I don't know, but we have to consider the possibility." Levi's phone buzzed with an incoming message.

Max returned with the ball again, but this time, Alan motioned to him. "Go lie down."

Max gave him his disappointed look but obeyed.

Beside Alan, Levi glanced at the screen on his phone. "This might be something."

"What?"

Levi turned his phone toward Alan so he could see the screen. "Our local intelligence has identified a large deposit in Matei Barone's account. Based on the amount, I'd say the museum employee is the one leaking information."

Forty thousand euros deposited the day after Victoria had arrived in Sereno. "Want me to go with the police to pick him up?"

Levi pondered for a moment before he shook his head. "They already questioned him once about the missing painting. It may be best to let the same officer have a go at him."

"I hope this guy will give us some answers. I really want to get Victoria out of the palace. She needs to experience the real world sooner than later."

"Cassie said Victoria and Annabelle are both still struggling." Levi shoved his hands into his pockets. "Even though she won't admit it, Cassie is rattled too."

"With good reason." Alan turned toward the palace, Victoria's balcony visible from where he stood. "Have you thought about bringing in a counselor to help them work through their trauma? It might help."

"Cassie and I talked about it. We're already in the process of vetting a psychologist who Dr. Marois recommended."

The physician for the royal family. "How long will that take?"

"I'm hoping it won't take more than a few days."

"The sooner, the better."

Levi pocketed his phone and took a step back as though studying him from a new angle. "Is something going on with you and Victoria?"

Alan wasn't typically one to kiss and tell, but there wasn't any reason to deny the change in his and Victoria's relationship, not when it was Levi asking the question. "Yeah." He let out a sigh. "I'm worried about her. She can barely walk outside without having a panic attack."

"I'll ask Dr. Marois to have a talk with her," Levi said. "He can determine if there's anything that can be done before she can meet with the psychologist."

"I guess that's better than nothing," Alan said. "There's one more thing I wanted to talk to you about."

"What's that?"

"I need your advice." Alan shifted his weight from one foot to the other. "Would it be wrong of me to ask for a reassignment?"

Awareness filled Levi's expression. "Because you want to stay close to Victoria?"

"Yes, but I'm also torn. It's my turn for a hardship post."

"It's not like you've never had one before. You started out in North Africa when things in that region were in a state of unrest."

"Yeah, but that was five years ago."

"If you care enough about Victoria to ask for a reassignment, it's worth putting in a request," Levi said. "And if you need me to make a call, just let me know."

Alan nodded. "Thanks."

CHAPTER 36

Victoria stepped out of her apartment as Alan approached.

"Hey there." Alan glanced at Giuseppe standing a short distance away and kept his hands at his sides. "I was just coming to see if you wanted to join me for dinner."

"Actually, Levi asked me to come to his and Cassie's apartment for dinner."

Disappointment etched his features. "Oh."

"Come on." Victoria stepped toward her sister's apartment. "You're invited too."

"Are you sure? I saw Levi a few hours ago, and he didn't say anything."

"I'm sure." Victoria knocked on Cassie's door.

Levi answered. "Oh, good. You're both here." He waved them inside. "Come into the living room."

Victoria followed him inside to where both of her sisters already waited. She greeted them before she asked, "What's going on?"

Levi waited for them to sit before he did the same beside his wife. "We found the person who helped Sheldon plant the bombs."

Hope bloomed inside her. "Are you sure?"

Levi nodded. "When pressed with the evidence, Matei Barone admitted to leaking shipping information."

"Did he identify Sheldon as the person paying him?" Alan asked.

"Not directly." Levi stretched his arm across the back of the couch, resting his hand on his wife's shoulder. "According to him, he doesn't know who was paying him."

"Can you trace the funding?" Victoria asked.

"As a matter of fact, the money came through a third-party app." Levi waited a beat before he added, "The funds were transferred from the cell phone found in Sheldon's apartment."

Victoria drew a sharp breath. "Then, he really was responsible."

"Yes."

"But why?" Victoria asked.

"We may finally have an answer to that," Levi said.

"Which is?" Annabelle prompted.

"It turns out Sheldon invested heavily in the Imperial Blu about six months ago."

"That's around the same time he started asking me out," Victoria said.

"I'm not a finance type," Alan said. "Spell this out for me."

"From the report I was given, the Imperial Blu had a few setbacks last year, first losing Lorenzo to the Royal Sands, and then suffering some damage in a kitchen fire," Levi said. "To help dig them out of their financial hole, they sold stock in their company. And the value of the company would triple if the Royal Sands didn't open."

Alan shifted on the couch so he was facing Victoria more fully. "He tried to kill you to get a better return on his investment?"

"That's what it looks like," Levi said.

"What about the other owners?" Alan asked. "Is there any chance any of them were also involved?"

"Not from what we can tell," Levi said. "In fact, according to the bank, Nico offered to buy back Sheldon's shares four months ago, but Sheldon refused. Apparently, he said he wanted to wait until next month."

"Which makes sense." Victoria's stomach churned uncomfortably. Her life had nearly ended because a man wanted more money. She shook her head. "If something happened to me, the value would go up as long as the resort didn't open. He would cash out at the high point."

"Obviously, his plan didn't work." Alan reached for her hand and gave it a reassuring squeeze.

Levi focused on Victoria. "Believe it or not, this is good news."

"That's right," Alan said. "Based on this new intel, Sheldon really was the person behind the threats against you."

"You're telling me I'm safe?" Victoria didn't feel safe.

"We'll keep the heightened security in place, but based on this information, it would be possible for you to return to the resort."

"I don't know if I'm ready to do that yet."

"You can take your time." Alan glanced at Levi and Cassie. "Right?"

"Of course," Cassie said. "We want you to feel safe."

Victoria sighed. "That may take a while."

* * *

Request denied. Alan read the email from personnel a third time. Despite his request and Levi's support, his orders to fly to the Middle East had not been altered. He would leave the day after Cassie's coronation.

Disappointment swept through him, but it wasn't the only sensation he was experiencing. His heart ached at the prospect of being so far away from Victoria. For several days, he had let himself get swept up in the possibilities that living so close to Victoria would open. Now he faced a reality he had hoped to avoid.

He pushed back from his kitchen table and crossed to the window. Late summer roses bloomed in the meticulously groomed garden. Grassy fields stretched out before him, the Mediterranean glistening beyond them.

In two weeks, he would be living on a military base, likely without a window, much less a view. Not that he would want to stare at rows of barracks or parked armored vehicles.

Max stood from his spot on the rug and sniffed the air. He padded to the front door and barked.

Alan's heart squeezed in his chest. He would leave Sereno; Max would stay.

Max barked again and scratched at the door.

"You need to go out?"

Max scratched at the door again.

"Come on." Alan opened the door, not bothering to grab Max's leash. He stepped into the hall, surprised to find Victoria standing between his apartment and the exit.

"Hey." Alan glanced at the guard standing beside the open door.

Max trotted out the door, and Alan let him go. The dog would come back when he finished his business.

Alan took another step toward Victoria. "What are you doing down here?"

"Shadow needed to go out." Victoria glanced at the floor as though ashamed that she had delegated the task to someone else.

"Still struggling to go outside?"

She lifted her gaze to his and sighed. "I know Levi said Sheldon was to blame for everything, but every time I think about going outside alone—"

"Hey, it's okay." Alan pulled her into his arms. "Moving past traumatic events takes time."

Giuseppe walked in with Shadow. Max trotted in behind them.

Alan released Victoria and took Shadow's leash from the guard. "Can you give us a minute?"

"Of course." Giuseppe moved a short distance down the hall.

Though Alan wanted nothing more than to pretend he wasn't leaving, he said, "I got an email today from personnel."

Hope lit Victoria's eyes. "And?"

Alan drew a deep breath before breaking the news. "They said no." The magnitude of the decision crashed over him. "I'm sorry. I wanted to stay."

Victoria pressed her lips together as though trying to control her emotions. For a moment, she didn't say anything. Then she asked, "When do you leave?"

"The day after the coronation."

"So soon?"

"I'm afraid so." Alan ran his hand down Victoria's arm until his hand found hers. "I'm sorry. I really wanted to make this work."

"Wait." Victoria stepped back. "Are you saying I won't see you again?"

"Victoria, I'm slated for a hardship post." Alan fought the urge to reach for her again. Their time together was coming to an end. Maybe it was best that they start adjusting to that reality now, before he fell any harder for her.

"For how long? It's not forever, right?"

"It should be for two years, but I can't ask you to wait around for me for that long," Alan said. "You won't be able to visit me, and it's unlikely I would be able to get away more than two or three times a year."

Victoria tipped her chin up, and her eyes met his. "Do you want to make this work?"

"Of course, but it's not fair to you."

"Alan, it's not fair for you to walk away from me." Her voice lowered to barely louder than a whisper. "Not when I'm in love with you."

"You—" Alan couldn't have heard her right. "You're in love with me?"

Her cheeks flushed, but she kept her gaze locked on his. "Yes, I am."

The tightness in his chest eased, the bands of disappointment fading beneath her revelation. Unable to resist, Alan lifted his hands to frame her face, and he lowered his lips to hers.

The sensation of the kiss swept through him, and a new future sparked in his mind. Two years of taking whatever time together they could and then a transfer back to Sereno. He could make that happen, especially if Levi put in a specific request for him to be assigned here.

He pulled back. "Two years. That's a long time."

"Some things are worth the wait."

CHAPTER 37

Victoria stood at the edge of the woods beside her horse while Alan went through his daily training session with Max and Shadow on the beach. For more than a week, she had fought against the terror that clawed through her every time she wanted to step outside. And for more than a week, she had waited for Alan to share those three little words with her. He still hadn't.

Maybe she was expecting too much from him. After all, they had only been dating a few weeks. Just because she had fallen in love with him didn't mean he wouldn't need some extra time to catch up. Assuming his feelings would ever mirror hers.

She had started meeting with the psychologist Levi had brought in a few days ago. Dr. Pampena was a kind woman who made it very clear that these daily outings were good for her. Supposedly, they would get easier with time. Victoria was still waiting for that to happen.

Today, she had the added challenge of being out in the open for the first time since the attempted break-in. Up until now, Alan had used the woods to hide the various training tools for the dogs to find.

It was like a game. That was how Alan had acted with the dogs anyway, like he was playing with them the whole time, encouraging them to win.

Shadow had yet to identify any of the bomb components Alan had put in her path, but she consistently responded to several commands now: sit, down, stay. Well, she mostly stayed. She was still working on that one.

Victoria stiffened when a sailboat came into view in the distance, just beyond the waters considered part of the royal estate. She instinctively searched for any sign of someone pointing a camera—or a gun—at her. Thankfully, the only people on board appeared to be the woman at the wheel and the man working the sails.

Alan finished his last commands with Shadow and gave her a treat and his usual praise. He then held up a stick, and the puppy wagged her tail. "Go get it."

Alan threw it down the beach. A second later, he sent Max's tennis ball after it. Both dogs bounded through the incoming surf, sending water flying with each step. Their pure joy brought a smile to Victoria's face.

She waited for Alan to return to her side before she said, "They're both going to need a bath."

"I expected as much." Alan did his own evaluation of the distant sailboat. "You doing okay?"

"I think so." She glanced out at the water again, a speedboat now also visible. "But maybe we should go in."

"Do you mind playing with them for a minute while I pack up?"

"That's fine." She hoped. She looked out at the two boats now on a parallel course to the coastline.

Alan whistled, and the dogs came running.

Max reached Victoria first and obediently dropped his tennis ball in front of her. She picked it up, only wincing a little when her fingers gripped the slobbery ball. She tossed it down the beach and then turned to Shadow, who bounded toward her.

Victoria leaned down to take the stick, but the puppy played tug-of-war instead of releasing it. "Drop it."

Shadow didn't follow her instructions, so Victoria pulled a treat from her pocket and held it out. Sure enough, Shadow opted for the treat over the stick. "Good dog."

She let the puppy have the treat and then grabbed the abandoned stick so she could throw it. The routine repeated twice more before Alan joined her, his pack already on his back.

He whistled again for the dogs, and they all headed toward where they had left their horses tied at the edge of the woods.

Victoria reached her mount and swung herself up into the saddle. "I can't remember the last time I've gone riding so many times in one week."

Alan untied his horse and climbed on. "It hasn't happened for me since I lived in Bellamo."

At Garrett and Janessa's home. "It's too bad Garrett and Janessa can't come for the coronation."

"Yeah." Alan urged his horse into motion. "But it will be nice to see Stefano and Alora."

Stefano and Alora. Not Prince Stefano and Princess Alora. The fact that Alan had omitted their titles caught Victoria's attention. She rode beside him and glanced at Alan. "Are you good friends with both of them as well?"

"I know Alora better than Stefano, but I've spent a decent amount of time around them."

"Any other dignitaries you're already acquainted with that I should know about?"

"Not really. I may have met a few over the years, being around Garrett and Janessa, but I prefer to stay in the background with the rest of the security team."

The vision of Alan and Max performing their duties while others socialized evoked an uncomfortable thought and caused her stomach to churn. "Will you be able to attend my sister's coronation? I was hoping you would attend with me."

"I'll have to talk to Levi about that." Alan ducked to avoid a low branch and guided her down a narrow section of the trail. When it widened and she once again took position beside him, he continued. "We might be able to close the gate a half hour before the ceremony so I can come up to be with you."

"I hope you can." Victoria pressed a hand to her stomach. "I really don't want to attend without you."

Alan slowed his horse and looked at her. "There are very few people who will be missed if they aren't there, and you're one of them."

"And you're one of the very few people I need to have with me that night."

A flicker of surprise flashed in Alan's dark eyes. He stopped his horse and leaned over to kiss her. "Then I will do everything I can to be there."

Unspeakably relieved, she kissed him again. "Thank you."

CHAPTER 38

Alan lifted his pistol and fired. His target today was a paper bull's-eye at the indoor shooting range, a huge improvement over a moving target who was shooting back. He shook that thought away. The shooting on Monday was behind them, and thus far, no one knew if the man he'd shot had survived.

He reloaded and squeezed off another round. He sensed someone approaching, so he set down his weapon and removed his protective gear before turning.

Levi stepped into view and leaned against the barrier that separated Alan's stall from the one beside him. "I thought I might find you here."

"Just getting in some target practice before Max and I make our evening rounds." Alan gestured with his hand to encompass the facility. "I have to say, it's nice having a range right here on the palace grounds."

"The king was smart to include this when he had the security office built."

"You mean the previous king," Alan said. "You're the king now."

"I'm the king consort, and even that is a title I never expected to have." Levi glanced over his shoulder and lowered his voice. "If it weren't for Cassie, I'd still be standing in the back of the room trying not to get noticed."

"Hey, you were at least used to being in the room. I rarely make it inside the building while anyone else is there," Alan said. "Speaking of which, Victoria asked me to be at the coronation."

"How is she?"

"She's getting outside every day, so I'm going to call that a win."

"I heard." Levi pulled his own weapon out of the holster attached to his belt. "I also heard that she's still struggling with it."

"It's only been a week and a half since the shooting. You can hardly blame her."

"You're right, but that doesn't change the fact that Cassie's coronation is in less than two weeks. A significant part of our security plan rests on the resort being open and able to accommodate our high-profile guests."

"Are you worried that she can't get everything done remotely?"

"I know she's doing everything she can from here, but the work is falling behind," Levi said. "The restaurant hasn't passed the final inspection, the staff hasn't been fully vetted, several deliveries have been delayed, the carpet installation is behind schedule."

"None of those problems is a result of Victoria working from home."

"No, but many of them might very well be resolved if her presence were felt."

"Are you telling me to get her back to work?"

"Yes."

"That's a big ask." Alan turned to face the target he had shot moments ago. Aiming a gun at a bull's-eye was simple. Hit the center, and you succeed. Helping Victoria move beyond her trauma wasn't something he was trained for or even knew how to accomplish.

Levi didn't speak for a moment, clearly understanding the complexity of the challenge before them. Finally, he said, "What if we have you work exclusively at the resort? That way she'd have the comfort of knowing you're always nearby."

"What about the palace?" Alan asked. "As you said, we're less than two weeks away from Cassie's coronation."

"We can set a delivery window for an hour or two either before or after you go to the resort so that everything coming onto the palace grounds is examined," Levi said.

"That's not going to work the last couple days before the coronation."

"I'm hoping Victoria will gain some comfort working on her own by then."

"And if she doesn't?"

"First things first. Help her face her fears so she can learn that life still exists outside the palace grounds," Levi said. "And if it helps motivate her, tell her I'll talk to security about breaking you free of your duties in time to attend the coronation with her."

"You're very manipulative sometimes."

"Only when I'm trying to help people I care about." Levi grabbed a pair of protective ear coverings and slipped them into place. He stepped into the stall beside Alan.

Alan slipped his own protective gear into place. He reloaded his pistol and shot at the target. How was he supposed to help Victoria without feeling like he was manipulating her? The answer to that question hit him instantly. The only way he could accomplish what Levi wanted was to be honest with her. From there, he would support whatever she was ready for.

He shot at the target until he emptied his clip. When he finished, he expelled the magazine and confirmed that the chamber was clear. When he turned, Levi stood behind him once more.

Both men removed their ear protection.

"Will you help me?" Levi asked.

"I'll try, but on one condition."

"What's that?"

"You have to promise you won't deny that we had this conversation."

Surprise lit his eyes. "You're going to tell her I asked for your help?"

"Yes. I'm not going to lie to her, and I'm not willing to try to manipulate her."

"Fine, but only if you make it clear that we only want what's best for her," Levi said.

Alan nodded. "Deal."

* * *

Victoria typed another email to the building inspector's office. She had been promised that the kitchen inspection would be taken care of this week. It was now Friday, and nothing had happened yet. It was almost as though they thought they could ignore her request since she wasn't at the resort to complain when they missed yet another appointment.

She read through her message twice to make sure her request to confirm an inspection appointment for today was firm and professional without coming across as a royal tirade. She hit Send with a bit more force than necessary and pushed back from the dining room table.

Leaving her laptop and her breakfast dishes behind, she crossed to the balcony doors and pulled one open. The roar of the waves filled the room, and the cool mist of the drizzling rain moistened her face and arms.

The weather would protect her from going outside today. She shouldn't be grateful for that, but she was.

Shadow slipped past her legs and made it onto the balcony. She sniffed at the puddle forming beside the railing.

"Get back in here." Victoria leaned down and picked her up. "We don't need you tracking water all over the floor." She carried her back into the living room and pulled the door closed behind her. A quick look at the puppy's damp paws gave her a new direction. "Should we take you out before I dry you off?"

Shadow wriggled in her arms.

"Come on." Victoria grabbed Shadow's leash on her way out the door, though she made it only as far as the bottom of the stairs before Alan approached with Max.

"Hey there. I was just coming to find you." Alan glanced at the guard standing near the main hall and tilted his head. The subtle signal was enough for the guard to step into the hall, leaving only his shoulder visible to them.

"What's going on?" Victoria asked. "Is everything all right?"

"Levi is concerned that a few things are falling behind at the resort because you aren't there."

The last thing Victoria expected from Alan was to hear a complaint about her efficiency at work. She straightened her shoulders and tipped her chin up. "If Levi is worried about the progress, why am I hearing about it from you instead of him?"

"Because he hoped I could help get you back to work on-site."

She wasn't sure which was more insulting: having her brother-in-law doubt her ability to get the job done or knowing he had been talking to Alan about her behind her back.

Alan put his hand on her shoulder. "Levi's worried about you. That's all."

Anger and hurt rose within her. "He's worried about the resort and the coronation."

"Yes, he is, but he's more concerned about you." Alan dropped his hand and motioned to Shadow. "Do you want me to take her out for you?"

She lifted her chin a little higher. "Are you afraid I can't handle stepping outside?"

"No. I was just offering to prevent you from getting wet."

"Oh."

"Let me take her. Max needs to go out too." Alan held out his hands, and after a brief pause, Victoria held out the puppy's leash to him.

"Thanks."

"I'll be right back." Alan took the leash and headed for the door.

With her hands now free, Victoria reached into her pocket and retrieved her cell phone. She pulled up Levi's number with the intention of calling him, but she glanced at the guard's barely visible shoulder and reconsidered. A confrontation with Levi was very likely in her future, but it needed to occur in private.

Why hadn't Levi talked to her directly? Had he been too worried that she would take offense when he brought forward his concerns? Okay, so the insult of her current failures wasn't lost on her, and she couldn't deny that simply making a request didn't carry the same weight as calling the inspector from the resort and him knowing she was waiting for him there.

And the carpeting installation. It was Friday. The likelihood of the contractors trying to cut off early was far higher when she wasn't there to prevent it.

Alan returned with the two dogs, his clothes damp from the rain.

"After I put Shadow in her kennel, will you drive me over to the resort?" she asked.

"Now?"

Victoria swallowed the bitter pill of truth and nodded. "Levi's right. I need to be there to get everything back on track, and I don't want to wait until the weekend to make it happen."

"I'll go get a car and meet you back here in ten minutes."

"Thank you."

Thirty minutes later, with her guards in place at the resort entrance and beside her car, Alan opened her car door.

"You ready for this?" he asked.

She couldn't answer past the lump in her throat. Her limbs grew heavy, as though they weighed a ton each. She looked up at Alan, willing herself to move but not able to make it happen.

"You can do this." He took her hand in his and helped her stand.

With her body now upright, she scanned the building before her. The sign for the restaurant had been mounted above the external entrance, and a uniformed doorman stood beside the double doors leading into the lobby.

"Come on." Alan let go of her long enough to shift his hand to her back. He applied gentle pressure to encourage her forward. "You can do this."

She nodded. Miraculously, her brain connected with her legs, and she managed to walk forward. As soon as she entered the lobby, she spotted the foreman for the carpet company.

He leaned against the welcome counter while chatting with one of his employees. The moment he spotted Victoria, he straightened.

"Pelayo, I was hoping I would see you," Victoria said.

"Your Highness." He bowed his head. "I wasn't expecting you here today."

Obviously. Victoria prevented the snide remark from escaping her and opted for a more subtle approach. "I understand your crew will need to put in some extra hours this weekend to get the installation back on schedule."

"Oh, well—"

"I'll need the updated schedule by two o'clock today," she said, not giving him the chance to contradict her.

Something flickered over his face, a sort of resignation. "Yes, Your Highness."

"Thank you." She turned toward the woman behind the welcome counter. "Will you please get the building inspector's office on the phone? Let them know that I am here waiting for their inspector and would like to know when I should expect him."

The woman nodded. "Yes, Your Highness."

She picked up the phone and made the call. Victoria caught a glimpse of the little smirk on Alan's face.

"Have you and Max already cleared the common areas today?"

"We did, but I haven't done your office yet." Alan moved toward the hallway leading toward her office. "I'll take care of that now."

Once Alan and Max had cleared the room, she entered, then closed the door and turned to face Alan. "Thank you."

"I didn't do anything beyond passing along Levi's concerns."

"Yes, but knowing Levi, he didn't want you to share them in quite that way."

"Maybe not, but you deserved to hear it straight." Alan settled his hands on her shoulders. "I'll be here until you're ready to leave."

Victoria glanced at the pile of mail on her desk. "I might be a while."

"That's okay." Alan leaned down for a brief kiss. "You're worth waiting for."

CHAPTER 39

ALAN PARKED THE SUV HE'D borrowed from the palace in the service area beside the restaurant. A second SUV parked beside him, and Federico got out of the driver's seat. Alan turned off the engine and circled to the back.

Federico opened the back door. "Where do you want to set up?"

"Let's use the beach. That will give the dogs the extra challenge of the scent and sound of the ocean."

"Sounds good."

Alan opened the back, where both dogs were kenneled. While Max could certainly ride in the car without needing to be contained, Shadow still had some learning to do in that regard.

Beside him, Federico pulled out a portable wagon and began transferring the training materials into it.

"Thanks for being willing to help out today," Alan said. "I'm still not comfortable with Princess Victoria being here without me."

"That's understandable," Federico said. "It can't be easy."

Alan had witnessed that truth firsthand, but he didn't comment. Victoria's emotions weren't a topic he was going to discuss with anyone outside the family, not even a trusted employee. "Go ahead and set up. I'll bring the dogs down."

"You got it." Federico grabbed the handle for the wagon and pulled the training materials to the edge of the patio. From there, he started lining up the water bottles, one of which contained potassium chlorate and another, ammonium nitrate.

Alan waited until he was nearly done before he opened Max's crate and clipped the leash on his collar. "Come on, boy."

Alan signaled for Max to climb down and then sit beside him. He didn't even manage to open Shadow's crate before the puppy's tail started wagging.

"You ready to get out of there?"

Shadow yipped in response.

Alan laughed. "Okay, let's go." He opened the crate and grabbed Shadow's collar before she could escape. After he clipped her leash into place, he lifted her down and set her beside Max. With a leash in each hand, he said, "Let's go." They reached the beach as Federico placed the last few bottles.

"Who's going first?" Federico asked.

"We'll let Shadow take the first turn today." Alan sensed Federico's eagerness and held out Shadow's leash. "Want to do the honors?"

His eyes lit up. "Yeah. That would be great."

"Just remember, go nice and slow. Don't let her skip anything."

"Got it." Federico guided Shadow forward before issuing the command. "Search."

A little surge of pride rose within Alan when Shadow lowered her nose to sniff at the first bottle. When she reached the tenth bottle down the line, Federico stopped, pressed on Shadow's rump so she would sit, and then rewarded her. Another failed attempt.

Alan put his hand on Max's head and scratched between his dog's ears. This whole exercise was probably a wasted effort. After all, he was leaving in ten more days. He didn't have long enough to train Shadow.

The pang in his heart was instant. He would be leaving Max, and he would be leaving Victoria. At least Federico knew enough now to keep Max going with his routine once Alan left.

Federico put Shadow back in motion, and they resumed their progress along the line of water bottles.

Shadow sniffed at a half dozen bottles. Then she lifted her head and sniffed the air. Federico gave the command to search again.

Shadow lowered her nose to the base of the nearest bottle. Then she sat and looked up expectantly.

It couldn't be.

Federico grinned over his shoulder before reaching into the pouch at his waist and retrieving a treat. He gave it to Shadow, showering her with an abundance of praise.

Pride burst through Alan, and it took all his willpower to keep from interrupting the training session. He waited impatiently while Federico and Shadow completed the course.

Federico's face was beaming when he approached. "She did it!"

"Which one did she identify?" Alan asked.

"The potassium chlorate."

"In that case, rearrange the bottles and add a second bottle of potassium chlorate," Alan said. "Let's see if she can do it again."

* * *

Victoria checked the area by the breezeway leading to the restaurant twice before stepping into the wide, glass-encased hallway. Behind her, a worker vacuumed the carpeted area in the common space by the elevators. The scent of fresh flowers hung in the air along with the underlying odor of lemon.

Lorenzo approached from the restaurant. "I was going to come find you. The inspector just left."

Victoria braced for the results. The inspector on Friday had failed them on a minor ventilation issue that the electrician had hopefully resolved yesterday. "Please tell me you have good news."

His lips twitched into the beginnings of a smile. "We passed."

A sigh of relief escaped her. "So, we're good to open?"

"We could open tomorrow if you wanted."

Victoria grinned. "That is fabulous news."

"I assume you want to stick with the original plan of holding the grand opening of the restaurant the same day as the resort."

"Yes." Despite the underlying security concerns of opening the resort to the public, a little trickle of excitement worked through her. Sheldon was behind bars. So was his accomplice from the art museum. The threat was behind them.

At least, this one was.

Lorenzo motioned toward the window. "Is your friend still going to be coming around every day through the grand opening?"

"Through the coronation anyway." She hoped. Victoria glanced out at the beach where Alan stood with Max. Federico was beyond him with Shadow.

Shadow sat down.

Victoria stepped closer to the window. When Federico leaned down and offered a treat to the puppy, she moved toward the door. "I'll be right back."

Victoria headed for the french doors leading to the patio and stepped outside, her focus on her puppy and the shower of praise she was receiving.

Alan turned as she approached, a huge smile on his face. "Did you see it?"

Excitement rose inside her. "Shadow found one?"

Victory flashed in his eyes. "She did. That was her third round. She's finding potassium chlorate every time."

"I'm sorry I missed it."

"You're here now." Alan motioned to the line of bottles on the beach. "Want to take her through the course once? That is, if you can spare a couple minutes."

She should check on the menu options for the days leading into her sister's coronation, but when Federico approached with Shadow at his side, her resolve wavered. "I suppose I can spare a few minutes."

Federico grinned. "I'll set it up again."

"Thanks," Alan said. He leaned down and scooped Shadow into his arms. "You're a good dog, aren't you?"

Shadow barked and wriggled in Alan's arms to try to lick his face. Max barked as though he wanted to join in the fun.

Alan looked down at Max and laughed. "You'll get your turn soon enough."

Victoria couldn't help but smile.

Alan set the puppy down and held out Shadow's leash. "Here you go."

Like a proud parent about to watch her child perform, anticipation danced inside her. Victoria took the leash and nodded.

Federico returned to where they waited. "Okay, we're all set. The targets are the second, fourteenth, and twenty-third bottles."

"Go see what she can do." Alan waved Victoria forward.

"Okay." Victoria guided Shadow forward and gave her the command to search.

Shadow lowered her nose to the sand and made it to only the second bottle before she sat. Delighted, Victoria leaned down and praised her dog.

Alan stepped forward.

"She did it!" Victoria straightened.

"Here. Give this to her." Alan passed a treat to Victoria.

Victoria leaned down and gave Shadow her treat, rubbing the fur on her neck as she did so.

Alan removed the bottle with the bomb element inside it. He handed her a pouch with more treats. "Keep going."

Victoria straightened and tugged her dog's leash. "Shadow, search."

The puppy missed the second substance, but she sat again when she reached the last one.

After Shadow was appropriately rewarded, Alan approached. "Good job."

Victoria turned to face him. "I can't believe she did it."

"She's a natural."

"I guess so." Victoria glanced toward the restaurant entrance, where Lorenzo currently stood. "I hate to say it, but I need to get back to work."

"Text me when you're done with work, and we can drive back together." He lowered his voice. "I'll be sure to call the kitchen so the chef will have dinner waiting for us."

Warmed by the thought of spending time with Alan after a long day of work, she smiled. "I'd like that." She stepped back. "I'll see you later."

"That you will."

Victoria headed back inside to where Lorenzo waited.

"Félix has the work schedule for the week of the coronation, but we're still short two servers," Lorenzo said. "Perhaps you can get those last few security checks expedited."

"I'll see what I can do." She moved toward the dining area. "In the meantime, check with the servers we've already cleared to see who would be willing to put in some extra shifts."

Lorenzo nodded.

Victoria glanced out the window at where Alan was currently taking Max through his training. It wasn't until Max sat beside one of the offending water bottles that the last fifteen minutes caught up with her. She had gone outside without looking over her shoulder or worrying that someone was aiming a gun in her direction. She had moved across the patio the same way she had the first day Alan had come to visit.

Perhaps the threats really were behind her. Thank goodness. She quite liked the idea of feeling normal again, especially if that normal included spending her free time in Alan's company.

CHAPTER 40

ANOTHER FORMAL DINNER, ANOTHER NIGHT wearing a tux. Only tonight, the venue was the resort, not the palace. The private opening celebration of The Royal Sands Resort was well underway when Alan entered the grand ballroom.

White lights hanging from the ceiling, potted plants around the room, elegant place settings on the linen-draped tables, a photo display on the far side of the room featuring the various amenities the resort offered.

He waited a moment for his eyes to adjust to the dim lighting and resisted the urge to tug at his bow tie. Victoria had been kind enough to tie it for him before he'd gone on duty, and he didn't want to risk messing it up. Heaven knew he would never be able to replicate her efforts. No matter how hard he tried, he could never get both sides even.

From the looks of the scene before him, the formal dinner portion of tonight's event had already concluded. Too bad. He had hoped to arrive in time for dessert, but with the steady stream of guests arriving for the coronation, his work of clearing luggage had taken longer than he'd hoped.

A short distance away, he spotted Victoria chatting with Stefano and Alora. Alan's smile was instant. He crossed to them and managed to resist greeting Victoria with a kiss.

"Your Highnesses." He bowed his head slightly but didn't manage to contain his grin.

"We were wondering when you would show up." Victoria smiled at him, her face absolutely beaming. She put her hand on his arm. "I believe you are well acquainted with our guests."

"Very much so," Alora said before Alan could respond.

"It's been too long." Stefano shook Alan's hand.

"That it has," Alan said. "How does it feel to be the first guests here at the resort?"

"Our rooms are beautiful." Alora turned her attention back to Victoria. "Truly, you've done a remarkable job here."

"Thank you."

"You really have," Alan added. "Everything looks incredible."

Two blurs of movement rushed forward from the seating area behind them, both with the same dark hair and dark eyes as Alora.

"Alan! Alan!" Seven-year-old Dante wrapped his arms around Alan's torso.

"Who is this young man?" Alan said in mock seriousness. "This can't be Prince Dante. He's much too tall." Alan fought to keep a straight face. "This must be Prince Giancarlo."

From his spot behind Dante, Giancarlo stood a little taller. "I'm Giancarlo."

Alan leaned down so he was closer to eye level with Giancarlo. "Are you sure? The Giancarlo I know is only nine. You look like you're at least twelve."

Giancarlo tilted his head in his thoughtful way. "You're teasing me."

"Maybe just a little." Alan's grin broke free, and he reached a hand out to draw Giancarlo into a hug. "I can't believe how big the two of you are getting."

"We got to come to the grown-up party," Dante said.

"So I see."

Alora put her hand on Dante's back. "And I'm afraid it's time for the two of you to go upstairs."

"Already?"

Stefano nodded. "It's that time."

Dante let out a heavy sigh. "Okay."

Brenna, the boys' nanny, stepped forward. "I'll take them upstairs."

"Thank you, Brenna," Alora said. "We'll be up in a little while to tuck them in."

Brenna ushered the boys toward the archway that led to the main hall.

Alan turned back to Victoria to find her staring at him. "Is something wrong?"

"No." She glanced at the boys as they left before she focused on him again. "Nothing at all."

"We'll have to catch up later." Stefano put his hand on Alora's back, a clear signal that it was time to move to the next conversation.

"Enjoy the rest of your evening," Alan said.

Stefano and Alora had barely moved away before Lord and Lady Romero stepped beside them.

"Princess Victoria, don't you look lovely tonight," Lady Romero said.

"Thank you." Victoria offered a polite smile. "You as well."

"I'm so glad your sister decided to hold this dinner tonight," Lord Romero said. "It's important that we all move past these ghastly security breaches."

Victoria stiffened. Clearly eager to change the subject, she motioned to Lady Romero's gown. "Your dress is lovely. Is that one of Gloria Gerard's designs?"

"It is." She lifted her chin slightly. "I told Marcelino that I wanted only the best to design my clothes for this week. After all, this will likely be the only coronation I attend in my lifetime."

"Gloria has certainly been busy the last few months, preparing for this event," Victoria said.

"I heard your sister decided to have your chef cater the event instead of bringing in outside help," Lord Romero said. "That's quite a lot of work."

"It is, but only family will be staying at the palace, so that will ease the burden on our kitchen staff significantly."

Not to mention, Félix would be preparing all the desserts for the coronation dinner in the resort kitchen. Alan kept that tidbit to himself. No point in sharing information with anyone who didn't need to know.

"Are you ready to transition into your new position?" Alan asked. "You'll be the new head of agriculture, right?"

"Yes, although I will likely be doing double duty for a few months. It will take that long to get Lord Cattaneo up to speed on the complexities of the contracts and finances."

"I can imagine." Alan couldn't really, but it seemed like a safe response.

Victoria tilted her head slightly. "Will you excuse us? The king asked to chat with Alan when he arrived."

"Yes, of course."

Alan escorted Victoria toward the corner of the room where Levi stood beside Cassie. "Did Levi really want to talk to me?"

"Levi always wants to talk to you," Victoria said.

Alan chuckled. "You didn't want to listen to Lord Romero go on about the economic progress of the new oil fields?"

"Not even a little." She stopped beside Levi. "You said you wanted to speak to Alan when he got here?"

"Actually, I'd love a minute with both of you." He lowered his voice. "The delegation from Spain is arriving on their yacht day after tomorrow. Alan, can you meet them and do a sweep with Max before their belongings are loaded and taken to the resort?"

"Yeah, but what about deliveries arriving at the palace?"

"The only ones we have showing up around that time are the desserts from the resort restaurant and Annabelle's dress from Gloria Gerard."

"If you feel comfortable with having the guards clear those deliveries, I'll make sure we don't have any issues with the Spanish."

"Thanks." Levi blew out a relieved breath. "Only a few more days of this craziness, and we'll finally be able to get back to normal."

"Yeah." Alan's stomach twisted uncomfortably. He wasn't looking forward to his new normal.

CHAPTER 41

Victoria was late. Her quick visit to the resort this morning had turned into an impromptu breakfast with Alan and Prince Stefano's family. Even though the casual meal had cut into the time she had allotted to get ready for the coronation activities, she couldn't regret spending time with Alan and his friends.

Victoria rushed up the stairs to Annabelle's room, Shadow trotting behind her. The coronation would begin in less than two hours, and Victoria was taking full advantage of having her sister nearby to fix her hair.

Besides the fact that Annabelle had a knack for such things, Victoria couldn't deny that she wanted to look her best today, not only to represent the royal family well but also because this would be her last full day with Alan before he left tomorrow. She wanted him to remember her looking her best.

She knocked on Annabelle's door, and it swung open an instant later.

"It's about time." Dressed in a white robe, Annabelle waved her inside. "We're supposed to be down in the chapel in an hour."

Twenty minutes for Annabelle to do her hair, five minutes to don her dress, shoes, and jewelry, three minutes to freshen up her makeup. Plenty of time. "Is Cassie already here?"

Cassie stepped out of Annabelle's bedroom, dressed in a full-skirted, gold silk gown. Her dark hair was already styled in a sleek updo that would readily accommodate the crown she would soon wear. "I am."

"And already looking gorgeous, I see." Victoria hugged her older sister. "Are you ready for today?"

"Ready or not, it's happening." Cassie glanced down at Shadow. "I see you brought your little friend with you."

"She's going to be cooped up so much today. I wanted to keep her out of her kennel for as long as possible."

"I don't blame you."

Annabelle tugged on Cassie's sleeve. "Come on. Let's get your hair done so we can get dressed."

"I still haven't seen your gown yet," Victoria said. "Did you find what you wanted?"

"We're about to find out." Annabelle headed for her bedroom. "I've been so busy helping set up for today that I haven't even had a chance to look at it."

"You haven't tried it on yet?" Victoria asked. "You're showing a lot of trust in Gloria."

"She's never let me down yet." Annabelle led the way into her room, where a large dress box lay on the settee at the end of Annabelle's bed. "Let me grab some scissors."

Shadow sniffed at the floor and at the legs of the settee. Then she put both front paws on the padded surface and sniffed again.

"Get down from there." Victoria leaned down to force the puppy off the furniture, but before she could, Shadow sat down and wagged her tail.

"Looks like all that training with Alan is paying off," Cassie said.

"Yeah. He's been great with her."

Annabelle opened her bedside table drawer and retrieved her scissors.

Annabelle circled the bed. Shadow remained where she was, her tail still wagging. The puppy looked up expectantly, as though expecting a reward.

Cassie edged forward. "Let's see this dress."

"You're going to love it." Annabelle opened the scissors and angled them toward the tape on top of the box.

Victoria looked down at Shadow again, and an impossible scenario rocketed through her mind. She reached out and grabbed Annabelle's arm. "Wait."

"Why?"

"Just back up for a minute." Victoria waited for her sisters to edge away from the box before she gently picked up Shadow and took her to the bedroom door. She set her back down and issued the common command. "Shadow, search."

She let Shadow guide her. The puppy sniffed at the floor, she sniffed at the bottom of the furniture, she sniffed at the air just below the dress box, and then she sat and wagged her tail.

"This isn't possible," Victoria said.

"What isn't possible?" Cassie asked.

Ignoring her older sister's question, Victoria turned to Annabelle. "When was your dress delivered?"

"Sometime yesterday. Why?"

Yesterday, while Alan and Max had been at the resort helping with security as their distinguished guests had checked in.

Her heartbeat quickened. Was she overreacting, or was it possible Shadow had found another bomb?

"Better safe than sorry," she muttered to herself.

"Better safe than sorry about what?"

"That." Victoria pointed at the dress box with one hand and pulled her phone from her pocket with the other. She dialed Alan's number.

His harried greeting came over the line after the fourth ring. "Hey, can I call you back? Max and I are in the middle of clearing the equipment for the band."

"No."

"No?" Alan asked, clearly surprised by her answer.

"I think Shadow just found a bomb."

* * *

A bomb? Alan couldn't have heard her right.

Victoria continued to talk, her stress obvious. "Shadow signaled twice right next to my sister's dress box," she rushed on. "Alan, it was delivered yesterday when you and Max weren't here."

The likelihood of Shadow finding a bomb was astronomical, at least it would have been had Max not already found two others in the past month. Not willing to take any chances, Alan turned to the guard beside him. "Take over, but don't let anyone else in until you hear from me."

"But—"

"Come on, Max." Alan rushed toward the palace, his phone still in his hand. "Where are you?"

"I'm in Annabelle's room." Her voice wavered. "What do I do?"

"First, get everyone out of there. Then call Levi."

"Okay." The line went dead, and Alan increased his speed.

Max matched his pace as though they were on a grand adventure, but this wasn't fun and games. This was real. And if there really was a bomb, either Sheldon had an accomplice, or he really had been framed.

Alan reached the palace entrance nearest his room. The guard stationed there immediately opened the door.

Levi was waiting beside his apartment door.

Alan rushed to him. “Victoria and Annabelle?”

“They’re fine. Cassie too.”

“Cassie was there?”

Levi nodded.

“That could have been disastrous.”

Levi reached for Max’s leash. “I’ll keep Max while you suit up.”

“Can you call Federico for me? I may need his help. And have him bring the portable scanner.”

“He’s already heading over here. He’ll meet us by Annabelle’s room.”

“Good.” Alan hurried into his apartment and quickly traded his flak jacket for his full protective suit. He tucked his helmet under his arm and returned to where Levi waited with Max.

“You get someplace safe.” Alan headed down the hall. “I’ll call you as soon as we’re clear.”

“Be careful,” Levi called after him.

Alan glanced over his shoulder. “I will.”

CHAPTER 42

Victoria and Cassie followed Giuseppe through the back hallway to the east wing, a half dozen guards surrounding them and Shadow wrapped in Victoria's arms. Annabelle had already been escorted to the south tower with her security detail. Cassie would take refuge in Levi's office, while Victoria would leave the palace walls entirely.

They reached Levi's office door, and Cassie stopped to face her. "Maybe I should be the one to go to the stables."

As much as Victoria didn't want to go out into the open, she shook her head. "No. It's safer for you here."

"It's safer for you here too," Cassie countered.

"But royal protocol is that unless we're in the panic room, we can't be together." And they couldn't be in the panic room because it was too close to a potential bomb.

Cassie pulled her into a hug. "Be safe."

"You too."

Cassie sniffled and released her. In a blink, her guards ushered her into Levi's office and closed the door between them.

"This way, Your Highness." Giuseppe gestured toward the staircase that led to the exit nearest the stables.

Victoria made it all the way to the bottom of the stairs before the panic started closing in on her. Even though she knew the answer, she asked, "Why are we going outside again?"

As though Victoria didn't know the answer, Giuseppe said, "One of you needs to be out of the palace in case we have any communication issues."

In case there really was a bomb . . . In case it went off . . .

Alan.

The thought of him rushing toward the danger, of possibly losing his life trying to disarm yet another bomb intended for her . . . But this one wasn't intended for her. This one had been sent to Annabelle.

"This way, Your Highness," Giuseppe said again, reminding her that she needed to continue forward.

Her heartbeat quickened, but she followed him to the exit.

Giuseppe spoke to whatever guard was on the other end of the communication device he wore in his ear. After a few seconds, he nodded and pushed open the door to reveal Sabine waiting for them. Sabine motioned for Victoria to follow her, while Giuseppe and the other three guards currently following Victoria took position beside her.

They moved down the path, Victoria glancing back toward the palace as she left the security of its walls, the walls that currently contained a bomb and everyone she loved. Her heart seized at the possibility of losing any of her cherished family members or Alan.

She caught a glimpse of movement on the terrace outside the chapel. Lord Romero and his wife had apparently opted for a few moments alone before the ceremony began. And now that ceremony could be postponed for unthinkable reasons.

Sabine moved quickly through the open stretch of the path, urging Victoria forward. The typical six-minute walk to the stables took barely half that time, and Victoria's breathing was labored by the time Giuseppe escorted her through the double wooden doors.

Another guard approached from inside. "The area is clear. The stable manager is in his office with two of the stablehands."

Giuseppe nodded his approval. "Sabine, you stay inside with Princess Victoria." Giuseppe motioned to two of the guards. "You two, take the rear entrance. Jorge and I will take the front." He waved at the doors they had just entered.

The four men deployed to their positions, leaving Victoria alone with Sabine.

"I'm sorry these aren't the most comfortable of accommodations," Sabine said. "If you'd like, we can have you join the stable manager in his office."

"That's okay." Victoria set Shadow down. The puppy shook herself as though proving that she was now free of Victoria's embrace.

Had Shadow really found a bomb? Or was it possible that Victoria was overreacting? After all, she had been the person Sheldon had tried to kill, not Annabelle.

* * *

Federico was waiting outside Annabelle's apartment when Alan arrived. Like Alan, he was dressed in full protective gear, right down to the astronaut-looking helmet.

Alan slid his own helmet over his head and locked it into place.

"You really think there's a bomb in here?" Federico asked.

"Let's find out." Alan opened the door. "Wait here until I have Max do a sweep."

Alan stepped into Annabelle's expansive apartment and took in the open space. With a sense of urgency, he pulled his phone from his pocket, dialed Victoria's number, and hit the speaker function since his helmet prevented him from holding the phone to his ear.

"Is there really a bomb?" Victoria asked.

"Tell me where to start looking."

"Annabelle's room. It's down the hall. Second door on the left."

With the phone still in his hand, he led Max down the hall. When he reached the open bedroom door, Alan said, "Max, search."

Max lowered his nose to the ground and started sniffing at the furniture. When he reached the bed, he lifted his nose into the air.

"Did you find anything?" Victoria asked.

"Not yet."

Max sniffed at a large box lying on a low couch at the foot of the bed.

"I'll call you after we clear the room."

Max sat.

"Or not."

"Or not what?"

"Victoria, I'm going to have to call you back." Alan took a step forward. "Shadow was right. We have another bomb."

"Be careful."

"I will." Alan ended the call and turned toward the door. "Federico! Bring the scanner."

Federico appeared in the doorway, holding the handheld scanner Levi had procured for the royal guard after the last bomb scare. "What are we scanning?"

"This box."

Federico stepped forward and activated the scanner. Alan moved closer so he could see the screen. Nothing.

Federico turned the scanner over and checked the power button. "It's on, and it's working." Federico ran the scanner over the length of the box again. "Maybe the fabric of the dress isn't registering."

"We should have been able to see the hanger though."

Alan pulled his knife from his toolkit. "Get out of here." He glanced at Max, still sitting at attention. "Take Max with you."

"But—"

"Just wait in the main hall. I'll holler if I need you."

Federico nodded and took Max's leash. "Come on, Max."

Alan waited until the two were out of the room before he slid his knife into the box a few inches from the corner and shaved away the outside layer without cutting all the way through the cardboard.

He ran his finger along the thin layer of cardboard that remained. No wires.

He put his glove back on and cut all the way through the box, then grabbed his pen light and shined it through the small hole he had made. Billowing fabric lay inside. Judging from the way it lay, he had cut into a spot near the bottom of the gown.

With a full arsenal of tools at his disposal, Alan retrieved the snake camera. He inserted the tip through the hole in the box and turned it to see the rest of the inside of the box. Despite the light shining from the camera, he didn't see anything beyond a silver dress. Silk, from the looks of it.

He set the camera aside and cut away a larger piece of the box. When he set aside the slice of cardboard, the inside of it reflected beneath the overhead light.

Alan ran his gloved hand along the surface. If he was right, whatever lined the inside of the box was a shielding that prevented the scanner from working. Perhaps it also contained an element that Max was trained to detect.

But Alan already knew that was wishful thinking. Max might be trained to detect dozens of bomb components, but Shadow had been trained on only three. None of those three would be used in packaging.

Little by little, he cut away more of the box until the entire top had been removed and Annabelle's gown lay before him. Two glittery straps crossed over the fancy hanger that filled out the bodice all the way down to the waist.

Annabelle would look stunning in the dress, assuming it wasn't really encasing a bomb.

Gently, Alan lifted the edge of the skirt, working his way through the entire lower part of the box without finding anything beyond yards of billowing silk and a shimmering overlay that sparkled beneath the light.

"Where is it?" Alan muttered the question to the empty room. He leaned closer to examine the bodice. He shined his light on the jewel-encrusted straps, which reflected the light in a million directions.

Alan shifted to the side. That was when he saw it, the nearly invisible silver wire running beneath the strap.

He looked closer. If his guess was right, that wire was connected directly to the detonator. The moment Annabelle slid the dress off the hanger, the bomb would have detonated, ensuring her death.

"Federico," Alan shouted.

He appeared at his side a moment later with Max. "Did you find it?"

"Yeah, I found it." Alan motioned to the spot beside him. "Come here. I'll need your help to disarm it."

Federico nodded. "Tell me what I need to do."

CHAPTER 43

Victoria's fingers remained wrapped around her phone, her mind spinning. "Why Annabelle?"

Sabine furrowed her brow. "Excuse me?"

"Twice someone planted a bomb that could have killed me. Assuming the same person is behind the bomb in Annabelle's room, why would they now go after her?"

"I don't know, Your Highness." Sabine shook her head. "I'm afraid none of this has ever made sense."

"No, it hasn't." Victoria paced to the nearest stall, barely aware of the horse that poked his head over the top of wooden door. Her thoughts still racing, she asked a new question. "What would have happened had Annabelle been killed today? Or if I had been killed in one of the previous bombing attempts?"

"Obviously, there would have been a period of mourning."

"And the coronation would have been postponed." This wasn't the first time that possible motive had arisen, and it didn't make any more sense now than it had when Alan and Levi had first discussed it.

Victoria paced across the wide space between the two rows of stalls. "What else would have been different?"

"If it had been Princess Annabelle, someone else would have taken on the patronage of the arts."

"But that would have been for her specifically, just like had I been killed, someone else would have taken over the resort."

Sabine tilted her head toward the palace. "And ultimately, the oversight of the economic council."

Victoria tried to remove her emotions from the possibilities. "Cassie would take that on if something happened to me, just like one of us would have stepped into the role with the foundation for the arts."

"Yes, after Queen Cassandra's coronation."

"After the coronation." Victoria stopped and turned. "Who would benefit if my sister's coronation were postponed?"

"Nobody." Sabine held her position by the door. "The laws are all set up for the coronation to happen within a year of succession, but theoretically, the government would keep operating as it always does."

"But it wouldn't be my sister running everything."

"Not technically—"

Victoria lifted her phone and dialed Cassie's number.

"Have you heard from Alan yet?" Cassie asked.

"He found a bomb." Victoria didn't want to think about the risks Alan was facing right now. "How familiar are you with the coronation laws?"

"I've been studying them for the past two years, ever since Papa got sick. Why?"

"What happens if your coronation is delayed?" Victoria forced herself to ask the unthinkable. "Is it possible our family could be forced from power?"

"No. I would still be queen. You and Annabelle would still be in line for the throne."

"Someone has to be trying to prevent your coronation," Victoria said. "That's the only thing that makes sense for why someone would try to kill me and then go after Annabelle."

"The only things that change after I'm crowned is that I no longer have to rely on the ruling council to approve staffing changes," Cassie said. "But if something happened to one of you, I could still move forward with that. It would just take longer."

"Months longer." Victoria paced the space between the stalls again.

"Yes, but what would a few months matter?" Cassie asked. "It's not like anyone would gain anything from staying where they are except—"

Victoria stopped midstep. "Except what?"

"The royal treasury."

"What about it?"

"Fifty percent of the income from our royal holdings go to the managing body."

"Yes. That's the king, or now, the queen."

"The crowned king or the crowned queen," Cassie said, emphasizing the word *crowned*. "The succession laws grant a one-year grieving period, during which the funds continue flowing into the royal treasury."

"And after the one-year period?" Victoria asked.

"The funds would be distributed to the various members of the ruling council based on whatever funds they are managing."

"So you're telling me that the only income our family would be in control of is the resort?"

"Yes," Cassie said. "Annabelle isn't managing anything income-based, and I handed over control of both of our new energy projects to the economic council when Papa died."

"That shouldn't matter since we don't have money coming in from those yet."

"Not yet, but the drilling starts in three weeks." The tension in Cassie's voice was palpable. "If you or Annabelle had been killed, our citizens would expect no less than a four-month grieving period before my coronation could be rescheduled."

"How much income is projected during the next four months?"

"Two hundred million on the low side," Cassie said. "But it could be twice that."

"And whoever is in charge of those funds would get half of that?"

"That's right. Lord Romero would become a very wealthy man, practically overnight."

"Sounds like we finally have a motive," Victoria said. "This would also explain why Lord Romero was outside with his wife when I was moved to the stables."

"You saw him?"

"Yes."

"Hold on. Levi wants to talk to you."

An instant later, Levi's voice came over the line. "Did I hear right? You saw Lord Romero?"

"Yes. He was out on the terrace, not far from the entrance to the chapel."

"Did he see you?"

"I don't know." Victoria barely registered that the couple was nearby, much less what they were doing. "I was a little distracted by the whole get-out-of-the-palace-because-there-might-be-another-bomb thing."

"Ask Giuseppe if his men can see them."

Victoria held the phone away from her mouth and spoke to her guard. "The king wants to know if anyone is still out on the terrace."

Sabine relayed the question to Giuseppe. A moment later, she shook her head. "It doesn't appear so."

Victoria lifted the phone again. "They aren't there."

"Then, where did they go?" Levi spoke the words as though he were asking himself the question rather than Victoria.

She responded anyway. "I think the better question is, How far away are they staying from where the bomb was planted?"

"You're right. That's an excellent question."

* * *

Alan cut away another swatch of fabric from the bodice of Annabelle's dress and dropped it onto the pile on the floor beside him. "Looks like there's another trigger here." Alan leaned down to look at the bottom of the bomb that had been built inside the fancy hanger shaped like a woman's torso.

Federico leaned down beside him. "Boy, they wired that tight."

"Yeah. Whoever built this wasn't taking the chance that someone could slip the dress off the hanger without it going off." Alan straightened and took a step to his left so he could take another look at the primary trigger. "With two triggers, we have to assume there's a fallback circuit."

"Meaning, if we disarm one detonator, the other one will go off?"

"I'm afraid so."

Alan separated the wires at the bottom of the hanger and determined the use of each. "Come here. Keep this green-and-white wire separated from the others." Alan waited for Federico to circle behind him before he took his previous spot by the top of the box. He traced the wire to the primary detonator and grabbed his wire cutters. He handed a second pair to Federico. "When I tell you, you're going to clip the green-and-white wire."

Federico's face paled. "If we don't clip these at the exact same time, this bomb will explode."

"I know. That's why we're going to do it at the exact same time." Alan pulled his phone from his pocket and set the timer for one minute. "We'll do a practice one. As soon as the timer goes off, cut."

Federico swallowed hard and nodded.

Alan held his wire cutters in the air as though prepared to cut a wire. Federico did the same. The alarm rang, and the two cutters snapped closed in unison.

"Okay, we did it that time." Alan reset his timer and set it on the low couch beside the box. "Same thing. Make sure you make a quick, clean cut through that wire."

Federico nodded. He slid his wire cutters into place as Alan did the same.

Alan glanced at the timer, his pulse increasing as the numbers ticked down. When it reached ten, Alan counted down out loud. "Ten, nine, eight. Remember, quick, clean cut."

Federico nodded again.

"Four, three, two, one." The buzzer went off. Alan snapped the wire in two. When nothing happened, he looked up to check the cleanly cut wire in front of Federico and let out a relieved sigh.

Federico leaned back on his heels, the tension releasing from his body. "Now what?"

"Now we find out who planted this thing."

"How?"

Though Alan knew he should call Levi first, he pulled up Victoria's number and hit the Talk button.

"Are you okay?" Victoria asked in lieu of a greeting.

"Yes, but I need your insight. Do you have any idea who would know your sister's gown was being delivered from her designer?"

"I don't know. I'm sure Gloria Gerard probably had her assistant send it. And, of course, the delivery driver," Victoria said. "Wait. Lady Romero mentioned something about Gloria Gerard at the dinner the other night."

"Why would she try to plant a bomb?"

"I don't know if she would, but her husband might," Victoria said. "Turns out, if my sister doesn't get crowned within a year of my father's death, Lord Romero is set to come into a lot of money."

"How much money?"

"A hundred million. Maybe more."

Alan whistled. "Sounds like we might have found ourselves a new suspect."

"That's what Levi said."

"I need to talk to him. I'll call you right back."

Alan ended the call and dialed Levi.

"Status?" Levi asked.

"The bomb has been neutralized." He looked down at the shredded fabric at his feet. "Unfortunately, so has Annabelle's dress."

"If that's the only casualty today, I'm going to consider us lucky."

"I just spoke with Victoria. It sounds like Lord or Lady Romero may be the culprit behind the bombs."

"I look forward to seeing their expressions when everyone walks into the coronation whole and healthy."

"Do you even know where they are?"

"I called Alora a little while ago to scout them out. Lord Romero and his wife are out on the terrace by the chapel."

"You said you had a naval vessel standing by off the coast, right?"

"That's right. Why?"

"Any chance you can get it to shoot off one of its guns? I have a feeling Lord Romero will assume the shot is the bomb going off."

"That's a good idea," Levi said. "Give me ten minutes. I'll have Alora keep an eye on the entrance to the terrace to see how Lord Romero and his wife react."

"Sounds good. Federico and I will get this bomb out of here so Annabelle can come back and figure out what she's going to wear for Cassie's coronation."

"I'll let Cassie break the news to Annabelle about the dress."

"Just make sure she tells Annabelle that the dress died for a good cause."

Levi chuckled. "I will."

CHAPTER 44

Victoria kept her phone in her hand, willing it to ring. Shadow sniffed at the ground, taking advantage of the full length of her leash. "I hate not knowing what's going on out there."

"It shouldn't be much longer."

A phone rang, but it wasn't hers.

Sabine lifted her mobile into view and hit the Talk button. She had barely greeted the person on the other end before she nodded. "Tell me when we're clear, and I'll bring her out."

"Bring me out where?"

Sabine hung up the phone. "King Levi has asked that you return to your quarters to finish getting ready for the coronation ceremony."

"Then, Alan disarmed the bomb?"

"That's my understanding." Sabine spoke into the communication device in her ear, ensuring the area was clear before escorting Victoria to the door, Shadow behind them. "As soon as the guards make a sweep of our path, we'll take you to your quarters."

The ground shook, and Victoria reached out and steadied herself on the edge of the door. "Alan!"

In an instant, her future fragmented.

Shadow barked. Victoria burst outside, but before she could rush toward the palace, one of the guards stepped into her path.

Giuseppe caught up to her and spoke in a low voice. "It wasn't a bomb."

A sliver of hope pierced through her panic. "Are you sure?"

"Yes, Your Highness." He lowered his voice. "Alan wanted the person behind the bombing attempt to think it went off."

Victoria pressed her hand to her chest. "I wish he would have told me."

"Wait here another minute."

Victoria adjusted her grip on Shadow's leash and held her position between Giuseppe and Sabine. She glanced at the terrace. Empty.

Her body tensed. "Do you know where Lord Romero went?"

Giuseppe repeated her question into his communication headset. The scowl on his face didn't bode well for Victoria's already frayed nerves.

"Lord Romero entered the ballroom right after the blast."

"What aren't you telling me?" Victoria asked.

"He isn't in the ballroom now."

"Then where is he?"

"We aren't sure," Giuseppe said. "He could be in the restroom."

"Or he could be somewhere else." Although how anyone could slip past the royal guards today was beyond Victoria's comprehension. Everyone was on duty. "Why wasn't someone watching him?"

"A guard was assigned to him, but somehow, he slipped through the crowd and disappeared from sight." Giuseppe spoke into his communication headset briefly, and then he motioned to the palace. "The king and queen want you back inside. We're going to take you around to the front."

"Why?"

"Because we don't know where Lord Romero is, and we would prefer to keep you and your sisters out of sight until your grand entrance at the coronation," Giuseppe said. "There's too great a chance he could be somewhere in that back hallway."

As long as Lord Romero didn't know she and her sisters had all survived the latest assassination attempt, they were safe. She quickened her step. The sooner she was out of sight, the better.

* * *

Alan unclipped Max's leash and picked up his end of the rectangular container that now encased the bomb. Federico carefully lifted the other end, and the two men moved to the door of Annabelle's apartment.

"Come on, Max." Alan heard Max come up beside him. "What's the status on the royal family?" Alan asked Federico.

Federico relayed the question through his comm set before answering. "The king and queen are remaining in the king's office until they are ready to enter the ballroom. Princesses Victoria and Annabelle are being escorted back to their apartments."

"Good." With any luck, Lord Romero would believe the explosion of a moment ago really was the bomb going off rather than a shot fired from the nearby naval vessel.

"The transport is outside the family entrance," Federico said.

Alan nodded his approval. They reached the door, and the guard standing beside it pulled it open for them. They passed through, and Alan helped Federico muscle the bomb container into the back of the waiting SUV.

Max sat obediently on the driveway as Alan secured the container into the back of the SUV using netting and bungee cords. No reason to take chances. As soon as he stepped back, he gently closed the rear doors and circled to the front of the vehicle. With the bomb now as stable as possible, he removed his helmet and unzipped his protective gear. He stepped free of it and stored it in the back seat. When he glanced at the empty front seat, he asked, "Where's the driver?"

"Helping escort Princess Victoria back inside," Federico said. "The key should be in the cup holder."

"Back inside?" He drew his eyebrows together. "Where was she?"

"At the stables. Protocol demands that, in situations such as these, the second in line to the throne be removed to an alternate location until his or her safety can be ensured."

The idea of Victoria outside, unprotected, sent a wave of apprehension through Alan. He wasn't going to rest easy until she was safely inside and Lord Romero was securely behind bars.

* * *

Victoria caught sight of Alan only an instant before Shadow did. The puppy yipped and jerked forward, pulling Victoria with her.

Victoria stumbled a step and bumped into the guard in front of her. Shadow's leash slipped from her grasp, and the puppy streaked toward Alan and Max.

Victoria took a step after Shadow, but Sabine grabbed her arm. "Let her go."

"But—" That was as far as Victoria got before Sabine pulled her back into the center of her protection detail.

A popping sound carried in the air, not unlike fireworks going off in the distance. Sabine cried out and fell to the ground. Another guard dropped an instant later.

"No!" Victoria dropped to her knees as the three other guards shifted to protect her.

Another popping sound. Another guard fell.

Alan shouted. "Get her inside!"

The urgency in Alan's voice. The blood on Sabine's shoulder. Both brought new clarity to the situation. That popping sound wasn't fireworks. It was gunfire.

Panic and fear surged through Victoria. Someone was shooting at them, and the only thing preventing bullets from reaching her was Sabine's body.

Dogs barked. More gunfire rained around them. Footsteps pounded.

Victoria looked up to make sure Alan was okay, but she wasn't able to see him before a guard dropped down and pushed her head lower. "Stay down!"

Now trapped behind Sabine, she eyed the closest entrance. The two guards had taken cover behind the concrete pillars. One of them fired off a shot before ducking back down.

Sabine spoke to Giuseppe, her voice tense. "You need to get her to safety."

"How?" Victoria asked. "We'll never make it."

"She's right." The guard closest to her fired off another shot.

"Keep the princess protected," Giuseppe ordered the other guards. He then spoke into his earpiece. "I need backup in front of the palace."

Giuseppe had barely spoken those words when more gunfire sounded, and another guard dropped to the ground.

Victoria ducked her head lower. Four of her five guards were wounded, and she had no idea how to get to safety.

CHAPTER 45

Only years of training and discipline prevented Alan from rushing to Victoria. He might make it all the way to her without getting shot, but the odds were against it.

Shadow streaked toward them, though, and Alan shot off another round. He couldn't see the shooter, but he could make sure whoever it was had to take cover.

The puppy reached him and burrowed into Max's side. The dogs were safe for the moment. Now to give Victoria that same gift, not just for her sake but for his too. He needed her, and one way or another, he had to find a way to break this stalemate.

Federico grabbed Shadow's collar. "How are we going to get them out of there?"

Alan evaluated the scene before him. Victoria and her guards were pinned down with no protection other than the bodies of those who had already fallen. The shooter's gunfire had originated from somewhere behind the line of limousines, although Alan had yet to get a good look at him.

Alan pressed his left hand against the side of the SUV. "We need to get this SUV between the shooter and Victoria."

"What happens if a bullet hits the bomb?"

"The bomb container should protect it from gunfire." The possibility of a stray shot cutting through the vehicle and the bomb container was low. The odds of a bullet hitting the detonator were nearly impossible. Nearly. "I don't see any other choice." Alan motioned to the dogs. "Get them inside."

Without waiting to see if Federico complied, Alan pulled open the front door and slid into the driver's seat. He hit the button to start the vehicle.

The engine roared to life, and he quickly put it in gear. He stomped on the gas and turned the car to put it between Victoria and the threat. Almost instantly, gunfire sparked off the hood, and a bullet impacted the windshield only inches from his face, the bulletproof glass cracking.

Alan ducked instinctively, but he kept going.

More gunfire. Two more bullets in the windshield.

Alan reached the spot right in front of Victoria. He opened the driver's-side door and climbed out, keeping his head low.

Giuseppe crouched closest to him, Victoria beside him with her hand on Sabine's shoulder.

"Are you okay?" Alan asked.

Victoria drew in a shaky breath. "We have to get the wounded out of the line of fire."

Sabine lifted her head. "Get her to safety first. You can come back for us."

"No." Victoria shook her head. "It's a miracle no one has been killed yet. I can't just leave you here with three wounded men, especially when you're wounded too."

"How bad are their injuries?" Alan asked.

"They all took hits in their vests," Giuseppe said. "Sabine has a bullet in her shoulder, and Emil took one in his leg."

Victoria motioned to the back of the vehicle. "Open the back. We can get them inside and drive them out of here."

"There's a bomb in the back."

Victoria stiffened briefly. "The back seat, then." She crawled to the back passenger door and pulled it open. "Help me get them inside."

Torn between wanting to get Victoria to safety and his moral desire to help the wounded, Alan opted for the fastest possible method. He followed the princess's order.

"Keep your heads down." Alan helped Sabine into the back seat. "And slide over."

Sabine winced as she moved, but she managed to use her good arm to army crawl across the back seat.

Giuseppe helped the man with the leg injury into the spot beside Sabine.

A new volley of gunfire sparked in the air.

Victoria yelped in surprise and ducked beside the rear tire.

"We aren't all going to fit," Giuseppe said.

"Victoria, when I tell you, climb over the front console into the passenger seat. Keep your head down. I don't know how many more hits the windshield can take." Alan spoke to the remaining downed guard, his only apparent injury sustained from the two bullets in his bulletproof vest. "Can you drive?"

He winced when he sat up. "I can try."

"I can drive," Victoria said.

Alan whipped his gaze to meet hers. Immediately, he shook his head. "No. It's too dangerous."

"It's no more dangerous than having him try to drive with broken ribs."

"She's right," Giuseppe said. "If she drives, the two of us can run alongside the car and lay down cover fire."

Alan's chest tightened. It was a miracle Victoria was still alive. Could he really let her expose herself to more bullets?

Victoria spoke in a surprisingly calm voice. "It's our best chance of getting all of us out of here alive."

Alan hated that she was right. He closed the back door and turned to Giuseppe. "Help him into the passenger seat."

Alan squeezed off a shot to keep the sniper at bay. As soon as the injured were settled into the car, Alan put his hand on Victoria's shoulder. "When I tell you, drive around the edge of the palace. Keep your speed at twenty kilometers per hour. That will let us run beside you and lay down cover fire."

Victoria swallowed hard and nodded.

"As soon as you get to the rear entrance," Alan continued, "you get inside as fast as you can."

"But—"

"Let the guards take care of the wounded," Alan said. "We'll be right behind you."

She nodded again. Keeping her head down, she slid into the driver's seat.

"One more thing." Alan waited for her gaze to meet his. "If Giuseppe or I go down, I need you to promise you'll keep going."

The protest flashed in her eyes before she could utter the words.

Alan put his hand on her knee. "Promise me."

Tears welled up in her eyes, and she pressed her lips together. A tear spilled over, and she nodded once more.

Her tears nearly undid him, but the new spark of gunfire brought Alan back to the immediate task at hand. "Don't forget. Keep your head down."

Giuseppe pressed on his earpiece and edged closer. "We have men in place to rush the sniper."

"Tell them to go as soon as the car moves."

Giuseppe relayed Alan's suggestion.

"Ready?" Alan asked Victoria.

"I'm ready for this to be over."

"I know. Me too." He eased back and closed the driver's side door. Then he glanced at Giuseppe to make sure he, too, was ready to spring into action.

* * *

Victoria kept her body scrunched down in the driver's seat. Her hands shook, and she gripped the bottom of the steering wheel to steady them. She could do this. She needed to do this.

The engine was still running, left on from when Alan had rushed out of the car to shield her and the others from the sniper's bullets. All she had to do was press her foot on the gas and somehow steer the vehicle to safety while not getting shot.

While not getting shot. Those words repeated in her mind as more gunfire sounded. Was it possible for her to survive yet another attempt on her life? And could she help protect Alan as she tried to save herself and the guards who had taken the bullets meant for her?

Alan thumped his hand against the side of the car, signaling her to move forward.

Victoria took a deep breath, peeked over the dash, and pressed on the gas. The moment the vehicle went into motion, two shots impacted the passenger-side window.

She ducked down again, keeping her head only high enough to barely peek over the dash. She checked to make sure Alan and Giuseppe were still beside her.

"Speed up!" Sabine insisted.

Victoria pressed harder on the gas and turned the wheel to drive toward the side of the palace. If she could get past the corner, the sniper would no longer have a shot. She hoped.

Three more bullets cracked the back window. Victoria ducked again before peering between the steering wheel and the dash. Just another few hundred meters, and they would be protected by the palace walls.

The back window took another hit and then another. Glass cracked. Victoria squeaked in alarm.

"We're almost there," Sabine encouraged.

Victoria checked again for Alan. He was no longer visible, but the side mirror gave her the assurance that he was still on his feet, still running beside the SUV, still shooting at whoever was hiding behind the limousines.

She glanced toward the shooter but couldn't spot him. Then, out of the corner of her eye, she caught a glimpse of movement. Suddenly, a flurry of gunfire filled the air.

CHAPTER 46

The moment Victoria drove past the corner of the east wing wall, Alan motioned to Giuseppe. "Stay with her. Make sure she gets inside."

He nodded and continued running alongside the SUV.

Alan turned to face the sniper and the half dozen guards who had rushed toward the assailant's position. When one of the guards lifted a hand and signaled to another that the shooter was down, Alan rushed forward. He needed to see for himself that the current threat was neutralized and to make sure there weren't any others heading their way.

His gun still in hand, he jogged across the football-field-length space between the palace wall and the line of limousines. Whoever had been shooting was clearly well practiced. He wouldn't have guessed Lord Romero to be the type to spend hours on the shooting range. Then again, he wouldn't have pegged him for someone who would try to murder a member of the royal family for money.

Alan reached the cluster of guards beside the limo, Federico standing among them. Past them, a man in a gray suit lay sprawled facedown on the concrete.

"Was it just the one shooter?" Alan asked.

"It appears so." Federico nodded toward the palace. "And don't worry about the dogs. I put them in your apartment. Shadow is in Max's kennel."

"Thanks." Alan glanced at the fallen man as one of the guards checked for a pulse.

He shook his head. "He didn't make it." The guard turned him over.

Alan stepped past Federico so he could see the body more clearly. His stomach lurched. The man before him was one he knew, but it wasn't Lord Romero. "He was here the day of the shooting."

"How did he get in here?" one guard asked.

"He must have come in disguised as a driver," another answered.

"Either that, or he was hiding in the trunk of the limo," Federico said.

"How he got in here doesn't matter right now." Alan took a step toward the palace. "He's a hired gun. Whoever brought him in here brought him as insurance."

"Which means we still have his employer somewhere in the palace," Darius said. He tapped on his earpiece and started barking orders to the guards inside the palace walls.

Alan didn't wait to hear his instructions to the others present. He sprinted toward the main entrance. He had to get inside to Victoria before Lord Romero found her.

* * *

Guards and medical personnel rushed out of the palace. Giuseppe opened Victoria's door and urged her out into the open space between the SUV and the servants' entrance.

For a brief moment, she couldn't move. Then she listened. The shooting had stopped.

"Your Highness, this way." Giuseppe urged her forward, and Victoria managed to put her body in motion.

She hurried up the short walk and through the single wooden door.

"I'm to take you to your apartment to get ready for the coronation."

Victoria couldn't imagine stepping out in front of a crowd right now, but the concept of stepping into the safety of her private quarters sounded like a wonderful alternative to where she was now and where she had been only moments ago.

She only had to close her eyes to hear the gunfire and the cracking of glass.

Giuseppe guided her down the hall that ran the width of the palace.

She was halfway to the front corridor before she thought to ask, "Why are we going this way?"

"Both the front and back hallways are open to the ballroom." Giuseppe motioned to the stairway. "We'll go upstairs before we cross to the family wing."

With only a single guard protecting her, what Giuseppe suggested made sense. They ascended the stairs and passed into the servants' wing. The hall was empty and eerily quiet.

"Where is everyone?"

"All of the guards are either protecting your family or are attempting to neutralize the threat." They moved past the line of closed doors. "We'll join the rest of your family's protective service when we reach your apartment. Your sister Annabelle is already there."

"What about the king and queen?" Victoria asked.

"They are in another secure location, awaiting the coronation." Giuseppe shot her an apologetic look. "We can't have all of you together until we're sure the shooter acted alone."

"It had to have been Lord Romero," Victoria said. "He's the only one who had a motive to kill me or Annabelle."

"I wouldn't have guessed Lord Romero would be that good of a shot," Giuseppe said.

"He couldn't have been that good if I'm still uninjured."

"You're only uninjured because the sniper never had a clear shot."

Thus, the reason she was hurrying through the halls with only one guard.

Giuseppe peeked into the adjoining hall before waving her forward. "This way."

Victoria moved into the upstairs foyer that overlooked the main entrance. She passed a potted tree. She was halfway to the two suits of armor in the center of the open space when the front doors burst open below her and Alan rushed inside.

He looked down both halls before he looked up. The relief in his countenance was palpable.

"Alan." Victoria took a step toward the curved stairwell closest to her.

"You need to stay up here, Your Highness," Giuseppe said, reminding her that she was expected at a destination that wasn't Alan's embrace.

She stopped but couldn't bring herself to continue in the direction she needed to go, not when Alan was rushing toward the stairs. A guard cut him off, clearly asking for information. Alan was still in the center of the entryway when a figure emerged from the hallway opposite her.

When that person stepped forward, Victoria's jaw dropped. Lord Romero hadn't been the person shooting at her. He couldn't have been since he now stood only a few meters away.

Surprise reflected in Lord Romero's gaze, but he quickly banked it. He bowed his head slightly. "Your Highness. I didn't expect to see you up here. I assumed you were getting ready for the queen's coronation."

Giuseppe drew his weapon but kept it by his side. "What are you doing up here?"

"I needed to stretch my legs." He took a step closer to the suit of armor and tilted his head in the direction of the ballroom. "It's quite stuffy in there."

"Is that why you were outside earlier?" Victoria asked. "Or were you making sure you weren't anywhere that you might be injured by the latest bomb you sent?"

An awareness flashed in his expression, and this time, he didn't manage to hide his surprise. "I don't know what you're talking about."

Fury pulsed through her. This man had done everything he could to cause her death without getting his hands dirty. He was a coward. A murderous coward.

"A hundred million euros." Victoria stepped forward. "Is that what my life was worth? Or Annabelle's?"

"I'm sorry, Your Highness. I am at a complete loss as to what you are referring." Lord Romero held his position, his posture relaxed. "I don't know what money you are speaking of."

Footsteps pounded on the stairs.

"Well, I'm sure that now that the guards know where to look, eventually, they'll find the connection between you and the people you hired to kill me."

Lord Romero's jaw clenched.

"Victoria, stay back!" Alan shouted as he approached the top landing.

Victoria didn't get the chance to react. Without warning, Lord Romero shoved the suit of armor at Giuseppe and lunged at Victoria. He grabbed her arm as metal clanged to the floor, and Giuseppe jumped back.

Victoria gasped and tried to pull free, but Lord Romero pulled her against him so her back was pressed against his chest. He hooked one hand around her throat, and she struggled to breathe against the sudden pressure against her windpipe. Then his free hand came up, and suddenly, something sharp and metallic pressed against her throat.

Giuseppe regained his balance and aimed his weapon. "Let her go."

Alan reached the top of the stairs, his gun drawn. "You heard him. Let the princess go. It's the only way you're getting out of here alive."

Lord Romero shook his head. "You're hardly in the position to make demands. I will get out of here alive, and you're going to do exactly as I say."

* * *

Alan's gaze met Victoria's, his fear for her future, for their future together, reflected in her eyes. They couldn't have come this far for it to end like this.

"You hurt her and you will regret it." Alan glanced at the dagger in Lord Romero's hand. From the looks of it, Alan suspected Lord Romero had obtained the weapon from one of the collections on display in the palace. That would explain how Lord Romero had made it through the metal detectors without incident. Or perhaps he had somehow bypassed security.

At this point, it didn't matter how he came into possession of the weapon. It only mattered that he didn't use it.

Alan took a step forward and then another, creating a loose triangle with Giuseppe at one point, him at another, and Victoria and Lord Romero at the third.

"Stop right there." Lord Romero took a backward step, dragging Victoria with him. The two knocked into the suit of armor that remained upright. A breastplate clanged to the floor beside the wreckage strewn between Victoria and Giuseppe.

Lord Romero looked behind him long enough to keep from stepping on any of the metal obstacles.

Victoria swallowed and spoke in a shaky voice. "Why are you doing this? You know the guards will never let you pass if you hurt me."

"You're coming with me." Desperation filled his voice. "You'll get me out of here." He took another step to the side and focused on Alan. "I want you to clear a path to the front entrance. And I want a car waiting for me outside."

"And then what?" Alan asked. "You've already tried to kill her multiple times. How do we know you won't follow through this time?"

"You can't prove I've done anything."

"You're right, but if you aren't guilty, why not let Princess Victoria go?" Alan asked.

"I'm not going to be someone's fall guy."

Alan's hope that he could reason with Lord Romero deflated. "Just let her go." He lowered his weapon to his side. "Take me instead."

"You won't matter to the guards." Lord Romero jerked Victoria back another step. "She will."

The movement loosened Lord Romero's hold ever so slightly. If Alan could get him to turn a bit more toward the staircase, perhaps Giuseppe could get a clear shot.

Alan shifted slightly to his left. "Then let me walk out with you. As soon as you're clear of the palace gate, you can let me and the princess go. We won't try to stop you."

Derision filled Lord Romero's voice. "You really think I'm going to buy that?"

"I can help you if you'll let me." Alan took another small step to his left. As he hoped, Victoria's captor shifted with him. "You know I'm connected. I can get you what you want."

He seemed to ponder Alan's words.

Alan took another step. "Think about it. All I want is the princess to be safe. But if you hurt her, I will kill you."

Lord Romero's face paled. "Help me get out of here, and I'll let her go."

"You're asking me to trust you. If I'm going to do that, I need a show of faith," Alan said. "Lower the knife."

"First, put down the guns." Lord Romero jerked his chin toward Giuseppe. "Both of you."

Though it went against protocol, Alan slowly leaned down and set his pistol on the floor. He stood and nodded at Giuseppe. "Do it."

The muscle in Giuseppe's jaw flexed, but he complied.

"Now lower the dagger," Alan said. "I don't want it at her throat."

Lord Romero tightened his grip on Victoria, but he lowered the dagger to his side. "Now, clear a path—"

That was as far as he got before Victoria threw her weight backward and knocked him into the suit of armor.

She broke free, and Lord Romero tripped, falling to the floor.

Alan rushed forward, stomping on Lord Romero's hand with one foot, the lord releasing a cry of pain. The dagger fell from his hand.

Giuseppe leaned down and retrieved his own gun. "Hold it right there." He took another step forward and kicked the dagger out of Lord Romero's reach.

Alan pulled Lord Romero to a stand and reached out to Giuseppe. "Give me your handcuffs."

Giuseppe complied, and Alan cuffed both of Lord Romero's hands behind his back. A phone rang, and Alan retrieved the cell phone from Lord Romero's pocket. He hit the Talk button.

"Hello?"

"Alan?" Levi asked.

"Yes. Why are you calling Lord Romero?"

"I didn't know that's who I was calling. I just dialed the last number off the phone the guards found on the sniper's body," Levi said. "What are you doing with Romero's phone?"

"He just tried to kill me, right after he took Victoria hostage." Alan stepped in front of Lord Romero. "That should eliminate any doubt that Lord Romero was the man behind the murder attempts."

Lord Romero pressed his lips into a firm line.

"Is everyone okay?" Levi asked.

"We're all fine, but I'm not sure where Lady Romero is. You might want to bring her in for questioning to see if she was also involved."

"I will," Levi said. "Have the guards process Lord Romero's phone into evidence."

"Will do. I'll talk to you later." Alan hung up and handed the phone to Giuseppe. "The king wants this treated as evidence."

Giuseppe nodded and took Lord Romero by the arm. "We'll get him turned over to the local authorities."

Alan nodded. Then he turned to Victoria.

She stood amid the pieces of armor, her arms folded tightly across her chest. "Is it over now?"

Alan moved to her and pulled her into his arms. "I sure hope so."

CHAPTER 47

VICTORIA FOUGHT FOR CALM AS she stepped out of her bedroom with Annabelle, both of them dressed for the coronation. Whether she and her sisters would be able to make it through the event, much less walk into the room, without a mental breakdown still remained to be seen.

Alan stood from where he waited on the sofa. "You look stunning." His gaze shifted to Annabelle. "Both of you."

"Let's hope the press is kind when they see that I'm wearing the same gown as last year's spring gala," Annabelle said.

Alan winced. "Yeah. Sorry about your dress."

Victoria crossed to him. "I think she'll forgive you."

"Eventually." Annabelle pressed a hand to her stomach. "I don't know if I can do this."

Victoria's thoughts exactly.

Alan stepped between them and hooked his arms through theirs. "You're both stronger than anyone realizes. And now that Lord Romero and his wife are in custody, we're certain there won't be any more incidents."

The calmness of his voice carried a certainty Victoria needed. "Do you really think Lady Romero could have been involved too?"

"We don't know, but Levi and the police will uncover the truth."

"Did you and Max do another sweep of the ballroom?" Victoria asked.

"We did." Alan leaned over and kissed her forehead. "Are you ready?"

"No," Victoria and Annabelle said in unison.

"Great. Let's go." Alan guided them forward.

He released their arms at the door. When they entered the hall, Giuseppe waited beside the door. Prince Stefano and Princess Alora approached.

"Princess Annabelle, we hoped we might accompany you to the coronation ceremony," Stefano said.

"We thought you might feel more comfortable surrounded by friends," Alora added. "Especially after the events of this afternoon."

"You know what happened?" Annabelle asked.

"King Levi trusted us with his concerns," Prince Stefano said.

"In that case, I'd appreciate you joining me."

Giuseppe signaled for them to move forward, and Annabelle walked beside Alora and Stefano.

Alan leaned down and whispered into Victoria's ear. "I'll be right beside you."

"For tonight."

"Yes, for tonight."

And tomorrow he would leave. "I wish tomorrow would never come."

"I wish I could stay," Alan said softly. "Truly, I do."

"I know it's your work that won't let you." Victoria wanted to ask him to stay anyway, to find another type of work. After all, Levi had worked for the CIA and had found a new career here. Alan could do the same if he really wanted to.

Even as those thoughts raced through her mind, she swallowed her words. If remaining with the CIA was what Alan needed, then she had to support that. She had to love him enough to let him be the man he wanted to be.

"Maybe for tonight, we need to live in the moment," Alan said.

"Yes." Victoria took a steadying breath. "As long as the moment doesn't include bombs or guns or knives."

"That's a reasonable request." Alan lifted her hand to his lips. "Thank you for asking me to be your date."

Victoria managed a smile. "Thank you for saying yes."

They made their way to the family chapel, waiting at the west entrance until the royal family's arrival was announced.

Despite the nerves tangled inside her, Victoria stepped into the chapel with Alan. Annabelle entered next with Stefano and Alora.

Victoria and Annabelle took their positions at the front of the chapel, where the coronation would take place. Then Cassie and Levi made their entrance.

The religious ceremony was blessedly short, and just shy of two hours later, her sister and brother-in-law were crowned queen and king. The motivation for the threats against her and Annabelle were no longer present. Maybe now she could finally live the life she had planned for herself.

She looked out over those in attendance, her gaze meeting Alan's. Her heart squeezed in her chest. He had protected her, given her the foundation for building her life, for finding her future. But deep inside, she already knew that true happiness would be forever fleeting unless she had Alan by her side.

* * *

Victoria was going to collapse if she didn't sit down soon. With Alan's help, she had managed to keep up appearances during the coronation and the banquet that had followed. She and Alan had eaten. They'd danced. They'd socialized with their guests. And for most of the evening, they had even managed to pretend that this wasn't their last night together for the foreseeable future.

A number of their guests had already departed, and Victoria prayed the rest would leave soon. She wanted time alone to process everything that had occurred today, both for Cassie and the rest of their family.

The orchestra ended its final song of the evening, a signal for those lingering that the festivities were indeed drawing to a close.

Alan leaned down and spoke in her ear. "Did you want to say your goodbyes and go upstairs?"

"I'd love to, but I'm not sure I can sneak away, not until I check with Cassie." Victoria scanned the room for her sister. Not surprisingly, she was standing beside Levi.

Levi motioned to Victoria. Or maybe he was trying to signal Alan.

"It looks like the king wants to speak with us." She tucked her arm through the crook of Alan's elbow. Together, they crossed to where Levi and Cassie stood.

"Is everything okay?" Alan asked.

"Better than okay." Levi paused and waited for Annabelle to join them.

"Giuseppe said you needed me," Annabelle said.

"We do." Levi nodded at Darius, who stepped in front of the cluster of family along with two other members of the royal guard to create a human barrier between them and the others who were still present.

"What's going on?" Victoria asked.

"I just received word from the police chief," Levi said. "The missing painting was recovered from Lord Romero's home."

"That puts the last nail in his coffin as far as proving he was involved with the second bomb," Alan said. "Did the interrogators get anything out of the wife?"

"You're assuming she was involved," Annabelle said. "I find that hard to believe."

"Believe it," Levi said. "She's already confessed to gathering information to help her husband."

Annabelle's eyes widened. "She talked to me about my dress designer."

"And she used her charity work with the arts council to find out which art pieces were being transported to and from the palace and the gallery," Levi added.

Annabelle shook her head. "All this time, I thought she was my friend."

"None of us ever would have expected either her or her husband to act the way they did," Cassie said.

Levi slipped his arm around Cassie's waist. "The good news is that with Lady Romero working with the prosecutors, we now know the details of who was involved and why."

"What about Sheldon?" Alan mimicked Levi and drew Victoria closer to his side. "Was he involved?"

"He and Marguerite did plan to create some sort of blackmail images to use against you on the eve of Cassie's coronation, but according to Lady Romero, Lord Romero was the instigator behind funding Sheldon's trip to Sereno and setting up him and Marguerite as the fall guys," Levi said. "It's possible she was more involved than she's claiming and is trying to lighten her sentence."

"It wouldn't surprise me if they weren't initially using Sheldon as a source of information," Alan said.

"The Romeros had to find out somehow that I was coming back to Sereno and would be working at the resort," Victoria said.

"As head of the economic council, he already had the basic information anyway," Levi said.

A memory pushed to the front of Victoria's mind. "What about the bombs being out of order?" she asked. "Do you have any idea why they planted two bombs?"

"Apparently, their bomb maker for the one at the resort got held up," Levi said. "Lord Romero panicked and hired someone in London to try to bomb the plane there instead."

"So they weren't trying to cover up forgeries?" Annabelle said.

"We don't believe so," Levi said.

"What about Nico Amando?" Victoria asked. "Is there any chance he or someone from the Imperial Blu was working with the Romeros?"

"He doesn't appear to have any involvement with the threats against us," Levi said. "Based on the financial information found at the Romeros' home, the police believe they'll be able to trace the payments made to the men hired to breach the palace, but all indications are that they were hired guns."

Victoria shuddered. "So, those men really were here to kill me."

"You, Annabelle, Cassie, me," Levi said. "It wouldn't have mattered."

"They just needed someone to die," Alan said, disgusted. "Someone the country would expect the royal family to mourn for."

"Yes." Levi nodded.

Cassie reached out a hand and put it on Alan's arm. "Thanks to you, they didn't get the chance."

"That was as much your husband's doing as it was mine," Alan said.

"Regardless, I am eternally grateful for your service," Cassie said. "You will be sorely missed around here."

Alan swallowed hard and glanced at Victoria before speaking to Cassie. "I will miss being here."

CHAPTER 48

He could do this. Alan repeated the thought as he squatted down beside Max and clipped his leash in place. After today, Max would no longer be his. He would belong to Victoria.

Alan had known this day would come. He took comfort in knowing Max would be with someone who would love him, someone he already loved. Alan's chest tightened. Max would be with the woman Alan already loved.

That thought broke through the cloud hanging over him and pierced his heart. He loved her. Yet he was leaving her.

He drew in a deep breath and let it out slowly. "It's only for two years." Alan ruffled Max's fur. "And I'll visit whenever I can."

Max barked as though his response were expected.

Alan stood and garnered his courage. He really hated goodbyes. "Come on, Max. Let's get this over with." Alan led Max to the door, where Alan's tux was encased in a hanging bag and draped over his single suitcase. He grabbed the tux and led Max out the door.

The halls between his apartment and Victoria's were quiet despite the numerous guards posted in the residential wing. Alan didn't know how long it would take for security to feel confident that the threats against the royal family were truly over, but he didn't mind knowing they were taking these extra precautions.

He knocked on Victoria's door, and she opened it a moment later.

"Hey." She focused on him for a moment before looking down at Max. "Think he's ready to move into his new home?"

"I hope so."

Victoria stepped aside and motioned them in. "When do you leave for the airport?"

"In a couple minutes." He held up his tux. "Any chance I can leave this with you?"

"Why? It's yours."

"Yes, but I'm not going to need a tux where I'm going." He wouldn't need anything but work clothes and his protective gear. "The only time I can imagine needing it is when I'm with you."

"In that case, I'm happy to hold on to it for you."

"Thanks." He laid it over the back of her sofa. Then he unclipped Max's leash and set it on the occasional table beside him. "There you go, buddy."

"I'll take good care of him," Victoria said with entirely too much understanding.

Alan had to swallow before he spoke. "I know you will." He squatted beside Max and pulled the dog against him for a last goodbye. Unable to speak, he straightened and faced an even harder goodbye.

Victoria stepped into his arms and pulled him close. Alan held her against him, inhaling the lingering scent of her shampoo.

Victoria sniffled. "I'm going to miss you."

"I'll miss you too." Alan rubbed her back before pulling away. "I'll come back to visit as soon as I can."

Victoria nodded. She leaned closer and tilted her chin up. Alan leaned down and kissed her, savoring this last moment together.

The grandfather clock chimed the half hour. "I should go."

Victoria gave him one last kiss. "I love you."

He loved her, too, but he couldn't push the words past the lump in his throat. Instead, he nodded and headed for the door. She followed, and Alan couldn't resist kissing her one last time before stepping back and slipping into the hall.

He closed the door between them and blinked hard against the tears trying to form. Giuseppe approached, and Alan willed for him to keep walking past him, but that wasn't to be.

"King Levi wishes to see you."

"I was about to leave."

"I don't believe the king's request is optional."

Though tempted to leave for the airport without facing another goodbye—saying goodbye to Victoria and Max had been hard enough—he made his way to Levi's office. Levi's assistant's desk was empty, and he stood in his open door as though he had nothing better to do than wait for Alan. Alan knew better.

"It's about time. I was afraid I was going to have to intercept you at the garage."

"Where's Renato?" Alan asked.

"At the garage, making sure you weren't trying to leave before I talked to you."

His emotions still churning close to the surface, Alan folded his arms. "What's so important that you needed to talk to me before I go?"

"You are." Levi closed the outer door and leaned against the front of Renato's desk. "So is Victoria."

"Victoria and I have already said goodbye."

"But you shouldn't have." Levi lifted a hand in a frustrated gesture. "It's not like you've never done a hardship tour before. You don't have to leave."

"I don't have a choice, and you know it." Alan unfolded his arms and shoved his hands into his pockets. "If the director wasn't willing to override personnel's decision, they must really need me there."

"Or they caved when a new dog handler whined about being posted in the Middle East."

"That's a stretch."

"Actually, it's the truth," Levi said. "The bomb tech who was originally supposed to take your post pulled some strings. Turns out, he's the assistant director's cousin—or cousin once removed."

Alan had been so certain that this assignment had come because it was his turn. Irritation rose within him, and he fisted his hands in his pockets. "That's why personnel reassigned me?"

"You had an aging dog, which made you an easy target."

Alan's sense of loyalty warred with his deepest desires. "Even if that's the case, it doesn't change the fact that to stay with the CIA, I have to leave. Today."

"You know, I always loved the story about how you and Max came into the agency together."

Some of the tension eased out of Alan's body. "We've been through a lot."

"Maybe you should consider retiring together too."

"Leave the agency?" Alan asked. "And do what?"

"You have options." He waved a hand to encompass the room. "You can come work for me. Or if you'd prefer, I can help you start your own business."

"Doing what? Most people don't need someone to come in and disarm bombs."

"No, but there is a shortage of trained ordinance dogs. You could help alleviate it."

"Become a trainer? I've never done anything like that before."

"Yes, you have. You've been training Shadow for the past month." Levi swallowed hard, as though fighting a sudden onslaught of emotion. "If you hadn't, my wife and two sisters-in-law wouldn't be alive right now."

Alan didn't want to think about that or the fact that he was about to leave Sereno and hope that Victoria remained safe in his absence.

"I know leaving the agency is a huge move," Levi continued, "but let me ask you one question: Are you in love with Victoria?"

There was no point in denying it. "Yes."

"Have you told her?"

"No."

A knock sounded on the door.

"Here's your chance."

* * *

Victoria had been so sure Alan would say he loved her, yet the moment had passed without him so much as hinting at it. A seed of doubt took root deep inside her heart. Now, to make matters worse, Cassie was insisting that Levi needed to talk to her. She wasn't in the mood to meet with anyone, especially so soon after saying goodbye to Alan, but it was easier to give in than to argue.

She sniffled back the tears that had been trying to fall since Alan had left her apartment and knocked on the closed office door a second time.

"Come in," Levi called out.

Victoria pushed the door open and froze when she saw Alan standing inside. "I thought you already left." New tears flooded her eyes, and she blinked rapidly. She wasn't going to cry. She wasn't going to cry. She wasn't going to cry. She sniffled again and turned to Levi. "Cassie said you wanted to see me."

"Actually, I think Alan's the one who needs to see you." Levi headed for the door. "I'll give you two some time to talk."

The door closed, leaving them alone.

Victoria clasped her hands in front of her. "I'm not sure I can handle another goodbye."

"I was just thinking the same thing." Alan looked out the window as though avoiding the reality before them.

Was he avoiding something? Her stomach turned to lead as a new thought surfaced. Maybe the reason Alan had never said he loved her was because he didn't. Maybe Levi wanted Alan to talk to her because he knew their relationship had no future.

Even though she wanted nothing more than to go hide in her room, she lifted her chin. "Is this going to be one of those kinds of goodbyes?"

Alan focused on her now, and his eyebrows drew together. "What kind of goodbye?"

"The one that ends with 'we can still be friends'?"

"What?" Surprise flashed on his face. "No." He closed the distance between them. "I don't ever want to have that conversation."

Victoria's rising despair ebbed and was replaced with her growing confusion. "Then why did Levi say you needed to talk to me?"

"I have a pretty big decision to make. I guess he thought I should make it with you."

"What kind of decision?"

Alan stepped forward and took both her hands. "Whether to change careers."

"Wait. What?" Victoria leaned back. "Why would you do that? You love your job. And you're amazing at it."

"I do love my job, but Levi gave me the idea of a new opportunity that would give me more freedom in where I live." He linked his fingers through hers. "How would you feel about me staying here and starting a business training bomb-detection dogs?"

"Stay here?"

"Levi pointed out that Max and I started with the agency together. It does seem fitting that we retire together too."

Hope fluttered inside her. "You would be a great trainer."

"Thanks. I've actually never thought of using those skills as a career until now, but the more I think about it, the more I like the idea."

Her hope for a future with Alan expanded, but with it came a new kind of doubt. "I would love for you to stay, but I don't want you to look back and regret walking away from your career. I couldn't stand it if you started to resent me for your decision."

"I could never resent you." Alan's gaze fixed on hers. "I love you."

"You love me?"

"Yes. You're the best part about me."

Tears sprang to her eyes. "My father used to say that about my mother."

"Then, he was a very lucky man too." Alan released her hands and slid his arms around her. "I love you," he repeated. "I want you to be my future, and I hope to always be part of yours."

Absolute joy filled Victoria's heart to the point of bursting. Alan loved her. He was staying. And he wanted her in his future. Her own future shifted in that instant, illuminating brightly in her mind. "I can't think of anything I would love more."

About the Author

TRACI HUNTER ABRAMSON WAS BORN in Arizona, where she lived until moving to Venezuela for a study-abroad program. After graduating from Brigham Young University, she worked for the Central Intelligence Agency, eventually resigning in order to raise her family. She credits the CIA with giving her a wealth of ideas as well as the skills needed to survive her children's teenage years. She loves to travel and recently retired after spending twenty-six years coaching her local high school swim team. She has written more than forty best-selling novels and is an eight-time Whitney Award winner, including 2017 and 2019 Best Novel of the Year.

She also loves hearing from her readers. If you would like to contact her, she can be reached through the following:

Website: www.traciabramson.com
Facebook page: facebook.com/tracihabramson
Facebook group: Traci's Friends
Bookbub: bookbub.com/authors/traci-hunter-abramson
Twitter (X): @traciabramson
Instagram: instagram.com/traciabramson